# KISS MY AXE

## MAY ARCHER

**ISBN:** 978-1-964685-30-4



**Cover Art:** Qamber Designs
**Editing:** One Love Editing
**Proofreading:** Jodi Duggan

*All the good bits are theirs, and any mistakes are my own!*

# KISS MY AXE

**Living in a treehouse? Unavoidable.**

**Falling for the grumpy lumberjack hottie next door? Unthinkable.**

After a viral PR disaster torpedoes my marketing career, I flee Manhattan. The only place left to land? A fairy-tale treehouse in a pickle-obsessed Vermont town, left to me by an uncle I barely knew.

Yes, I said pickles.

No, I'm not okay.

But I'm only here temporarily. Just long enough to regroup, let the notoriety die down, and figure out my next steps in peace.

Unfortunately, my new neighbor has other ideas.

Beckett "the Axe" Axford–cranky local heartthrob and unapologetic tree-murderer–claims Uncle Jim made him promises about the forest around the treehouse, and he's none too pleased when I won't take his word for it.

Unfortunately for *him*, I'm done playing by other people's rules. I'm not backing down just because some sexy–I mean *grumpy*–lumberjack says so, and I can handle whatever he dishes out.

Tree climbing? No problem.

Pickle festival popularity contest? Sign me up.

Kissing my unexpectedly-tender, flannel-clad nemesis in the woods after dark? I can take it, bro. And take it. And t–
*Ahem*. You get the picture.

I'm tired of losing, so I'm not giving up my inheritance *or* my heart without a fight.

And if Beckett thinks differently, he can kiss my axe.

# PROLOGUE
## GRIFFIN

FORTY-TWO STORIES ABOVE TIMES SQUARE, the rooftop of the Knickerbocker Hotel offers an unobstructed view of Manhattan. Below me, half-sized humans scurry around, jackets buttoned against the spring chill. Traffic honks and sirens wail.

But up here above it all, everything's calm. String lights twinkle overhead, and heaters scattered around the perimeter of the patio chase away the worst of the wind that whips between the skyscrapers.

The whole setup screams *expensive*. Screams *luxury*. Screams *control*. Which is exactly what Bill Tiden wanted for the Rise Athletics billboard launch.

I adjust the collar of my navy Tom Ford coat and check my phone. Six minutes until showtime. Around me, the party hums with anticipatory energy. The paid lifestyle influencers with their sculpted abs and perfect teeth cluster by the open bar, drinks in hand and phones already primed for optimal lighting. The team from Rise hovers to one side while Bill, with his high-and-tight haircut and perpetually constipated expression, holds court.

I'm not nervous. I've toiled seven years for this day. More, if you count all those unpaid internships in college. I've spent late nights, weekends, and major holidays at my desk, and my phone is never turned off. I've been building my own name as carefully and steadily as I've built campaigns for my clients. Crafting my own narrative, you might say: lower-middle-class kid from Brooklyn pulls himself up toward the executive suite through hard work and talent. And now, finally, it's all coming together.

"Griffin!" Sarah Kim from our creative team appears at my elbow with a champagne flute. "This is it! The big moment! This is going to be huge for the Nelson Group."

"It is." I take the champagne from her, but I can't drink. My nerves are humming like live wires in the best possible way.

This night, this campaign, isn't just huge for the company; it's huge for *me*. As project lead on the campaign that will catapult Rise from a mid-level sports and leisure company to a leading activewear brand... well, I shouldn't get ahead of myself, but I don't think it's too out-there to think this will lead to a promotion.

The campaign I designed for Rise—*Work Hard, Grind it Out, Rise Up*—isn't just about athletic wear. It's about aspiration. Becoming your best self, as my friend Milo says. It's about broadening horizons and making people feel empowered.

Which, yeah, is a tall order for a $70 pair of leggings. But with help from my team, and thanks to an amazing model... we nailed it.

My phone buzzes with a text from former classmates in our business school group chat.

> **JESSICA**
>
> Best of luck tonight!
>
> **TREVOR**
>
> So jealous I could puke.
>
> **AMINAH**
>
> Can't wait to see your new place Saturday and to hear EVERYTHING about your launch!

Eight or nine years ago, we'd all been scrambling for internships. Now, I'm launching a campaign that will be seen by millions. And yeah, the speed of that still astounds me sometimes, but I swear I've earned it.

My mothers didn't just teach me how to make poster board protest signs and march for justice. They instilled in me a good work ethic by example, and after seeing them struggle to support our family, I know you have to put in the effort if you want good things to happen.

I take out my phone and snap a quick picture of myself and text it to them with an excited-face emoji. A millisecond later, my phone buzzes with messages from them.

> **MAMALAINE**
>
> So proud, Griffy.
>
> **MAMATISH**
>
> We love you!

"Griffin." Alan Nelson's voice cuts through my thoughts.

"Alan. Hi." I slide my phone away and turn to find my boss approaching, his silver hair slightly windblown. He's followed by his secretary and his entourage of VPs, but my attention catches on the young man trailing slightly behind.

Erick Nelson, Alan's son, is officially an intern and unofficially the prince of nepotism. With the kind of effortless beauty that belongs in a cologne ad—word on the street is that his mother, the former Mrs. Nelson, was a model—and a resume that includes a list of chichi private schools, he shouldn't have to work hard. But when Alan assigned him to my team a few months ago, I was pleasantly surprised to find that while Erick needs to polish up his poker face when dealing with shitty clients, he's generally eager to please.

"Erick." I extend my hand. "Thanks again for all your effort on this. You should know, Alan, that Erick took charge of the final graphics package after Bill's last-minute color tweak. He was an absolute lifesaver."

Erick's handshake is firm, but there's something off in his expression. Nervous energy radiates off him like heat waves, and he drops my hand almost immediately. "Nah. I didn't do much."

"Not true," I argue, mostly for Alan's benefit. "I know you were dropped into the deep end of the pool, having this as your first project. The hours were long, and the client was… tricky," I say diplomatically.

Alan gives Erick a fond smile. "Chip off the old block."

Something flickers across Erick's face—guilt, maybe?—but before I can ask him if he's okay, Bill Tiden's laugh booms over the party chatter. He's regaling a cluster of influencers now with some story that involves aggressive hand gestures, and he's making his way toward us.

"…so I told the guy, look, this isn't San Francisco," Bill's saying. "Rise is a family company with family values. We don't cater to every special-interest group that comes knocking."

One of the influencers—a fitness model with kind eyes and, according to his Instagram, a husband and child at home—shifts uncomfortably, and Erick's jaw clenches.

"I think inclusivity—" Erick begins.

"Inclusivity." Bill waves dismissively. "Marketing buzzword. Our customers are real Americans who want real products. Not political statements."

I slide into the conversation smoothly. "Bill! Come over here so you can get the best view of your billboard."

I wish I could explain to Erick that challenging clients like Bill gets you nowhere. That it's better to charm your way around their rough edges and focus on the work. But that's the kind of lesson it took me *years* to master.

"Griffin." Bill nods. "The man of the hour. Ready to earn your millions?"

I keep my smile firmly in place. I make enough to afford some luxuries, like a one-bedroom apartment and a parking space for my car, so I can theoretically visit my moms more easily, but it for sure ain't millions.

"Two more minutes," I say, checking my phone again.

The crowd gravitates toward us like they're drawn by magnets, and we all crane our necks toward the massive LED display.

I'm sweating inside my coat like this breezy rooftop is the surface of the sun. Pride and satisfaction swamp me. *I've proven myself*, I think. *I've reached the top of the mountain.*

I'm vaguely aware of Erick hovering at the edge of the group, his face pale in the string lights. When I frown at him quizzically, he looks away.

"Thirty seconds!" someone yells.

We go quiet, all forty of us with phones raised, holding our breaths, looking over the edge of the building at the beautiful chaos of the city…

And the billboard flickers to life.

For a split second, my brain can't process what I'm seeing. Like when you wake up in a strange hotel room and the shadows fall all wrong, panic grips me, and I think, *Where am I? What is this? Why?*

The image on the screen is familiar. The model I chose stands against the royal blue background Bill insisted on at the last moment. He's wearing Rise's signature compression leggings, which practically *glow* in the lighting. But the text…

My god, the text.

My carefully crafted tagline—*Work Hard, Grind it Out, Rise Up*—isn't positioned at the bottom of the image in sans serif block letters where it belongs.

Instead, it's wrapped around the model's crotch, the letters following the contours of his prominent dick bulge.

It's perverted. It's porntastic. It's…

"An *outrage*." Bill's voice cuts through the silence like a whip crack. "An outrage of epic proportions!"

Someone—one of the influencers, I think—lets out a strangled snort. "He *is* pretty epically proportioned. Goddamn."

"Wouldn't mind *grinding it out* with him," another snickers.

"I… that's not…" My mouth works from side to side,

but no coherent words emerge. I can't *think*. I can't *imagine*. I don't *know*. "This isn't the file we approved."

"You're damn right it's not!" Bill says. His face has gone crimson, and when he turns to face me, his eyes are blazing. "Was this supposed to be funny? Some kind of joke?"

"No! No, I swear! This was an accident! It had to be—"

"I won't be made a fool of." His voice drops to a dangerous whisper. "And my company will *not* be associated with this kind of juvenile, degenerate, *indecent*—"

Around us, phones are out and recording. The influencers hired to promote the launch are now documenting its spectacular failure. I can practically see the TikToks being uploaded in real time.

"Alan!" Bill spins toward my boss, who's gone white as paper. "You assured me this campaign would be handled by professionals. This is unacceptable."

Alan's gaze finds me, and when I look back on this moment, I will see my future evaporating in his expression. "Griffin, what happened here?"

"I don't know!" I sound loud and panicked, and I hate it. "The files were perfect when I reviewed them. Then Erick sent the graphics package—"

My eyes dart to Erick, who's standing there frozen.

"Don't you dare blame an intern for this," Alan says, avoiding the fact that the intern in question is his son. "This was your project, Griffin. You assured me you could handle the responsibility. Clearly not."

The words hit me right in the stomach and leave me winded. I open and close my mouth, but no sound comes out.

Around us, the party's descended into uncomfortable

murmurs and barely concealed laughter, and with a quick glance around, Alan's clocked it too. I recognize the moment when he realizes he needs to deflect the stain of this from the Nelson Group… and when he decides to use me as a human shield.

"The Nelson Group will be parting ways with you, effective immediately, Griffin Mercer," he announces loud enough for everyone and their TikTok followers to hear. "Please leave your key card here, and we can make arrangements for you to collect your personal belongings."

The terrace spins like a tilt-a-whirl.

This can't be happening. It legit *cannot*. Aren't there supposed to be HR people involved when you're fired? Shouldn't there be some kind of trial where I can provide evidence?

I did the work. I put in the effort. I *earned* this success, and it's supposed to be mine.

I was so fucking close.

I look at Erick, silently begging him to speak up, to explain, but he won't meet my eyes. His face is a mask of guilty silence that says he sees me going under, and he's not gonna throw me a rope.

"Alan," I manage. "Please hear me out. Give me a chance—"

"You had your chance," Bill says, turning away and dismissing me with a gesture. "And you can bet every agency in this city will hear about this disaster!"

Believe it or not—and I really can't—the party continues around me. People have gotten a spectacle, even if it wasn't the one they came for, and they're pouring champagne while thanking the heavens they're not in my shoes.

Meanwhile, I stand there, frozen, as everything I've built disappears before my eyes. The corner office, the promotion. Hell, the *paycheck*. The respect of my colleagues. The life I'd carefully constructed.

My limbs are frozen solid, and ice is seeping through my chest as all of it crumbles into nothing, forty-two stories above the city I love.

# CHAPTER ONE

"This might sound dramatic, but hear me out," Milo says. "I think Vermont is trying to kill us."

I snort, but… he kind of has a point.

The trip from New York to Vermont was supposed to take five hours, but we're now crawling into hour nine after being stuck in a conga line of logging trucks, caravans of tourists scouring the backcountry of New England for autumn vibes, and people who think blinkers are optional.

My back hurts. My left leg's cramping. My phone's lost signal three times in the last hour, and every attempt to check my messages drains the battery faster than Milo chugs from his giant water bottle. It's like with every mile closer to Winsome, Vermont, the universe invents a new way to test me.

And, FYI, I am absolutely failing those tests even *before* Milo starts tapping his foot so hard the passenger-side floorboard might give out.

I reach over and push his knee to still him. "Best friend

or not, babe, if you break my car, Vermont won't be the thing that kills you."

Milo pouts. "The tapping distracts me from the fact that I've had to pee for, like, twenty minutes."

I feel like it's only been twenty minutes since we stopped for Milo's last pee break, but the man insists on hydrating like a pro athlete and carrying around a pink water bottle as big as his head.

"The GPS says there's only 1.4 miles to go, but I can pull over." I gesture at the thick forest that lines the road.

Milo gasps. "I do not *urinate* in *woodlands*, Griffin. Besides, it's chilly out there. I am a hothouse flower, as you know, and I only thrive in very specific climates." He sniffs delicately. "Ideally, north of Houston and east of Bowery."

I roll my eyes. "Yet you insisted on coming to get me settled."

"Because friends don't let friends do dumbass things alone!" he fires back. "Especially when the dumbass thing is *moving to Vermont*, which is a serious overreaction to a… a career blip." He pauses for effect. "You could've stayed and fought, you know. You could've slept on my couch. You could've taken your story to the media! You didn't have to give up."

I keep my eyes on the pothole-riddled road and grind my teeth. I'm well aware that Milo thinks my retreat from Manhattan was a mistake. My ears are still ringing from his screech when I told him I'd be moving north for a while. And I don't know that he's wrong. I've spent months wondering if I could have done something different. Could have fought harder.

But the moment the Rise Athletics billboard dropped, I stopped being Griffin Mercer, rising star in Manhattan's corporate marketing community. I became Griffin Mercer, unemployable walking punchline.

The guy who trusted the boss's nepo-baby son and got burned.

The guy who learned the hard way that your job doesn't, as my moms had tried to warn me, love you back.

No marketing company in New York will touch me now, and I know this because I've contacted them all, even the rinky-dink ones I wouldn't have given the time of day last year.

The people I thought were my friends—all those former classmates and coworkers, people whose weddings and dinner parties I've attended—stopped returning my texts.

And my moms and Milo have tried to keep my spirits up by distracting me with cat memes (and, in Milo's case, shockingly awful television shows), but if I have to see one more kitten clinging to a rope, reminding me to *just hang on*, I might scream.

At a certain point, just hanging on felt an awful lot like drowning.

So when I got a letter two weeks ago saying I'd inherited a cabin in Vermont… well, let's just say it felt like the universe might be doing me a solid for the first time in ages.

Giving me a belated thirtieth birthday present or something.

If not saving me from drowning, then at least showing me which way to swim.

"I'm not giving up," I tell Milo now. "I'm getting out of range of the firing squad long enough to fucking reload.

Three months in Vermont to regroup and figure out my next steps. It'll be *great.*"

He sighs.

"Which one of your mindfulness gurus always says the hardest part of any decision is making it? Well, I've made a decision. And now, things'll get better." I push at his knee, inviting him to see the humor. "Vermont can't actually kill us."

The moment the words are out of my mouth—literally, the very second I utter them—a moose lumbers into the road directly in front of us like Vermont is saying, "*Bet.*"

"Shit!" I yell, getting both hands on the wheel and yanking left.

I swear, the enormous beast has the audacity to side-eye me as we whiz past.

"Oh my fuck. Vermont, we are so sorry," Milo moans, clutching the oh-shit bar.

I let out a shaky breath as adrenaline courses through my body. "Fuck that. Victory over the moose invasion! Vermont is gonna have to try harder if—"

Before I can even gasp, a big-ass red pickup barrels around the curve ahead. It blasts its horn, and I manage to swerve right just in time to avoid an accident.

"What the *fuck*?" I yell at the truck's taillights in my mirror.

We bounce onto the gravel shoulder, directly into the pottiest of potholes, and the car lurches violently. One of the brand-new tires I'd bought as an investment in relia-bility gives up the ghost and starts making a *thwack-thwack* noise, and the car decides it doesn't want to steer.

*Well, fuck. So much for victory.*

We limp to a stop.

"You need to stop pissing Vermont off," Milo warns.

I massage my forehead with one hand and reach for my phone with the other. "We're fine," I tell Milo firmly. "Totally, completely fine. This is why I paid for the auto care package. A tow truck will come and get us. Easy peasy."

But it turns out that with only one bar of cell service, it's neither easy nor peasy.

"You owe me… so huge." Milo pants as we push my car the remaining half mile to our destination. The air is damp and chilly, despite us working up a sweat. "When you get sucked into some flannel-wearing cult, marry a lumberjack, and adopt four children—as you inevitably will—you're henceforth required to call them Miletta, Milolo, Milon, and…" He stops pushing to consider the question.

"Milo," I say.

"Eh." He shakes his head, walking beside me as I push. "Nah. Too obvious."

"*Milo.*"

"Well, if you insist, but won't it get confusing when—"

"*Milo!*" I yell. "We're nearly there. Run and turn the steering wheel so we can steer the car into the driveway, huh?"

"Yeesh. Okay, okay. And we're sure this is your driveway?" Milo wonders.

"Positive," I say. "It's right there on the map the lawyer's office sent over with the key and the letter from my uncle."

Though at this point, I don't blame him for verifying, because impossible as it sounds… I'm starting to think he might be right about Vermont having an axe to grind with me.

From what I found online regarding trusts, there's a whole bunch of paperwork missing in the packet I received, but with Uncle Jim's lawyer out on medical leave, I'm picking my battles. What I know for sure is that seventeen acres of land and a one-bed, one-bath, seven-hundred-square-foot house are definitely *mine*... and that's all I really need to know, right?

We end up leaving the car at the end of the driveway, grabbing our suitcases and Milo's beloved drinks cooler, and covering the rest of the distance on foot.

The path to Jim's house branches off from the paved driveway, a hundred feet of moss and rocks that lead to a shadowy clearing. But there's still enough light for me to see that there were definitely a couple of additional things I needed to know.

I stare at the vision before me, not sure if I want to laugh or cry.

"It's a... it's a *treehouse*," Milo breathes.

It is indeed. And not like a child's backyard treehouse. This thing is adult-sized, two stories tall in spots, and appears to have crash-landed in the middle of an oak tree, straight from Middle Earth.

"This isn't... your uncle's place?"

I nod. It definitely is, exactly where the map said it would be. And the way my luck's been running, this feels somehow on-brand.

The treehouse is chaos incarnate. Like the blueprints I'd draw in the margins of my notebooks as if a little kid went on an ayahuasca retreat. There's a whole patchwork of different types of wood and twisty railings, strewn with glittering stained glass windows—a moon, a star, a mush-room, a… *fuck,* is that a dildo? But the pièce de résistance is an enormous… turret-type thing… shaped like a whiskey barrel that's cantilevered on the edge of the roof, complete with a small pine tree growing from its roof and a rope bridge disappearing into the trees.

"Holy shit! There's a mailbox on a pulley!" Milo drops his luggage and runs ahead, eyes glowing with rare, unironic excitement. "Griffin! I used to daydream about having a place like this!"

"I… I did too," I admit. "I was obsessed with stories about running away to live in the woods. No moms making me go to bed on time. No school. No chores."

Of course, all of that went away when I became an adult. Before I learned that going to bed on time is the linchpin of adult happiness. Before I learned the difference between fantasy and reality.

Then again, my reality's been less than stellar lately.

I climb the steps more slowly, dragging my luggage, and find Milo chortling to himself as he inspects a line of carved and painted wooden mushrooms that guard the window at the top of the stairs.

"Griff," Milo says, turning his head to look at me. "This dead uncle of yours… how much recreational drug use are we talking?"

I exhale a huff of laughter and try to dredge up memo-ries of the old neighbor I used to call Uncle Jim… but there's not a whole lot there, honestly. Which feels shitty, considering he left me his, ah, house-type structure.

"I was only eight last time I saw him. I have no idea what he was into. I remember he was older and had gray hair that stuck up all over—"

"Aww, just like you, boo." Milo lifts a hand like he's going to ruffle my hair, which was a mass of blond, dandelion-fuzz cowlicks back in college, before I learned the wonders of pomade.

I shoot him a glare and whack his hand away tiredly before he can disturb the carefully combed strands. "No touching."

Milo is used to my personal-space forcefield and just rolls his eyes. "Go on. What else?"

"I dunno. He called me Sprout? He liked to lay in the grass on summer days in the park near our building and tell me what the clouds were whispering to each other?" I shrug. "He wore these long, flowy sarongs to, ah, 'let things breathe.'"

Milo presses his lips together.

"Oh!" I add as a long-buried memory surfaces. "And he was always going on road trips in an orange VW bus he called the Magic Mushroom Mobile."

Milo laughs out loud, like he can't restrain it anymore. "So a *lot* of drugs, then?"

I run a finger over the gnarled railing and wince. "Maybe. Yeah. In retrospect."

I look around, but there's no VW bus in sight, which either means Jim sold it sometime in the last twenty-plus years—*likely*—or that he was out on a road trip when he died. I don't know which it was, and that also feels shitty.

But there's no way forward but through, so I hold up the keys. "Wanna see inside?"

"Fuck yes," Milo says, grabbing them and opening the lock.

The rounded hobbit door opens into yet more chaos—a purple velvet couch that looks like it was stolen from a bordello, red wing-backed chairs, a lime-green coffee table in the shape of a toadstool. Everything smells of woodsmoke and peppermint. Stained glass windows throw rainbow sprinkles across shelves packed with books and mushroom trinkets. Best of all, it's *warm*, which is great because I'm always cold.

Directly across from the front door, a fire extinguisher box attached to the wall says "Good Luck Charm! Break in Case of Emergency!" but the glass door to the box is hanging ajar, and the only thing inside is a tennis racket… which might or might not be the good luck charm.

"It's… cute," I say, surprised. "And appears structurally sound."

Milo nods once. "It's a vibe," he admits, which, given his current dislike of the entire state of Vermont, is a ringing endorsement.

I head right toward the kitchen where a pink Smeg fridge sits beneath polka-dotted mushroom curtains, and a purple unicorn wearing Uncle Sam's top hat points at me from a framed poster saying "I Want YOU to SPARKLE!"

Milo heads to the back and calls my name. "Griff, there's a trapdoor in the bedroom ceiling. Pretty sure it's a portal to another dimension."

I find him standing in the middle of a room just big enough to hold a tidy queen-sized bed and a small wooden dresser. He points at a large square of dark, shiny wood that stands out against the white ceiling.

"Pretty sure it leads to the barrel-shaped room we saw," I correct.

Milo's eye roll says I've missed the joke. "Same difference, boo."

We take turns tugging on the tasseled bell pull dangling from the door, but nothing happens.

"What the hell?" I toe off my shoes, climb on the bed, and tug harder, but it won't budge.

I really shouldn't have missed so many arm days, back when I had a gym membership.

Milo, who's thrown himself down on the bed to watch me, like my struggle is free entertainment, pops back up with a shrug. "Don't suppose your uncle left you magic words to whisper?"

I shoot him a look.

"Just asking! I'm gonna go get my bags and inspect the bathroom situation. There will be no repeats of that woodland experience I was forced to endure while we were pushing the car earlier," he says with a warning glare. "And we will not discuss it further."

But after Milo leaves, his offhanded comment about Jim's magic words makes me think. I get my backpack from where I dropped it by the door and find the letter Jim's attorney forwarded. The paper it's written on smells pepperminty, just like the house, and it's already worn along the crease from how many times I've unfolded it in the past week, just to make sure this was really happening.

> *Heya, Sprout!*
>
> *By the time you read this I'll already be at the Big Drum Circle in the Sky!*
>
> *Wish I coulda seen your face when you heard about the Griffin Mercer Trust—priceless!—but my true love's been waiting on me and it's past time I joined her. We're gonna dance barefoot 'round the stars, just like in the old days, and discover all the secrets of the universe. (If I find out what*

*happened to the house keys I lost in 2012, I'll come back and tell you. Pinky swear.)*

*In the meantime, the forest and the treehouse are yours, kiddo. Use them wisely or whatever.*

*Love,*

*Jim*

*PS - trapdoor's a little sticky but I oiled the pulleys and the rope bridge is strong*

*PPS - when the mushrooms talk, listen*

*PPPS - wifi password's FUNGUY (Get it? Fungi?)*

*Later!*

I laugh, but it comes out like a sob, and I realize my eyes are wet, which is crazy. There's nothing in this note to cry over, and I'm not a crier by nature.

I didn't cry when I handed over my apartment keys or when Alan Nelson fired me. I didn't cry when I nearly hit a moose or when I had to listen to Milo singing sea shanties while I pushed my car half a mile down the road.

So what the fuck's my problem now?

Maybe I'm just tired. Or maybe knowing a guy I haven't seen since I was a kid remembered *me* as he prepared to go to the "drum circle in the sky" is so freaking sweet it slips past my defenses. Or maybe it's that this place—this impossible, whimsical treehouse—feels like every childhood dream I gave up when I learned that dreams don't pay bills.

Everything I worked hard for evaporated, and then I got this gift I didn't earn. It feels… unbalanced. But now that I have it, I'm going to use it wisely, just like Jim said.

"Aw, honey." Milo drops his luggage in the hall and

rushes in to hug me. "It's finally hitting you that you've left New York, huh?"

"What? No," I protest, but it's a sign of how overwhelmed I am that I submit to Milo's hug, even though I'm stiff and awkward. "I haven't *left*-left. This is… this is temporary."

But we both know that's not entirely true.

I built my whole life around New York—the energy, the diversity, the momentum, the people who keep changing and *becoming*. Even as a kid, I used to climb out on my fire escape at night so I could listen to the sirens and the neighbors playing music through the open window and revel in the knowledge that I was part of something bigger.

I know other cities have their charms, and since I need to find a job, I'll end up in one of them soon. I might even love it. But a big-shot career in New York has always been the dream, and now that dream's gone, and I'm finally letting myself feel that loss.

Still, crying is annoying and useless, so when my phone chirps, I take the opportunity to pull away and wipe my eyes.

The screen shows a message from my moms.

MAMALAINE

Let us know when you've arrived, Griffy!

MAMATISH

Your mom genuinely won't be able to sleep unless she gets her weekly Proof of Griffin's Life and Safety pic.

My mothers are the best, even if they did choose to spend their retirement running a bed-and-breakfast in the Berkshires with their friends. The B&B work suits them—

they love the hospitality and flexibility, even if it'll never make them rich, and it gives them plenty of time to organize protests to save the bumble bees, or underprivileged children, or whatever else is being endangered in Williamstown.

They've more than earned the right to choose passion over profit after all those years of financial stress when I was younger.

I show Milo the screen, and he grins.

"Your mothers could not be more lesbian if we stuck them in a Subaru ad," he sighs happily. He snatches my phone, snaps a quick picture of me, and sends it, along with the caption *"I'm alive. Vermont hasn't caught me yet."* But when I reach for the phone, he refuses to give it back.

"Nuh-uh. You can make your five billion to-do lists tomorrow," he says, shooing me back to the living room and the lurid purple brothel sofa. "For tonight, we're watching *Extreme Wilderness Adventure*."

"Oh, god, Milo, why? Haven't I suffered enough?" I demand.

He rolls his eyes. "You love to pretend you hate this show, but you *just* admitted you wanted a treehouse as a kid, and I've seen you lusting over the flannel-clad eye candy. No one can resist the allure of the mountain-man wannabes."

There's a lot I could say about the silliness of watching C-list celebrities trying to filter pond water using a pair of Crocs and a paper towel, while survival experts look on, shaking their heads and making sure the celebrities don't kill themselves.

But Milo's right. There's something satisfying about watching people attempt the kind of wilderness survival I used to fantasize about, even if they're doing it badly. And yeah, the eye candy is particularly sweet.

I'm so worn-out, sleep should come the second I close my eyes. But even after Milo conks out on the opposite end of the couch, I can't get there. I wriggle out of my jeans and shirt, pull on a blanket, and spend hours tossing and turning on the surprisingly comfy sofa, just listening to Milo's soft breathing.

The house is quiet.

Deep quiet.

*Too* fucking quiet.

And sure, there's something to be said for hearing yourself think. For having the space to plan. But for a person who thinks of sirens and subways and honking horns as white noise, that absence is weirdly disorienting.

When I finally fall asleep, I have weird dreams, not about Times Square for a change, but about throwing mushrooms at a faceless foe and hitting them dead-on.

Sometime later, the *beep-beep-beep* of a truck and loud male voices shouting pierce my consciousness, and I smile a little to myself.

*Trash truck,* I think groggily. *And Mr. Graziano in 1B, brandishing his baseball bat because someone's letting their dog shit on our stoop.*

But then I pay attention to what the voice is saying.

"—just another tourist who decided to take a hike and leave their car wherever the fuck they felt like. Fucking tow it out of there, Freddy!"

I suck in a breath heavy with woodsmoke and pepper-mint and remember where I am.

My eyes pop open.

"If the fucking tourist wanted to have it towed *proper,*

Ed, he shouldn't have fucking left it in the middle of my fucking road!"

Hold up. What car? *My* car?

Oh, fuck no.

"Milo!" I call as I bolt to my feet, shove them in my beloved Common Projects Chelsea boots, and grab Uncle Jim's lucky tennis racket in lieu of Mr. Graziano's baseball bat. "Come on."

I don't wait for him. I stomp down the stairs and across the mossy path to the driveway, where I find half a dozen very large men in work gear hovering near my car. One guy is squatting down to attach a rope to my bumper.

I am so *over* people fucking with me. So *done* with things not going my way.

"Unhand that," I demand, brandishing the racket like I'm a knight in a fairy tale and this is my trusty sword. *"Immediately."*

Six pairs of eyes turn toward me, and I realize two things at once.

First, tennis rackets are not swords.

Second, I've misplaced my shining armor. In fact, I'm buck-ass naked aside from my boots and booty short underwear.

I lift my chin higher. "You heard me! Back off right this minute."

"Who the hell are you?" the guy with the rope demands, rising to his full, impressive height.

The man is large. Extraordinarily so. Like a Greek statue come to life and decked out in distressed jeans, a flannel shirt, and a beard so beardy the guys on *Extreme Wilderness Adventure* would weep with envy.

Past Griffin might have found him attractive. Fire-hot,

even. But I have had it up to *here* with entitled jackwads stomping around my life.

"I'm the guy who owns the car you're vandalizing and the land you're standing on," I say, making a swipe with my racket. "So, once again… back the fuck away from the car."

The other five giants take hasty steps out of swinging range, but the biggest guy doesn't move.

His eyes blaze with annoyance. "Bullshit. This land belongs to Jim Grange, and he never has visitors. So stop playing games and move this piece of crap so I can get down my road to do my job…" He folds his arms. "And if you shake a leg, maybe I won't call the sheriff and tell them someone's been camping out at Jim's place."

*Camping?*

*His road?*

*Shake a fucking leg?*

There's a lot I don't know about my inheritance—like why Jim built a hobbit habitat in this forest, or why the hell he left it to me—but I have pored over the map the lawyer's office sent me the same way I've read Jim's letter ten times.

Which means I know for a fact this gravel drive is on *my* land. Which means this person is a) dead wrong, b) probably lying, and c) definitely trying to bully me into backing down.

A few months ago, I might have been able to muster a smile, turn on some *let's be friends* charm. Too bad for this guy, though, because I left that Griffin on the roof of the Knickerbocker.

"Stop calling *my* driveway *your* road," I say through gritted teeth. "And if *you* shake a leg and move your big-ass trucks off my property, maybe *I* won't call the authorities and tell them you're trespassing."

Look, I know what you're thinking. That I'm overreacting. That I'm making this guy a stand-in for Alan and Erick Nelson, for every random TikTok troll who dragged me online. That I'm taking out my frustrations at all the power imbalances and injustices in the world on this one incredibly large, incredibly smug, incredibly rude man.

And you might be right.

But I have already retreated once, and I'm not doing it again. No matter what indignities and injustices Vermont throws at me.

And if this thick-headed hunk of lumberjack thinks otherwise, he can kiss my ass.

# CHAPTER TWO

## BECKETT

THIS GODDAMN DAY, I swear.

First, I skipped out on a command performance at an Axford family birthday breakfast, which means I'm not only missing my mom's sausage casserole and homemade donuts, but I'll also be catching shit from every one of my siblings for not going to my parents' place to celebrate my dad.

Then Mikey—the newest, most promising guy on my crew—calls five minutes before the start of his shift to quit, and Freddy tells me with a guilty shrug that he heard Mikey signed on with my biggest rival because "Mike's got a baby on the way, boss, and Derek Sullivan's offered him a bonus."

Cue me mentally rearranging the crew assignments for the week, figuring which jobs can be delayed without losing contracts and which will need overtime to keep on track.

Then, after calling Rocky in on his day off, we finally get underway an hour late... only to find a shiny little SUV with New York plates parked diagonally across the Grange Cut, ass-end kissing the drainage ditch and nose-end cocked toward the woods, comprehensively blocking our path. There's no way to ease around it with our giant brush-clearing equipment.

This isn't the first time an out-of-towner has decided someone's private land would make a good driveway for their impromptu hike, so I do what I usually do. I scan the ditch, the shoulder, and the tree line in three quick passes, automatically calculating if I can winch the SUV into the clearing without damaging it, and realize it's faster to haul it straight back.

So I'm hooking up the bumper to do just that when the car's owner scurries out of Jim's house half-naked, brandishing a racket at me like he's gonna serve me a Wimbledon-style beatdown.

Worst of all, my own brain's decided to go on strike at the sight of the guy. It hiccups and stutters, focusing in on the jut of the man's hip bones beneath his tiny underwear with Terminator-like intensity despite the fact that I'm on the clock… which is so unlike me I can't even tell you.

I don't ogle strangers. I don't ogle *anyone* when I have work to do.

And as if I wasn't already hangry, horny, and pissed off enough, the sexy tourist lifts his chin and throws my own words back in my face. *"Move your big-ass trucks off my property. And if you shake a leg, maybe I won't call the authorities and tell them you're trespassing."*

Despite my immediate, overwhelming annoyance, part of me wants to laugh.

I know some folks in Winsome find me intimidating.

I assume that's because I'm not exactly the friendliest

person in town. I hate gossip, which is Winsome's favorite pastime, and I'm not a happy joiner when it comes to town activities. I also have no patience for the outsiders who blow through Winsome, leaving a trail of car accidents, missing-hiker searches, and broken hearts in their wake. And… yeah, okay, it's probably also because I'm built on the larger side of "big" and don't smile a lot, which gives me what my youngest brother calls "Resting Intimidation Face." It's a real thing.

Whatever the reason, I don't go out of my way to change this impression because it means people in town—at least those who aren't named Axford—tend to leave me alone, and I like it that way.

I already have plenty of shit to deal with from the fuckers who share my DNA.

But the fact that this guy doesn't seem intimidated in the slightest? It's… let's say, unusual.

He's squaring up to me, clutching that damn racket, like he doesn't realize he's practically naked, several inches shorter than me, and built lean—*like a dancer*, my wayward brain supplies, which is a thought it's never had about anyone before, even actual dancers.

I reluctantly admit this guy has balls. But if a man won't back down when he's outmuscled, either he's bluffing or he has a plan, and I need to know which it is. Also, those balls of his are practically *on display* in his skimpy underwear, and I'm fighting the urge to pull off my own shirt and cover him up, which is all kinds of wrong.

"Once again, who the hell are you?" I demand.

The guy raises his chin so high it's practically pointed at the sky. "Who wants to know?" he taunts in a distinct

New York accent, like we're kids on the playground and he is rubber, I am glue.

Behind me, Freddy clears his throat and steps forward. He's bigger in circumference than I am, and I've seen him literally throw a man through a wall for mouthing off to his sister, but right now, he's all sheepish smiles for Mr. New York. "We're from Axford Lumber. I'm Fred Munson. That's Hussein, Rocky, Carlos, Bunsen—"

"Adam," Bunsen corrects, stepping forward, wiping his big hands on his jeans, and giving the guy—I shit you not—a chipper little wave, like we're at a goddamn tea party. "Adam Berner. But since middle school, everyone's called me Bun—"

I shoot Bunsen a furious look, and he finishes with a strangled "Um. Never mind."

"And that's the boss, Beckett Axford," Freddy finishes in a rush, pointing at me. "His great-something-grandfather started the company, and—"

"Jesus," I mutter. "Anything else you'd like to share with the guy who's fucked up our morning and made himself at home on Jim's land?" I turn in place and eye each member of my crew. "Social security numbers? Mother's maiden names? Astrological signs?"

"Virgo," Carlos says, raising his hand. "But I don't really know what that means. If it means virgin, then it's bullshit, and you can ask Bebe Jones if you don't believe me."

I exhale like I'm breathing fire and decide Carlos will be doing all chainsaw maintenance for a month.

Mr. New York gives a startled, genuine laugh that changes his whole face, and suddenly, I'm looking at him again. *Really* looking this time, at the bits of him *above* his underwear.

He's—fuck, okay, I admit it—he's beautiful. His skin is milk-pale all over and dusted with golden hair, and his face belongs on magazine covers. But his perfection is skewed just a little. The hair on the left side of his head is sticking straight up, like half of him was electrocuted. And between the blue shadows under his eyes, the glint of a blond beard growing in, and the red creases on his cheek, it looks like Mr. New York's had a rough night.

Possibly marauding through town, holding innocent Winsomefolk at racket-point.

But it's his eyes that sock me in the gut. They're so clear and light I can see them from a foot away—green with a sunburst of amber in the middle—and surrounded by thick, down-tilted eyelashes that make him look like a baby deer. And when he smiles—

*Dear god.* I blink and shake myself all over, like my parents' old Labrador retriever when she's taken a dunk in the river. *What the fuck is happening right now?*

I change my mind. Carlos is doing chainsaw maintenance *permanently*. And so is anyone else who makes this guy smile. His smile is way more dangerous than his stupid tennis racket.

"Hey. I'm Griffin Mercer," the guy says, with five friendly nods for each suddenly smitten member of my crew and a glare for me.

"Oh, goody," I say with exaggerated excitement. "Now I'll know whose name to put in my diary tonight when I write all about the special boy I met." I roll my eyes. "What the fuck are you doing here, *Griffin*? Why are you blocking the road to my land?"

His face and neck go red. "It's *my* road now," he proclaims, which is utterly ridiculous.

I consider the possibility for point-two seconds and shake my head. "No way. Jim Grange loves this place. He'd never sell."

But even as I say it, there's a niggling thought in the back of my head.

*Fucking fuck, what if he* did?

Jim Grange has owned this patch of Winsome for twenty-ish years, give or take, since he won it in a poker game from my idiot uncle. He's a good guy and an easy neighbor. He was happy to win the land so he could build his wacky little treehouse. But once he won it, Jim had no problem letting Axford Lumber cut through his property to get to our forest. When I took over running the company and wanted a formal easement agreement—a legal document that would guarantee me the right to use this road—Jim agreed.

But god knows Jim wouldn't be the first person to sell off land without warning. My own father did the same, just last year, which was a whole other clusterfuck. And my dad's a trustworthy, responsible, steady sort of person.

Jim's... not.

He used to leave on long road trips, like the one where he met my uncle, without telling a soul, and the only way we'd know he was gone was when the postman would alert my mom that his mailbox was full, so one of us kids could run over to collect his mail. We'd only know he was back when the Magic Mushroom Mobile was parked in the driveway—or, on one horrifying occasion a few years ago, when I went to collect the mail and found Jim sunning his asshole on his roof.

Now that his traveling days are mostly behind him, Jim likes to take "herbal supplements" and "stroll around the forest" to "let his mind wander"… which has necessitated at least three search and rescue calls that I know of because he's wandered himself into trouble. He *agreed* to the easement months ago, so I got a lawyer to write the damn thing up. But he still hasn't filed it with the town, and I'd bet money those papers accidentally ended up in his compost heap despite his best intentions.

And Jesus, don't get me started on Jim's mushroom thing.

All of which is to say, it's not a total surprise when the hot tourist—*Griffin, his name is Griffin*—opens his mouth and tells me Jim has pulled the ultimate unexpected move.

"You're right. Jim didn't sell it," he says. But before I can feel smug, he adds, "I inherited it." A flicker of sadness passes over his too-pretty face. "Jim died."

Carlos whistles low. Hussein shakes his head sadly and murmurs something under his breath that sounds like, "Ah, shit." Freddy glances at me with a wary look I've seen before, usually when I start grinding my back molars so hard the noise carries.

"Died," I repeat, though I can barely hear myself over the blood roaring in my ears. "How? When?" I ponder, then add, "Where?"

I know it can't have been here in Winsome. The town gossips, led by my mother and my brother Holden, would've spread the news in a heartbeat because they can't help themselves… which is why I always try to avoid doing or saying anything where they can see, or hear, it.

"I… I don't know," Griffin admits, dropping the racket to his side. "Uncle Jim's lawyer's out on medical leave, so I don't have a lot of details yet." He frowns. "You didn't know?"

My guys exchange looks. Each shakes his head.

"Back up," I say. "You don't know when your own uncle died? And since when does Jim have a nephew? I thought he didn't have family."

"We weren't blood related. Jim was an old family friend. A neighbor. N-not that it's any of your b-business." He shivers but ignores it and crosses his arms over his chest.

My jaw goes so tight my body vibrates.

He's right. It *isn't* my business.

Just like it's not my business that it's unseasonably chilly this morning, and this mostly naked idiot's turning himself into a popsicle.

Except it literally *is* my business—the part about the inheritance, anyway—because there are Swiss-cheese holes in this guy's story, and I really need him to be lying.

If he's not, Axford Lumber's fucked. And since the family business is my responsibility now, I'm fucked too.

"Jim and I have an agreement where I can use this road to access my family's land back there." I nod past the guy's car to where the Grange Cut disappears into the trees. "As his quasi-nephew, I'd think you'd know that."

Uncertainty flickers on his face for half a second before he lifts the damn racket again. "I have no record of that, Mr. Axford. There's not a word about your supposed agreement in the paperwork I received from Jim's attorney's office. My map of the property line shows this road is absolutely within the boundaries of *my* land."

*Fuck.*

"It was a gentleman's agreement," I snap. "That's how things are done in Winsome."

Now I'm the one lying, sort of.

Handshake deals were how my father and his contemporaries did business, which is why Axford Lumber has an amazing reputation and a very shaky bottom line.

That was the past, though. Nowadays, we have access to the internet just like everyone else and plenty of unscrupulous people in town ready to take advantage of the unwary... which is why I'd insisted on the formal easement.

Or tried to.

*Fuck, fuck, fuck.*

"Griffin!" a voice calls from back near Jim's house. "Are you okay? I called the sheriff, and they're sending someone out, so whoever's bothering you had better—ohhhh."

The man who steps off the path is shorter than Griffin with a head of wild curls. He's dressed head to toe in slouchy black clothes that are probably trendy and holding a cell phone like a weapon.

He sidles over to Griffin, clutches his forearm, and whispers like he's trying not to move his lips, "Is this some kind of Vermont-induced psychosis, or are we being invaded by lumberjacks? Holy fuck, and it's not even my birthday!"

The way Griffin shakes off his hand makes it pretty clear that the two men aren't together.

I mean, not that I noticed. Or care either way.

"Jesus, Milo. Focus. Did you actually call the sheriff?" Griffin demands.

"Uh, *yes.* Obvi. I told the dispatcher my best friend's

home was under siege." Milo tosses back blond curls. "She promised the sheriff himself would be here in five, which —honestly? Kind of impressive. I assumed a small-town cop would be kicking up his feet, eating donuts."

I huff out a breath. *He is. The sheriff's right now eating my fucking donuts. And probably my portion of sausage casserole too. And no wonder he's coming fast, since he's half a mile down the road at our parents' house.*

Sure enough, moments later, the crunch of gravel announces the arrival of a familiar black-and-gold sheriff's SUV. The middle of my three younger brothers climbs out, wearing his full uniform and the same damn sunshine smile he's had since birth.

"Morning, boys!" Holden calls, and at the sound of his voice, every person in our little group—Winsomefolk and New Yorkers alike—relaxes a little.

Holden's always been this way. A friend to all, a golden boy, a high school quarterback, a helper of old ladies who need groceries carried.

Yes, it *is* highly annoying, thank you for asking.

He claps me on the shoulder just a little too hard and strides forward to shake hands with the newcomers. "Welcome to Winsome!"

But Milo seems immediately wary. He stares at Holden's outstretched hand like it's a crusty sock.

"Charmed," he says, not sounding remotely charmed… and also not returning his handshake.

Griffin elbows him. He casts a sidelong glance at me, then extends his hand to Holden with a small smile. "Thank you. It's been a journey."

I watch Griffin's hand disappear into Holden's as he introduces himself and his friend. His fingers are cold, I can tell, and I have the wildly inappropriate urge to warm them myself.

"I'm really sorry to drag you out here, sir—" Griffin continues.

Pretty sure Holden gets off on the *sir* thing because his chest puffs up like a fucking prize rooster.

"No problem. Just doing my job," Holden replies in his aw-shucks voice. If he had a hat on, he'd probably tip the brim like a cowboy in a spaghetti western.

It's insufferable.

"Rachelle said we had a possible trespass situation?" Holden glances at me, one brow lifted like he already knows I'm about to explode.

"No," I say shortly.

"Y-yes," Griffin insists, though his delivery loses a little conviction since he's visibly shivering in the chilly air.

Holden frowns and holds up a hand. "Hang on. You're freezing."

He can't exactly give Griffin his uniform shirt, Milo's sweater wouldn't fit, and my guys are standing back and watching like this is an amateur drama they bought tickets to. Which means…

Holden turns to me with a meaningful cock of his head.

I sigh loudly and unbutton my flannel, peeling it off and holding it out like it pains me.

"Here," I mutter, as though I haven't been half wanting to offer it all along.

I can see that Griffin doesn't want to take it. The *I'd rather freeze* is written all over his face. But with Holden looking on, everyone's always on their best behavior.

"Thanks," Griffin says, his tone pure *fuck you.*

"Yeah," I say in the same tone.

He shivers again as he slips his arms into my shirt and pulls it around himself like he's savoring the warmth of my body. It hangs halfway down his thighs, nearly swallowing him whole, and something low in my gut clenches so hard it's nearly audible.

*I am not attracted to this guy,* I remind myself. *Attraction is for one-nighters at the Shed. Not for anyone who might start to get ideas, and* definitely *not for assholes from out of town who want to get into an arbitrary territorial dispute.*

It's easier to remember all this when I notice Griffin hasn't let go of his damn tennis racket. Does he plan to practice his backhand on me right in front of the sheriff? I almost wish he would.

"So?" Holden prompts, hands on his hips. "Trespassing?"

"Yes. As I was telling your angry lumberjack friend—" Griffin jerks his chin toward me. "—I recently inherited this land from Jim Grange."

Holden turns to me, eyebrows raised. I give him a tight shrug. *Was news to me too.*

"Inherited?" Holden repeats. "Meaning… Jim passed? My condolences. He was a good man."

Griffin looks uncomfortable, but nods.

"I assume you have proper documentation of the inheritance?" Holden goes on. His eyes narrow a little—a reminder that there's actually a brain beneath that golden-retriever charm.

"A letter from Jim's attorney stating that I'm the sole beneficiary of the trust that owns this land. The Griffin Mercer Trust." Griffin swallows. "I also have a handwritten note from Jim confirming it. And a map."

"Well. Okay, then. Easy enough to verify." Holden shoots me a look that says *this doesn't look good*. "Mr. Mercer—"

"Griffin."

"Griffin. None of us were aware of Jim's death or that the land had passed to a new owner. I assure you, my brother didn't intend—"

"Hang on. Brother?" Milo narrows his eyes. "You two are related?"

He shifts his gaze back and forth between me and Holden like he's searching for similarities. There are plenty to find, though Holden gets his coloring, love of gossip, and bizarre friendliness from our mom.

"Oh, sure," Rocky volunteers cheerfully. "You can't throw a stone in Winsome without hitting an Axford. They run the inn, the garage, the clinic..."

Holden shrugs, not at all embarrassed. "Side effect of our family staying in one place for generations," he says lightly. "But as I was saying, I know my brother didn't intend to trespass, and this was all a big misunderstanding. Beckett's very sorry for disturbing you. Right, Beckett?"

"*I* wasn't the source of the disturbance here," I hear myself say sourly. "Which means the apology needs to come from *him*."

Yeah, I know I should keep my mouth shut. I'm well aware. But something about this whole interaction... okay, fucking *everything* about this interaction... is getting under my skin.

Predictably, both Griffin and Holden glare at me.

"What?" I demand. "We've been using this road for

years. I didn't do anything different than I've always done. Why does Jim's death have to change things?"

"A fair point," Holden allows. To Griffin, he explains, "Arrangements like the one Jim made with our family are common here. They're called prescriptive easements. Jim still owned the land but allowed us to use the road. It's the same way the Parsons let hikers cross their pasture to get to the Falls." Holden gives him his *I'm everyone's pal* smile. "It's not official, but it's been done that way so long, there's an expectation that it'll continue."

Griffin frowns thoughtfully, but then Milo speaks up.

"Think carefully, Griff," he declares. "Your uncle made some shady, half-legal verbal agreement? Fine. But that ended when he died. If you *keep* letting this guy use the road, it's like *you're* entering into an agreement. What happens when you want to sell so you can buy a new place somewhere? Everyone knows easements decrease property value."

Holden forces a chuckle, trying to keep things light. "Hang on now. There's no need to make this into a big legal issue—"

"You're his brother. Of course you'd say that," Milo scoffs.

Holden lets out a disbelieving laugh. "But I'm also the sheriff—"

Milo purses his lips and lets his silence speak several skeptical volumes.

For a second, Holden looks like a puppy who's been smacked with a newspaper. I might enjoy the novelty of it if my business wasn't on the line.

"Milo's right," Griffin finally says, giving Holden an apologetic shrug. "I appreciate your time, Sheriff Axford.

I'm grateful you came out here. And I'm sorry to disappoint you guys," he tells my crew, "but until I've had a chance to explore the legal ramifications and make sure I'm not being taken advantage of, I can't afford to have *this person* using my road." He waves a hand in my direction.

*This person?*

*Taken advantage of?*

"This might be your land, but everything beyond that tree is *mine*. My family's forest. You can't just march in here waving a tennis racket and deny me access to it."

"And *you* can't bully me into an agreement when I haven't had time to research it." Griffin twirls the racket like a cheerleader baton, then gives it a little flourish. "Legally, this land is mine, and I'm going to protect it."

*Protect it? From me?*

The comment stabs me in the chest.

I have three shit-stirring brothers, a smart-assed sister, a cousin who lives to tease me, and a billion neighbors who won't mind their business, but I still can't think of a time I've been this fucking provoked. Not since I was a teenager.

Something inside me snaps, and before I know what I'm doing, I've grabbed the damn tennis racket out of his hand and hurled it toward the sky.

The satisfaction is fleeting. Even as it's spinning through the air, I'm thinking, *Beckett, you immature asshole, what have you done?*

But then the racket spins through the air in a perfect arc... and lodges in the crook of a pine tree twenty feet off the ground.

For a second, we all stare in stunned silence.

Holden groans.

Milo gasps.

My guys wince.

And Griffin makes a noise like the whistle on a teakettle. "You absolute—! That racket was an *heirloom!*" His chest heaves, lips parted and face flushed as he gets up in my face.

"Oh yeah? Are you the nephew of *Lord* fucking *Wimbledon* now too?" I shout.

"You better get off my property," he yells back, "or I will… I will… I will sue the pants off you!"

"I'd say the same," I growl, "but you don't *have* any pants!"

Milo and Holden step between us at the same time, Milo murmuring something to Griffin and nudging him toward the treehouse, while Holden grabs my arm and frog-marches me down the driveway to my truck like he forgets I've got several years and fifty pounds on him.

"What the hell was that?" he demands once we're out of earshot.

I heave a breath. "I lost my temper."

"Yeah, no shit."

"But can you blame me?" I pace a tight circle in the leaf-and-pine-needle strewn gravel between my truck and Holden's SUV and throw out a hand toward the treehouse as Griffin disappears through the door, the flannel edge of my shirt skimming the backs of his thighs. I suck in a breath and try to focus. "The *nerve* of that guy. Typical fucking tourist. Last year, one of them smacked into my truck in the parking lot at Chapel Island. Just yesterday, one nearly ran me off the road when I was heading to the office. And now, this asshole's destroying my business—"

"Except he's not a tourist, and *he* isn't the only one at

fault here." Holden watches me pace. "Don't you remember anything Mom used to say about catching more flies with honey?"

"Who the fuck wants to catch flies?" I demand. "I want to do my damn job. I have contracts to fill. I need to be clearing brush in the Far Tract right *now* so we can start staging next week. Axford Lumber can't compete if—"

"Beckett." Holden's voice sharpens. "If Griffin's telling the truth, and I think he is, you're shit out of luck when it comes to accessing the Far Tract unless you take him to court and get a formal judgment or he changes his mind."

Hearing the truth laid out so baldly throws a wet blanket over the fire burning in my chest, and I bend over, bracing my hands on my thighs.

I cannot believe one pale, pretty city boy with a pair of sexy legs has so comprehensively fucked up my life.

My brother puts a hand on my shoulder. "Take some time to cool off, and then talk to him. For all we know, he'll be reasonable when he has a chance to get his feet under himself."

"I don't have time," I mutter. "I have contracts waiting—"

"Well, you're going to have to find a way. A *legal* way." Holden's eyes, brown like our mom's, watch me steadily. "Do not bring your crew back out here unless you have his agreement, or I'll have to arrest you." He flashes a grin. "And if that happens, I promise you, I'll print your mug shot on a T-shirt and wear it every fucking day for the rest of my life. Understand?"

I straighten and glare at him. "You have donut crumbs on your uniform," I say in lieu of an actual answer.

He glances down at his shirt, dusts himself off, then

lifts an eyebrow. "Jealous? Because Mom *outdid* herself for Dad's birthday breakfast this year." He licks his lips like he's savoring the sweet honey glaze. "She did something with pumpkin spice flavoring that was amazing."

"Petty fucker," I mutter.

"Learned it from my big brother," he shoots back. Then he adds more gently, "We missed you. Eliza and Luis were talking wedding stuff. Ames brought some kind of baked oatmeal thing because it's supposed to be good for Dad's heart. Even True showed up." Holden laughs. "Carved dad another bird."

"Yeah?" I push a hand through my hair. The adrenaline's leaving my system, and I feel like I've finished a ten-mile run. "Dad must have a whole flock of them by now."

"Well, the man spends his whole life birdwatching and doing crosswords since he retired," Holden points out. "And True claims he can't carve a crossword, so…"

That actually pulls a laugh out of me, but then I think about our dad, who used to be all about brawn and constant motion, larger than life, and the laugh dies.

Our father does have one other hobby, but I'm not sure how even a talented woodworker like True could represent "making comments about how Beckett's running the family business" in a wood carving.

"He asked for you," Holden adds after a pause.

I lean my ass against the door of my truck and squint up at him. "Who, Dad?"

"Mm. Well, more like Mom fretted about you not being there, and Dad said you were too busy with work to make time for family and to leave you be."

That stings more than I want it to.

"I would've come," I tell Holden. "But I really did have to work. Sullivan's breathing down our necks. You know he underbid me on the Timberline project by fifteen percent? He can't even be making a profit at those rates! And he's leaning hard into this whole eco-consciousness schtick, when I don't see how he could be producing as much lumber as he seems to be if he's truly doing it sustainably."

Holden shrugs. "Maybe his operation's bigger than you realize. He's sure buying up plenty of land."

"Yeah, including the plot he bought from Dad on the other side of the Far Tract," I say bitterly. "But Dad told Derek from the beginning that he couldn't get a permit to harvest timber on that land because of the water table. So if he's this green warrior who's trying to save the planet, tell me why he's been trying off and on to pull a logging permit for that plot anyway when he knows it'll never go through."

I can't help thinking that if Dad had bothered telling anyone—namely me—that he was planning to sell off land in the first place, all of this could have been avoided.

But here we are.

My hands clench into fists, and Holden notices.

"See now, I was thinking you didn't come to breakfast because you and Dad are having a months-long pissing contest," he says conversationally.

I force my hands to relax. "We're not. At least *I'm* not. Dad and I have different opinions about how to run the business. He still believes in loyalty credit and handshake deals, but that's what got us into trouble." I thrust a thumb over my shoulder toward Jim's—*fuck, Griffin's*—road.

"Hell, it's *still* getting us into trouble. You should see our P&L from last quarter."

"Criminal justice, bro," he reminds me, tapping his chest. "Profit shit is not my wheelhouse."

I snort. My B.S. in Forestry hadn't prepared me for this stuff either. Dad always held the reins tight on the front end of the business. Opening QuickBooks after his heart attack last year had been an eye-opening education.

Holden's expression softens. "You want some advice?"

I roll my eyes. I swear, if I spent any more time around my siblings, my eyes would stay permanently glued to the heavens. "Do I have a choice, Sheriff Axford, *sir*?"

He knuckles my biceps, hard, and I yelp. "Ow! Fucker."

Holden shakes his head. "When you're in a hole, Beckett... stop fucking digging."

I blink. "What's that supposed to mean?"

"It means, sac up and face the fact you've handled things poorly, then fix them."

"Which things?"

It's a serious question, but Holden snorts like I'm being funny on purpose. "Making nice costs you nothing and will save you a fuck-ton of heartburn and headaches down the line. So pour on some honey and catch some damn flies. Give the guy a chance to cool off, then talk to him. Maybe throw in an apology if you're feeling wild."

I squint. "Still not sure if you're talking about Griffin or Dad."

Holden smirks and pats my shoulder again before heading to his SUV. "Figure it out, bro."

The most annoying thing about my brother—and there are many, many things—is that he's so often right, especially when it comes to reading people. So after I reassign my crew to jobs back at the mill, I make a mental note to try to talk to the guy.

To… Griffin.

But not until I've cooled down. Not until I can do it with some strategy and a little less aggression.

Because if Griffin Mercer holds the key to my land, I can't afford to keep pissing him off.

Even if part of me really, really wants to.

# CHAPTER THREE

## GRIFFIN

THE NEXT MORNING, I march out of the Winsome Town Hall like I've just claimed victory in a war.

This is my favorite kind of war because nobody's going to get hurt, but one person—one arrogant, unfairly sexy, ridiculously broad-shouldered person who gives lumberjacks a bad name—is gonna get his pride trampled, while another innocent and generally delightful person—aka me —gets to savor the smug feeling of triumph.

I can't lie, I had my doubts when I first located the records office. The place smells like sad, stale coffee, and the ancient records clerk greeted me with a dead-eyed stare from behind a towering stack of papers, like I was her first human visitor in years. I thought for sure Vermont was about to do me dirty again.

But I shouldn't have doubted Sylvia—my new favorite sixty-something; don't tell my moms—because once I explained why I was there, she spryly jumped up from her desk, popped a piece of bubblegum, stuck a pencil in her Reagan-era perm, hopped over to one of the many, many file cabinets, and produced the deed to the Grange property in about thirty seconds flat.

I clutch the rolled-up papers Sylvia copied for me as I skip down the stairs to join Milo, who's sitting on the low wall in front of the building, basking in the late-September sunshine.

"I have good news," I say, bouncing in front of him. "The *best* news. Guess!"

Milo glances up from his phone and taps his lip thoughtfully, pretending to consider. "Hmm… Erick Nelson admitted to sabotaging you, his dad offered your job back with a bonus, and we're going home to forget all about treehouses with stained glass windows that look like big green dicks?"

"What?" I scowl. "No."

"Oooh, I know! The hot mechanic who fixed your flat tire called you back and asked for my Instagram handle so he could send me some NSFW snapshots!"

"Milo." I smack his arm with my rolled-up papers. "I feel like you don't know how this game is played."

"Sorry, sorry." He snickers, then morphs his face into something angelically eager. "Why, I can't imagine, Griffin! Please share your excellent news!"

"Much better." I grin. "The deed is, in fact, in the name of the Griffin Mercer Trust!"

"Which… is pretty much exactly what you thought." Milo sounds unimpressed.

"Yes, but! The hand-drawn property map the lawyer sent me is actually part of the official property record, and it shows the road—by which I mean *my driveway*— running right over my land. They also have a copy of the trust on file."

He nods. "That makes sense, since the trust owns the land."

"Right? It says…" I unroll the papers and read, "All property, both real and personal, tangible and intangible, including intellectual rights, of whatever nature and wherever situated, shall be distributed to Griffin Mercer."

"What intellectual rights are we talking about?" Milo asks.

I shrug. "Not a clue. Maybe he wrote some mushroom poetry. But are you ready for the best part?"

Milo sits forward, takes a deep breath, cracks his neck side to side, and shakes out his hands, making a huge production of it. "Okay. Yeah. I'm ready. Lay it on me."

I rock back and forth on the balls of my feet giddily. "There's no easement on record! Nary a clause nor a footnote. So, there!" I add, speaking directly to the ghost of Beckett Axford that's taken up residence in my head.

"Okay, yeah." Milo nods. "That *is* good."

"It's excellent," I correct. "Damn, I wish I could courier these copies directly to Beckett's house encased in a glitter bomb." I drop down on the wall beside Milo and tilt my face up to the sun. "And then be there hiding in the bushes to watch him open it!"

The idea of Beckett with glitter clinging to his messy dark hair, his beard, his broad chest, and his big, thick thighs makes my heart rate kick up excitedly.

Because of the glitter. Obviously.

"Griffycakes. My precious lamb." Milo pushes up his designer sunglasses so they're nestled in his curls, and his serious gaze meets mine. "Don't you think you might be getting a little too invested in this?"

I laugh incredulously. "Uh, *no*. I'm exactly the right

amount invested in this. You were *there*, Milo. You saw how rude Beckett was. How dismissive. How cranky. And he threw Jim's lucky tennis racket into a tree!" Even a day later, the memory of it makes my hands clench into fists.

I spent a fucking *hour* last night trying to shake the tree —not my most logical endeavor, I grant you—and throwing rocks at the racket to dislodge it. All I had to show for it was a blister on my thumb.

"He did," Milo agrees. "And I'm not defending him…"

"Really?" I demand hotly. "'Cause your tone sure suggests you are."

"Griffin Alexander Mercer. I will ride with you to Beckett's house and glitter bomb the hell out of him right now if you want. I will toilet paper every tree in his forest. You know this! But what I want to know is… why are you wasting your time and energy on Beckett the Lumberjack when you have so much other shit to worry about?"

"Because…" For a second, I flail. "Because if I let the man bring his noisy trucks and his noisier crew down my driveway, they're going to use chainsaws all day, Milo! That's the opposite of the peace and quiet I'm looking for. Besides, *you* were the one who said allowing Beckett access would set a new precedent and might lower the value of the property when I sell it!"

"Yes, but I mostly said that because Officer Smiley was getting under my skin, and someone needed to put him in his place." He narrows his eyes like he's thinking of Holden. "No one's actually that friendly, mark my words."

"Yeah, well… whyever you said it, you were right."

"As I usually am," Milo agrees. "But, boo, if you get ten percent less when you sell, it's still a huge windfall, right?"

I huff. "Spoken like someone who hasn't lost his

income *and* his ability to make more in his chosen career anytime soon."

Milo looks chastened. "I know. I'm not saying the money's not important. I just... I feel like this is about more than money. You're taking it personally."

"Hell yes, it's personal," I answer without thinking about it. "And not just because Beckett's an asshole," I add.

He lifts one eyebrow. "You sure about that?"

"Yes." I blow out a breath. "Look, when I got the letter from Jim's lawyer about the trust, I didn't have the... the mental bandwidth... to question it. You know that better than anyone."

Milo nods. He was there for my lowest points this summer. He saw how the relentless silence from potential employers and the colleagues I'd thought were my friends weighed on me even heavier than the avalanche of bill reminders. He knows that what hit me hardest wasn't just losing my career or my six-figure salary; it was the ego hit of thinking I'd built myself an unsinkable life—one where I wouldn't be forever struggling at the whims of fate like my moms had been—only to have it all go full-on *Titanic*.

"When you're drowning, you don't ask *why* someone's throwing you a rope, you just grab it," Milo says softly.

I glance at him in surprise. This is the closest he's come to acknowledging that he understands why I chose to relocate temporarily rather than simply sell off the property sight unseen, the way my moms expected me to, or mortgage it to pay for a wrongful termination suit against the Nelson Group, the way Milo wanted.

"Yeah." I sit forward, bracing my elbows on my knees, and watch my fingers knit and unknit themselves. "But now that I'm here, now that I've seen the treehouse, I can't stop thinking *why*. Like, why build a fairy-tale funhouse in the first place? Why Winsome?" I wave a hand, indicating the tiny town with its cute clapboard shops, single stoplight, and overabundance of trees. "And why *me*? People don't just leave whole-ass properties to kids they haven't seen in twenty-plus years."

"You forget that your moms have shown me your scrapbooks." Milo nudges his arm into mine. "You were a *very* adorable child. And very precocious, with all those reading trophies and gold stars for writing stories."

I roll my eyes. "I'm being serious."

"I know." Milo shrugs. "But there are a million possible reasons. Maybe Jim remembered you fondly. Maybe he didn't have any family." He lowers his voice and nudges me with his elbow. "Maybe the mushrooms told him to."

I snort. "Maybe, yeah. But that's what makes it so personal."

Milo frowns and shakes his head. "Explain for the class, babe."

"If I'm the closest thing Jim had to family, if he remembered me fondly as someone he wanted to leave his treehouse to, then... then it's on me to take care of it. You know? To make sure it goes to someone who'll appreciate it. To keep it as intact as possible until then. I wasn't there for Jim when he died—hell, I still don't even know how or *where* he died—"

"Because that lawyer still hasn't called you back," he grumbles.

"But the least I can do for the man is to protect this treehouse he entrusted to me until it's time to sell it."

*Maybe then I'll feel like I've done something to deserve it.*

"But you will sell it," Milo says with narrowed eyes.

It's not a question, but I answer it anyway. "Of course." I nudge his arm back. "I'm immune to Jim's mushroom magic. I cannot imagine chucking my whole life out the window to become a…" I frown. "Winsomer? Winsome-man? Winsomite? Whatever. But it's like I told my mom when she texted this morning to give me the contact info of a real estate agent she knows: I'm not ready to think about selling until I know where I'm going next."

"And not until you solve the Mystery of Why Jim Left You A Treehouse, Encyclopedia Brown?"

I snort. "That too, I guess. And in the meantime, for all those reasons, I'm not letting Beckett get his grubby paws on my land."

A grin cracks Milo's face. "But maybe you wouldn't mind if he put his paws on other things?"

"Ugh. Stop." I push to my feet, horrified to find that Milo's words are having an effect on me. "You're such a child."

"Oh, I'm thinking *very* grown-up thoughts, I assure you. Lumberjack Beckett looked like he wanted to lick you when you put his shirt on," Milo continues in the same sing-song voice.

I whirl back. "He did not!"

"Like an ice cream cone." Milo sucks a tooth. "And since you *slept* in said shirt last night, I have to assume you'd be amenable to a little licking, even if you're sworn enemies or whatever."

"That…" I choke lightly. "That is a false interpretation of events, Milo Fitzgerald."

He hums thoughtfully. "I was *this-close* to taking a picture of you as proof."

"You wanted the window open! I was chilly!" I remind him. I feel a defensive blush climbing up my face. "A-and I didn't want to dig through my suitcase to find a sweater in the middle of the night because... because it would have been loud, and you were sleeping, and I'm *thoughtful*! The shirt was right there, so I grabbed it. That's all!"

"Mmm."

"And... whatever laundry detergent the guy uses *happens* to smell really nice," I press on, trying not to remember the crisp cedar scent of the shirt or to imagine it still lingering on my skin. "Probably some niche local brand."

"You think Vermont sells some kind of Mountain Man Sex–scented Tide Pods?" He laughs. "Goddamn. I'm changing my whole opinion of this state."

I snort. "*Pfft*. Sex was your word, not mine. I do *not* want to have sex with Beckett Axford."

"No, of course," he agrees cheerfully. "You just want to cuddle with him."

This brings up a whole host of ideas—big-armed, broad-chested, flannel-coated ideas—that I have no business thinking. Not on a public street in broad daylight. And definitely not about jerkus maximus Beckett Axford.

"I mean it, Milo! I legit cannot remember the last time I was as purely angry as I was when he showed up yesterday."

And that's saying something. Not just because of the last few months but because of how many hours I've spent over the years dealing with clients who think waving their hands and saying "make it, like, *pop*" is actionable creative feedback on an ad campaign.

Milo looks at me and his smile flickers. "You know… I can't either. He really gets under your skin, doesn't he?"

"Like a splinter the size of a fucking troll."

He laughs and pushes to his feet. "He can't be all that bad. The man was wearing a Meals on Wheels T-shirt. He feeds the homebound, Griff."

I huffed. "He probably stole it off a little old lady."

"Little old lady with impressive shoulders and pecs, amirite," Milo said through a grin. "Okay, ignore me. I've probably reached the stage of malnutrition and dehydration where I'm no longer making sense. I'm literally wasting away to a gorgeous husk right here on this quaint little street. You know what Silvano says about proper hydration being essential for cellular health. Vermont is murder on my mitochondria, Griffin."

I roll my eyes because I know way too much about Milo's mitochondria *and* about his various wellness "experts."

"Then let's go," I say, pointing toward the lone grocery-store-ish building in the town center. "I have a shopping list."

Milo links his arm with mine as we head down the sidewalk. "Of course you do."

"And I researched a few simple recipes we can make."

"Really hoping you've suddenly taken to using the royal *we*."

"Hang on." I pull away smoothly, handing him the papers, and take my phone out of my pocket. "I need to add laundry detergent to the list."

Milo's smile says he's not offended.

As we stroll down Whether Street, Winsome stretches out before us like a storybook town. There's a hand-painted sandwich board outside a place called Ruby's Diner advertising apple cranberry as their muffin of the day, and it's making the air smell like a scented candle. Wind chimes dance on someone's porch, gently clinking above pots of mums. And every shop door is standing open to let the warm breeze waft in.

Milo's right. It *is* a quaint little street. A bit heavy-handed on the Americana, but lived-in and real. The cars parked along the curb with license plates from all over New England suggest I'm not the only one who thinks so. The Abigail Inn's lot seems pretty full, and peeking in the windows of the restaurant next door, there seems to be a decent crowd for a Tuesday.

I guess I can see why Jim chose Winsome. Maybe that part's not a mystery after all.

"Fucking asshole," Milo mutters down at his phone, drawing my attention away from the scenery.

"Who?"

"Eh. Just a TikTok troll. Nothing to worry about."

My stomach flips. "Commenting on something you posted?" I ask hopefully.

Milo's started making a name for himself as a health and lifestyle influencer, and every time he posts about spirulina extract, resin shots, or his beloved red-light therapy machine, someone comes for him.

Fortunately, Milo enjoys getting into it with those folks.

"Nah." He clicks the screen off. "Some guy who runs a hot dog stand in Ohio stitched the billboard TikTok into a discussion of marketing standards and didn't like it when I educated him." He smiles. "All good now."

My stomach sinks anyway. "Milo, you don't need to

fight these battles for me. It changes nothing, and I don't want any of it blowing back on you—"

He waves a hand. "I'm an adult, Griff. I can take care of myself."

"I know," I say. "But—"

"You know, I've been thinking it's time for *you* to join the influencer game, babe. Hear me out: cottage-core rebrand! Griffycakes123 lives in a mushroom-themed house! He has a tragic backstory! He has an adorable best friend! He gets hot for the lumberjack next door—"

"Stop with that." I shove Milo, who laughs and feigns stumbling. "And I'm telling my mothers you think my childhood was tragic. Just because we didn't have much money didn't mean I wasn't safe and happy."

"I meant your *recent* backstory, obviously." He pretends to rub his arm and adds in a teasing tone, "Though I remember the story your moms told me about your toast sword. You were a fighter even back then. Kind of foreshadowing the tennis racket incident, when you think about it."

I roll my eyes. Milo loves this story—the one where my lesbian moms were determined to raise me with non-gendered, non-violent toys and were shocked the first time I bit my toast into the shape of a sword and started parrying imaginary foes at the breakfast table.

"It's not that I want to fight anyone," I tell him honestly. "I just don't want to lose anything else I care about."

Milo pats me on the shoulder understandingly, and after I playfully shove his hand away, we continue our walk in silence.

The Basket looms at the end of the block, looking like a

cross between a rustic event barn and a Trader Joe's. When we step through the automatic doors, the air is cool, and we're greeted by a wall of signs.

One says "Fox Creamery Hand-Churned = Udder Joy" under a picture of a cow in lotus pose. Another says "Sugar House Jam of the Week: Peachy Keen, You Sassy Bean!" A third has a picture of a smiling, anthropomorphic pickle wearing a gold crown and a T-shirt that says "You're a Big Dill to Someone in Winsome, Vermont!" They're all cute, but I don't know what any of them *mean*, which is kinda the point of a sign.

Part of me wants to explain this to the friendly-looking guy behind the lone cash register, who's watching us with the avid look of a man who hasn't had fresh shoppers in a while. But since Milo's hangry-ness is growing with the gravitational force of a black hole, instead, I focus on completing our shopping before it sucks me in.

Fortunately, the store is small and well laid out, and we quickly find all the items on my list... with one crucial exception.

"Excuse me, sir," I begin as I set my basket down by the register.

"Perky!" he says.

For a second, I think he's describing himself as a form of greeting, and I'm almost tempted to blurt out, "Over-tired and cynical!"

Then he points to his name tag—Perkins (Perky) Halloran, Owner Since 1998.

*Oh.*

Milo elbows me aside. "Hi, Perky, I'm Milo. Could you *please* direct me to your selection of functional hydration beverages? I'm looking for aloe juice, ideally with pulp.

Possibly a reishi mushroom elixir—I'm not picky about brand. And at this rate, I'll take literally *anything* with hibiscus tonic."

I duck my chin to my chest and rub my forehead. I'm not sure where Milo thinks those beverages would be hiding since we've already been up and down all ten aisles.

Sure enough, with each suggestion, Perky seems more confused. "We got water, soda, and fruit juice in aisle seven," he offers.

Milo seems crushed and frazzled. He gives me a look that says *Griffin, do something,* which kinda belies the whole "I'm an adult, I take care of myself" thing from before. But unlike certain best friends, *I* don't point out *my* best friend's peccadilloes and inconsistencies.

"Do you have anything with electrolytes?" I suggest.

"Ohhhh!" Perky brightens. "Of course. Why dincha say so? We got a whole display of local pickles in aisle four."

"Pickles," I repeat, sure I've misheard. *Hoping* I've misheard.

"Sure thing. Pickles are the original electrolyte, boys," Perky says confidently. "Sugar-free. Full of sodium and potassium. Rehydrate the body and the soul."

"*Pickles,*" Milo breathes like Perky's become his newest health expert. "I never thought..." He grabs a fresh shopping basket and heads off.

Meanwhile, I stand there frozen, certain my horror's showing on my face.

Perky laughs as he scans my purchases. "Not a pickle fan, I take it?"

"Uh. No." More like I *hate* them.

"Guess that means you fellas aren't in town for the Brine, then?" He weighs my bananas on a cute little scale.

I shake my head. "What's that?"

Perky pauses to push up his glasses and stare at me in surprise. "The *Winsome* Brine," he clarifies.

I shrug apologetically.

"It's our biggest festival! See, the Fletcher Pickle Company used to have their headquarters just up the street." He points vaguely north. "The factory closed ages ago—it's an artists' workspace now—but we Winsomefolk still celebrate our proud pickling heritage every autumn, and we crown our Big Dill, of course."

He's saying a lot of things here, but my brain gets stuck on *we Winsomefolk*.

Dear god. How is *Winsomefolk* so much weirder than any of the possibilities I came up with? Is he including me in that term? Am I one of them now, even temporarily? Because legit, the proud pickling heritage might be a deal breaker.

"So if you're not in town for the festival, what brings you to Winsome?" Perky asks, dragging my brain back to reality.

"Oh. I, ah, inherited some property—"

He gasps. "So *you're* Jim Grange's nephew from New York! I heard all about you from Rachelle when I was at the diner earlier."

My immediate thought is, *Who the fuck is Rachelle, and why is she talking about me?* Is this normal small-town stuff? Because that might be a deal breaker too.

"I'm sorry for your loss," Perky goes on with a little cluck of his tongue.

I nod stiffly. Just like when the sheriff offered condolences the day before, it feels strange to accept them over someone I barely knew.

"I imagine Jim took the bus out for one last joyride when he knew it was his time. He sure loved his adventures." Perky gives me a commiserating smile. "He used to say his heart wasn't made to be planted in any one spot. But I like to think at least part of it put down roots in Winsome. That's why he shared his mushrooms with us."

There's a lot to unpack here, like the fact that Perky clearly knew Jim better than I ever did. But also…

"Jim…" I lower my voice and lean in. "…shared his mushrooms with you?"

I can't tell if he's talking about the kind of mushrooms you make ravioli out of or the ones Jim suggested might talk to him.

Maybe for Jim, they were one and the same.

Perky looks at me like *I'm* the one who's not making sense. "Well, sure. I'd bet those mushrooms are why half our visitors come to Winsome! Speaking of which, what happened to the Magic Mushroom Mobile? Because I'd really love to—"

He pauses mid-sentence and narrows his eyes when a voice behind me says, "Morning, Perky."

I whirl around, half expecting to see Beckett Axford in all his flannelly glory—honestly, that's how my luck's running these days—but I don't.

Which is *good*. Which is *excellent*.

The last thing I want is to see him again. Obviously.

Instead, I find a man in a sleek windbreaker and hiking boots. He looks like he's in his fifties, with salt-and-pepper hair, expensive cologne, and a charming smile.

"Sorry to intrude," he says, directing that smile at me.

"But I couldn't help overhearing. Derek Sullivan." He holds out a hand. "Sorry to hear about your uncle. Jim was a good man."

"Right." I force a smile as I shake his hand. "Guess it's true what they say about gossip in small towns, huh?"

"You have no idea," Derek says. His eyes glint with humor. "Especially when you're not from around here… and especially when you dare to stand up to one of the town's golden boys."

I wince. "You heard about that?"

"About your easement argument with Beckett Axford?" Derek chuckles. "Hell yes. Pretty sure everyone has."

I dart a look at Perky, who bites his lip guiltily, suggesting Rachelle isn't the only gossip in town.

"Well, I'm not sure what you've heard," I say defensively, "but Beckett—"

"Oh, you don't have to tell *me*," Derek interrupts, still sounding amused. "Beckett's had it out for me since the day I arrived. The man hates outsiders. There's a reason he's called the Axe."

Perky scoffs, "You made that up yourself. No one calls him that except you."

Derek shrugs. "Well, they should. God knows he's a *pain* in the axe."

A startled laugh bubbles out of me because I had almost that exact thought when I first met Beckett.

Derek smiles and pulls a business card out of his pocket. "Listen, Griffin, I know we just met, but if there's anything I can help you with, please let me know. I've got an excellent Boston lawyer on retainer—"

"Oh. Not necessary." I hold out a hand to wave him off.

"I own the land. The deed's on file at the record office and everything. Axford Lumber has no legal claim to it."

"And anywhere else in the world, that would be the end of it," he agrees. "But around here, it doesn't work that way. If Beckett sues you for access, first, the Winsome town council is required to make a recommendation to the court. Easements, like logging permits, fall under the town's zoning laws." He sighs. "Ask me how I know."

My mouth falls open, and suddenly, I feel like I'm forty-two stories above Times Square again. "But that's not…"

"Fair? Mmm, tell me about it. Now, I don't know the specifics of your case, obviously. But I can tell you I bought some land here over a year ago, and every time I've tried to get a permit to use it, I've been blocked." He sighs wearily. "I'd hate to see you suffer from the same frustration. We outsiders have to stick together, don't we?"

He presses the card into my hand, and without thinking, I curl my fingers around it.

Derek nods to Perky, who nods back stiffly, then turns for the door.

Milo rejoins me at the register, arms loaded with jars and bottles labeled Garlicky Replenish and Fermented Fresh. His eyes track Derek as he exits the store.

"Who's the silver daddy?" he asks in a low voice.

Perky adds Milo's pickle haul to my bags with a disapproving frown. "Derek Sullivan of Sullivan Timber. Started a new eco-conscious lumber company a couple years ago, and he's been buying up land around here like crazy. He owns the land on the other side of the Axfords' place from Jim's… I mean, yours. And he thinks it's the Axfords' fault he can't get a permit to cut down trees there. Like they're blocking him on purpose." He snorts in amusement and peers at me over the top of his glasses. "It's not true."

"Huh," I murmur, studying the business card still clutched in my hand. "Well, he seemed nice enough."

Perky could not look more horrified if I laid out a pentagram on his linoleum floor and summoned a pickle demon. "Don't confuse smooth with nice."

I nod because Perky's right. I've met a million guys like Derek, selling gen-u-wine Rolexes on Canal Street and sitting across from me in Midtown boardrooms. Beware the guy who offers to "collaborate" while angling to own the project.

But that doesn't mean those people can't be helpful in their own way. In fact, it's good to know up front that someone's looking out for themselves first… rather than, say, having that lesson spelled out for you in six-foot-tall, semi-pornographic letters on a Times Square billboard.

And while I know better than to believe Derek's biased view of events, I don't buy Perky's blind loyalty either.

So, I casually tuck Derek's card in my pocket. Because the enemy of my enemy is my friend, as they say. And Derek Sullivan might have an axe to grind with Beckett Axford…

But so do I.

# CHAPTER FOUR

## BECKETT

THE TEXT COMES at 5:22 p.m., just as I'm finishing up at the lumber yard office.

I've spent the afternoon running numbers, reshuffling work schedules, and wondering if I can squeeze in a quick run before dark so I don't explode out of sheer frustration.

Obviously, this isn't the first schedule delay I've ever dealt with. Equipment breaks down and weather turns shitty all the time, so I've got alternate felling sequences mapped out that will help us make our next few deliverables. But this isn't like a normal delay.

When the weather turns, I wait out the storm. When equipment breaks, I fix it. But this clusterfuck? I have no idea how to solve it, and I have a couple of months max before winter shuts us down.

Forestry's a delicate business, and it doesn't work like people think. You can't just point to a patch of woods and start cutting unless you want to lose the forest for good. Every tract's on rotation and managed years in advance with an eye to conservation.

The Far Tract is the one that's ready now. The other parcels I can reach might look fine to the naked eye, but they're either too young, too thin, or—like the parcel Dad sold to Derek Sullivan—too wet and too close to the river to get equipment in without devastating the whole area.

My margin for error is razor-thin, and if I can't start cutting soon, I'm going to have to cancel contracts, which means Axford Lumber slides deeper into the debt pit I've been trying to claw us out of.

So, the obvious answer is to talk to Griffin, right? Like Holden said. Be reasonable and whatnot.

Except every time I even *think* about talking to him, I remember our interaction yesterday—how he looked in my flannel, which I assume he's burned in effigy now, and how I lost my cool—I feel the opposite of reasonable.

Am I supposed to apologize to him? Am I supposed to grovel? Because there's no way.

All of which is to say that when my phone dings with a text alert, I'm almost grateful for the distraction… until I turn over the phone on my desk and see the message from my youngest brother.

AMES

We need you at the farmhouse, Beck. Right now.

My blood turns to ice water, and I don't even bother shutting down my computer. I bolt up the long gravel driveway that connects the lumber yard to my parents' farmhouse, thankful for once that the lumber office is only a few hundred yards from my parents' house.

My work boots pound against the packed earth as worst-case scenarios cycle through my head—another heart attack, a stroke, an accident with one of the tools in Dad's workshop.

The last time there was a family emergency, there was no text. I was standing right there when Dad collapsed, and when I close my eyes sometimes, I can still see it. One minute, he was explaining new safety protocols to Rocky, a smile on his face. The next, he was crumpled on the sawdust-covered floor, clutching his chest and gasping.

I'd never felt so fucking helpless in my life.

By the time I burst through my parents' back door, my lungs are burning, and my heart's thudding against my ribs.

"Ames?" I demand, scanning the kitchen for signs of crisis. "Did you call an ambulance? Where is… wait, *Dad*?"

I belatedly spot my father sitting at the big farmhouse table. There's a can of root beer in front of him, his reading glasses are perched on the end of his nose, our old dog is spread out like a rug over his feet, and he's tugging at a lock of his gray hair.

When he spies me, his expression brightens. "Beck! You'll do. Celestial body, six letters."

"I don't… are you having chest pains?" I demand, my heart still ricocheting around my chest. "Shortness of breath?"

"Planet!" he says, pulling a pencil from behind his ear. "Or wait, Saturn? No, has to end in *T*. Planet it is."

I have absolutely no idea what's happening at first, but then I notice a few things.

A few *suspicious* things.

The kitchen smells strongly of sweetness and spices. Pots steam on the stove. The wooden table around my dad is set with bowls and napkins for a crowd.

Then the back door opens behind me, and Mom bustles in, hanging her jacket and purse on the peg by the door without even looking at us. She's wearing navy slacks, a flowery headband, and a cream sweater with her name tag still pinned to the collar, like she's fresh from the front desk of the Abigail, our family's inn.

"Wilder's right behind me, but he insisted on checking my wiper fluid, even though I told him—oh!" She turns finally and notices me. "Beckett! What a wonderful surprise! And you're the first to arrive, looks like!" She busses my cheek, then thumbs away her lipstick residue and holds my chin in her hand as she assesses me. "You look stressed, honey."

"Yeah, getting a text that there's an emergency at home does that to a person," I fume. I pull away and bellow, "Ames! Get your ass in here!"

"Language." Mom swats my hip as she moves to check the pots on the stove.

Footsteps gallop down the stairs, accompanied by the sound of laughter, and my brother appears in the kitchen.

"Told you it'd fit," Ames says over his shoulder. "You're not much bigger than me, Rob. You just pretend you are."

His best friend and permanent shadow lumbers in behind him, wearing an old Axford Lumber sweatshirt that's at least two sizes too small for him and makes him look like Winnie the Pooh.

"Guess you're right," Robbie says, agreeing with whatever ridiculous thing pops out of Ames's mouth, as usual.

"Ames," I say sharply, gesturing at my phone. "What the fuck was this about?"

"*Language*, Beckett James," my mom repeats.

"Well, I just thought…" Ames begins with a sheepish shrug.

Before he can reply, the back door opens again.

"Hey, hey! The whole gang's here for Tuesday dinner, huh?" Holden saunters inside, still wearing his uniform. He's got one arm slung over our sister Eliza's petite shoulders and they're trailed by our cousin Wilder and then our brother True.

True makes a wide arc around everyone and immediately slides into his spot at the table.

"If I'd known Beck was coming tonight, I'd've gotten here earlier." Wilder slaps my arm with easy humor. "Gotta make sure I get some of Ames's maple cornbread before this one hoovers it all down."

I glare at him while moving over to give my sister a hug. "I was *lured* here under false pretenses." I drop a kiss in Eliza's hair. "How's the bride?" I murmur.

She beams up at me. "Good now you're here."

Ames ignores us. "I made three trays of cornbread, Wilder. You act like you don't come to Watchfire for cornbread nearly every day."

"And get the friends and family discount," Robbie adds with a grin.

Mom laughs, and though Robbie is a heavily muscled firefighter half a foot taller than she is, when she shakes his shoulders like he's a little kid, he not only allows it, but he gives her an adoring look, not unlike Greta the dog when my dad rubs her belly.

Mom looks beyond him and narrows her eyes. "Truett Andrew! And you, Wilder Thomas! Have you washed your hands?" she demands.

True looks at his hands, then looks at Wilder, who shrugs. They both head for the kitchen sink.

"So why is it," Eliza asks, "that you only come to family dinner if you're lured here under false pretenses, Beckett?"

I can't think of a single thing to say to that. My eyes flash toward my dad almost against my will, but he's sitting there focused on his crossword, tuning out the chaos.

"I didn't mean—" I begin, then stop. "It's not that I don't…" I hesitate. "I've been…"

"Working?" Eliza, Holden, Wilder, Ames, Robbie, my mom, and even True finish simultaneously.

Dad doesn't take his eyes off his crossword but harrumphs loudly.

"Well, you're here now," Mom says, patting my cheek. "So let's eat."

The smell of Ames's famous honey chicken is making my stomach growl. And the truth is, I've missed these fuckers, even if I can't remember why at the moment, so I move toward the table.

My mom, who's busy moving trays of cornbread from the oven to the counter, says without even turning her head, "Ah ah ah. Hands, Beck."

I roll my eyes as I stomp my thirty-six-year-old self to the hall bathroom to wash up.

By the time I get back, everyone's seated. My usual spot—at the end, across from my dad, beside True—is waiting for me.

"That's quite the outfit you're wearing," Holden's telling Robbie while he holds out his bowl for Ames to fill. "Shopping the kids' section, are we, Roberto?"

Robbie blushes, but Ames is the one who answers as he serves Holden some chicken. "Robbie was out with *Alyssa* earlier, and she got chilly, so he gave her *his* sweater, and he borrowed one of mine."

"Lissa," Robbie mutters, blushing harder. "She goes by Lissa."

"Bart Cagney's daughter?" Wilder hoots. "I was just working on his Lexus earlier in the week. I told him he needed new brakes, and he asked me with perfect seriousness if he should just junk the car and buy a new one."

"More money than sense," True agrees.

"Well, I think Lissa Cagney's a very sweet girl." Mom hands Robbie a basket of cornbread. "And so stylish!"

Ames passes me a bowl of honey chicken and rice. For a little while, I sit there, filling my stomach and letting their overlapping conversations wash over me. I'm in a shit mood still, so I don't say much—which makes our half of the table pretty silent since my dad and True don't speak either—but otherwise, it's like a million other dinners I've had in this kitchen.

Eliza's talking about adding a second doctor to her practice before she and her fiancé, Luis, get married. Mom's slammed at the inn because the Brine is coming. Wilder's thinking about taking his Harley on a road trip before the cold weather sets in, and Robbie asks him about business at the repair shop. Ames tells a story about one of his regular customers at Watchfire, who claims she's voting for Ames as Big Dill this year, and when Holden teases she'll be the one and only vote for Ames Axford, Robbie argues loyally that he'll vote for Ames too.

This scene is so comfortably familiar, my shoulders loosen. I take a deep breath for the first time in days…

And then Mom pushes back her bowl, turns to me, and says, "So what's this I hear about you threatening to murder Jim Grange's nephew, Beckett?"

I aspirate some rice, and I have to choke down water while True whacks me on the back.

"You shouldn't listen to Winsome gossip, Mom," Holden chides. "Beckett didn't threaten to murder anyone."

I shoot him a grateful look through watering eyes.

But then the fucker goes on, "Not out loud anyway. Although if looks could kill…" He whistles low.

While I try to remember how to breathe without gasping, Holden goes on to give a technically accurate but highly biased version of yesterday's events, complete with dramatic gestures and sound effects.

"So there's Beck…" He stiffens his shoulders, puffs out his chest, and makes a *grrr* noise, because apparently, I'm an enormous growling rooster. "And then there's this other guy, pretty much naked, holding up a tennis racket like it's Excalibur…" He narrows his shoulders, messes up his hair, widens his eyes, slumps in his seat, and clutches his fork with both hands, jiggling it like he's terrified. "And the whole time, I'm thinking these two need a room, 'cause the sexual tension was off the chaaaaaarts—"

Everyone laughs. Truett elbows me, inviting me to share the joke, but I don't.

"It wasn't like that!" I choke out. "Please tell me you weren't spreading this around, especially when you got your facts wrong, wrong, *wrong*. For one thing, Griffin's not tiny; he's just not as tall as you."

Holden is the tallest of us—even taller than me, which, yes, is a heinous miscarriage of justice since he's the fourth sibling out of five, but I rarely give him the satisfaction of commenting on it.

"And Griffin wasn't afraid. He was prepared to… volley me to death," I continue.

This earns a snicker from Wilder and an "awwww" from my mom, who can't be listening properly to any of this because if she was, she'd know it's *not* an aww-worthy story.

"And he wasn't naked either," I finish.

Just saying those words, the mental image hits me all over again—Griffin's long, pale legs, the sharp jut of his hip bones above the waistband of those ridiculously small briefs, the way my flannel shirt had swallowed him whole when he put it on.

Holden wrinkles his nose. "Looked pretty naked to me."

"He was wearing underwear!" I insist. "Skimpy black underwear that barely covered his ass—" I dart a look at my mom. "—*assets*, but still. And you know very well I gave him my shirt to put on. So, no, definitely not naked." I shake my head. "Did they not train you to be observant when you went to policeman summer camp, asshole?"

"*Beckett.*"

"Sorry, Mom," I huff. "What I meant to say was that I'm concerned that my beloved brother Holden, a well-trained law enforcement officer, *needs his fucking eyes checked.*"

Mom heaves a long-suffering sigh.

I glare at Holden, and his eyes twinkle back merrily.

"Well, you'd know since you were the one ogling the guy," he concedes. "And since my vision's so bad, I prob-ably also mis-saw the part where you threw Griffin's tennis racket into a tree like you were auditioning for the Olympic hammer throw, and he started shrieking like a siren—"

"Banshee," True interrupts. Since he doesn't interrupt often, everyone stops to look at him, and he shrugs. "Banshees shriek. Sirens sing."

"I meant like a police siren, not the mythological character, but point taken," Holden agrees. "He started shrieking like a *banshee*… about how Beckett and his crew are forbidden from his land."

"That was a… a misunderstanding," I say. "And I'm handling it. It's handled."

This is only half-true. Handling it means staying ahead of whatever Griffin tries next, and now I'm behind. My original plan of taking Holden's advice to calm down and talk to the man is still stuck on step one.

I specifically don't look at my father to see how he's taking this news.

"*Huh.*" My mother tilts her head at me. "Do we know if Griffin's planning to stay in Winsome permanently? Does he have a job in town? What does he do for work?"

Vivian Axford is usually a pretty sharp customer, but once again, I feel like she's missing the point here.

"We didn't exactly exchange lists of hopes, dreams, and future plans, Mom. And I don't care where he ends up, as long as he lets me—"

"Because he could have simply sold the land," she goes on. "Plenty of people would buy it for Jim's treehouse alone. But instead, he came all this way, and I heard he went grocery shopping today like he's settling in."

"Probably because I did something bad in a past life," I say sourly. "And Griffin Mercer is my punishment."

She smiles. "Well, I think Griffin sounds like a very interesting man, Beckett."

It's not so much *what* she says but *how* she says it that makes my head whip toward her while Ames, Robbie, and Wilder chuckle.

She calls Griffin *interesting* the same way she says Robbie's Lissa's a "sweet girl."

The same way she used to say True's ex, Kelly, was a "pretty little thing."

Like she approves of him, somehow.

Like he's *mine*.

"Mom, no. You've gotten this all wrong. I was only trying to move the guy's car—"

"Tow it," Holden corrects.

"Improperly," Wilder adds.

I feel my face get hot. "—and he came at me with a *weapon*, then banished me from accessing the Far Tract! He's not interesting; he's a fucking menace. And if he thinks he can keep me from our land, he can—"

"You know, Beckett..." Mom's apparently too absorbed in her own thoughts to notice my language... which is frankly terrifying. "I was just telling your father the other day that it's been so long since you were out and about in town. Wasn't I, Grant? I said, 'Honey, I'm worried Beckett's been working too hard. He used to go to the movies with Gupta Perryman's daughter all the time—'"

I gape at her. Maybe *she's* the one having a stroke, not my dad. "Mom, Jalissa and I haven't gone out since high school—"

"'—and then he dated that nice boy Kevin from Calbee for a while—'"

"Kevin and I weren't dating," I argue. "We went out

twice. Maybe three times. Also several years ago." Winsome-folk had immediately begun thinking of us as a couple, which is why I've made it a point not to "date" anyone since.

"—and he used to go to the Shed every weekend to have a drink and make new friends—"

"Mmhmm. I heard a rumor Beckett once made two friends at a time," Wilder agrees around a mouthful of chicken. He bounces his eyebrows at me where my mother can't see, and my cheeks go hot.

"Beck's skill at picking up friends is inspiring," Holden chimes in.

"You mean it *was*," Ames chips in. "I haven't heard about him making any friends in a while."

I glare at my brothers and cousin so hard they'd burst into flame if there were any justice in the world.

"See, Beckett? Everyone agrees. You need to socialize more," Mom says. "So why not kill two birds with one stone? I'm not saying you should marry the guy—heck, we have enough wedding excitement already with your sister—I'm just saying take some time off work and have a little fun. If you ask Interesting Griffin out for a drink and show him around Winsome, you can see if—"

I shake my head wildly at her. "Not only no, but hell—*heck* no," I say, and I mean it with every ounce of my being.

Because yes, fine, I admit I'm attracted to the guy, against my will and all common sense.

But my mother's transparent as glass. She's not talking about me and Griffin becoming friends, and she's sure as fuck not talking about me picking Griffin up at the bar and banging his brains out.

She's trying to matchmake me... with the worst possible contender.

Eliza's laughing into the sleeve of her sweater, True's openly grinning, and Robbie won't meet my eyes, which says they recognize it too.

I know my mom wants nothing more than for me and my siblings to have loving, committed partnerships like the one she has with my dad. She thought True had found that once, but then Kelly left him a few years ago. Right now, Eliza's the only one of us with a steady partner, which means Vivian Axford's fired up like a matchmaking locomotive.

But I refuse to be the only one she's aiming for.

"Holden was making eyes at Griffin's friend Milo!" I announce, sliding my brother directly into my mom's path.

To my surprise, Holden merely laughs and shakes his head. "You mean Milo Fitzgerald, aka @MilotheWunder-twink, who hawks health potions and talks about his cellular regeneration all over Instagram? He's only twenty-eight," he tells my mom seriously. "Too young for me. Also, prickly as a cactus and born and bred in the city. Not my type."

Mom nods, accepting this—which is weird enough since Holden's *thirty*, not eighty-two, so I'm not seeing the problem—but then the rest of what he's said hits me.

I gawp. "You ran a background check on him?"

"Mmhm. One of the many useful skills I learned in policeman summer camp." Holden sits back in his chair, hands locked behind his neck, and smiles smugly. "Ran one on Griffin Mercer too."

"Don't care," I say, but I don't sound convincing to my own ears.

Holden shrugs. "Good, because I wasn't planning to hand out his personal information. But I didn't find anything that would help your case, anyway."

*My case?* To my shock and shame, it takes me a second to realize what he means—that the only reason I'd want Griffin's personal info was so I could prevail in court.

"Right. Good. Well." I clear my throat. "Like I said, I'm taking care of it."

"Yeah? How are you doing that, exactly?" Dad speaks up for the first time.

It hits me, when my gaze swings to him, that though we're seated across from each other, this is the first time I've really looked at him since we sat down.

The man looks tired. Even... *old*. There are lines of strain around his eyes that didn't used to be there, and I fucking hate that.

Dad's voice softens. "Why not give David Halloran a call and let him—"

"Because I don't need a lawyer," I say with as much patience as possible. What I don't add is that we don't exactly have the money to enter into a protracted legal battle with anyone over property rights. If I go in guns blazing with an attorney, there's no telling how Griffin will react.

Dad shakes his head sadly, and I bet I know what he's thinking: *Axfords are the heart of Winsome. Relationships make the business. Friends and family are what it's all about.*

Those are all things he's reminded me over and over since he—*theoretically*—left the running of Axford Lumber to me, and he's right.

But my great-whatever-grandfather who started Axford Lumber didn't have to worry about sustainable harvesting practices. He didn't operate in a global economy where he was competing with pine from Chile and plywood from Guangdong. He didn't have Derek Sullivan magicking up giant piles of lumber and convincing my customers that his lumber's the cheaper *and* more eco-conscious local choice. And he didn't take over the business while his dad was in the hospital, only to find out we were extending our customers credit to the point where we'd sold off land to pay our bills.

My dad's a smart man. He *should* understand all this. But he doesn't seem to get it.

It sucks because I'm a grown-ass man myself, but my dad is still my role model. He's always been in my corner. And my dad's part of the reason I fell in love with the forest and the lumber business.

Right now, I'm working my ass off to keep Axford Lumber afloat, but instead of pride, every time I look at him these days, all I see on his face is anger or sadness.

It takes me a minute before I notice the table's gone silent, and my mom and siblings are exchanging looks. *That* really sucks too.

If you want to know the real reason I've avoided family dinners and birthday breakfasts for the last little while, it's this. I could probably handle the tension myself, but it kills me knowing that it's hurting everyone else. It's easier to just keep my distance, at least until I can get things at Axford more stable. Until I can prove to my dad I know what I'm doing.

Just as I'm pushing back my chair, ready to make my excuses and leave, Holden leans forward.

He's not laughing anymore as he says, "I don't know if a lawyer's gonna help, Beck."

I sit my ass back down. "Why not?"

"Because…" He glances around the table. "I also spent some time today researching how easements work here in Winsome. Any dispute over fair use of land goes to the town council for mediation before it goes to court." He shrugs. "It's a zoning issue, like with Derek Sullivan's logging permits."

Dad perks up. "Well, there you go, then! This town's loyal to its own. They'll understand it's nothing personal with this Griffin guy, but we need to access our land. They won't vote against us. Heck, I've personally helped every member of that council at one time or another. I coached Jenn Pratt's softball team. I practically built Mark Diaz's entire front porch—"

"You did," Holden says slowly.

"So… what's the problem?" Dad looks up and down the table.

Mom gives me a commiserating look and reaches over to pat Dad's hand.

"You're not running the company anymore, Dad," True says gruffly, when it's clear no one else wants to point out the obvious. "You're not the face of Axford Lumber these days. Beck is."

"So what? I can handle a town council meeting, you guys," I say. "Come on."

"You can," Ames agrees, but there's something in his tone that makes me want to flick him in the back of his head like I used to do when he took the last Gatorade from the fridge on the days I had football games.

Holden clears his throat. "There's, uh, something else

you should know. I heard Griffin was seen at the Basket today, talking to Derek Sullivan."

Everything goes still. The room, the conversation, the blood in my veins.

"Talking," I repeat.

Holden shrugs. "That's all I know, man. Sullivan gave him his card, but that doesn't mean they're teaming up or whatever—"

The chair scrapes against the floor as I push back from the table, anger flooding through me so fast it makes my vision blur. Derek fucking Sullivan is already moving in for the kill. To lock down the access road so Axford Lumber can't access it ever again.

Because of course he is. *Of course.*

"Beck, where are you going?" Mom asks as I head for the door.

"Out."

"Beckett," Dad calls, concern in his voice, but I can't stop.

I need air. I need space. I need to run until my lungs burn and my legs shake, and I can't think about anything except putting one foot in front of the other.

I jog down the porch steps and into the gathering dusk. The September air is crisp and clean, carrying the scent of burning wood and dying leaves, and I fill my lungs with it as I run down the road.

I make a pit stop at my truck and grab my sneakers from my gym bag, and then I'm running in earnest. Past the lumber yard, across Goodfellow Road, and out into the trails that cut through the forest.

My brain is full of too many thoughts, so I run without direction, letting muscle memory guide me down familiar trails and back roads. The rhythm of my shoes against packed earth slowly works its magic, unknotting the tension in my shoulders and clearing the noise from my head.

It's nearly dark out now, with deep sunset pinks peeking through the gaps between the trees, but I know these woods like the back of my hand. Not quite *every* tree and sapling, not *every* bump and root in the paths my father and grandfather and great-grandfather cleared, but pretty darn close. Still, it's not until I hear the burble of the Winsome River—just a trickle, this far out of town—that I realize where I've headed.

*Go home*, I tell myself sternly. My own cabin's practically across the road, and if I keep running, I could be there in five minutes or less. I could shower, pour some whiskey, sit on the porch—

No, *better* plan, I'll go back to the lumber yard, get my truck, head for the Shed, and pick up a tourist for the first time in months. What I need is one good orgasm that doesn't involve my own hand on my dick—

But I don't do either of those things. My feet are suddenly like lead, incapable of movement. So I stand there, bent over at the waist, hands on my knees and breath heaving, unsure of what to do next.

Until I hear the swearing, and suddenly, the choice is made for me.

I scan the trees through the dusk, looking for the source of the noise. But then there's a crash of breaking branches, followed by a truly imaginative string of curses.

I glance *up*…

And I find Griffin Mercer, official Pain in My Ass, twenty feet up a massive pine. He's wearing a light-colored hoodie and a pair of pants this time, and he's clinging to the trunk, his face red with exertion.

"Milo!" he whisper-cries, like too much noise might make him lose his grip entirely. "Miiiiloooooo!"

"What the fuck?" I demand.

Even as I'm yelling, my eyes sweep the tree, tracking his grip points, the lean of the trunk, how far he is from a safe drop. If he slips, I'll need to get under him fast.

Sure enough, my voice startles him, and he nearly loses his hold. He grips the tree harder and glares down at me through the branches. "What are *you* doing here?"

"Rescuing you from whatever dumbass thing you think *you're* doing," I say, stepping closer. "I still haven't worked out what the fuck that is, but I'm ninety percent sure the headline's gonna start with 'Local Idiot Dies By.'"

"I'm… inspecting my property," he says haughtily.

"Really."

He nods once.

"By climbing a tree with no safety equipment and no helmet?"

"Ugh. Go away."

"Sure. Yeah. I'll do that. One quick question first… Are you actually insane? Because you didn't *seem* insane yesterday, but admittedly, I was kind of distracted."

"This is *my* tree," he says in that same haughty tone. If he could raise his chin while still looking down at me— and without, you know, falling to his death—he would. "I can climb it if I want to!"

"Ahhh, there we go," I say. "Local Idiot Dies… Because He Can Climb His Tree If He Wants To. A fitting epitaph. Griffin died as he lived, five hundred pounds of entitled city boy in a hundred-forty-pound frame."

"Go *away*," he repeats.

For a second, I watch him stretch and strain, his hiking boots dislodging chunks of bark. It looks like he's *climbing*.

"One more quick question. Are you aware that the ground is down *here* and that you're going the wrong...?" And then I get it. "Jesus fuck. Are you risking your life to retrieve that stupid tennis racket?"

"That's Jim's *lucky* tennis racket," he corrects. "Which you *stole*. Leaving me no choice but to—*fuck!*"

His foot slips, and his hands scrape the bark, which has to hurt like a bitch. He wraps his arms around the tree again, pressing his face to the trunk and clinging for dear life, panting.

My heart jumps into my throat, and without thinking, I sprint forward and start climbing. It's not just instinct—it's calculation. He's tired, his hands are scraped, his footing's not great. One more mistake and he's on the ground with broken bones or worse.

"Fucking *fuck*," I mutter under my breath. "You know, rescuing an asshole stuck in a tree wasn't on my bingo card for tonight. I was *supposed* to be getting laid."

"Ha! So you're s-saying I saved some poor, innocent p-person from having to spend time with your ch-charming self? Make *that* my epitaph."

The pine is old and thick, with plenty of handholds, and I'm a hell of a lot more experienced at this than he is, not to mention taller. Within seconds, I'm close enough to wrap an arm around his waist.

"I've got you," I murmur, feeling the tension in his body as he leans into me. "Let me help you down."

"But the racket—"

"Can stay there," I insist.

I keep my voice low and steady—the same tone I use with newbies working a sawline for the first time. Calm keeps people moving.

"I can *do it*," he pants, but the fight's gone out of his voice.

"Sure, city boy. You were doing great so far."

I guide him down slowly, my chest pressed against his back, one hand on his waist and the other showing him where to place his feet. I can smell his hair product—something orangey and probably expensive—and feel the heat of his body through his sweatshirt.

His scraped hands are shaking from exhaustion and adrenaline. I know he has to be scared out of his mind, but he doesn't freeze or panic.

*Griffin is brave.*

I mean, he's a hell of a lot of other things—stubborn and foolish come to mind—but for the second time, I find myself reluctantly admiring this idiot.

We're about five feet from the bottom when Griffin's boot slips on a patch of loose bark. His weight shifts wrong, throwing us both off-balance.

"Shit," he breathes, and an instant later, we're both falling.

We hit the ground hard, a tangle of arms and legs and pine needles. I manage to twist at the last second so I take the brunt of the impact, Griffin landing half on top of me with his face inches from mine.

We're both breathing hard, staring at each other in the fading light, too stunned to move. His eyes are even more incredible up close—that impossible green with flecks of gold, framed by the longest eyelashes I've ever seen on a human.

And then, without thinking, without planning, without any goddamn sense at all, suddenly we're kissing.

*It's the adrenaline*, I think. But the second our mouths touch, something electric shoots through me, and I'm kissing him like my life depends on it.

He tastes like apples, and he makes a small, surprised sound against my lips that goes straight to my dick. His hands fist in my shirt, and for a second, I'm sure he's going to push me away.

Instead, he kisses me back. *Desperately.*

This isn't like any kiss I've ever had. It's like we're fighting with our lips, arguing with our tongues. Neither of us wants to yield any ground. Neither wants to be the first to pull away.

There's a corner of my brain that sees just how ridiculous this is. Griffin Mercer's a pain-in-the-ass city boy who's trying to destroy my livelihood. I should not be kissing him like he's the answer to every question I never knew I had. But once again, my brain's been hijacked, and I can't make myself let him go.

When we finally break apart—simultaneously—we're both breathing like we've run a marathon.

My head's already trying to shove the moment into a mental box marked "complication." The problem is, the damn box doesn't want to close.

Griffin's pupils are blown wide, his lips swollen and pink even in the semi-darkness, and there's a flush spreading down his neck that's practically begging me to follow it with my tongue.

"That didn't happen," he says, quickly scrambling off me to stand.

"Pfft. *What* didn't happen?" I counter, rolling to my feet. "I don't even know what you're talking about."

"Good! So don't… don't kiss me again," he says, and… yup, like clockwork, that chin is back in the air. "Because I dislike you. *Greatly.*"

"Oh, Jesus, not nearly as much as I dislike you," I inform him. "But just to be clear, baby, you kissed me."

"Like hell!" he squawks. "Believe me, if I kissed you, you'd know… *baby.*"

I snort. "Like I'd ever kiss someone so—"

At the same time, he makes that teakettle whistle noise he made yesterday and says, "You are so arrogant, so controlling—"

"—so fucking *stubborn,*" we yell simultaneously.

Somehow, we've gotten close so that our breath is mingling again. Like opposing magnets, we don't seem to have a choice.

Griffin's milky skin's practically glowing in the darkness. His hair's sticking up like a halo. His shirt—the kind of high-tech, expensive shit people wear when they're pretending to be outdoorsy—is half bark chips and half pine needles, and he looks like a human porcupine, which is pretty fucking accurate. There's not a single attractive thing about him, I swear to god.

So tell me why—please tell me why—when his gaze drops to my lips, I close the distance between us.

This time, I'm almost sure he kisses me first.

It's fiercer than before, like he's trying to prove a point. My hands fist in his shirt, and I back him against the pine tree, pressing him into the rough bark as I kiss him back just as hard.

He makes a low sound in his throat, and his hips

punch forward, grinding against me. I can feel every inch of him through our clothes, and when I shift my weight, pinning him more firmly against the tree, he gasps into my mouth. If my brain hadn't already packed its bags and gone on a walkabout, the press of his dick against mine would have done it.

It lasts maybe ten, maybe thirty, maybe a hundred-twenty seconds before we break apart, breathing like we've been submerged.

"That was..." Griffin starts, then shakes his head. "No."

"Ha. Definitely no. Never to be repeated," I agree roughly.

"Or discussed."

"Absolutely not."

We stare at each other for a long moment, and then he swallows hard.

"You should..." He waves a hand toward the road.

"Oh, I'm going. Hell, I'm practically gone," I tell him, though my feet don't move, and my arms fold over my chest. Out of my mouth come the words, "Just as soon as you admit you started... this thing we're not talking about."

He snorts. "No fucking way! You're a controlling caveman!"

"Oh, please. Spoiled city boy."

"I guess now I know why they call you the Axe." Griffin folds his arms over his chest, mirroring my pose.

All at once, I remember who this guy is and who he's been talking to and the heat in my blood chills so fast it makes my head spin. Or, hell, maybe it was already spin-ning. Every single thought and action I've had since I got here is blurred and melded, light filtered through raindrops.

Either way, I take a quick step back.

Griffin frowns like he's confused about how there came to be several feet of space between us.

"Let me guess where you heard that," I say. "You've been chatting with your new BFF, Derek Sullivan, right? The man who's been in Winsome for all of five minutes and doesn't know shit about shit? The man who can't even come up with an original nickname for a guy named Axford?" I roll my eyes.

He lifts his chin in his signature move, and I want to kiss him again so badly I force myself to take another step back.

"Be careful of Derek Sullivan," I say, knowing my words will fall on deaf ears. "You can't trust him."

"Oh, unlike you, right?" Griffin's hiss slides through the night like a knife.

I brush pine needles off my arms. "Yeah," I say. "Unlike me."

I walk away without looking back, though every instinct I have is screaming at me to turn around. To apologize. To kiss him again until we're both senseless.

I refuse.

Because Griffin Mercer might be the most beautiful, infuriating, impossible man I've ever met, but right now, he's also my enemy. I owe it to myself and my family to remember that.

No matter how tempting it is to forget.

# CHAPTER FIVE

## GRIFFIN

Sleepless nights provide many hours to concoct elaborate revenge schemes. They also leave you feeling ornery and strangely horny.

So after two of the longest, horniest nights of broken sleep in recorded history, I decided I needed to stop daydreaming about sexy glitter bombs and do something real. Something effective. Something reasonable.

I should have known that *reasonable* wouldn't work in Winsome.

"Well, that was a waste," I mutter as Milo and I settle in the window booth of Watchfire, the restaurant across the road from Winsome's one and only attorney's office.

"Not entirely," Milo argues, sliding back his sunglasses. "The lawyer gave us a lunch rec, right? Think the butternut soup's as life-changing as he claimed?"

I grunt.

The inside of Watchfire is all warm amber light, exposed beams, and wood floors. It smells of bacon, butter, and maple syrup—some of my favorite things. And the double-sided fireplace in the center of the space has an actual, honest-to-god wood fire burning in it, which I appreciate from a marketing standpoint since it really sells the theme.

But though this place practically requires you to relax and enjoy yourself when you step inside, I stubbornly refuse to get on board.

A lunch rec was about all we got from meeting with David Halloran. He'd been kind, but he'd confirmed what Derek Sullivan told me. Before pursuing a legal route to protect my land, I'd have to put my case before the Winsome town council, and at least four of the eight members were likely to favor Beckett, no matter how strong my case was.

*"Winsomefolk are loyal, and after generations of goodwill and community service... well, the Axfords are beloved. Kind of like local royalty. You understand, right?"*

Oh, I understand. Another nepo baby's going to take something that's mine, simply because his family has power and I don't. My three-month fresh start is looking pretty damn similar to the bullshit I escaped in Manhattan.

Things in Jim's treehouse aren't going much better.

Jim cleaned out everything but a couple of boxes of books labeled *Donate?* and several rolls of antacids.

Jim's attorney's office hasn't returned my calls about Jim's death *or* about the easement situation.

I still can't figure out how to open the trapdoor to the barrel room, and after my tree-climbing debacle the other night, every time I consider climbing up the side and smashing a window, I hear a voice in my head say, *"Local idiot dies by..."*

I swear I can hear Jim's lucky racket clacking against

the tree when the world goes quiet every night, and it taunts me.

And although Milo assures me the Rise billboard's no longer trending on TikTok—I've been replaced by a clip of a gopher with a leaf blower, which I'm honestly not sure how to feel about—I still haven't gotten a response to any of the resumes I've sent out *or* any calls from the former colleagues and business school classmates I've reached out to.

I'm feeling powerless as fuck, and I hate it.

Milo makes a triumphant noise and jabs a finger at his menu. "There it is. Butternut Soup. Now, how big do we think the bowl is, and, scale of 1-10, how weird would it be to ask for a tureen?"

I ignore him and keep my gaze on the menu, but I'm not really reading it. My brain keeps recycling David's words.

*Beloved. Generations of goodwill. Local royalty.*

*Fuck.*

"Hey." Milo kicks me lightly under the table, and I startle. "Stop it."

I startle. "Stop what?"

"Making that weird whistling noise. You've been making it off and on since you went out to get Jim's tennis racket the other night and came back looking like you'd been mauled by a pine tree."

He tilts his head in silent question, and I consider how to answer.

*That's because I was mauled, Milo.*

*By the world's most infuriating asshole lumberjack.*

*Who kissed me like he'd die if he didn't.*

*And even two days later, my lips feel low-key bruised, and I hate how much I like it, m'kay?*

"Mauled? Pfft." I wave his words away, knowing I'm blushing and unable to stop it. "I tried to retrieve the racket, the tree fought back, the end."

Look, I don't lie often, especially to my best friend, but some things defy explanation and don't merit discussion. What happens in the Winsome woods *stays* in the Winsome woods... and, yes, possibly in my shower fantasies.

I'm not proud of it.

Fortunately for me, a server with a honey-blonde bob, a floral apron, and a name tag that says *Vivian* hustles over before Milo can question me further.

"So sorry for the delay, guys." She sets two glasses of ice water on the table. "The Brine Planning Committee's having their final meeting before things kick off this weekend. They've been at it for hours, and they've kept us hopping."

She nods her head toward the far side of the restaurant, where several tables have been pushed together to form one mega-table, and all twenty seats around it are filled by people who look like they stepped out of a decades-old L.L.Bean catalog.

It's a sign of just how adaptable humanity can be that when a woman wearing big glasses and a T-shirt that says *You could Lose Some, but Why Not Winsome?* glances back at me and waves, I lift my hand in greeting too... though I cannot imagine why anyone would wave at a perfect stranger.

"Doesn't seem to matter how much we plan for the Brine in advance, every year, there's always a scurry at the last minute," Vivian goes on with a sigh. "Too many people in charge, you know? But Ames called in the family as reinforcements, so we'll have your lunch out in a jiffy."

"It's no problem," I assure her, both because it's true and because I want her to stand right there and distract Milo from his interrogation as long as possible. "I'm still looking. So many great options."

I gesture down at the printed sheet, and now that I'm actually looking, I see things like "Relish the Brine Grilled Cheese" and "The Big Dill Pickle Burger." I shudder a little, realizing I genuinely might need help finding something that won't make me vomit.

I mentally shake my fist at the sky and think, *Fucking Vermont.*

"Do you serve anything that's not so…" I clear my throat. "Pickle-forward?"

Vivian laughs and leans in like she's conveying a secret. "We don't usually lean into the pickles. This menu's special, for the Brine. Some folks love it, but feel free to ask for substitutions."

"Really? So I could get the, ah, Relish the Brine Grilled Cheese without any relish whatsoever?"

"Absolutely." She pulls an order pad from her apron pocket and shoots me a wink. "We're very pickle-flexible in Winsome."

Despite my mood, I can't help smiling back.

"I'd like a vat of butternut soup," Milo says. "And the maple cornbread. And the *Dill*-icious Lemonade. Seems hydrating."

I bite my tongue.

Vivian nods her approval. "It is. Ames grows the dill himself. Drink for you, sweetie?" she asks me.

"Just a Diet Coke." But because you never know in this town, I add, "Also with no pickles."

She laughs again and pats my shoulder maternally. "You poor thing. I take it you're not here for the Brine, then?"

"The pickle festival? Afraid not," I say, prepared to leave it at that.

But Milo seems to have caught whatever illness makes people in small towns overshare, because he immediately volunteers, "I'm only here for one more day, but Griffin's going to be living here temporarily."

I scowl at him, but Vivian gasps delightedly. "Oh, *you're* Griffin! So you must be Milo!" she says, like we're a well-known duo.

I paste on a polite smile. I can only imagine what she's heard about us and who she's heard it from. For the second time in just a few months, it feels like someone else is in control of my reputation, and I fucking hate it.

Milo, on the other hand, preens. "That's us."

"I've been meaning to come over with some of my apple cake and see how you're settling in," Vivian says. "Just remember, boys, if you need anything, you only have to speak up. You're part of our community now, and the best part of living in Winsome is that you never have to go it alone."

I feel my smile grow strained. I want to say, *Am I really part of the community, Vivian?* and *Is it really so different in Winsome? Because it sure seems like the powerful people run shit here just like they do everywhere else.*

But of course, I keep my mouth shut. Vivian doesn't deserve my foul mood.

"That's very kind, but—" I begin.

"Actually," Milo cuts in. "Would you happen to know anyone who's handy with carpentry things? Because there's this trapdoor in the ceiling that leads to the barrel turret room thingy, and Griff and I have been trying for days, but we can't—*ow! Griffin!*"

"Ooops. I'm so clumsy," I say innocently, tucking my boots back under my own chair. To Vivian, I add, "We're all set. I've got everything under control."

Vivian's lips twitch in a smile, and she murmurs something that sounds like, "That sounds familiar."

I frown, but before I can ask her to explain, the front door to the restaurant opens with a jangle of bells.

I can't actually see the door since Vivian's in my way, but somehow, I swear, I immediately know who's walked in. Maybe I'm becoming clairvoyant now that I'm thirty. Or maybe it's just that the barometric pressure drops when the giant storm cloud that is Beckett Axford gets near.

Either way, it's no surprise whatsoever when Beckett steps into view, just as shoulder-y, scowl-y, and beard-y as I remember, his dark hair gilded copper and honey by the overhead lights. He's beautiful enough to make me forget what I was saying mid-conversation, which is simply un-fucking-fair.

I swallow, and in my mind, I'm back in the shadowed woods. The air's sharp with pine and the hum of night insects. Beckett's hands slam against the tree on either side of my head, caging me in. His mouth claims mine in a way that leaves no room to breathe. The hard heat of him is pressed against me like he's daring me to shove him away. And he's growling in the back of his throat while his hands clutch me possessively, and he's saying—

"Griffin?" Vivian asks in concern. "Honey, are you alright? You're making a kind of whistling noise—"

"He does that," Milo says with a smirk. "I'm concerned he might be allergic to pine trees."

I briefly debate kicking my beloved best friend again, harder this time.

But Beckett's scanning the room like he's looking for someone, so without even thinking about it, I sink down in the booth until Vivian's blocking my view once again. Because if I can't see him, he can't see me, right?

To be clear, I'm not playing ostrich because I don't want to go toe to toe with Beckett. *Fuck, no.* In my current mood, I'd like nothing more.

But I know if I see Beckett again, I will turn the color of a ripe cranberry—my pale skin hides nothing—and Milo will misinterpret it to mean that I'm actually interested in Beckett and give me another round of shit for it.

"Pine trees," Vivian repeats, staring at me. "Interesting! You know—"

"Hey, Mom," Beckett calls. His head appears over Vivian's shoulder as he gets closer, and I sink further into the seat. "Ames said he needed volunteers to work—"

I know when he sees me because both of us freeze, like an oversized lion in work boots encountering a pomaded, urbane gazelle.

"Beckett!" Vivian says cheerfully. "Hi, sweetheart. Look who's here."

Belatedly, I process that Beckett is calling Vivian *mom.*

That she's calling him sweetheart.

That she *produced* this giant, cranky human.

That she, herself, is an Axford.

I suck in a breath and sit up sharply, and the minute I do, Beckett's blue eyes lock on mine. Heat rushes through me as I remember the press of that body against mine. My hand unconsciously moves to my lips before I catch myself and drop it to the table.

My whole face suffuses with heat.

The kiss didn't happen. We *agreed* it didn't happen.

"Milo." He nods. "Mercer," he says in a growl that sends a shiver down my back.

"Hey," Milo says with a little wave.

I nod regally. "Axford."

"*Interesting,*" Vivian says again, and I'm pretty sure this time she's not talking about my supposed pine allergy.

Beckett's cheeks redden. "It's not. At all. I came by because Ames texted the family chain that he needed help." He shoots me a glare. "And since my crew can't start clearing brush in the Far Tract this week, I have time."

I'm about to fire back something unwise when Vivian interrupts.

"Oh, how perfect! Griffin and Milo were just telling me they need someone to help them open a trapdoor in Jim's treehouse. I was going to suggest True or Ames, but if you're free—"

Beckett's eyes widen in panic, and I nearly snort-laugh.

Until Milo, the traitor, says, "Oh, yes! Griffin would really appreciate it."

My eyes widen too, thinking of having Beckett in my space. Especially since Milo has to leave tomorrow for a big-deal wellness retreat in Arizona.

"Nope. Not necessary! I've got it all under control," I say quickly. I can feel my pulse in my cheeks now, and I'm guessing I've passed cranberry and turned some shade of ultra-red that the human eye cannot fully process.

"Hmm. Well, if you're sure, honey." Vivian shrugs. "Probably just as well since the Brine starts this weekend. Remember what we were talking about at dinner the other night, Beck?"

"Uh. No?" He swallows, and his face goes nearly as red as mine, like he does remember. "Anyway. Better go see what Ames needs." He strides away without another word.

Vivian watches him go with a fond smile. "Poor Beckett. He's probably the least social of my boys—"

"You don't say," I mutter.

"—but he's such a lovely man. Big-hearted. Responsible. And he's been working night and day, running the family lumber business since his father had a heart attack and retired last year."

For a second—less than a second, a *millisecond*, really—I feel bad for the guy because that can't have been easy.

Then Vivian lowers her voice and goes on, "Now, I absolutely *hate* spreading gossip…"

"Oh, same," Milo breathes, leaning toward her.

"…but I heard the other night that several people in town are thinking of voting for a *certain Axford* to be crowned Big Dill at the Brine." She bites her lip excitedly.

"Really," I say with polite disinterest. "That's… some sort of homecoming king, but with pickles? How perfect."

I mean this sincerely. I cannot think of a more appropriate fate for a man who could out-salt and out-vinegar a vat of brine than for Beckett to be crowned Winsome's Pickle Prince.

Vivian lets out an inelegant snort, which I have to

admit is really charming. "I suppose it is, sort of. It's mostly a ceremonial thing—turning on the tree lights at WinterFest and things like that—but the Big Dill also advocates for important issues that can improve the town. Fresh ideas, you know? Like, last year, Aubrey Sprague gave a speech about pollinator gardens that got us all talking, and a whole bunch of us started one this summer as a result."

It's hard not to roll my eyes. I can't imagine Beckett would find much to improve as Big Dill since the Axfords already seem to run Winsome. Unless, of course, it's to give the town a Griffin-ectomy.

"Oh, and the Big Dill gets to cast the tiebreaking vote if the town council's ever deadlocked on an issue." Vivian gives an exaggerated shrug like she can't imagine how that would be important.

I pause with my water glass halfway to my mouth, sure I've heard wrong.

*Did she just say a tiebreaker vote on the council?* It's like a religious awakening, how suddenly the clouds in my mind part.

"And, ah, Beckett's campaigning for this thing, you say?" I set my glass down with a *click*.

"Oh, not *campaigning*, per se." Vivian shakes her head. "There isn't an official ballot for Big Dill. Not like when we elect the town councilors. It's all write-in votes, you see. But we get an idea of who'd like to serve by seeing who takes part in the Brine events. And through gossip, of course."

"Of course," I echo.

"Well," she says with a satisfied grin. "I'll just go put

that order in for you boys." She shoots Milo a friendly wink.

"Griffin," Milo warns the second Vivian walks away. "Don't even think about it."

"He's running for this thing, Milo," I whisper hotly. "This has been his plan all along."

"You don't know that! Vivian specifically said—"

"I heard what she said." I wave a hand. "But you saw how he was! All... *Mercer*," I say in an impression of Beckett's deep, growly voice. I scoff. "Like... who *does* that?"

"Greet someone by name?" Milo shakes his head. "You're right. That *bastard*."

"He's smug and broad and... and... *smug*!"

"Boo, he really wasn't—"

"All because the whole time, he knew he had this thing in the bag! He knew he couldn't beat me fair and square on the merits of his case, so he'd win by scoring the tie vote! And now there's only one way to stop him." I jab a finger into the scarred wooden tabletop. "I need to win Big Dill."

"How did I know you'd say that?" Milo closes his eyes and huffs. "Griffin, have you considered upping your green tea intake? There's research that L-theanine can boost your calming neurotransmitters, and let's be honest, you need some calming—"

Milo keeps talking, but I've stopped listening. I'm already making lists in my mind, planning out what I'll need to do.

I know how to run a campaign. I know how to sell a vision, build a narrative, connect with an audience. I've done it for corporate clients for literally a decade. Why not for myself? Why not for *Winsome*?

"You know, I could actually do some good for this town," I interrupt.

Milo stares at me. "What?"

"No, seriously. Like… like… like creating a tourism marketing plan," I say triumphantly.

When Milo's other eyebrow climbs to join the first, I dig deeper, selling him on my vision.

"We know they already get tourists here, but that's for this pickle-fest thing. I bet there's still a huge untapped market out there, the rest of the year. What if an outsider —" I tap my chest. "—gave them ideas about things that might draw more tourists? Like… I don't know… Better roads with no potholes? Adding some signage so people know where the fuck they're going? Adding some cell towers so people can call when they accidentally almost hit a moose or get sideswiped by a fucking truck?"

Milo nods slowly. "Go on."

"Then, once the infrastructure's in place, the rest is pretty straightforward. You said yourself the town's quaint. And fuck knows it's quirky. And inclusive too. I don't know if you clocked it, but there's a rainbow flag outside the bar down the street."

He shakes his head sadly. "It's like you don't even know me. It was the *first* thing I noticed."

"So the real question is who *wouldn't* want to come here? We get some influencers to talk about the health benefits of the local pickles—" I lift a hand to Milo, who tips his head. "We make a list of the places around town with beautiful views, or quirky history, or whatever. I can go to the library and research—"

"Okay, hold up." He puts out a hand. "That's great and all. Seriously. But babe… you don't live here."

I frown, considering. "You think there's a length of residency requirement? Like I haven't lived here long enough?"

Milo stares at me like I've grown three heads. "No, dumbass. I think you're *leaving* in three months. That's what you said, Griff."

I open my mouth, then close it again, feeling myself deflate. "I am. Of course I am. But I'm sure there'd be a runner-up person who could take over for me. I mean, previous Big Dills must have had stuff come up that prevented them from finishing their… reigns."

"Sure. But while you're spending all this time campaigning, how are you getting a new job?"

This… is a good question. A damn good question. And the answer is…

"I don't know." I blow out a breath. "Look, I know you think I'm not trying hard enough—"

Milo squawks. "That's not—"

"—but I *have* been. It just feels like I've been swimming against the tide all the damn time. And I…" My voice clogs with unexpected emotion, and I stop to sip some water.

Milo's whole face softens. "Griffy—"

"No. *Ugh.* I don't want pity. This land… it feels like my responsibility. I told you that. And… I want to win this, Milo. For Jim. For me. For every little guy who doesn't feel like he gets a say in his own damn life because the system is rigged. And if I can prevail this *one* time, win this *one* thing, then… maybe all the other shit I have to deal with will start to feel possible again."

Milo studies me for a long moment with a pucker between his eyebrows that's going to make him a candidate for Botox before thirty if he keeps this up.

"And you're sure this has nothing to do with you wanting to win against your hot lumberjack nemesis for personal reasons?" He leans toward me and lowers his voice. "Because if you want the man, you could probably lure him out to the treehouse by promising to give back the flannel shirt I happen to know is tucked in your dresser."

I'm blushing again. Or maybe *still*. "You're an asshole," I say without heat.

Milo grins… then frowns and gnaws his lip. "You know, maybe I should skip the retreat."

"What for?"

He shrugs. "Because you might have great ideas for the town, Griffin, but you're not operating at peak friendliness these days. In fact, I've seen cacti that are more approachable."

I dunk my finger in my water and flick droplets at him. "*Asshole*," I repeat.

He laughs, and I'm suddenly overcome by affection for the man. *This* is why he's my best friend.

"There is no way you're skipping this retreat," I tell him. "You danced around your living room when you heard they invited you. This is how you're going to level up *your* career."

I refuse to let my own career crisis derail both of us.

"Here we are," Vivian says, coming toward us with a tray of dishes.

I stand automatically and take the far edge of the tray so she can lower it without straining.

"Thank you, sweetheart." She beams as I sit back down, and she sets my plate in front of me.

My stomach immediately growls like I've been starving for years and haven't noticed. The thick-sliced bread is buttery and perfectly golden brown, gooey cheese melts out the side, and it's served with chips that look homemade.

I immediately dive in and groan. "Oh my god, this is amazing."

Vivian laughs as she sets a basket of cornbread and the largest bowl of soup I've ever seen in front of Milo.

Milo barely seems to notice.

"Vivian," he says, "could you tell us more about these Brine events you mentioned? What does it all entail?"

"Mmm, let's see. There's a scavenger hunt, a road race, a talent show, a craft fair, food trucks, speeches..." She ticks the items off on her fingers.

"And which would you say are the biggest events?" he wonders. "The, ah... prerequisites for letting people know you want to be Big Dill, so to speak."

Vivian's gaze ping-pongs between us excitedly. But when she speaks, it's with a studiously casual tone that mirrors Milo's.

"Hmmm. I'd say the Wild Gherkin Chase. Definitely. That's the kickoff event, this Saturday. It's a scavenger hunt. *Highly* competitive."

Milo and I exchange a glance. I can do competitive.

"And then probably Hello, Winsome," she continues. "It's a fun way that people get to know their neighbors. You can make a speech, you can do an interpretive dance... anything you want, really."

I choke on a potato chip. "So it's a talent show?"

"Sounds fun." Milo shoots me a look that screams *cactus*, and I scowl, which probably only proves his point.

*Shit*. Milo's right. I really do have to make more of an effort to be friendly.

"It's a long-standing tradition," Vivian explains. "When Carmine Esposito talked about removing the metered parking on Whether Street, there wasn't a dry eye in the house. He didn't win Big Dill, but they did remove the meters."

I nod. I don't waste a minute worrying about *that* event. Prickly I might be, but public speaking is my jam. There's a reason Alan Nelson had me pitch to all of our toughest clients. I'll figure something out.

"So, hypothetically, if a person wanted to get involved in these activities," I wonder, "what would they need to do?"

"Well, for everything except the Wild Gherkin Chase, you'd simply show up. But—" Vivian looks almost theatrically alarmed and presses a hand to her chest. "Oh, wait! Griffin, *you're* not thinking of trying for Big Dill, are you?"

I lift my chin. "Maybe. Possibly. Yes."

"But sweetie, I really don't think..." She shakes her head forlornly. "I'd hate for you to be disappointed. You know, when Beckett was ten, he read a story about a boy who whittles, and he spent three whole weeks using his little pocketknife to turn scrap lumber into cereal bowls for himself and his siblings. Once he really wants something, he doesn't quit. So if Beckett has his heart set on this..."

I'm pretty sure I read the same book Beckett read, and it's annoying to think we have this in common.

"Oh my god!" Milo exclaims. "Griff, that's just like the story your moms tell about the time you insisted on making your own ink out of crushed-up berries because you read about it in a book. They said you were pink for weeks—"

"But *hypothetically*," I insist, ignoring him.

"Welllll…" Vivian draws out the word and purses her lips. "I suppose *hypothetically*, you'd want to write down your contact information on a piece of paper like this one." She pulls her order pad and pen from her pocket and sets them on the table by my hand. "Then you'd give it to the correct member of the committee." She points to the mega-table. "Ada Wickham, who runs the Pickle Jar. The lady in head-to-toe pink. And if you were to charm her and compliment her earrings, she'd probably make an exception and get you registered for the Chase." Vivian bites her lip. "But I *cannot stress enough*, honey, that you really should *not* under *any* circumstances consider going up against Beckett—"

I'm already reaching for her pen and notepad. I'm not sure my handwriting's even legible. Then I stand and stride over to the big table to level the playing field.

The planning committee meeting is breaking up as I approach, so I make a beeline for the lady in pink. As I get close, I realize the woman is a whole foot shorter than me… unless you count her hair, which is arranged in a large, red bouffant. She's wearing earrings that I guess are meant to be cucumber pickles, but… pink, so they look like something else entirely.

"Excuse me, ma'am," I say. "I'm Griffin Mercer."

The woman narrows her eyes, and they disappear into a sea of wrinkles. Her bright red lips thin.

"Who," she demands, "are you calling 'ma'am,' whippet?"

My eyes widen. "Oh, god. I'm so sorry. I—"

She bursts out laughing, and it sets her earrings swinging. "Ah, gets 'em every time. What can I do for you, Griffin Mercer?"

"Uh. Well." I lick my suddenly dry lips. "I'm new to Winsome, but Vivian was telling me about the Brine, and I... I'm really eager to participate. Could you help me get registered for the scavenger hunt?"

"Well, well." She darts a look at Vivian, quirks a smile, then looks me up and down. "So you're the man who owns Jim Grange's treehouse now."

The way she says it is different from the way other people do. Not unfriendly, but no-nonsense. She's not offering condolences like Jim was actually my uncle, like maybe she knows better.

"That's me."

"Hmm. And what exactly did Vivian say that got you so excited to take part in these events?" She quirks one bright red eyebrow.

The rest of the meeting's broken up, and a couple of people touch Ada's shoulder as they leave, but she doesn't so much as turn her head.

Meanwhile, I shift my weight from foot to foot, unsure how to reply. "I, uh... well, I'm new in town, like I said, and I thought—"

*Fuck.* I really did use to be good at public speaking, I'm almost sure of it.

"I heard you and Beckett Axford got into it the other day," she interrupts. "That true?"

"I... suppose," I admit, my voice a bit strained.

Ada leans closer. "Is it true you were naked, and he kissed you with tongue, right there in front of god and everybody?"

"What?" My face goes from warm to wildfire, the prickling heat racing up my neck like a fuse toward a stick of dynamite. "No!"

"Figured someone had embellished that one. Beckett's not one to put on a show." Ada laughs again, and it sounds surprisingly young. Musical, almost. "So tell me, Griffin. Are you entering these events because you're hoping to curry favor with the town council when it comes to your land dispute?"

I open my mouth, then close it again. *Fuck*, the gossip around here is *insane*. Do they know my shoe size and the contents of my vibrator basket too?

"Perfect!" she declares, though I haven't actually said anything. "I'll make sure your name's on the list for the Wild Gherkin Chase. Be at Chapel Island Park at eight thirty Saturday morning."

"Really?" I let out a relieved breath. "Thank you—"

"No need to thank me. I have a feeling this is going to be highly entertaining." She collects a large red purse from the arm of her chair and tucks it under her arm. "Besides, any friend of JG Flummery's a friend of mine."

I frown. "Who's—?"

"Come on by the Pickle Jar one night next week," she instructs. "Bathsheba will want to meet you. Let's say Monday—no, wait, Monday's my manicure. And the farmer's market's Wednesday. Better make it Tuesday evening to start," she says. As she heads for the door, she calls over her shoulder, "And bring Bathsheba donuts from Fox Creamery because we need to talk strategy, and she thinks better with donuts."

"Uh… okay." I nod. "Donuts. Strategy. Got it."

I have no idea what kind of strategy is involved in a scavenger hunt, but then again, I've never chased a Wild Gherkin before either.

I'm damn well going to learn, though.

Beckett Axford has no idea what's coming for him.

# CHAPTER SIX

## BECKETT

I ROLL up to the little parking lot at Chapel Island on Saturday morning in a state of complete disbelief over the fact that I'm here.

Festival bunting flutters from every lamppost, each strip of green and gold catching the sunlight until the whole street looks like it's been strung with liquid light. There's a giant banner stretched between two maples that reads "WINSOME BRINE: GET YOUR PICKLE ON!" in green glitter paint so aggressively sparkly and loud it has to be violating a noise ordinance. And I think to myself, *Holy fuck, is this what an out-of-body experience feels like?*

I swear to you, the idea of being Winsome's Big Dill has never crossed my mind. Not once in my thirty-six years in this town. Not in the "maybe someday" sort of way, like when you think about how great it would be to climb Kilimanjaro while scarfing potato chips on your porch. Not in the "maybe if I were drunk enough" kind of way, like when I heard about Gary and Gordon Lapierre dressing up in tights and doublets for King Richard's

Faire. Not even in the "maybe if you paid me" way, like when my mom prodded me to audition for *American Idol* back when I was a sullen teenager who could strum precisely two songs on my secondhand guitar.

But three things happened in quick succession that led me to this place.

First and foremost: Griffin Mercer, King of Chaos and Lucky Tennis Rackets, came to Winsome.

I keep telling myself I can't stop thinking about him because I'm worried about access to my land. About my company. And that's fucking *true*.

But in the dead of night, when I finally give in and jerk myself off just to get to sleep, it's not the damn financial projections that have been looping around in my brain. It's the way he kissed me like he was a fire and I was oxygen. It's the little moans he made when I kissed him. It's how his body fit under my hands.

Apparently, there's no room in this town for Griffin and my common sense.

Second: My mother stopped by the office two days ago and oh-so-innocently mentioned that Griffin was running for Big Dill.

Her exact words were: "You shouldn't even *try* to compete, Beck. Absolutely not. I know it's tempting, since the Big Dill gets the tiebreaker vote on the town council and could influence their recommendations about the easement at the treehouse, but I know how much you hate these silly town events. Besides, from what I saw of him, Griffin's pret-*ty* determined. And so sweet. He'll definitely win."

Vivian Axford's acting skills are terrible, and her reverse-psychology game is transparent as glass. But apparently, I'm still falling for it because I actually considered the idea.

But the third and final straw… was the fucking *sign*.

I'd been walking down Whether Street yesterday morning, on my way to do Kurt Trachtenberg a favor and look over some storm-damaged trees in his yard, when I'd spotted a half-dozen Winsomefolk gathered around the front window of the Pickle Jar, gasping like they'd just witnessed the second coming of Cucumber Christ.

I'd rolled my eyes and kept on walking, obviously, because the only thing I wanted *less* than becoming Winsome's Big Dill was to gossip about whatever new tourist crap Miss Ada was selling. But then Perky from the grocery store shifted just as I was walking by, and I caught a glimpse of what they were gawking at, and I stopped dead.

A sign in the window read GRIFFIN MERCER: FRESH IDEAS FOR WINSOME.

"Gotta hand it to the kid. He obviously wants to be Big Dill, and he's pulling out all the stops," Perky said admiringly. "I heard he's got Ada's vote, and Bathsheba might endorse him."

"You can't be serious, Perky." That had been my dad's voice, and my head whipped around to find him in the crowd. "Griffin's been in town less than a week. He doesn't understand a dang thing about what Winsomefolk like or need. He doesn't even realize we never do campaign posters for Big Dill!"

"But maybe we should," Miriam Tringali said thoughtfully. "Sure would make things easier. I think I might like his 'fresh ideas.'"

"And I think Griffin understands more than you give

him credit for, Grant," Mrs. Chen from the post office chided. "He stopped by the library Thursday night to do some research on the town, and while he was there, he offered my Celine some advice on her science fair poster. He suggested gluing real leaves to the trees, rather than just coloring them with markers. To add texture, he said. Turned out *beautiful.*"

There were appreciative murmurs from the crowd. I caught the words "so kind!" and "dang thoughtful" and even "genius."

"*I* heard he's committed to doing every single Brine activity." Old Walt Lehmann gave an indulgent chuckle. "Makes me more excited about it than I've been in years, getting to see it through a newcomer's eyes."

"Anyway, he's not just a random tourist," Perky pointed out. "He owns the treehouse, which means he's one of us now."

"Think he'd be open to advocating for a crosswalk at the intersection of Quilter Road once he's Big Dill?" someone else wondered.

Predictably, everyone ignored this lone sensible suggestion.

Dad turned his head and caught my eye. He looked pretty damn concerned, and I can't say I blame him since it's been almost a whole week and I *still* haven't come up with a solid way to approach Griffin about accessing the Far Tract—aside from getting acquainted with his tonsils and the little moans he makes when he's aroused, which was counterproductive.

I'm concerned too.

So here I am, forcing myself out of my truck, dodging kids hopped up on sugar, hotfooting it over the bridge that spans Chapel Creek, and following the excessive signage to the check-in table for the Wild Gherkin Chase—the unofficial kickoff to the Brine-related festivities.

The check-in table is staffed by two women, only one of whom I recognize: Mrs. Pratt, my no-nonsense fifth-grade teacher who's not exactly a big Beckett Axford fan. The other is younger and has long, blonde dreadlocks, a nose ring, and a baby strapped to her chest.

"Hey. I'm, ah, here to check in," I say, forcing my voice into something resembling civility.

"Why, Beckett Axford, it really *is* you." Mrs. Pratt looks me up and down like I'm still ten and she wants very badly to ask about my math homework and why I haven't returned my copy of *My Side of the Mountain* to the school library. "When I saw your name on our list, I told Posy there had to be a mistake," she adds, nodding toward the other woman.

Posy doesn't seem to catch her disapproving undertone because she beams at me. "But here you are!"

"Here I am," I grind out. I give the registration papers in front of Mrs. Pratt a pointed look. "If you could check me in—?"

"Good morning!" a throaty and annoyingly familiar voice says from beside me. "I'm Griff Mercer. I'd like to check in for the scavenger hunt, please."

I turn my head, and there's my new rival, all golden, tousled hair and a smile that could probably power half of Vermont. He's in head-to-toe tourist gear— formfitting jeans, a pristine cream-colored fleece, and boots made for city streets. I should scoff—I mean, I *do* scoff, under my breath—but the first thought in my head is *I wouldn't mind getting this guy dirty.*

Hearing my scoff, Griffin gives me the briefest side-eye —a look that could freeze hellfire—before turning his megawatt grin on the volunteers.

"Griffin!" The Posy person clasps her hands together. "So nice to meet you. I was sorry to hear about your uncle Jim. I met him at the bookstore maybe a year ago, and he was a treasure."

"Oh." Griffin's smile flickers for just a second, and I catch a glimpse of something uncertain underneath before he locks it down. "Thanks. Thank you. That's… very kind."

I have to admit—grudgingly—that Griffin's got a decent poker face. Better than mine.

"Well now," Mrs. Pratt says. "Isn't this exciting?"

Her gaze bounces between the two of us, and I wonder if she's expecting us to throw down right then and there. If so, she's destined to disappointment because there is no realm in which I'm going to allow Griffin to out-charm me in front of these women.

Today's contest isn't just about winning the scavenger hunt; it's about winning hearts and minds or some shit. And it begins here and now.

"*So* exciting." My voice is dripping with enough false cheer to sweeten an entire pitcher of iced tea. "I've been looking forward to it all week."

Three sets of skeptical eyes swing my way—which is honestly fair, since at least two of them must see on their paperwork that I hadn't decided to do this damn thing until yesterday morning.

But Griffin's smile never wavers. "Same. Everything's so festive! You're fortunate you've had the opportunity to do this for years, Beckett."

My name on his lips makes complicated things happen in the neighborhood of my groin, but it's not enough to distract me from his game.

"Alas," I say, shaking my head sadly, like *alas* is a word I say out loud all the time. "I haven't had the pleasure before, so this is my first time too. I've been busy working for Axford Lumber, my family business." I shrug modestly, letting the unspoken weight of the Axford name hang there.

This isn't something I do often—not consciously anyway—because I don't actively try to be a douche, but Griffin Mercer brings out my worst impulses.

I'm slapped down for my bad behavior almost instantly.

"Oh, yes! Your dad helped my wife pick the hardwoods for our whole downstairs," Posy gushes. "Grant's amazing. Must be so awesome working for him, huh?"

I really hope my poker face is functional. "Awesome," I manage. "Every single day is just… awesome."

"And how are you settling into town, dear?" Mrs. Pratt asks Griffin. "I hope you've felt welcomed?"

"How could I not?" Griffin's smile cranks up another notch so the ladies are full-on basking in it. "I had a welcoming committee greet me the morning after I arrived." He shoots me a look that could strip paint. "I don't think I've had a chance to thank you for that, Beckett."

I *tsk*. "We had a small misunderstanding, as you've probably heard," I explain to the women with a wink and a shrug. "My bad. A… swing and a miss, you might say." I mime swinging a tennis racket.

Griffin's eye twitches, and I half expect cartoon steam to come shooting out of his ears.

"I did make up for it later, though," I assure the women. "When I saved Griffin's life."

"Oh!" Posy says, blinking rapidly between us. "Wow, that's…"

"Untrue!" Griffin begins at top volume, then lowers his voice, remembering our audience. He shakes a finger at me faux-playfully, while his hazel eyes skewer me dead. "Hah. Beckett, you… jokester. You know I was doing just fine until *you* tried to rescue me."

"Poor Griffin got stuck up a tree and needed an assist," I tell Mrs. Pratt confidingly. I lower my voice to a whisper. "He's a little embarrassed. Isn't it cute?"

I say this to be provoking, and it works. Griffin's eyes are now shooting tiny laser beams into my face. But the galling truth is… I'm not lying. His cheeks are flushed, his eyes are bright, and it's really fucking hard not to stare at him.

"When he says *assist*, he means he climbed up and dragged us both down," Griffin says with a brittle laugh. "You know what they say about the bigger they are, the harder they fall? Well, the only thing bigger than Beckett's ego is his… *ass-istance*." He darts a pointed glance at my backside.

"Nice of you to notice," I say with a cheerful wink, and he turns a shade redder.

"So… you two are friendly, then?" Mrs. Pratt demands. Her eyes zing back and forth between us. "Because the way I heard it—"

"Mrs. Pratt." I shake my head sadly. "You know better than to listen to town gossip. I'm an Axford, and Axfords have been welcoming newcomers to town for generations." I throw an arm around Griffin's shoulders, fully expecting him to elbow me away. "Right, buddy?"

He doesn't throw me off. His whole body freezes—seriously, I don't even think he's breathing—and his pounding pulse ricochets into me at every point where we're connected.

But clearly, I underestimated his commitment to this bit because, to my surprise, he wraps his arm around my back and squeezes my waist. "I guess so… pal."

His fingers dig in like he's trying to leave marks, each press sending a bright shock through my skin that settles low in my gut. Heat radiates through the fleece, ghosting over my ribs, and for one insane second, my body leans toward him before my brain can issue the order to move away.

It's not comfortable, it's not safe, and I sure as hell don't like it… but for one weird, unguarded second, I let myself breathe in the orangey scent of his hair product—

A sharp *braawwwp* from a bullhorn, and someone calls, "Five minutes to start!"

Griffin jerks away from me like I'm contagious, his face tomato red.

"If I could just finish registering now?" he asks Posy. "Don't want to be late!"

"Oh, sure," Posy says. "We'll just get your wristbands. Ramona?"

Mrs. Pratt consults her list, then sorts through the little plastic bin on the table. She hands Griffin a strip of blue-and-orange paper.

Then she hands an identical one to me.

I frown, turning the band over to inspect it. "All the bands are the same?"

Posy laughs. "Gosh, no. You two are the blue-and-orange team! Feel free to make up a team name."

"You were both late registrants, and neither of you signed up with a partner, so you were paired together," Mrs. Pratt explains. "You can't do a scavenger hunt alone."

"Can't you, though?" Griffin wonders. "I really think I could."

"Same," I say. "Hard same. I was expecting to, in fact. I'm good on my own."

"But you'll be better together," Posy chirps, rubbing her baby's back and looking way too chipper. "Since you're friends and all."

I can practically hear Griffin's internal screaming, which harmonizes nicely with my own. We don't look at each other, but I can tell from the way he raises his chin to the sky that he's realized we're stuck.

Other teams are clustered around, chatting and laughing, looking like they're actually excited about spending their Saturday morning traipsing around town solving riddles and taking pictures. We stick on our wristbands and trudge toward Chapel Island's massive gazebo in loaded silence, maintaining distance like we're opposing magnets.

"Just so we're clear," Griffin murmurs once we're out of earshot, "I'm winning this thing."

I snort. "Then I guess it's lucky you hitched your wagon to me, huh?"

Griffin takes a breath like he's about to verbally unleash when a man with a microphone steps into the gazebo. I recognize him as one of the people standing outside the Pickle Jar yesterday.

"Hi, everyone! I'm Ry Marek. Some of you parents and kids may know me as Mr. Marek from Proctor School, the unapologetic crosswalk advocate—"

The crowd laughs appreciatively.

"—but for today, you can call me Captain Fun!"

"*Jesus,*" Griffin and I mutter at the same time. Our eyes meet, and we both quickly look away.

I have to stifle a smirk. I *knew* Griffin's happy-joiner thing was all an act.

Ry explains the rules with the kind of enthusiasm usually reserved for announcing lottery winners. Each team gets seven riddles leading to various historic or quirky locations around town, all in a different order so we can't simply follow each other. We solve the riddles, take a picture of each location, text it to the phone number on our wristbands, and we'll be texted the next clue. We get points for speed, creativity, and—god help us all— "team spirit."

"Ready for your first challenge?" Ry asks, and a cheer goes up from the crowd that makes me wonder if someone spiked the whole town's coffee.

Volunteers hand each team a sealed envelope. Griffin and I both reach for ours at the same time, our fingers touching as we grab it.

The brush of his fingers against mine is a bare flicker of skin on skin, but it lights up a nerve all the way to my shoulder. My grip almost loosens, like my body's considering treason, and I clamp down harder just to prove I'm not that weak.

"*I'll* read it," Griffin says, trying to tug it away.

The air horn blows again, and the other teams take off, giggling and grinning.

"I'm capable of reading, city boy," I counter, keeping my grip on the envelope. "Went to college and everything."

"Well... I have a degree in marketing, so I bet I have better handwriting analysis skills."

"How would that... It's a *typed* clue, you ass."

Griffin tears the envelope away from me and rips it open with more force than strictly necessary. But I catch the card inside as it flutters toward the ground.

"*Cross the bridge where true love's sealed, kissed beneath and fate revealed,*" I read aloud. "Easy. That's the—"

"Kissing Bridge," Griffin says immediately.

I narrow my eyes. "How the fuck did you get that?"

"I read and I know things," he intones in a perfectly bastardized *Game of Thrones* quote.

I snort-laugh before I can help myself, then turn it into a scowl as the dumbass starts running west through the park.

"Hey, Tyrion Lannister, the bridge is this way." I hook a thumb over my shoulder and begin walking backward in the correct direction.

For a second, he looks like he wants to protest, and then he scowls and takes off at a full run past me, sunlight flashing in his golden hair like Mother Nature's conspiring to make him look good.

I roll my eyes. This is going to be the longest morning ever.

We run toward the eastern edge of the park, weaving around other teams who are still debating, trying to solve their riddles. When he starts jogging north, I whistle sharply and point him in the right direction.

"You could let me lead," I yell. "Since I'm the one of us who's lived here his whole life and actually knows where he's going."

"But you're too slow," he calls over his shoulder. "All that *bulk*."

Once again, the asshole startles a laugh out of me. "You weren't complaining when this bulk broke your fall the other night."

"I have no idea what you're talking about, since the other night didn't happen," he says smartly.

"And that's the second time today you've mentioned my ass," I point out. "Keep it up and I'll think you're obsessed with it."

"You wish."

In front of us, the Kissing Bridge arches low over Chapel Creek, its pale, sun-bleached planks and bright green beams glowing in the late-morning light.

"There's a legend about this bridge," Griffin says, barely slowing down. "Before it was the Kissing Bridge, locals called it the Lantern Bridge. During a fierce winter storm in 1819, Winsome's postman and his faithful steed got stranded on the far side of the creek, and townsfolk hung lanterns along the bridge to guide him. To this very day, they say that if you carry a light from one side of the bridge to the other without letting it go out, you'll always find your way home."

I'm so stunned, my legs stop working for a second. "Jesus Christ. Did you memorize a Winsome travel brochure, Mr. Marketing Degree?"

"Maybe. The library's full of useful information," he says smugly. "Big-Dill-Winning information."

I force myself into a run to catch up with him. "What kind of useful shit would that be?" I demand. "An ancient grimoire full of curses? Because that's the only way you're gonna win this thing, city boy."

It's his turn to laugh out loud against his will, and then he shoots me a dirty look like he blames me for his slip. He slows down as we approach the bridge.

I admit to myself I'm glad because I hadn't intended to *run* today, and I was starting to get a cramp. City boy has stamina.

"I don't need curses to beat you, Beckett," he says matter-of-factly. "I have skills."

"Just not when it comes to opening trapdoors, apparently." I snort. "You know the door's probably just locked, right?"

"*Locked*?" Griffin turns and presses a hand to his chest, his pretty hazel eyes wide. "Ohmigosh, *locked*. Why... I never considered! What a revolutionary concept! *Locked*. He doesn't just drag people out of trees, ladies and gentlemen."

"Excuse me, we both know I actually *did* save your ass."

He scowls but doesn't argue. "If you must know, there *isn't* a lock on the trapdoor," he mutters. "Not that I've found. Yet."

"Why would Jim hide a lock?" I wonder.

Griffin scowls, but for once, it's not entirely aimed at me. "I don't know! Why the hell would you build a treehouse in the woods in the first place? Why leave it to a guy you haven't bothered to contact since he was eight, who didn't know the house existed until he inherited it? Why clear out everything because you knew you were getting ready to go to the drum circle in the sky but not *warn* a person that you were dying?"

I'm not sure which of us is more shocked that he blurted all that out, but I can tell from the blush staining his face that he immediately regrets it.

"Whatever. Doesn't matter. Back to the hunt." He focuses on the bridge. "I think we should—"

"You're winging it," I say. "Learning as you go. I get it."

Griffin's eyes flash to mine, like he thinks I'm going to mock him.

Instead, I'm thinking about taking over Axford Lumber on my own, trying to figure shit out, feeling like I'd been dropped into a pool so deep I didn't know which way was up. Not knowing what I was doing, but not wanting to burden anyone else in my family while they were still reeling over almost losing my dad. Wanting to demand answers from my father, but not wanting to upset him further.

Hell, I'm still in that place.

Not that I want Griffin or anyone in town to know just how dire the situation is for Axford Lumber. God, no.

Griffin's situation's completely different than mine, but it also seems bigger and more overwhelming than I'd considered, and some parts are familiar.

After a second, I say, "I had a great-great-uncle who once built a wooden bridge halfway across the Winsome River, where it crosses the land behind my cabin. Literally, halfway across." I shake my head. "When I was a kid, I was convinced there had to be a reason why there was only half a bridge, you know? Like, did a storm wipe out the other half? Did they run out of wood? Did great-uncle-whoever die before he could finish?" I give him a half smile and a shrug.

He blinks. "And?" he says expectantly. "What'd you find out?"

"I didn't. That's my point. Guy died long before I was born. Sometimes you don't get to know why."

"That… is the worst pep talk I've ever heard," Griffin says wonderingly. "Wow. Like, amazingly bad. Zero out of ten."

I scratch my beard and shrug. "Now that I hear myself saying it out loud, it's not as inspiring as I thought."

His face ripples like he's not sure what expression he's supposed to be wearing, and he lets out a helpless laugh that makes me feel things I have no business feeling.

I clear my throat. "So. What's the plan? We take a picture of the bridge—?"

He straightens his shoulders. "We both have to be in the shot," he reminds me. "But we get points for creativity, they said. So I say that we take a picture commemorating the lantern guy's ride."

That's actually an excellent plan. And not one I would've considered. "It's not the worst idea ever," I allow.

Griffin huffs. "You remind me of Milo. God forbid either of you lets me think I know what I'm doing."

"Yeah, where *is* your sidekick today? Why isn't *he* your partner?"

"Because he's gone to Arizona for work," Griffin says with a shrug. He sets his camera on the ground facing the bridge, propping it up on a rock and checking the angles.

I frown as I watch him. *So he's living in Jim's house, dealing with the trapdoor all alone?* This makes me feel some kind of way… for no logical reason I can fathom. I mean, fuck, I live alone, and I'm perfectly happy about it. Thrilled, even.

Before I can think about it more, Griffin makes a *gimme* motion. "Hand over your phone. My camera's on a timer. I'm going to cross the bridge, holding your phone's flashlight up like a lantern—"

I pull my phone from my pocket. "Hang on, why *you*? You said we both have to be in the picture."

"We will." Griffin smiles widely. "You'll be my faithful steed. Get down on all fours, and I'll ride you."

I suck in a sharp breath as images slam into my brain— Griffin straddling me, fingers curled in my shirt, head tipped back in that exact way it did when I kissed him. My hands on his hips. His legs wrapped around my—

"I mean *r-ride*, like a horse!" he blurts, cheeks going crimson so fast I almost hear the sizzle. "Like g-galloping. Trotting. Whinnying. *Neeeeiiighhh.*"

I let my mouth curve slow and wicked. "I never whinny on the first date, Mercer. That's a hard *neigh* from me."

He squeezes his eyes closed and sucks in a breath through his nose. "I hate you so much."

"Back atcha," I say happily, which of course is when the asshole plucks my phone from my hand and runs onto the bridge.

"Hey! Give that back," I shout, following him.

I'm taller, but I guess his legs must go up to his armpits because he's genuinely faster than me. By the time I get to the center of the bridge, he's already standing there, grinning with my phone held aloft and the flashlight turned on. I reach up to grab the phone too… and Griffin's phone camera makes a clicking sound.

"Damn it. We'll have to reshoot," he says.

"Like fuck we will. Text the picture, get the next clue," I instruct, stealing my phone back.

Griffin fetches his own phone, muttering under his breath the whole time about *group projects* and *uncooperative steeds.*

Our next clue comes through, and I read it over Griffin's shoulder. "*Where knowledge sleeps in hallowed halls, seek the founder behind brick walls.*"

"Library," we say together, then glare at each other for our synchronicity.

"Specifically, the picture of Elias and Temperance Fletcher, the town founders, which is on the second floor," I add, grateful for the first time in my life that my second-grade class took a field trip to the library, just so I can see that flash of annoyance in Griffin's eyes.

Our pattern of one-upmanship continues through our next three clues—which leaves us at three for me and two for him, not that I'm keeping score or anything.

We bicker about everything. Which of us reads the clues and texts the pictures—usually him, since apparently we're using his phone. Whether Griffin's artsy photo ideas are genius or a waste of time. Who runs in front—*me*, not only because I know where I'm going but because, as Griffin points out, I make a good battering ram, and the crowds on Whether Street clear out of the way when they see me coming toward them.

Despite all the arguing, though, somehow it's working. We're not friends, but we're efficiently hostile. Two stubborn bastards working as a team. Enemies united by a common cause—in this case, taking down a team of frat bros from Hannabury College that I swear are ringers since I don't recognize any of them from around town.

For a little while, I forget this guy's holding my future hostage and find myself having fun. And I keep noticing things. Like how Griffin's hair still smells like oranges. How he gets a crease between his eyes when he's concentrating on lining up a camera shot. How his laugh, when it's genuine, is low and rough and twines itself around my insides.

Then everything goes to shit in a way I should have seen coming.

We're standing outside the Sugar House after solving riddle five involving a kind of Sassy Bean peach jam that somehow Griffin knew about. It's just after 11:00 a.m. Between the bright sun and all our running, we've both shed our jackets, and I'm thirsty as fuck, but the frat bros are machines, so I refuse to suggest a break.

Then Griffin's phone dings with our second-to-last riddle.

"*Where spirits meet and shadows play, find the stage of yesterday,*" he reads.

I grin. "Easy peasy. Back to the park, city boy. They mean the gazebo at Chapel Island. My sister used to do drama camp there every summer." I stride off in that direction, and it takes me a full beat to realize Griffin's not with me.

"What's the problem?" I demand, turning.

He points at his phone. "Shadows play. They mean a movie theater. Where do you have a movie theater?"

"We don't." I scratch the back of my neck. "I mean... I

guess they show second-run movies in the community center sometimes, but—"

"That's it, then. The stage of *yesterday*. Second-run movies." His hazel eyes light up eagerly. "Which way is the community center?"

The man is so pretty and so damn wrong. "Stage implies it's live, buddy. Like theater."

"Yeah? Which shadows play in the middle of the park, *pal*?" he shoots back. "They don't."

"They do! Because... because the trees make shadows on the ground," I say smugly. "And spirits meet because... people sometimes meet their friends there."

He makes a rude scoffing noise. "Unlike at the community center, where, I don't know, the whole *community* might meet?"

"You're overthinking this."

"Well, you're *under*thinking it, which is way worse."

We're standing in the middle of the sidewalk, voices raised, drawing stares from a bunch of fucking tourists who probably think we're providing some kind of small-town Vermont street theater experience.

"If we do it your way," Griffin goes on, chin jutting out in that way that makes me want to kiss him and throttle him at the same time, "and we come in dead last to those college boys because you were too pigheaded and controlling to consider—"

"Me?" I demand. "Oh my god. What about *you*? You come in here and assume you know—"

"—an alternate way of looking at things—"

"—better than anyone here—"

"—because you're from the fucking royal family of Winsome—"

"Are you serious right now?" I hiss.

I grab Griffin's bicep, and despite his squawking, I tow him down the alley between the Sugar House and Fox Creamery, then further, pushing open the gate that leads to the dining area behind Ames's restaurant. At this hour, the restaurant's still closed, and there's not a soul in sight.

"Once again, you have no idea what you're talking about, Mercer. I work my ass off to keep my family's business going—"

"You're trying to keep your business going by taking over Jim's land! All you care about is maintaining your own wealth and reputation! You think because I don't have family money and connections, I'm some weakling you can use as a pawn!"

I legitimately have no idea where this is coming from. All my "wealth" is tied up in land owned by my family's LLC. I don't have a reputation—not one that's worth a damn, anyway, which is why I'm participating in this farce of a scavenger hunt.

A distant part of me is clanging a warning bell that I need to calm down. To ask questions. To be rational. But somehow… *fuck*. I can't let it go.

"You're wrong. You could not be more wrong," I tell him. My voice comes out low and deep, rough enough to scrape. More like a growl than actual words. "I'm not trying to use you for anything. And I don't think you're weak!"

"Yeah, right—"

"I think you're stubborn as fuck! I think you're fucking *infuriating*. And I think you're… you're beautiful."

The words hang in the air between us, almost tangible, and I immediately want to take them back.

*One of these things is not like the other.*

Griffin scowls and shuts his mouth so quickly his teeth clack together. His hazel eyes search mine, looking for the joke or the hidden insult.

Later, I'll think back on this and wonder if this was the moment when I could have played it off. Stepped back, defused things.

Or maybe it was already too late.

Because when Griffin opens his mouth and utters a single confused "Beckett...?" I don't make a conscious choice to step toward him...

I simply *do.*

# CHAPTER SEVEN

### GRIFFIN

AN INSTANT LATER, his mouth is on mine.

This time, there's no danger, no pretense of adrenaline. This is pure want, and I'm kissing him back before my brain can even form a protest.

Beckett's hands frame my face, thumbs stroking along my cheekbones as he deepens the kiss. He nips at my bottom lip with his teeth, and I make a sound that's part gasp, part moan. His minty-sweet tongue tangles with mine, and I feel like I'm one of the balloons the little kids have been running around with all morning. I'm floating. Untethered to reality.

I'm not the Griffin who stared down at Times Square and imagined having it all. I'm not the Griffin who lost everything in one fell swoop. I'm not even the Griffin who literally can't find his way into a pickle barrel. I'm just a beating heart, an aching chest, a creature of the here and now.

And I can't get enough.

"Fuck," I whisper when we come up for air. My head is spinning. "We—this is—"

Beckett growls, "I know," but he doesn't stop and—*fuck, again*—neither do I. In fact, I grab his shirt in both hands and yank him closer.

His mouth moves to my jaw, then my neck, and I have to bite back a whimper when he finds a spot just below my ear that makes my knees go weak. His teeth graze my skin, sending shivers down my spine, and I can feel the heat pooling in my groin.

For the first time, I realize we're in some kind of enclosed garden. The big patio space is filled with empty wrought-iron tables and chairs, giant planters filled with late-season herbs, and fairy lights strung overhead that glint in the sunlight. A heavy-duty fire door leads into a building.

Beckett has me backed against the fence just like he backed me against the tree the other night. And there's a part of me that thinks I should, at the very least, object to consistently being the back-*ee* instead of the back-*er*…

But another part is wondering if they make shirts with lumbar support—or lumb*erjack* support—because I apparently have a latent fetish for this lumberjack backing me into things.

With Beckett's body solid and warm against mine, I can feel how hard he is through his jeans. The realization sends heat shooting straight to my dick, and I arch against him helplessly. His hands slide down to my ass, squeezing and pulling me closer, the friction between us almost unbearable. I swear I can feel every ridge of his cock through the fabric of our pants.

"Jesus, Griffin," he breathes against my throat. "What are you doing to me?"

I want to tell him I have no fucking idea, that it's *him* doing it to *me*, that he needs to stop because we don't even like each other.

Instead, I slide my hands under his shirt and run my palms over the broad expanse of his chest.

Beckett's skin is fever-hot and scattered with soft hair. When I brush my thumbs over his nipples, he makes a guttural, wounded noise, so I do it again… and again. Then I pinch them lightly, and his hips buck against mine.

"This," I gasp. "I'm doing this."

He growls again, low and rough, like the sound's been pulled out of him. Then he kisses me, hungrier this time, and I give up all pretense of resistance. My hands map the muscles of his back, the solid width of his shoulders, while his hips press forward in a rhythm that's driving me fucking crazy.

Craz*ier*.

Whatever.

Beckett's hands are everywhere, touching, exploring, claiming. One hand slides down to cup my cock through my jeans, and I let out a startled moan into his mouth.

"We should stop," I manage to say when he breaks away to suck at the spot where my neck meets my shoulder again. "Someone could come out here—"

That's not even number one on my list of reasons I shouldn't be doing this, but all the real reasons are slip-sliding through my brain like water.

"I know," Beckett groans, but his hand is still shaping me through my jeans. "We should definitely stop."

I should make the call. Be the strong one. And any

minute now, I *will*. Because I prefer my hookups uncomplicated and well-planned, with guys who know exactly why we're there, so there's no risk of messy emotional entanglements.

Beckett Axford is six-plus feet of complication. A Gordian knot of entanglement. But with his mouth hot on my skin and his body moving against mine, I can't remember why any of that matters. All I can think is that, in my entire life, no man has ever made me feel as good as this man I shouldn't want.

"Don't stop," I whisper, arching into him. I thread my fingers through his dark hair and tug until he lifts his head to look at me.

Beckett's blue eyes are wild, his pupils blown wide, and there's something almost vulnerable in his expression that makes my chest tight... probably because I feel that same vulnerability in *me*.

His lips are a little chapped, like he's been chewing them all day—probably literally biting them so we could solve clues without fighting. I find myself wanting to kiss them gently. To fix that small thing for him. To make him feel better, like he tried to do for me earlier.

And whatever this fever that's gripping us is, it's not *that*.

It's not a *let me make you feel better* thing.

It can't be.

"Griffin?" he says, like it's a question or a plea.

In answer, I surge up to kiss him again, pouring all my confusion and want and frustration into it. He responds immediately, one hand sliding up to cup the back of my neck while the other fumbles with the button of my jeans.

Then my zipper is down, and his hand is sliding inside, wrapping around my cock.

The feel of Beckett's hand on my bare skin is so fucking electric, it's like I'm a teenager having his first behind-the-gym frot again—totally primed, coiled, and ready to explode just from that one simple touch.

It should be mortifying. It's not.

Because it turns out grumpy-as-fuck Beckett Axford—who's also surprisingly intelligent, shockingly funny, and even unexpectedly kind in a way that isn't sticky with pity—wants me badly.

Despite all the reasons he should, he can't walk away any more than I can.

So for a second, I forget the last few months of heartache and bullshit. All the stuff that's made me question who I am and what I'm worth and all the things I've done wrong. And I let myself feel *powerful*.

I reach for his jeans, my own fingers trembling as I undo his button, pushing the fabric down when his zipper won't cooperate because I need to get my hand on him too. When I finally do, his mouth opens on a soundless groan.

Beckett's fucking huge, which isn't a surprise but is nevertheless a *thrill*. He's hot and thick, his tip already slick with precum that I use to lubricate my strokes.

We start moving together, our hands working in tandem, tugging and squeezing… driving each other wild like we've been doing this for ages. Like we know each other. The sensation of his cock in my hand is like a drug, and I'm addicted to the way it twitches and throbs in time with my heartbeat.

But then Beckett nudges my hand away and wraps his larger hand around both our cocks, his grip firm and sure.

He starts to jerk us together, his cock moving against mine, his strokes long and deliberate, driving us both closer to the edge.

Pleasure makes my whole body coil tight.

"Fuck, *yes*," he moans when I bite down gently on his shoulder, and his hips stutter.

I'm right there with him, the pressure building low in my belly made so much worse by the way Beckett's looking at me, soaking in every flicker of my reaction like he can't look away.

"Beckett, I—" I start to warn him, but then his mouth is on mine again, and I'm gone, coming into his hand with a muffled cry against his lips. He follows a second after, his whole body shivering and shuddering as he buries his face in my neck.

We stand there reeling and clinging to each other, like we've just had a tornado blow over us. Beckett's hand curls around the back of my shirt in a tight fist, like he's anchoring himself. His breath ghosts over my skin in uneven, shallow bursts. His heart hammers against my chest, and the smell of pine and sweat feels almost familiar. Comforting, or something.

And that—the sensation of comfort, the most innocuous thing in the midst of this whole... un-innocuous encounter—is what makes my brain plug back in and say, *What the fuck, Griffin?* Because comfort equals complication.

Of course, the universe decided my first real orgasm in months would come from a guy I—almost definitely—dislike.

I let out a shaky breath and aim for humor. "So. Have I,

uh… convinced you that we should head to the community center yet?" It comes out raspy and wrecked.

Beckett lifts his head and looks at me, and then he laughs—not the bitter sound I've heard him make before, but one that's warm and wraps around me like a hug.

"You're ridiculous," he says, and the affection in his voice makes my heart flutter.

*Red flag. The reddest of flags. Danger, danger.*

We both hear a scuffling sound, followed by the dull *thunk* of a lock being turned on the opposite side of the fire door. "Yeah! You can come over whenever, Robbie. Since when do you ask? Did you want me to— Oh, I see. No, of course she can. I mean, she's your girlfriend, so—"

Beckett and I jump apart like we've been electrocuted, scrambling to right ourselves. Before I even register what's happening, he shifts in front of me—his broad back suddenly between me and the fire door, shielding me from view as we fumble with our jeans.

The gesture is instinctive, protective, and somehow hits me as hard as the orgasm.

I tuck myself away, pull up my pants, and try to adopt a casual expression. I don't know what Beckett's doing to clean his hand, and I refuse to think about it.

A few seconds later, a dark head pokes out the door, and a pair of blue eyes locks on us. The man is built on a slightly smaller scale than Beckett, with a rounder face, but they have the same broad shoulders, thick muscles, and piercing gaze.

"Gotta go, Rob. My brother's here," the man says into the phone, shutting it off without looking away from us. "Beck? What's going on? I thought you were doing the Wild Gherkin Chase."

"Ames!" Beckett says in a too-loud, too-jovial voice. "H-hey, man. We were. I mean, we are! Griffin and I, we, um…"

He waves a hand at me like I'm supposed to pick up this part of the story.

Fortunately for Beckett, I used to be good at this shit.

"We were arguing," I say with a rueful grin, because the most polite lies start with a grain of truth. I step forward, extending my hand. "Sorry, we haven't met yet. I'm—"

"Griffin, the guy who inherited Jim's place and immediately put the kibosh on Beckett being able to access our tract." Ames shakes my hand without taking his eyes off Beckett.

I can guess where he heard this interpretation of events, and I glare at Beckett over my shoulder.

My glare fades instantly, though, when I realize what caught Ames's attention. Beckett's lips are bright red, his cheeks are flushed, his hair is sticking up in about twelve different directions, thanks to my hands, and his fleece is half caught in the waistband of his jeans.

I force a laugh, drawing Ames's attention to me. "That's one side of the story. Your brother has trouble acknowledging there's another side to consider… which is kind of a theme for him. If he wasn't so stubborn, we'd be finishing up the sixth riddle by now, and we wouldn't have blown our lead."

Beckett huffs, and I can't tell if he's genuinely annoyed or just committed to selling the act. "I think you mean it's thanks to *your* stubbornness that we're probably trailing behind the frat bros—"

"And if you'd listened to my ideas, we wouldn't be—"

"Guys? Didn't you hear them blow the air horn?" Ames points a finger, presumably toward Chapel Island Park. "I guess someone must've solved all the clues. The scavenger hunt ended like ten minutes ago."

Beckett and I exchange a look.

"Oh," Beckett mutters. "Fuck. We, uh… We must've been… arguing too loud to hear."

"That." I nod, knowing my face is the color of a ripe apple.

Beckett clears his throat and sticks his hands in his pockets. "Right. Well. I should get back to work. Invoices. Schedules. Stuff." He runs a hand through his hair. "Good hunt, Griffin. I'll see you around."

"Wait, Beckett—" Ames begins.

But he's too late. Beckett's already gone, so fast I'm surprised there's not a cartoon hole in the fence in the shape of a lumberjack.

That was supposed to be *my* dramatic exit, damn it, and he beat me to it.

"Nice to meet you, but I should probably go too," I begin. "Stuff to, ah… do."

Ames looks me up and down, and his lips twitch. "Come inside," he instructs, turning away so he can prop the back door open.

Oh, god, I really, *really* don't want to.

I'm sweaty and probably reek of sex. Worse, my adrenaline rush is about to crash out, and when it does, I'll have no choice but to confront what I just did. I'd rather have privacy for that because it's not gonna be pretty.

But Ames doesn't leave me much choice. He walks back into the restaurant, expecting I'll follow. And since the last thing I want is for him to immediately send up a smoke signal or text the Winsome Gossip Chat speculating about what he might have seen… I do.

Beckett owes me *huge*.

The fire door opens straight into the restaurant—the same warm, homey place where Milo and I ate lunch the other day. I follow Ames past the bar, where rows of liquor bottles glow like stained glass, and through a swinging door I somehow missed before. It leads straight into the kitchen, which is wide open to the bar and, beyond that, the dining room, so anyone sipping a drink or lingering over dinner can watch their food being chopped, grilled, or plated.

Back here, it's all gleaming stainless steel and professional-grade equipment, but somehow, it still feels as warm and welcoming as the dining room. With the whole restaurant empty—no servers or sous-chefs yet—the space feels serene. Almost… cozy.

Or it *would*, if I had a clue what the fuck I'm doing here.

Ames doesn't stop until he's standing by a stainless steel prep table. He motions me toward a handwashing sink, "just in case you need to wash up," and my face is on fire like I'm a toddler whose hand's been caught in the cookie jar.

Except, you know, in this case, the cookie jar was *his brother's pants*.

When I'm done, he motions me to one of the stools on the other side, then fixes me with a look every bit as fierce as his brother's.

I try to stave off whatever he has in mind by blurting, "It's lunchtime, right? Why aren't you open?"

A crinkle appears between his eyebrows. "Oh! We do

breakfast until ten on Saturdays and brunch on Sundays instead of lunch."

"Oh. Right. Uh… I bet it's good." I find a stool and pull it out.

"I certainly hope so. Hey, is it true…?" he begins.

I freeze with my legs bent and my ass halfway to the stool, waiting for him to finish that sentence.

*…that you're locked in a weird rivalry with my brother?*

*…that you were fucking around with that same brother on my back patio?*

*…that you were the guy in that billboard TikTok?*

*…that Jim left you his house for no reason whatsoever and you totally don't deserve it?*

"…that you don't like pickles?"

"Oh." I huff out a relieved laugh and drop the rest of the way onto the stool. "Your mom mentioned that, huh? Yeah, it's true. Though it feels like kind of a liability to admit that in this town, especially during the Brine."

Ames grins. "Meh. Maybe it's time the vinegar-hating minority of Winsome had representation." He grabs a loaf of crusty, golden bread from the cooling rack next to an industrial oven and begins carving it into thick slices with quick, practiced motions.

"I think your brother might feel differently," I say lightly. "I think he'd like the pickle majority to stay firmly in power."

Ames's smile doesn't falter. "Beck would happily control the whole universe if he could just find the right levers." He flicks a glance at me. "Wouldn't we all?"

"Some of us would just like to have control over what happens to our own lives," I point out. "And our own land."

"Touché." He winks. "For now, how about you control what kind of sandwich you want. Grilled cheese again, or are you feeling adventurous?"

"Oh." I immediately shake my head. "No. Thank you, but you don't have to do that. Like I said, I should probably—"

Of course, this is the moment when my stomach decides to remind me that I've been running around town for hours, had a quickie in a semi-public space, and haven't eaten since breakfast.

The growl it makes is loud and mournful and reverberates around the little kitchen.

Ames laughs. "Adventurous it is." He eyes me across the table. "Sit back and calm down, man. You look like you're expecting me to torture you for information, but I promise, I'm not that guy." He gestures toward himself with his knife. "Baby brother. Former Eagle Scout. Current volunteer fireman. A lover, not a fighter."

I'm not sure I believe his cute and innocent act. He is, after all, Beckett's brother. But Ames manages to achieve the same wide-eyed cherub look Milo gets at his most cunning, and it's so familiar I can't help but laugh.

From the giant refrigerator, Ames pulls a roast chicken, a jar of something suspiciously green, and a block of cheese. As he assembles the sandwich, he moves around the kitchen with easy efficiency, all the while giving me the life story of every ingredient—the cheddar's from Fox Creamery, the spread's made from garlic scapes he grows out back.

It's so chill and pleasant that by the time he's slid the plate in front of me, I've relaxed in spite of myself. And when I take the first bite, I groan. "Oh my *god*, Ames! You're amazing."

"That's what all the boys say." He winks. "Did you want some butternut soup? I think I have some in the fridge I could heat up."

"Nah. My friend Milo's the soup fiend. But he's in Arizona on a wellness retreat for a couple weeks at some big spa with a bunch of other influencers." I lick a bit of garlic sauce from my finger. "Kind of a coup to get invited," I hear myself volunteering.

"You sound like a proud mother." He grins. "Must be weird, being here without your wingman, though, eh? I'd be sunk without mine."

"It's… a little weird." I chew thoughtfully. "Milo and I have been friends since college, and we've been through a lot together. Family drama—mostly his—guy drama, career drama—mostly mine. But, I mean, I'm fine on my own," I add quickly. "And even if I weren't, I want him to be happy."

I wonder what the fuck is in this sandwich that's making me such a share-er all of a sudden.

"Yeah." Ames sets his elbows on the counter and blows out a breath. "Yeah, I get that," he says softly.

The kitchen door swings open, letting in a rush of cooler air and a man who fills the doorway.

"Amesie!" the newcomer says, striding in with a paper bag clutched in one giant hand. He's wearing a polo with a Winsome Fire Dept. logo over the breast, and it's barely containing his huge shoulders and biceps. His grin's nearly as big.

In the next breath, his free arm is slung around Ames's

shoulders like it belongs there. "Who's the best friend in the entire history of friendship?" he demands.

Ames's face softens, just a little, in a way I haven't seen yet, but he pulls a face and pretends to think about it. "Hmm. Bunsen, maybe? He's really nice…"

"Oh yeah? Did *Bunsen* come to help you *and* bring your favorite apple cranberry muffins from Ruby's?" The giant shakes the bag.

Ames laughs. "No, Robbie. You're the best friend ever, Robbie," he recites dutifully.

"Damn straight I—" he begins, and then he suddenly realizes I'm sitting there. He frowns. "Oh."

A tall brunette stunner strolls in, her heels clicking softly against the tile. Her camel coat swishes around her, and her flawless hair seems to wave in its own breeze. "Hey, Ames," she says softly. "Good to see you again."

"Lissa," Ames replies, bright enough to be polite and flat enough to be… something else I'm not really catching. "Hey."

Her eyes turn to me and light up. "Oh, gosh. I'm so sorry. We're interrupting you and your…"

"Griffin," I supply, giving both of the newcomers a casual wave. "And you weren't actually—"

"We weren't interrupting," Robbie tells her, frowning like he can't imagine where she came up with that idea. "I told you, I always come hang with Ames on Saturday afternoons and help him with dinner prep, especially during the Brine. That's why I can't come to your parents' garden party thing."

This earns him a flicker of something from Lissa—just a quick glance at where his arm is still slung over Ames. Robbie doesn't seem to catch it, but Ames does.

Ames makes a grab for the muffin bag, which gives him the perfect cover for shifting out from under Robbie's arm. It's subtle and well-executed, and I might not have noticed if I hadn't perfected the move myself, since my best friend is a touchy-feely-hugger and I'm not.

This, Robbie definitely notices. His brows pinch, and he frowns at me again before his face smooths out like he's decided not to ask.

"You know I always love having you here, Rob," Ames says, clutching the muffin bag to his chest like a life preserver. "Always. But if you want to go with Lissa, of course you should. I can handle dinner prep."

"See?" Lissa says, aiming a fond, exasperated look at Robbie. "It's like I told you. Ames doesn't need you chatting at him while he's chopping veggies. You're friends, honey, but you don't have to live in each other's pockets. Right, Ames?"

Ames opens his mouth, but only air comes out. He shrugs helplessly.

"Besides," she adds. "How's Ames ever going to find a boyfriend so we can double-date if you never let him chat up a nice guy?" She tosses me a wink.

I keep my expression neutral, expecting Ames to correct her, but he doesn't, though his face flushes and his fingers clutch the bag so hard I'm pretty sure the cranberry muffins are now cranberry crumbs.

"Oh. Shit. I didn't…" Robbie shoots Ames a look that's both guilty and… hurt. "I mean. I guess we should go to your parents' thing, then," he says, the same way I might say, "I guess we should order the deep-fried pickles."

Lissa laughs like he's adorable. "You guess?" she teases, looping her arm through his. She lifts up on her tippy-toes because even in her heels, she's got nothing on Robbie's height, and presses a kiss to the corner of his mouth. "It's a good thing you're so cute," she whispers loud enough for all of us to hear.

Robbie turns red as a beet and makes a strangled noise.

Lissa laughs again and tosses Ames and me a smile as she leads Robbie away. "See you later, guys."

They're gone a moment later, the door swinging shut on her laughter. Silence settles over the kitchen.

"Wow," I say. "So. That was…"

"That was my bestie. Yep." Ames clears his throat. He turns away and makes a big production about finding exactly the right spot on the counter to put the muffin bag.

"How long have you had feelings for him?"

He freezes. "I, ah… I think you've got the wrong idea there, Griffin. We're friends. Best friends. But Robbie's straight. Totally and completely."

I tilt my head. Ames's voice is tight but absolutely firm. He does not want to discuss this.

"Got it," I say, turning back to my sandwich. "Well. He seems nice."

"He is." Ames's smile is much more natural now. "Rob's literally the best guy on Earth. He's supportive and kind. We met in high school, and I don't think we've gone a single day since without talking. When he wanted to be a volunteer firefighter, I joined too. And after I finished culinary school and everyone said, 'Ames, you need more experience before you open a restaurant,' Robbie was the first one to say, 'You can do it, I know you can.' He helped me make my dream a reality. So that's what I want for him too." He spreads his hands. "Like you said with Milo, right? I want him to be happy."

This is the first time I've ever seen a person overshare as a way to share nothing at all. I wonder if that's a secret you learn, living in a small town.

"And you think Lissa makes him happy," I surmise.

"Hmm? Oh. Probably. If not her, it'll be someone. And she's pretty, right? Not *my* type." He shoots me a flirty wink that's two shades too desperate to be believable. "But she's smart too. And her dad's Bart Cagney. You know, from Cagney Bank and Trust?"

"I've seen the building in town."

Ames nods. "They've got a bunch of branches all over Vermont. If Lissa and Robbie get married and have kids, I bet Bart would set them up in a nice house. And Robbie deserves that, you know? The whole picket fence thing, not having to worry about money."

I frown. "How long have they been dating?"

"Since April or so?" Ames shrugs like he's not sure, but I bet if I pushed, he could tell me the exact date and time.

"And they're already discussing picket fences?" I demand. "Jesus Christ. The straights have got to *chill.*"

Ames laughs weakly. "You know, I'm supposed to be prepping for the dinner rush, but I'm, ah… suddenly not feeling all that great. I think I might call Jenna and ask her to come in early to prep."

I don't know Ames at all, but the look in his eye—the one that says his *actual* dream, which in his case has nothing to do with his restaurant, is slipping through his fingers and he's helpless to stop it—is achingly familiar.

God knows, I have no advice to offer Ames about this. So far, I've dealt with my own dying dream by exiling myself to a new state, starting a small-town land war, and then getting hot and heavy with my nemesis for reasons I can't begin to explain, even to myself.

But when I was at my lowest point a few months ago, when my career imploded and the rest of the world stopped answering my calls, at least I had Milo to stand beside me. To talk about nothing. To keep me distracted.

And though I'm sure Ames has a million friends in this town, none of them are here right now, and his *best* friend's currently locking lips with a woman who looks like she's never met a brine she didn't like. So…

*Fuck it.*

I don't know what I'm doing in this town—or in my life—but at least I can do this. Be useful. Be here.

"How about I do you one better?" I say, coming around the counter. "I'll help prep."

"*You* will?" Ames's brow lowers even as his lips lift. "Really?"

"Sure." I shrug as I head for the handwashing sink. "I don't know what Robbie usually does, but I can wash and chop. If you want anything else done, you're gonna have to explain it like you're my mothers and I'm five years old," I warn.

His mouth twists up in a lopsided smile. "That's really kind, Griffin."

"Well, Jesus, don't cry on me or whatever," I say with a wink. "I'm only doing this so you'll decide to share your soup recipe with me, and then I can dole it out to Milo in chunks over his next three birthdays."

"Oh my god." Ames sputters out a laugh. "Oh my *god.*"

I dry my hands on a paper towel. "You think I'm kidding."

"No, I think Beckett's met his match." Ames's smile is genuine and stretches from ear to ear. "Whether he knows it or not."

My face goes nuclear. "That's not… we're not… I don't know what you think you saw, but your brother and I can't stand each other. We just… happen to both enjoy hotly debating scavenger hunt clues, that's all."

"And that's exactly what I saw," he says solemnly. "Two men debating. Hotly."

I huff, but as Ames gets out zucchini for me to chop, my mind floats back to Beckett's blush when I joked about him being my steed, Beckett's hands on my cock and his mouth against mine. The way he jumped in front of me and shielded me without hesitation. The way he scowled and walked away.

The way I'm infuriated with the man, the way I should absolutely hate him for the threat he poses to Jim's land if nothing else… but also the way I know that if he were here in this kitchen again, I wouldn't be able to keep my hands or my mouth off him.

And I think if I'm Beckett's match…

One or both of us is going to burn.

# CHAPTER EIGHT

### BECKETT

I WAKE up Sunday morning feeling like I've been hit by a logging truck, and it takes me a full ten seconds to remember why.

Griffin Mercer, smiling in the sunshine as we raced around Winsome.

Griffin's lips. His eyes. His hands. His *cock*.

His face when I took off.

Sitting up, I drag both hands down my face. My stomach twists in a way that has nothing to do with the tumblers of whiskey I knocked back last night.

I heave myself out of bed, turn on my phone, and immediately regret it when I find three texts from my family, each one a special kind of torture.

MOM

How did the scavenger hunt go, sweetie?
Did you and Interesting Griffin have fun?

WILDER

[Image attached] Look what you missed, cuz. These college boys are loving their golden gherkin trophy. Maybe next year you'll actually FINISH the hunt instead of disappearing 😏

AMES

Thanks for bringing Griffin by yesterday! Really enjoyed getting to know him. He's great.

The last one stops me cold, and guilt pits my stomach.

*Getting to know him?* I'd assumed Griffin had cut out when I did. Did Ames interrogate Griffin after I left?

What am I talking about? Ames is Vivian Axford's son. Of course he did. While I ran off to nurse my wounded pride and pretend I hadn't had the best orgasm of my life with a man who's got my company by the balls.

*Christ. Dick move, Axford. Even for you.*

I just keep fucking up where Griffin is concerned. From literally the first minute I met him, I've been thinking with the wrong head. Feeling back-footed time after time. Reacting in the worst way possible.

I keep *saying* I'm going to do better, but then I get within five feet of the man, start feeling things, and my good intentions go *poof*.

After yesterday, I don't even have the excuse that I don't like the guy anymore. Those rare flashes of vulnerability Griffin showed were like a backlight, and suddenly, the shape of everything he was hiding came into focus. The fear and loneliness. The mask of haughty anger.

I feel a strange kind of kinship with the guy. I know a lot about prickly shells.

I get coffee brewing and drag myself to the shower, thinking about how I could repay this debt I feel for leaving him to face Ames's interrogation alone. If I were Ames or my mom, I'd bring Griffin some food, but me poisoning him wouldn't help anything. If I were Holden, I'd do something cringey sweet like bring flowers and apologize, but I was tragically born without the ability to charm.

Then it hits me.

I pull on yesterday's jeans and a clean henley, and before I can talk myself out of it, I grab my toolbox from my truck and march across the road to Jim's—Griffin's—treehouse.

The morning air is crisp and clean, carrying the scent of woodsmoke and dying leaves. Autumn's settling over Winsome like a comfortable blanket, painting the trees gold and crimson.

Normally, I'd stop. Breathe it all in. But today, all I see is Jim's house… and how Griffin must see it.

The house has been here since I was a teenager and I've been here plenty of times over the years, usually to collect Jim's mail or check up on him after one of his longer "herbal adventures." I'd knock on the door, Jim would answer, we'd chat for a minute on the porch or just inside his living room, and that was it. Jim liked his privacy. I respected that.

But now, as I peer up at the house, I remember Griffin asking *why*… and I'm asking the same question.

Dad helped Jim design and build this place when he first came to Winsome. Studying it now, I can see Dad's influence in the solid bones of the structure—the way the foundation hugs the natural slope of the land, how the support beams are positioned for maximum stability.

But everything else? The stained glass windows, the rounded doors, the pickle-barrel turret, the rope bridge extending from the barrel like something out of a kids' adventure movie? Pure Jim Grange chaos. A child's fantasy come to life.

When Dad's brother gambled away part of our land that had been his inheritance from my grandparents, my father was *pissed.* I remember my parents having heated conversations behind closed doors. I remember my dad looking nearly as sad as when Grandpa Tom died.

So why did Dad then help the guy who'd won the land build this weird house? How much had it cost him, emotionally, to do that? I hate that the distance between us means I can't just call him up and ask.

I'm climbing the steps to the front door when the whine of a saw splits the air. It cuts off abruptly, followed by Griffin screaming, *"Fuuuuuuckkkk!"*

For the second time, hearing Griffin yell turns my blood to ice. I drop my toolbox. Storm inside. Follow the sound to the back of the house.

"Griffin?" I bellow.

What I find isn't bloody carnage, but it does make my chest tight.

A simple, wood-framed bed is covered with an old, paint-splattered drop cloth, and there's a ladder set up beneath a massive wooden trapdoor in the ceiling. A circular saw sits abandoned on the floor, along with a lineup of tools —a rusty crowbar, a drill, a whole collection of screwdrivers and hammers. And in the middle of it all sits Griffin, leaning against the footboard of the bed with his knees drawn up to his chest. He's wearing his city boots, work gloves, and big safety goggles… and he looks like he's about to cry.

"What the fuck?" I demand, falling to my knees beside him and gripping his chin firmly. My heart's still jackhammering wildly. "Are you hurt? Are you—"

"Of course you're here at this exact moment," Griffin groans. He jerks away from my touch, then scrubs both hands over his face, knocking the glasses to the floor. "Of course you are."

The relief that floods through me when I realize he's not hurt is so intense, it makes me lightheaded. But protective anger follows close behind, surprising the hell out of me.

"What the fuck were you thinking?" I yell.

"I was *thinking* I was going to take care of a problem like a fucking adult." He thrusts a hand at the ladder and the tools. "But apparently, I can't fix anything these days. Not with you. Not with my inheritance. Not with the Big Dill. Sure as hell not with my career since I'm fucking unemployable." His breath catches. "Not even with a goddamn trapdoor. I really think Milo had it right. Vermont is trying to kill me."

Every instinct screams to pull him against me, but I hold myself back. He wouldn't want that, and let's be honest, I'd probably suck at it anyway. I'm not the guy anyone turns to for comfort.

I stick my hands in my pockets. "Vermont, as in the entire state?" I whistle low. "We're a pretty peace-loving place. You must've worked hard if you made all of Vermont pissed off."

"Go ahead and make fun of me," he continues, lifting

his chin stubbornly. "But I cannot use that saw. I tried! The second I turned it on, it freaked me out, so I shut it off."

"Good," I say firmly.

"No, it isn't," he shoots back. "Because I—"

"Don't know what you're doing and could have cut your fucking head off?" A shudder runs through me, imagining it. Before he can work up an angry retort, I continue. "You did the right thing."

The fight goes out of him for a second.

But he recovers quickly and scrambles to his feet, not quite meeting my eyes.

"Glad I have your approval." He strips off his gloves and wipes his palms on his jeans before looking down at where I'm still squatting on the floor. "What are you doing here, Beckett?"

Right. *That.*

"I, ah…" I push to my feet and run my fingers through my hair nervously. "I came to apologize. For yesterday."

"Yeah?" Hands on his hips, he eyes me up and down. "Which part of yesterday? And is yelling some kind of Vermont-style apology, or was that special for me?"

"Neither." I shoot him a rueful look. "You're not the only one who can't seem to get things right recently."

Griffin makes a dismissive sound.

"I meant for yesterday when we…"

"Frotted against a fence and came our brains out?" he suggests.

His voice drops, goes sultry and teasing, and I have to squeeze my eyes shut and will myself not to react.

"Yeah," I breathe. My eyes pop open. "I mean, *no.* Unless you want me to apologize for that part too?"

I honestly can't remember how things started yesterday, just that we were suddenly *in it*, and I'd never wanted anything so badly.

"I was apologizing for leaving you to deal with Ames," I explain. "I suck at making shit up, if you couldn't tell, and I knew he'd see right through anything I said. But I shouldn't have left a man behind." I meet his eyes head-on. "I'm sorry about that. It won't happen again."

Griffin's lips pull up on one side, and I replay my own words.

"I mean, not that I think we'll be in that situation… or any situation… *hell*." I rub at the back of my neck.

He lets out a quiet laugh. "I accept your apology, Beckett. Ames is cool. I, ah, stayed and helped him with dinner prep." He takes a deep breath. "And you don't owe me an apology for anything else. What happened was… insanity. Obviously. But it was mutual insanity."

I nod once.

"If you're in an apologetic mood, though, you *could* say you're sorry for losing us the scavenger hunt. How about something like, 'Griffin, I apologize profusely for my failure to listen to your brilliant suggestion of going to the community center.'" He flutters his long eyelashes and it makes my stomach clench.

"Mmm…" I scratch my cheek, pretend to think about it, and purse my lips. "Nah."

His smile makes the stomach-clenching thing worse. "I figured. Come on."

Frowning, I follow him back to the living room. He takes in the front door, still hanging open, and my tool bag unceremoniously dumped on the floor, but doesn't say anything. He leads me to a tiny pink kitchen just big enough for the two of us to stand in and gestures me to a white stool that's sturdier than it looks.

"Have a seat. I need coffee. And…" Griffin grabs a takeout container and cracks it open. "Robbie brought Ames cranberry muffins, and Ames shared the wealth. Help yourself."

He pours us each a coffee, then leans back against the counter, sipping his, with his feet crossed at the ankles.

"So." My throat feels tight. "Do I want to know what you and Ames discussed?"

Griffin's eyes meet mine over the rim of his mug. "Oh, all of your deepest, darkest secrets, naturally. Which I'm going to exploit to win Big Dill."

"Yeah?" I reach for a muffin.

"Mmm. There's your emo guitar-playing exploits, your teenage obsession with David Hasselhoff, your love of motivational cat posters, your habit of practicing your Winsome Lumberjack of the Year acceptance speech in front of the bathroom mirror. *'I'd like to say a few words to tell you all how I feel about this momentous event,'*" he says in a deep voice I think is supposed to be mine.

I smirk around a big bite of muffin. "Liar. Ames knows I loved Sarah Michelle Gellar, that the only two songs I ever learned to play were oldies, specifically so I could impress Thad Gates sophomore year, and that if I ever tell any of the assholes in Winsome how I'm feeling, it means I've been replaced with a pod person. As for the cat posters…" I grin. "No comment."

Griffin laughs so hard he snorts coffee, and it feels like the sun outside got a little brighter.

"So what you're saying," he teases once he's able to

speak again, "is that there might exist actual photographic evidence of teenage Beckett playing guitar?"

I shake my head. "I never got a chance to play for Thad before his family moved away to Boston, *whomp whomp*. And I have obtained and destroyed all copies of me practicing. If you want to see me play, you're gonna need a DeLorean."

Griffin's grin is wide. His eyes sparkle. And this competitive banter between us feels natural. Like we're friends... or something... instead of enemies. Like yesterday's insanity actually changed things.

Dangerous fucking territory.

I pop the rest of my muffin in my mouth and stand. "So, back to the trapdoor. I'm guessing the saw was a last-ditch effort to open it?"

"Yeah." Griffin straightens and sets down his mug. "I can't see a lock, not that I'd have the key anyway. In the letter Jim left me, he mentioned the door was sticky, but why have a dainty little pull cord if you're gonna need a crowbar every time you open it?"

"What about another entrance? Another staircase. Outside, maybe?"

He shrugs. "We can look, but I doubt it. The way the whiskey barrel's cantilevered over the side of the house—"

I snicker. "*Pickle*."

He gives me a look like my mother when she says, *Language, Beckett*. "Pardon?"

"Back in the day, they used to store pickles in barrels," I explain. As we're talking, we're moving outside and down the porch stairs. "So Jim made this a pickle barrel as a tribute to Winsome. Just like he put pickles in the stained glass windows. See?"

Griffin steps close, follows the direction of my pointing finger, and narrows his eyes. "Hooooold up. Those are *pickles*?"

I breathe in a lungful of his citrus shampoo, and my voice comes out rough. "Yeah. What'd you think they were?"

He shakes his head, laughing. "Don't ask. I guess we don't have to wonder what all the mushrooms were an homage to, huh?"

I grin. "Nah, that one's obvious. Everyone knows about Jim's talking mushrooms."

Griffin grins back, and the moment gets charged. But this time, Griffin steps away first and points up at the treehouse.

"Um. See what I mean about the cantilever? The only area where the barrel's connected to the main house is right where the trapdoor would be, inside." He slaps his palm against the trunk of the tree growing up through the barrel. "I thought about climbing this bad boy, figuring out some kind of jumping fingertip hold that would let me reach the outside wall of the barrel, then swinging out and holding on with one hand while breaking the window with the other—"

I stare at him. "You're not serious."

"No," he laughs. Then he gives me a pointed look. "Though we both know I'm an excellent tree climber."

I roll my eyes. "So excellent. In fact, you remind me a lot of the contestants on this show called *Extreme Wilderness Adventure*—"

He gasps and points at me accusingly. "Hey! You take that back. I've never tried to karate-chop firewood."

I shrug. "Not yet. But if the fancy city boot fits…" I nod

down at the scuffed leather on his feet, which probably cost more than every item in my closet put together.

He hmphs and turns back to the house. "Anyway. I also considered buying a really tall ladder," he continues. "But I decided to try the saw first."

I shake my head, exasperated. "Or you could've asked *me*, an actual tree expert with climbing gear and no interest in watching you die, to help you."

Griffin's chin lifts stubbornly. "Ask *you* for help? A man who's been trying to stop me from exercising my own free will about *my* property?"

"Right." I shoulder past him into the trees.

"Where are you going?"

"There's a rope bridge attached to the window," I grit out. "I'm following it."

"You could just ask me where it goes," he argues, hurrying along behind me.

"Ask *you* for help?" I parrot back. "A man who refuses to allow me to access my own land?"

Griffin draws in a breath, but instead of exploding at me, his voice sounds almost conciliatory when he says, "I've already followed the rope bridge. Milo and I did. It gets all tangled in leaves and branches a couple hundred feet back here."

I ignore him and push through the undergrowth, following the rope bridge's path. The forest canopy above us is a mixed hardwood stand—sugar maple, American beech, some yellow birch. I automatically catalog the diameter at breast height, crown spacing, and natural regeneration patterns.

It calms me, a little. Not enough, but some.

Then Griffin points at a moss-covered stone wall cutting through the trees and stops short.

"That's weird. Who put a wall way out here?" he asks.

"Old farm line," I say tersely. "This was pasture once."

"Pasture," he repeats. "In the forest?"

I huff. "No. This used to be farmland. Clear-cut. For hundreds of years, people planted crops and raised animals right here. When they were tilling their fields every spring, farmers would collect the stones that pushed to the surface that winter and turn them into walls, mostly for lack of anything else to do with them. But over time, people stopped relying on farming. They stopped clearing, and the woods started creeping back. First brush, then poplar and birch, then hardwoods. The forest came back to itself in stages. Reclaimed the land. That's why you'll see different types of wood side by side."

Griffin looks around and frowns skeptically. "Some of these trees are massive. Feels like it's been forest forever."

"Not even close." I brush my hand across the rough stones and feel the same sensation of connection that I always feel out here. "Most of what you see now is second or third growth. The true old growth—trees that had been standing for centuries—that was cut out a long time ago. But we can push things back in that direction if we're careful."

"Careful how?" he wonders.

"Selective harvesting." I nod at a tall maple. "See that one? Straight trunk, good crown. That's a crop tree. You thin out the weaker ones around it—the bent ones, the crowded ones—so the strong ones have sunlight and room to thrive."

He makes a thoughtful noise. "But wouldn't it be better

if we just… left the land alone? No human intervention? Logging's bad for the environment, everyone knows that."

I huff. "*Clear-cutting's* bad. Logging, when it's done right, means the forests will last long after we're gone and provide habitats for all the creatures that live here."

"I… I didn't know," Griffin says, still wearing a frown that says he doesn't like not knowing things, especially things *I* know.

I give a short nod and start walking again. "Most people don't, especially since we grew up hearing about people clear-cutting rainforests and that kind of thing. But the truth is, the early settlers here—including my own family—shaped the land. Now, the land's trying to shape itself back."

"Until people go and build treehouses in the middle of it." He rolls his eyes. "For who knows what reason."

"My father actually helped Jim build and plan his house," I volunteer as we duck under some low branches. "That's why I'm confident he would have made sure there was a second exit, even if it's via a weird-as-fuck rope bridge."

"Your dad did?" His voice brightens with excitement. "I hadn't even considered that Jim probably had help. Why don't we call your dad and ask if he has plans or blueprints or—"

"No."

"Why not? You expect me to ask you for help, but *you* won't ask your dad?"

"No need. I've got this." I keep walking, hoping he'll drop it. He doesn't.

"What if *I* call him—"

I stop walking and whirl to face him. "What if you just

*listen* for once?" I snap. "It's complicated, okay? My father and I have had some disagreements since I took over Axford Lumber. Dad wants things done old-school, the way *he* did them. I don't. And before his heart attack, he sold some land on the other side of our property because—"

I bite my tongue. I refuse to explain that he did it because he was trying to keep Axford going.

The last thing I want is pity *or* to be gossiped about.

"—because he thought it was a good idea," I say instead. "I didn't take the news well."

"He sold to Derek Sullivan, right?" Griffin winces. "Sorry. I shouldn't listen to gossip."

"Yeah, well. Him selling the land's not exactly a secret. Derek's been jawing about it since the minute he bought it, claiming Axford Lumber's blocking him from being able to pull a logging permit. Which we're not," I add, before Griffin can ask. "If I had that kind of power, I sure as fuck wouldn't be tossing my name in the ring for Big Dill."

He nods.

"Anyway, I'm not calling my dad because I don't want to hear what he'd say about how I'm handling… any of this." I wave a hand to indicate the land, Griffin, the business… my life in general. "Okay?"

Silence follows. For a moment, we stand there listening to the wind rustling the trees, making the boughs creak.

"Huh," Griffin says at length.

"What?"

"Nothing, nothing. Just… thinking about how different it was having two moms. We had to talk everything out to the bitter end. No secrets, no hiding your feelings. Just unconditional support and acceptance. It was sweet, but I was utterly unprepared for real life." He offers a wry smile. "Had to learn to be an asshole on my own later."

I grunt in acknowledgment. Yep, that's familiar.

Looking up, I find that the rope bridge is tied off to a red oak. Its trunk is easily three feet in diameter, and it looks to be a hundred years old based on the furrows in its bark. The canopy's so thick, I can't see through it to get an idea of how the bridge is attached, so I shift around the tree for a better angle.

"For what it's worth," Griffin offers, "it's obvious you care about your business. Shit, even *I* can see that, and I've known you two minutes. And Ames looks up to you—not that he said that out loud or anything. So, whatever your dad thinks… seems like you're doing okay."

I frown at Griffin, surprised to find that hearing this does help, a little.

I suppose I've come to accept that people see me as the least-friendly Axford. Maybe I even see myself that way since I haven't exactly made time for my siblings or friends since taking over the business.

Whereas my dad is a good man, a paragon of the community, so I need to defend myself ten times harder— even in my own mind—when I disagree with him.

Griffin's not my friend, but he also has no reason to lie.

This easy rhythm between us keeps happening—the feeling that Griffin gets me, though he's my polar opposite in so many ways, the feeling that we're on the same team. It's hard to remember that we're not. That I'm here because I fucked up yesterday, and I want to make things right. *That's all.*

"Thanks," I say, refocusing my attention on the tree.

And that's when I spot something embedded in the oak's trunk a few feet up.

"There we go," I murmur. "Griffin. Look."

He follows my gaze and sees them too—metal handholds, nailed into the back side of the massive tree like climbing spikes in a neat ascending pattern.

"Oh my god." He laughs wonderingly. "You know, when I was a kid, I was obsessed with this book about a kid who lives in a hollowed-out tree and has all these ingenious ways of getting around the forest—"

"*My Side of the Mountain?*"

Griffin's head whips toward me. "You've heard of it?"

"I may have forgotten to return my copy to the school library for a solid year," I confirm. I look up at the tree and shake my head. "But Jim actually decided to live it. At the risk of sounding like you… *why*?"

I examine the handholds more closely. They're galvanized steel, old but well-maintained, and it looks like they lead up to where the rope bridge must be anchored. I grab the rung closest to my head and hang off it. It's strong, probably anchored into the heartwood.

"It's a smart design," I say. "Using the tree's natural load-bearing capacity instead of fighting it."

"You think it'll hold our weight?"

"You wanna go up first, or should I?" I say in answer.

"Pfft. Like that's actually a question."

Griffin ascends first, and I follow, keeping my gaze on his ass… for safety reasons.

And yeah, okay, because it's a truly fine ass, and it's hard not to look at it.

It's surprisingly easy ascending the tree to a narrow platform that's also been firmly secured to the trunk. And that's where we find that the rope bridge isn't a rope bridge at all.

"Are those steel cables wrapped in rope? And… treated wood planks?" Griffin laughs out loud. "Oh my god, this is epic."

It is. It's an engineering marvel, honestly, and it's at least as impressive as the treehouse itself. The bridge barely sways under our weight when we cautiously step onto it.

After the epic adventure of figuring out how to get up here and journeying across the bridge over the treetops, it almost feels anticlimactic when Griffin slides open the large, unlocked window and we step into…

"An empty room?" His voice, heavy with disappointment, echoes off the rounded walls.

It's not entirely empty. There's a simple wooden desk sitting beneath a stained glass skylight that throws colored patterns across the floor. A couple of boxes are stacked on a rickety folding chair in the corner. And the trapdoor we'd been trying to access from below is actually a folding staircase that's been bolted shut from this side, like Jim last left via the rope bridge.

"I don't understand," Griffin whispers, which is the same thought I'm having.

I unlock the trapdoor, and the stairs slide down easily, right beside the pile of tools in Griffin's bedroom.

"Yay. More books to donate," he says, kicking a box with the toe of his boot. "Not exactly the treasure I was hoping for."

"Hey, hey! Be gentle with those. They could be—" I crouch beside the box and open the top flap. "Yeah, they are! First editions of *The Whispers*. Not One-Eyed Willie's hidden pirate ship, I grant you. But I bet they're worth a fuck of a lot to someone."

Griffin looks at me blankly. "Sorry. First editions of the what?"

"*The Secrets of the Whispering Woods* by JG Flummery? Aka *The Whispers*? Aka Jim's silly mushroom books?"

He continues to stare at me, eyes widening.

I take a breath. "Okay, let's start over. You do know Jim wrote children's books, yes?"

Griffin shakes his head. "H-how would I know that? I keep telling you, I haven't seen the guy since I was eight. Twenty-two years, man."

"Right." I scratch my beard. "Okay. Wow. It's just… *The Whispers* have been a really big thing in this part of the world for years. Lots of folks think they're set in the Winsome woods, so tourists come to hike and have the full Sprout experience. Sprout's the main character," I explain when Griffin's hazel eyes go big as saucers. "He gets lost in the woods and learns to talk to mushrooms, and they teach him about friendship and courage." I shrug. "Ames read them. He could probably tell you."

Griffin sinks into the folding chair, stunned. "Uncle Jim used to call me Sprout."

I frown. "So… he named the character after you?"

"Or nicknamed me after the character? When I was little, Jim used to sit with me in the park and tell me what the clouds were whispering. And sometimes he'd point at mushrooms in the grass and say they were gossiping about rabbits or complaining about the weather. I'd laugh every time."

I crouch down beside him. "So he was testing out story ideas on you? That's cool, right?"

"I just… I don't know how this is the first I'm hearing about it. I feel like my moms must've known."

I stand and watch over his shoulder as he types out a text.

GRIFFIN

Hey, guys. Did you know Jim wrote books about talking mushrooms, like the stories he used to tell me as a kid?! And if so, why didn't you tell me?!

"Still with the whys about Jim, huh?" I tease.

He laughs a little. "I guess so."

A pine needle clings to his hair, and I brush it aside. Griffin looks up at me, and suddenly, I want very badly to kiss him again.

*Too easy*, my brain whispers. This—sunlight dappling his face, stained glass on the floor, my fingers in his hair—this is how it happens.

Not just a kiss or even another shared orgasm, but the *slide*. Me losing track of who I am and what I need to do. What my priorities are.

I haven't thought about Axford Lumber once this afternoon, and I have a million things I should be doing. The cables on the log loader are starting to fray, and I promised Hussein I'd check over the equipment main.tenance logs. I have bid calculations to do for a job near Lebanon.

Worse, I barely know Griffin. And what I *do* know is that he's standing in the way of me protecting everything I hold dear.

I can't afford to forget that.

"Well." I clear my throat. "This was one hell of an

adventure, Mercer, but if we're out of secret rooms for now, I should probably—"

Griffin's phone buzzes again. He glances at the screen and makes a face before tilting it toward me.

MAMATISH

We need to talk. Call us when you can.

MAMALAINE

We're both home. No rush but… soonish, okay?

"I was half expecting them to say they didn't know what I was talking about," he says lightly. "Guess I was wrong about the whole *lesbian moms keep no secrets* thing, huh?" He makes a dismissive noise and pockets the phone like it's no big deal.

I can see the confusion on his face, though. He's thrown by this revelation, and every stubborn inch of him seems braced, which is reasonable, given those texts he just got.

Once again, I think, *Fuck*. I know that look. I've *worn* that look. I know what it's like to be absolutely stunned that a person—well, *people*, in his case—you trusted and thought you understood has done something totally out of character.

"Anyway." Griffin shuts the window leading to the rope bridge, dusts his hands, picks up the first volume of the *Whispers* books, and heads for the stairs without looking at me. "Thanks. For coming today. But I should probably call them back."

He doesn't ask me to stay. Doesn't even glance my way. But I get that too. His head is full of questions that I definitely don't have the answers to.

"Yeah." I hesitate at the front door and for some reason I feel compelled to add, "But there's a magnet on Jim's fridge with my number on it if you need... fuck, I don't know. Anything."

Wary hazel eyes meet mine. "I won't." It's half warning, half apology.

I shrug. "You say that now, but if Vermont's really trying to kill you, you might need backup at some point. A guy with insider information, maybe. A bodyguard, let's say."

He huffs, but I can see he's hiding a smile. And fuck if that doesn't make my heart beat faster, like it's the wildest, most dangerous thing I've seen in a day full of adventure. Because I'm starting to realize I really fucking like seeing Griffin smile. Enough that I want to make him smile again. Or maybe even all the time.

And that's not good at all.

"Don't touch the circular saw," I can't help but call out over my shoulder.

As I force myself to walk away from him.

# CHAPTER NINE

GRIFFIN

I SIT on Jim's purple velvet brothel sofa, staring at my phone screen while my heart gallops around my chest like a whole herd of rampaging moose. I really wish I hadn't asked Beckett to go, and that knowledge only makes me more anxious.

If you'd told me a week ago that I'd spend the last twenty-four-ish hours doing a scavenger hunt with my nemesis, getting hot and heavy against a restaurant fence, helping prep dinner for said nemesis's brother, nearly decapitating myself with a circular saw—slightly dramatic, I know, but go with me—and then embarking on a magical adventure through the treetops to discover a secret treasure room… I'd have laughed in your face.

Now, if you'd told eight-year-old Griffin, I probably would've said, "Cool! When do we start?" Because that's exactly what I thought adulthood was going to be like— one epic adventure after another, with mysterious rope bridges, hidden rooms, white knights to guide you through the forest, and maybe even a few sword fights thrown in for good measure.

I know better now. I know adulthood is all about spreadsheets and health insurance and trying to plump up your 401(k). It's about trying to be the absolute best at your career so that you never have to worry that you won't make rent. It's less about adventure and more about trying to avert disaster.

But today… today felt like something kid-Griffin would've dreamed up.

At least up until the part where I got those cryptic texts from my mothers.

*We need to talk.*

*Soonish.*

My mothers have never been cryptic people. *Ever.* In my thirty years of life, Lainey and Tish Mercer have been relentlessly, exhaustively transparent about everything. They've made sure I know more than I need to about their finances. When I chose to major in business, they'd been forthcoming with their opinions—*But you used to want to be Indiana Jones, Griffy! What about archaeology? Do you really want to spend your life working for The Man?* One summer, when I was eighteen or nineteen, they even initiated a discussion about which lubes were the best depending on what kind of sex you're having. And no, to answer your question, I have not forgiven them for that.

So this careful, measured response to my question about Jim's books? It's unprecedented. It's weird.

And because I seem to have become incapable of keeping a handle on my emotions since hitting the Winsome town line, the weirdness has transmuted into fear… though I can't imagine what the fuck I'm afraid of.

I hit the FaceTime button before I can lose my nerve.

Both of my mothers appear on screen almost immediately, sitting side by side on the floral couch in their cozy sitting room at the B&B. Mama Laine's graying auburn curls are pulled back in her usual messy bun, and she's wearing one of her paint-splattered cardigans over a Planned Parenthood T-shirt. Mama Tish, as always, looks more put together—her silver hair's cut short, and she's wearing a crisp button-down with the little dragonfly earrings I got her for her birthday a few years ago.

But they both look strained. Like they're holding their breath. Even during their worst financial struggles, I don't think I've seen them this tense.

"Griffin!" Mama Tish says with forced brightness. "How are you settling in, sweetheart? How's Vermont treating you? We've been eager to hear."

"I've heard it's *beautiful* up there this time of year," Mama Laine agrees. "My friend Daina—you remember Daina, who helped us organize that big protest a couple years ago?"

"Against Derwin Sherwin—" Mama Tish interjects hotly.

"Derwin Simpkins," Mama Laine corrects.

Mama Tish eyes her. "You sure?"

"Positive, baby."

She waves a hand. "Fine, then. Derwin *Simpkins*, the shady developer who tried to pave our paradise and put up a half-baked 'luxury eco resort' parking lot."

Mama Laine pats her knee. "In any case, Griffin, Daina moved to Vermont and built a yurt. Not quite as exciting as your little treehouse in the woods, but still so fun! We'll have to come visit both of you once things settle down here."

"If Griffin's still there and only if he'd like us to visit," Mama Tish reminds her. "We know you're planning to move on soon, Griff. And we recognize that you're an adult now. We respect your autonomy, and we never want to cross your boundaries."

She sounds like she's been watching therapy Instagram reels again or reading a self-help book called *Mothering Independent Children Whose Life Choices You Don't Understand*. For a second, I feel this overwhelming wave of affection for her. For both of them.

But then I remember the point of this call. "So you did know Jim built a treehouse, then? You stayed in touch."

They exchange a look—one of those wordless conversations that come from thirty-plus years together.

"Griffin," Mama Laine begins carefully, "we—"

"Then did you know he wrote these children's books?" I hold up the book I brought down from the pickle turret. "Why didn't you tell me? I asked you what you remembered about him when I told you I inherited this place, and you said you hadn't talked in years. I didn't think we *did* secrets in our family."

I'm a little hurt, but mostly confused.

"We don't." Mama Tish rubs a spot between her eyebrows. "We certainly never set out to."

"It wasn't entirely our choice," Mama Laine says. Then her face twists. "Except that everything's a choice, isn't it?"

This time, Mama Tish pats *her* knee.

"Could you clue me in on what the heck we're talking about here?" I demand. "Why was it some deep secret that

Jim wrote books and built a treehouse? Why not tell me? Warn me?"

"We didn't want to tell you, because…" Mama Laine nods at Mama Tish, who takes a deep breath, then continues. "We knew if we did, we'd also have to tell you Jim wasn't just an old neighbor, baby. He was our friend."

"I know that. I remember it, sort of. So?" It feels like my mothers are hoping I'll pick up some thread they're laying down, but… I'm sitting here threadless.

Mama Laine wets her lips and takes up the story. "Jim moved into our building when we were living on Prospect Park. He moved around a lot—he used to say he was like a mushroom, and he could pop up anywhere—but Brooklyn was his home base for a while. He knew we were struggling financially, and he knew we wanted a child, so—" She spreads her hands. Tilts her head. Screws up her mouth.

I still don't get it… and then suddenly, I *do*.

"Oh, no." I laugh. "No way. You can't seriously mean…"

In no realm did I expect this to turn into some soap opera confessional situation. *Griffin, your real father is…* That shit never happens to me.

Then again, I also never got fired or inherited treehouses, so maybe it's time I stop being so surprised by the twists and turns life takes.

"Jim didn't want you to know that he was your sperm donor," Mama Tish says. "He loved his adventures. His freedom. And that was fine with us since we'd planned to use an anonymous donor in the first place. But later… it became hard, having him in your life as an uncle. It started to feel like we were lying to you every day. And I think it was hard for Jim too. You were… an adventure he never expected to have, sweetheart. But he truly believed he wasn't meant to settle down. So he decided it was time to leave New York."

Mama Laine nods. "He didn't want to hurt you by being half in and half out of your life, Griffin. He stayed in touch with your mother and me here and there for a few years after he left. We knew he was writing some books. We knew he'd gotten his hands on some land and built himself a treehouse. But I promise you, we haven't heard from him in at least fifteen years, and we had no idea he planned to leave the place to you. I think the fact that he did shows that he loved you in his own way."

The world is tilting sideways. I grip the edge of the sofa so hard my knuckles go white.

I stare at them, these two women who raised me, who taught me everything I know about love and family and *honesty*. Who are now telling me they've been lying to me my entire life about something fundamental.

"We told ourselves that if you ever tried to find your biological father, if you ever even hinted that you were interested, we'd tell you everything. Your well-being has always been our highest priority, Griffin." Mama Laine's voice is pleading.

"But I did ask," I say softly. "About Jim. About why he would've left me this treehouse. You said nothing."

They exchange another look. "That's… that's true," Mama Tish admits. "But you'd just been through the wringer, losing your job. We thought—" She takes a deep breath and blows it out. "Okay, *I* thought—that was enough upheaval for a man who loves stability. I thought you didn't need another difficult thing to deal with." She gives me a tremulous smile. "I'd hoped when you'd figured things out with your career, when you'd processed your grief over that, you'd be in a stronger place. I hoped we could explain in person. Maybe at Christmas…"

Mama Laine nudges their shoulders together. "Full honesty, honey? We avoided it. We knew you'd be upset—rightfully so—and we left it too long. We messed up. And we are truly sorry, baby. That you're hurt. That we kept this from you. Our only excuse is that we made what we thought were the best choices at the time. The ones we thought would keep your heart safe. But we forgot safety isn't always the answer."

Both of my mothers are crying now, which makes my own eyes burn.

I hate this. I hate crying, I hate feeling out of control, and I especially hate that I'm doing both while sitting alone in a treehouse built by a man who was my father… but never wanted me to know it.

"We love you so much, Griffin," Mama Tish says through her tears.

"I know," I assure them, because I can see how much this is hurting them, and they don't deserve that. They've been nothing but loving and supportive my entire life. "I get that you were doing your best. And I love you both too. I just… need some time to process this, okay?"

"Of course," Mama Laine says immediately. "Whatever you need. Would it be okay if we called to check on you? Could we plan to come visit?"

We end the call with promises to talk soon, with reassurances that I'm not angry (though I'm not entirely sure that's true), and with my agreement that they were welcome to come visit, though the treehouse would be way too small for all three of us.

When the screen goes dark, I set my phone aside and just sit there, staring silently into space as the sun sets through the stained glass windows, throwing rainbow patterns across the floor.

My *biological father* designed those windows, I think, trying out the words. But it feels strange and disconnected. Like it should matter—should be this huge, seismic thing—but isn't. Like it's happening to some other Griffin, and I'm standing several feet away, thinking, *Bad luck, buddy.*

I spent my whole life thinking I had the full picture of who I am. I didn't really care to know anything more. Now, it's like someone tilted the frame and showed me something I didn't know was there.

And I really don't know how I feel about that.

As the last slivers of sunlight disappear, the silence starts to feel heavy. Like the numbness blanketing me has a weight to it. And I realize that for once, I don't want to sit and think and think and *overthink* this. I don't want to ask *why*.

My gaze darts to the kitchen. It's totally dark, and I can't see the fridge from this spot anyway, but I know exactly where Jim's wood-cut-shaped magnet with Beckett's number lives. And I think maybe I need a body-guard after all.

"Hey. Is Vermont after you again?" Beckett answers on the first ring. His tone is teasing, but I can hear the worry beneath it, and… fuck, I like that. I shouldn't. I don't want to. But I do.

"Let me guess," he goes on. "You tried to fix your porch steps with a blowtorch. Local idiot dies by…"

I let out a laugh, but it's high and thin. "No. Definitely not. I just…" I swallow. "I talked to my moms, and I didn't want… It's just that Milo's not here, and I…" *Jesus*, what am I doing? "You know what? Never mind. This is stupid—"

"Yeah it is. Spit it out, Mercer," he insists. "You need food? Whiskey? For me to give your mothers a stern talking-to?"

*Fuck*. It's weirdly comforting thinking he'd read my mothers the riot act for me. That feels wrong, but I decide I don't care.

I take a deep breath and say maybe the hardest words I've ever spoken. "I don't want to be alone."

"Then you won't be," he says like it's just that easy.

When he disconnects, a kind of panic grips me. Like I've whispered some kind of incantation, set something in motion I can't take back.

This is a terrible idea. The terriblest.

If I've learned anything over the past few months, it's that relying on anyone but myself—and Milo and my moms… until today—is a losing proposition. Once you have nothing to offer the people in your life, you're a liability, and they can disappear without warning.

I'm still standing in the kitchen, regretting this, when work boots echo against my porch steps.

I open the door, and as soon as Beckett sees my face, his expression darkens, and he steps inside. "Okay, what the fuck? Have you been *crying*? Because I was kidding before, about giving your moms hell, but…"

His hands come up like he's going to touch my face, but he rethinks it at the last minute, and they hang there awkwardly before he drops them into fists at his side.

"What'd they say? I take it they knew about *The Whispers*?"

I nod once. "I don't... I don't want to talk about it, okay? I'd actually prefer not to *think* about it if I could."

"Yeah?" Beckett leans back, and those blue eyes assess me. I can't imagine what they see, but I know any mask of okay-ness burned away a while ago. "What *do* you want, then?"

His eyes glitter like sapphires, and I can tell from his deliberately teasing tone and the smirk playing on his lips that he knows exactly what I want; the asshole just wants to hear me say it.

"Kiss me," I grit out. "Just kiss me and let me forget for a whi—"

I don't even get the words out before Beckett's hand's wrapped around the back of my neck, his mouth is slanting hot over mine, and the cedar smell of him is in my nose.

It's overwhelming, all-consuming. I can't think of a single thing but Beckett's big body and his tongue sliding against mine, which is exactly what I want. Every place our bodies touch—his hands on my neck and back, his chest against mine—is so warm, so *hot*, my toes curl. It feels like I've been cold forever, and now all those frozen bits of me are thawing. Coming back to life with pins-and-needles prickles.

This time, there's no fear of being caught. We take our time, learning the shape of each other, the sounds we make, the places that make us gasp and arch and beg for more. When he slides his hand inside my shirt, I think I might actually die from how good it feels.

"Good?" he whispers against my throat.

"So good," I manage, then prove it by tugging his henley over his head and running my hands over the solid muscles of his chest and shoulders.

It's just so damn *easy* with him. In this one area, anyway. We fight and tease and bicker about everything else, but in this… there's no pretending. No hiding. The second we give in and let this fire kindle, everything else melts away.

Beckett's skin is feverish under my palms, scattered with dark hair that I want to explore with my mouth. When I brush my thumbs over his nipples, remembering what it did to him yesterday, he makes a guttural sound that goes straight to my cock.

"Fuck," he breathes, his hands working at my shirt. "You make it impossible to think straight."

"Good," I say. "Not-thinking is exactly the plan. I prefer you not-thinking."

He huffs out a laugh that's more like a groan. "You would."

We somehow end up on the brothel sofa—the scene of my earlier silent freak-out—and I only realize this when Beckett's hands roam down my back and pull me onto his lap. But unlike before, when I didn't know what to think or how to feel, now I'm nothing *but* feeling. All in on sensation.

Am I distracting myself with this purely physical encounter? Oh yeah.

Do I care? Not one tiny bit.

I straddle him, the hard ridge of his erection pressing against mine through our jeans, and the friction makes us both groan. His fingers dig into my hips, holding me still as he rocks up, grinding against me.

"Fuck," I breathe.

Beckett's calloused palms slide up my sides, and I arch into the touch. He leans in, lips trailing down my throat, then lower, his breath warm and humid against my collarbone. I can feel his heart pounding, matching the frantic rhythm of my own.

"Griffin," he murmurs, his voice rough, and the sound of my name on his lips sends a jolt straight to my cock.

I reach for his belt, fumbling with the buckle in my haste, and he chuckles, low and dark, before helping me push his jeans down his hips.

His cock springs free, hard and just as huge as I remembered. I wrap my hand around it, stroking him slowly. He hisses, his head tipping back, and the sight of him like this—undone—makes my own cock ache.

"Clothes off," he growls, his hands going to my waistband. I lift my hips just enough for him to drag my jeans and boxers down, and then we're both naked, our cocks brushing against each other, slick with precum.

Beckett's big hand closes around us both, stroking us together just like yesterday, and the sensation is almost too much. I moan, tangling my fingers in his dark hair as I pull him into another kiss.

But I want more. I want to taste him.

It's been a hot minute since I've done this, so my tongue is almost tingling with anticipation as I slide off his lap and kneel between his legs. Beckett sinks down into the velvet, and the incongruity of it—the plush, velvet sofa, the acres and miles of hard, naked man—is like something pulled out of my deepest fantasies. A want so deep I've never articulated it to myself.

I take him in my hand again. His breath hitches, and—

*fuck.* I'm swamped with that same feeling as the last time we did this. Knowing he wants me. Knowing he wants me *this much*...

I lean in, my tongue flicking out to taste the salty bead of precum at his tip. He groans, and his fingers grasp my hair, my head, the back of my neck as his head tilts back into the sofa cushion.

Then I take him into my mouth, savoring the weight of him, the way he fills me. My tongue wraps around him, tasting and teasing, as I try to figure out what lights him up.

"Yeah. Oh, fuck. Just like that," he gasps, his fingers tangling in my hair. "Shit, you're good at this, city boy."

The unexpected praise makes me work harder, taking him deeper, until he's cursing under his breath and his hips are moving in small, helpless thrusts.

I love the way he tastes, the way his breath catches when I hollow my cheeks, the way his thighs tense beneath my hands. All that power, undone for me. It's addictive.

When he tugs at my hair, trying to pull me up, I resist at first. But then he says, "Griffin, stop, or I'm gonna—" and I let him guide me back up his body.

I'm just not ready for this terrible idea to be over...

And that's another thing I'm not gonna think about right now.

"Your turn," he says against my mouth.

I want to protest that he doesn't have to, like someone somewhere is keeping score, but then he's pushing me back against the couch cushions until our heads are at opposite ends. As soon as I realize what he has in mind, all rational thought leaves my brain.

"Beckett," I gasp when he takes me in his mouth. The wet heat is almost too much, and I have to grip the couch cushions to keep from bucking up into his throat.

"Beckett," I whine again, for once not caring how needy I sound. *"Beckett, Beckett, Beckett."*

He's relentless, using his tongue and lips and just enough teeth to make me see stars. He takes me deep—because he's competitive like that—and when he hollows his cheeks and sucks hard, I cry out, my whole body arcing toward him.

I quickly reach for him and take his cock in my mouth again, my hands moving greedily up and down the curved muscles of his thighs and ass.

We move together, our mouths working in tempo, each of us driving the other closer to the edge. The sofa creaks beneath us, and the air's filled with the sounds of our ragged breaths, the wet slide of lips and tongue.

"Fuck, Griffin," Beckett groans, breaking off. His hips shift restlessly in tiny motions like he wants so badly to thrust but doesn't want to hurt me.

I wrap my hands around his ass and pull him closer, showing him exactly how I want him to use me.

"Fuck," he says again. "You're gonna make me—"

I hum out my wholehearted agreement, and then he's coming down my throat.

As soon as his orgasm has rolled through him, Beckett dives for my cock like a starving man, pinning my thighs against the cushion and swallowing me down.

I swear, that's all it takes. My body tenses, my cock pulsing as I spill into his mouth.

For a long moment, we just lie there, breathing heavily, our bodies pressed together. I'm still trembling with aftershocks. Then Beckett levers himself off me and sits on the edge of the sofa.

"That was…" he begins, then stops like he's not sure what to say.

*…fucking amazing and earth-shattering?*

*…a simple biological reaction to a really messed-up, emotional day?*

*…a huge mistake?*

*…another thing we won't discuss?*

"Yeah," I agree softly. Because, honestly? All of those things might be true. *Are* true.

But when Beckett leans down to press a swift kiss to my lips, I decide for this moment that the weight of all the shit in my life—my job, my inheritance, my father, my future, whatever the fuck Beckett and I are doing—can hold *itself* for a little while.

Because life is short, and Beckett is gorgeous, and while it feels like the whole world is conspiring to make me doubt who I am… when I'm with him, I feel more like Griffin than I have in a long damn time.

And that realization is scary as fuck.

# CHAPTER TEN

## BECKETT

APPARENTLY, three days weren't enough to make me stop thinking about the taste of Griffin Mercer's cock in my mouth. Or the feel of his fingers digging into my ass cheeks.

Or the sound of his small voice admitting he didn't want to be alone.

And if the man had given me any indication he'd wanted me to stay after our epic encounter... hell, I'd probably still be there right now instead of at the damned Winsome Farmer's Market making a Big Dill appearance.

The outdoor market's in full autumn swing when I arrive Wednesday afternoon, and for the first time in months, I let myself slow down and actually take it in.

Food trucks line the perimeter of Chapel Island Park like a colorful wagon train. The Mac Attack's serving their famous lobster mac and cheese. Fox Creamery has donuts and a maple creemee machine in theirs. And a guy I don't recognize has a giant Argentinian flag draped in front of his truck and is serving up empanadas that make my stomach growl.

Kids weave between the stalls, clutching caramel apples, while their parents trail behind carrying bags of produce those kids are never gonna eat.

And the community center has a pumpkin-painting table set up that's drawn a surprising (or not so surprising, if you know Winsome) number of adults. Perky Halloran's currently turning his pumpkin into some kind of abstract art piece with globs of purple paint, while his husband-but-not, David, watches from afar and tries to pretend he isn't.

It's exactly the kind of wholesome small-town scene that usually makes me feel claustrophobic. Like I'm trapped in a Norman Rockwell painting with people who simultaneously know me way too well and not at all.

But today… I don't know. It feels different. Maybe it's the crisp air or the way the late-afternoon sunlight slants through the colorful maples, turning everything golden. Maybe it's because I haven't been to one of these things in ages, and I've forgotten why I hate them. Or maybe it's because I spent the day—and a good part of the night— with Griffin on Sunday, and that shifted the way I see things.

I shove that thought away with a huff before it can take root.

Sunday was tension relief. A hookup. Nothing more.

Even if I haven't been able to stop thinking about it for three days straight.

"Beck! Hey, Beckett!"

I turn to find my sister jogging toward me, her dark hair escaping from its ponytail. She's wearing scrubs under her jacket, which means she came straight from the clinic.

"Perfect timing," she says, giving me a slightly breathless hug. "I've been looking for you everywhere. We need to have a Big Dill strategy session."

I blink. "Oh, surely not."

"Hush and just listen." Eliza opens a checklist on her phone and waves it at me so enthusiastically I can't read it. "I ran the numbers, Beck. Based on voting patterns from previous years, demographic analysis, and some very scientific polling I conducted on my patients—don't look at me like that, it was voluntary—you have a real shot at winning this thing—"

"You sound so surprised."

"—but only if you actually participate in the events." She flips through several pages of what appear to be charts and graphs. "Your performance at the Wild Gherkin Chase was…"

I snort. "Suboptimal?"

"Actually, no. People saw you and Griffin laughing together and getting along, which was kind of a boost. And *technically*, you could say it was a boost for both of you, but you're the one with the reputation for being grumpy—"

"I'm not a happy joiner. That's not the same—"

"—which is why we need a plan. The Brine and Dandy is this Friday, and it's crucial that you nail this so you can pull ahead. You need to be charming. Approachable. Smile at least twice." She peers at me seriously over her phone. "Think you can manage that?"

"I wouldn't put money on it," Holden says, coming up behind us. He's somehow managing to balance three cups of cider and a paper plate of sugary funnel cake. "Remember how he asked Jenny Castellano to prom? '*You wanna go with me or what?*'" he says in a deep growl that I guess is supposed to be an impression of me.

"Well, it worked," I remind him. "Sort of."

Holden and Eliza exchange a look. "If you call Jenny agreeing because Mom called her mom and said you were 'going through a phase,' then I guess so."

Eliza clears her throat. "So. Two-smile minimum, yes? And I mean, really big smiles. Make sure they're visible. No smirking into your drink."

Since I am, at that very moment, smirking into one of the cups of cider Holden passed out, I cough and nearly choke.

The truth is, I know they're right. I've never been one for social niceties. Not the way the rest of my family is. I'm too apt to be hot-tempered and impatient. But I also can't help but feel that this whole Big Dill thing is getting out of hand.

"Speaking of phases," Holden continues with a shit-eating grin, like he can hear my inner thoughts, "how's your rivalry with Griffin going? Still planning to defeat him with the power of your sparkling personality?"

My face heats up, and I nearly choke on my cider again. If only he knew how close we'd come to *defeating* each other on Sunday.

"It's fine," I manage. "We're… managing."

"*Fine,*" Eliza repeats, making a note in her phone. "Well, that's promising. You know, from what I've heard around town, Griffin's actually quite likable. Maybe you could learn something from his approach."

"What approach?" I ask, though I'm not sure I want to know.

"Mmm, apparently, he spent last night at the library doing research." Eliza sips her cider. "Yesterday, he helped Ada Wickham at the Pickle Jar, and Bathsheba likes him. You know that cat's accurately predicted the Big Dill for seven of the last ten years, right? And Griffin's been asking people about their concerns for the town too. Very grass-roots political campaigning."

"If she got it right seven out of ten times, that means she was wrong three out of ten! So who cares if Ms. Wickham's cat endorses him?" I ask. But the pit in my stomach says that's *exactly* the sort of things people in this town care about. And of course Griffin's been doing actual campaign work while I've been… what? Avoiding him? Jacking off to memories of Sunday while telling myself it meant nothing?

*Not* a winning strategy.

"Meanwhile," Holden adds, "you've been hiding at the lumber yard, haven't you?"

"Working isn't hiding," I retort, but the looks my siblings give me say they don't believe it.

I'm saved from having to defend myself by the arrival of my cousin Wilder, who emerges from the crowd wearing his leather jacket and carrying a cardboard container that smells like empanadas.

"Uh-oh. Family meeting on the town green?" he asks, taking in our little circle. "Should I be worried?"

"Beck's Big Dill campaign strategy session," Eliza explains.

Wilder laughs. "Do tell. What's the strategy, then? Win at all costs, take no prisoners?"

"Apparently, I need to be more charming and less dedicated to my actual job," I mutter.

"Hmm. You know, I've always thought Beckett had a reservoir of charm buried deep. And I mean real, *real* deep," he says with a grin that makes me want to put him in a headlock like I did when we were kids…

And possibly steal his empanadas while he's incapacitated.

"We also need to work on your ideas for Winsome," Eliza says, consulting her phone screen again. "Griffin's doing a tourism marketing campaign, and I've heard it's phenomenal. I bet he's going to present it at Hello, Winsome. What are you going to do? What's your plan for Winsome?"

I open my mouth, then close it again.

The honest answer is that I never really thought about it beyond getting the tiebreaker vote for the town council and beating Griffin. Which suddenly seems like a pretty shitty reason to do a thing.

"See, this is what I'm talking about," Eliza says, throwing up a hand. "You can't just stand there looking grumpy whenever someone asks you a question, Beck. You need a vision. A raison d'être. What do you stand for, Beckett?"

Before I can answer—not that I *have* an answer—Ames calls across the green.

"Beck! Holden! Get over here and help me with this!"

I turn to see my youngest brother wrestling with one corner of the Watchfire tent that seems determined to become airborne and take him with it. Fortunately, the folding tables he set up under the tent don't seem as flimsy, and the vats of warm soup he's selling remain unscathed by the time we get over there.

"Thanks," Ames says when we finish tying down the recalcitrant corner flap. "Robbie was going to help, but he's busy."

"With Lissa?" I scan the crowd. Robbie's so big it'd be impossible for him to hide.

Ames shakes his head, but I swear, for some reason, his cheeks flush. "No. He's, um, doing a Touch-a-Truck thing for the little kids out in the parking lot. Hey, would you check the other stakes to make sure they're all good?"

I grunt, but it takes me a minute to even process what he asked. Instead, I'm still scanning the crowd, only now I'm looking for a familiar head of blond hair. Not that I'm expecting to see Griffin, necessarily. I mean, he could be here. He probably *should*, if he's taking this contest seriously.

And of course, he *is* still taking it seriously, right? Because Sunday was just… Sunday. Too much tension and emotion and proximity. A blip. We're still opponents, even if it didn't feel that way.

Still, when I finally spot him near the community center table, crouched next to a little girl who's painted cat ears on her pumpkin, I get a jolt like someone spiked my cider with a triple espresso.

He looks good. Really good. The afternoon sunlight catches in his hair, making it gleam red and gold like sugar maple leaves. He's wearing that too-perfect cream-colored fleece again, the one I happen to know makes his hazel eyes look more green than brown, and when he laughs at something the girl says, he forgets to be prickly, and his whole face lights up.

I watch him help her draw whiskers on her pumpkin cat—probably helping her market the pumpkin, since he's Mr. Marketing Degree, after all—but I can't make myself look away. I watch his hands on the paintbrush and remember them on my skin the other night. How he gasped my name when I took him in my mouth, and—

"Beckett!" Ames says.

I whip around. "What?"

"The other tent pegs," he reminds me.

"Sorry. I was thinking about… work stuff."

Holden's standing off to one side of the tent with his arms folded, wearing a shit-eating grin. He one hundred percent knows where my attention was.

"You know," Ames says casually as he dishes out some soup for a customer, "Griffin stopped by a little while ago."

"So?" I snap back instantly.

This only makes Ames amused too, and now *two* of my asshole brothers are smirking at me.

Seriously, why do I love these fuckers?

"Sooo… he mentioned you helped him figure out his trapdoor situation," Ames says. He cuts a look at me. "That was cool of you."

I shrug. "You make it sound like I'm not nice, Ames. You know better than that."

"To me?" Ames says. "Of course you are. You'd wrestle a bear for me without thinking twice. Same for Wilder and Eliza and True. Even for Holden, except when he's being full of himself, and even then you'd still do it, you just might stop to consider for a minute."

"Hey!" Holden says.

"But to outsiders?" Ames shrugs. "You're not always friendly. You know this."

I protest, "I was nice to Kelly… before she ditched True with no warning or explanation and moved back to fucking *Portland*."

Holden pulls a face, and I realize I might have yelled the last word. "You have big feels about that, bro?"

"Obviously. Don't you?" My ex-sister-in-law is definitely and permanently on my shit list.

"Excuse me? Beckett?"

Ed Hawkins appears beside Ames's tent. He's a small-time contractor who's been coming to Axford Lumber approximately forever. He's also the customer we've extended the most credit to. He's wearing the kind of expression that usually precedes him asking for that credit to be extended further.

"Ed," I say, stepping away from the tent. "Hey. How's it going?"

"Uh. Well." He shifts uncomfortably.

I stifle a sigh.

"I know we discussed that lumber order for the Morrison job. The, ah, pressure-treated deck boards and dimensional lumber for framing."

I nod. I remember it perfectly. We only quoted the job last week, and he seemed eager to move ahead with it.

"Right. Well. The thing is…" Ed clears his throat. "Cash flow's been a bit tight lately…"

"Tell me about it." I shake my head sympathetically. "This economy's a killer."

"It is! It is. And actually, ah, cash flow's been more than a little tight. I had a job cancel at the last minute, and I need to pay my guys. So I was wondering if we could work out a payment plan, like we've done before? I can put half down now, then pay the rest in thirty days when Morrison settles up with me."

Inside, I groan.

Look, despite my siblings teasing me, I don't *like* being a hard-ass. I feel for Ed and for all the other contractors out there. Ed's a really nice guy, and he's feeling the pinch, big-time. If I had all the money in the world, I'd float him, no problem.

But I have guys to pay too, despite the fact that they were sitting around holding their dicks last week while I rejiggered our cutting schedules. Rocky, Carlos, Bunsen, and the others aren't floating *me*—nor would I ever want them to. So… where does it end?

"Ed, I appreciate the honesty," I tell him. "But—"

"Heya, Ed!" a cheerful voice booms.

The voice that calls from behind me is warm and familiar. I don't need to turn my head to know who's put down his crossword puzzle and decided to join us.

Dad claps Ed on the shoulder like they're old friends, because they are. Grant Axford knows everyone in three counties.

"Grant!" Ed's face brightens immediately. "I was just talking to your Beckett here about a lumber order. We were working out some payment terms."

"That right?" Dad glances at me, then back at Ed. "Well, I'm sure he'll try to work something out with you. We've been doing business with you for… what? Fifteen, sixteen years now?"

"Eighteen," Ed says with a relieved smile. "Ever since I started."

"Well, there you go." Dad spreads his hands. "Family takes care of family, that's what I say. Don't I, Beckett?"

"Yeah," I grind out. "That's what you say."

This is so fucking typical. Grant Axford, leading with his heart instead of his head. Making promises without knowing a damn thing about the books anymore. Assuming things will work out because they always have in the past.

Except it's *not* working out. That's exactly the point.

Ed beams and shakes both our hands, thanking us profusely. Then he heads off, probably to tell Morrison that he can start the job next week. Meanwhile, I grind my molars into dust.

The moment he's out of earshot, I round on my father.

"What the hell was that?"

Dad frowns. "What do you mean?"

"You just committed us to a payment plan without even asking me. Without checking our cash flow. Without asking whether we can afford to carry that debt, or—"

"But it's Ed Hawkins, Beck. Why wouldn't we want to help one of our longest-standing customers? I've known him since he was a kid. His word is good."

"But his *word* doesn't help us meet payroll." I huff. "It doesn't cover our operating expenses when we're waiting sixty days to get paid. You undermined me in front of him, Dad. As if I'm not the one running the company."

Dad's face flushes. "I was trying to help! Last I checked, it was still *Axford* Lumber over the door, not *Beckett* Lumber. The way I figure it, we wouldn't have half our loyal customers if we hadn't built relationships in this town—"

"Half the customers or half the debt?" I hiss, trying to keep my voice down. From the look on his face, my shot hit center mass. I squeeze my eyes closed and take a breath. "Dad, I love you, but you lead with your heart, not your head. That makes you a great friend and a good man, but the company's suffering. I'm trying to fix things. I'm already dealing with not being able to access the Far Tract, I'm cutting costs everywhere I can, I'm working sixteen- and eighteen-hour days—but you're making my job harder every time you—"

"Every time I what?" Dad's voice isn't as low as mine, and it draws attention from nearby vendors. "Every time I remind you that doing business isn't just about spread-sheets but about people?"

"Every time you make promises we can't afford to keep!"

The words hang in the air between us, sharp and ugly. Dad's face goes through several expressions—anger, hurt, sadness—before settling on one that looks uncomfortably like resignation.

"Maybe," he says, finally lowering his voice, "if you'd ask for help once in a while instead of trying to do every-thing yourself, you could find a new way that actually works. Your head and your heart don't have to be mutu-ally exclusive. I know I didn't do the best job at balancing that, Beck. But you're overcorrecting. You could try to learn from my mistakes."

Before I can respond to that—before I can even figure out how to respond to that—movement in my peripheral vision catches my attention.

Griffin's maybe twenty feet away now, standing near

Rose Levy's maple syrup booth, but he's not alone. Derek Sullivan's with him, and from their body language, they're deep in conversation.

Griffin looks… wary isn't the right word. Serious, maybe. Like he's trying to commit every word he hears to memory.

Dad follows my gaze and lets out a heavy sigh. "And what's happening with that?"

I don't know if he's talking about Griffin or Derek or both, but I decide it doesn't matter. "I'm handling it," I say.

Dad eyes me. "Why don't you reach out to David Halloran? Have him handle the easement negotiations?"

I swallow hard. For some reason, the idea of sending our local attorney in to "handle" Griffin doesn't sit right with me, even if David would agree to that. And Dad's suggestion that someone else could succeed where I've so clearly failed makes me angry again.

"I said, I'm handling it," I snap, trying not to think of all the ways I've already handled my prickly new neighbor.

"All by yourself, right?" Dad says with a sigh. "You don't need any help."

I'm still formulating a response—hell, trying to find a clear thought in the chaos in my head—when Dad walks off toward the river, his shoulders set in a way that tells me this conversation's over.

*Fuck.*

I look back toward Griffin and Derek, but Griffin's disappeared. My first instinct is to go after him, to question him about what Derek wanted. But then I see Derek himself walking toward me.

The guy looks put together, I'll give him that. In his spiffy polo and tailored chinos, every hair perfectly in place, he's the kind of guy you might accidentally trust to get you a deal on a used Toyota and leave you owing eighteen percent interest for the rest of your natural life.

When Derek appeared in Winsome with the idea of starting an eco-conscious lumber company a couple of years back, my dad welcomed the competition. So did I. We were confident in the quality of our product, the expertise of our guys, our cutting-edge sustainability practices. I *almost* understand why my dad didn't think it was a big deal to sell the guy some land we knew we'd never be able to harvest as a way to improve our cash flow.

But Derek pretty quickly started undercutting us on jobs. Started wondering out loud whether "old" companies were the best choice for the modern world. Started pitching himself as the greener choice but still "hometown." Opened a mill on the edge of town and started stamping his lumber with "Milled in Winsome." Started luring a couple of members of our crew to work for him.

I keep running the numbers, but I honestly don't understand how Sullivan Lumber's able to make good on the contracts they've signed. The number of harvestable acres Derek owns in the area simply won't give him the yield he needs, unless he's bought acreage I don't know about. And even if he has, the prices he's offering mean he has to be operating in the red… at least until he's put the competition out of business.

He's the freaking Walmart of lumber.

Customers don't always think about that stuff, though. Some are thrilled to get a (supposedly) more earth-friendly choice at rock-bottom prices. Or maybe they simply can't afford to make a different choice.

Folks in Winsome have stayed loyal so far—which, yes, means Dad has a point about the way he did business bringing value beyond the financial. But when Derek's telling everyone and their brother about how *mean* the Axfords are for selling him land and then "blocking" his permit to cut on land that was never meant for cutting… well, I wouldn't be surprised if public opinion swung in his favor eventually.

"Beckett!" Derek's smile is wide and friendly, meant for other people to see. It doesn't reach his eyes. "Good to see you out and about. How's business?"

"Great," I say curtly.

"Glad to hear it." His smile sharpens. "I heard you were having some access issues with your timber stands, but I guess that's just idle gossip?"

Every muscle in my body tenses. "We're doing just fine."

"Of course, of course. But you know, if there's anything I can do to help… I mean, we're neighbors now. We should look out for each other."

*Not if he was Noah and I was the last man on Earth without a fucking Ark ticket.*

I give him a tight smile.

"Actually," he continues, all friendly and casual, "I was just talking to Griffin Mercer about that very issue. Neighbors looking out for neighbors."

"Were you."

"Mmm. Nice young man. Very… practical. We talked about some restaurants we both like in New York. Poor guy's itching to get back to civilization." Derek's smile turns predatory. "So I made him an offer to buy his entire property. Because that's what good neighbors do. So much more efficient than dealing with that messy easement business."

The bottom drops out of my stomach. "I wasn't aware he wanted to sell."

Derek gives me a satisfied smile. "Well, he's been very discreet about it. Professional. I appreciate that in a person. Of course, I can understand why he'd want to move on. All this legal uncertainty, the pressure from certain parties to give up his rights…" He shakes his head, still smiling. "Can't be pleasant."

The implication is clear: I'm the unreasonable one. I'm the one pressuring Griffin. And Derek Sullivan's swooping in to play the hero.

"I hope he can trust you to follow through on your promises," I say, keeping my voice level despite the anger burning in my chest. "You know how it is in small towns. People *say* one thing, then try to pull a permit to do another."

Derek's pleasant mask slips for just a moment, revealing something much colder underneath. "I think Griffin's perfectly capable of making his own decisions about who to trust, don't you?"

Before I can respond, Derek walks away, leaving me standing there with my hands clenched into fists and my mind racing.

*Is Griffin really planning to sell? Is that why he was so focused on Derek during their conversation a minute ago? Because he's considering the offer?*

My first instinct is to be furious. At Griffin, for even entertaining Sullivan's bullshit. At Derek, for being a manipulative asshole. At myself, for reasons not just about the business.

But underneath the anger is something like… well, hurt. Because after Sunday—after seeing glimpses of the real Griffin beneath his defensive anger—I thought we were starting to understand each other. To find some kind of common ground. To trust each other a little.

I head for the parking lot without saying goodbye to my family, needing to get away from the crowd and the noise, when I hear one last familiar voice call my name. The one I've been listening for all evening.

"You leaving so soon? Gotta get home for the latest episode of *Extreme Wilderness Adventure*, don't you?"

I stop without turning around. "Something like that."

Griffin catches up to me. His cheeks are flushed from the cool air, and when he smiles, it feels like he's smiling just for me.

"I don't have any more secret rooms to discover, but if you're up for another adventure, maybe we could… I don't know. Get coffee? My treat."

The offer catches me completely off guard. After three days of radio silence, after whatever conversation he just had with Derek Sullivan, Griffin wants to spend time with me?

I almost say yes. The word's right there on my tongue, because honestly? I want to spend time with him too. I want to know more about his family situation, about why he looked so lost when he talked about his career, about what made him brave enough to climb a tree in the dark just to retrieve a tennis racket.

I want to know if Sunday meant anything to him or if I'm just another complication in his already complicated life.

But then I remember Derek's predatory smile, his talk of Griffin being "practical," and my dad telling me that I need to think about people, not spreadsheets, and I decide to ask him straight up.

"Are you selling Jim's place?"

Griffin's eyes shoot wide in surprise. He opens his mouth to respond and stops, takes a breath, and starts again. "Can we just get coffee without talking about the property?"

I clamp my teeth together, remembering that this issue isn't the difference for him between success and failure. Between making payroll and destroying lives.

And that he doesn't know it's like that for Axford Lumber either.

Because I don't want him to.

"Can't," I say briskly, before sheer want makes me do something stupid. "Gotta work."

Griffin catches my tone, and his expression shifts immediately, like a door slamming shut. "I see." He takes a step back, his hands shoved deep in his pockets. "Okay, then. I'll see you around."

He's already starting to turn away when I can't help but call after him.

"You definitely will. We're still competing for Big Dill, right?"

Griffin pauses, glances back over his shoulder, and for a moment, I think I see vulnerability in his expression. Then he lifts his chin in that goddamn stubborn way of his and gives me a bright, brilliant smile that's not Griffin's smile at all.

"Beckett, Beckett. *Competing* implies there's an actual competition," he scoffs. Then he disappears into the crowd.

Leaving me wondering why focusing on winning... feels so damn much like losing.

# CHAPTER ELEVEN

## GRIFFIN

THE AIR IS SO FREAKING cold Thursday morning that my breath makes big, puffy clouds in front of my face as I walk down Whether Street. It's barely seven o'clock, but I've learned that's the best time to get fresh donuts in this town. I'm clutching a white paper bag from Fox Creamery to my chest like it's a precious treasure—which it is; their sugar donuts are *chef's kiss*—and the warmth of the donuts is the only thing keeping my hands from freezing off.

Since it's not quite October yet, this does not bode well for my perpetually chilly ass.

"Morning, Griffin," Mrs. Chen calls from the post office steps. The office isn't open yet, but she's already busy, arranging a display of autumn gourds that must violate, like, seventeen safety codes but looks charming as hell.

I lift a hand in a cautious greeting. In New York, we walk fast and never make eye contact—it's a point of pride. Here, it's the polar opposite. I'm still not used to this whole... gratuitous friendliness thing. Especially not at this hour.

Case in point, a fire truck rumbles past, and Robbie calls, "S'up, Griffin!" from the driver's seat, which makes me jump.

At this rate, I'll get acclimated just as I'm ready to move on. The thought makes my stomach twist.

"Griffin! Hey! Hey, Griffin!"

This time when I'm aggressively waved at, I manage not to startle. The guy who emceed the Wild Gherkin Chase jogs across the street to meet me. Judging by the big white grin on his tan face, the "Captain Fun" moniker wasn't a one-day thing but his entire personality.

"Perfect timing!" he says, slightly out of breath. "We haven't officially met yet. I'm Ry Marek. I teach fourth grade at the Proctor School."

"Nice to meet you." I shift my donuts so I can return his handshake.

"I heard you're thinking about infrastructure improvements if you're crowned Big Dill. That true?"

I nod. "Among other things."

"Fantastic! See, I've been advocating for a crosswalk near Proctor School for ages. The kids have to dodge traffic every morning." He wipes his sweaty brow. "If you want, I can show you the exact spot I was thinking?"

"Maybe another time? I promised to help Ada with her window display again today." I gesture down the street toward the Pickle Jar.

That's code for *Ada's "teaching me to win Big Dill" while I do unpaid physical labor and she eats donuts.* I like to imagine it's a sort of wax-on, wax-off, Karate Kid–type situation, except that my Mr. Miyagi has a bouffant.

"Sure! Thanks for being open to it." Ry grins. "I appreciate that you want to hear about the town's needs instead of assuming you know what's what."

"Oh, I'd never assume that," I say dryly. "Believe me."

And if I ever tried, Beckett would set me straight.

As we say goodbye and I keep walking, I replay my video call with Milo last night. He'd been glowing about his wellness retreat—connections he'd made with some major supplement brands, talk of a collab.

I'd almost hated to bring the vibe down by catching him up on *my* news, but I'd known he'd be pissed if I didn't.

"Wait, hold up," Milo had said, his face pixelating slightly on my laptop screen. "You broke into the Pickle Turret and learned Mushroom Jim's not just a stealth bestselling author, he's also your biological father? Oh, my sweet baby boy! That's it, I'm leaving tonight—"

"Milo, no. Absolutely not."

"Um, absolutely *yes*! This is huge. Life-changing! Your emotionally constipated self needs someone to help you process. You shouldn't have been alone! I blame myself."

"I… wasn't. Alone, I mean. Beckett came over. I called him after the, ah, FaceTime with my moms. And he helped."

And by "helped," I'd meant *"he made me orgasm so hard, my brain tilted sideways and allllll my thoughts slid off, so I slept like a rock."*

There'd been a moment of silence so charged it had literally lifted the hairs on my arms.

But when Milo spoke, it was only to say a breathy "Well. Well, well, well."

"Milo," I'd groaned.

"Don't you *Milo* me, Griffin Alexander Mercer," he'd

said, pulling out my full name like my mothers when I'm in trouble. "You slept with him, didn't you? That's how he 'helped.' He helped you with his big lumberjack penis!"

"No! I mean, yes. I mean… We fooled around twice. Possibly two and a half times? Irrelevant." I'd waved a hand. "I called, and he came over. It was… nice." I'd cleared my throat. "Hey, tell me more about these collab opportunities, huh? They sound *amazing*."

Milo had sat there frozen for so long I'd wondered if the internet had cut out.

Then he'd exploded.

"Who the fuck are you right now, Griffin? I'm not talking about the hookups—you wanna tonsil tango with your flannel-wearing nemesis? *Great*. I've been hoping for that since day one. You wanna touch his dick—two and a half times? *Here for it*. You wanna take him and his big dick on a woodland adventure and prison-break your locked treehouse? *Weird, but okay*. But you going mushy as a black banana for a guy you've known less than two weeks? Ha! Fuck no. Not on my watch."

"Who said I'm mushy? I'm not mushy," I'd protested, but even as I said it, I'd known it wasn't entirely true. I might not be mushy, but I was definitely… overripe.

"Griffin. You don't tell people when you need them. You only told me about your billboard situation when I saw it on TikTok, and I'm your best friend! But you called the Angry Lumberjack and asked him to come over?" He hesitated, then added, "Look, I don't wanna be that guy, babe, I really don't, but… how do we know Beckett isn't getting in your pants so he can get in your head? Sweeten you up so you stop fighting about the easement? I'm just saying… you gotta think. Enjoy the dick without getting dick-stracted from your goal."

Coming on the heels of my chilly interaction with Beckett at the farmer's market yesterday, in which he'd only seemed interested in whether I was selling Jim's land, Milo's outburst had been the ice-cold reality shower I'd needed to wake me up.

He's right that I don't trust people easily. You can't make it in the corporate world wearing your heart on your sleeve, and recent events have reinforced those trust issues.

So why'd I reach out to Beckett? Why was my first thought, when Beckett blew me off at the farmer's market, to worry about him?

It's perilously close to mushy behavior, which is the last thing I need.

I don't think Beckett's deliberately using sex to "dick-stract" me from my Big Dill run. But he's still my Big Dill rival. His priorities are directly in conflict with mine. We're not on the same side.

I need to put him out of my head—and shower fantasies—for good.

I push through the door of the Pickle Jar and immediately get assaulted by the scents of old wood, lavender sachets, and the dill-scented pickle candles Ada sells.

You're taught early in marketing that there's a buyer for every product, if you know how to pitch it, and this store crammed with antiques and pickle-themed tourist tchotchkes is proof. Fancy walnut grandfather clocks tick beside a display of T-shirts with slogans like "I Got that Big Dill Energy" and "In a Pickle? Head to Winsome!" and "I got pickled at the Brine and Dandy in Winsome,

Vermont," which features a pickle with a monocle, a top hat, and a shot glass. But like so many weird things in this town, the combo works.

"Griffin, is that you?" Ada calls. "I smell donuts! Bring 'em here!"

I follow her voice through the maze and find her in the back room, surrounded by cardboard boxes full of what appear to be old Brine posters, and her judgmental tortoiseshell cat, Bathsheba. The cat twines itself around my leg twice before jumping on a nearby shelf to give herself a bath, which according to Ada means Bathsheba likes me.

"Found these beauties in my cellar," she says, pointing at the boxes. "Thought you could incorporate them into the window display."

I set the donut bag on the table, shuck my fleece, and take a closer look. The posters span decades of festivals, with artwork ranging from hand-drawn illustrations yellowed with age to clip-art computer graphics from twenty years ago.

"These are perfect. We could do a Winsome Through the Ages thing?" I suggest.

Ada beams, her bright red lips already covered in cinnamon sugar. "Exactly what I was thinking. You have a real knack for this stuff. Winsome's been needing someone with your skills."

I chuckle. A *knack*. Also a business degree and over seven years' experience working on demanding, high-profile accounts, but okay.

"Winsome only has me for another couple months," I remind her. "Until the end of the year at the most."

She waves this away with a hand covered in jewelry and sugar. "You keep saying that, but a girl can dream."

Chuckling, I gather up an armload of posters and head to the front window.

Ada chatters about strategy while I work, but I'm only half listening as I arrange the display. But just after I've gotten out the stepladder to string up some bunting, one of the posters catches my eye, and I freeze.

*Come see JG Flummery, Author of The Whispers!*

There's a small author photo in the corner of a man with gray hair that sticks up in tufts just like mine, grinning at the camera in what looks like the 1990s. *Jim.*

"Oh, now that's a good one," Ada says, noticing where I'm staring. "Your uncle Jim was quite the local celebrity."

I swallow hard.

This week, I've tackled a bunch of things that needed to be done regarding Jim's estate, like emailing his attorney to ask whether the intellectual rights mentioned in the trust include a series of kids' books I've never read. I've managed my moms' increasingly worried texts. And I've sat and stared at the cover of the *Whispers* book on my coffee table for hours, like it's the ancient grimoire of curses Beckett joked about.

But I'm still not sure how I feel about the revelation that Jim was my biological father. I know Milo would say my detachment is strangling my mitochondria, which is the true cause of my back pain, rather than tree climbing and brothel-couch acrobatics, and I do sort of sense that there's this giant wall of emotions in the back of my brain, just waiting to tip into a landslide, but at this exact moment, they're not touching me.

"Ada…" I hesitate, then push forward. "You knew Jim,

right? Did you, ah… did you know he was my biological father?"

She goes very still, then sets down her donut and really looks at me. Her expression shifts from casual to assessing, like she's seeing me for the first time.

"Well, I'll be damned," she says finally. "I didn't know, but maybe I should've. You've got the same hair—golden spun sugar. Same spirit, too, in some ways."

"Me and Jim?" I snort. "I'm a professional with a career. I have no desire to talk to mushrooms or build a wacky treehouse. Or to donate sperm to create a child but insist on keeping it secret until I'm dead."

I blow out a breath. That came out sounding judgy when I'd been aiming for blasé. I've been telling myself I have no feelings whatsoever about this, but maybe I do.

"Jim was a sweetheart, but he had a vision of what he thought his life should be," she says carefully. "He thought he was meant to be a free spirit. Time and again, he had opportunities to put down roots and build lasting relation-ships, but he'd pick up stakes and leave. I think at a certain point, he knew the life he was trying to get wasn't what his soul actually needed. But for all his free-spiritedness, the pigheaded man didn't know how to adapt."

"That's not me," I tell her, stung. "The person you're describing isn't like me at all. I *never* wanted to leave New York. I want roots. I *had* roots. All kinds of roots."

But even as I say it, I wonder if those roots were as deep as I'd thought. New York let me go pretty easily, and no one but Milo seems to care that I'm gone.

"Glad to hear it, for your sake," Ada says mildly. "There's a reason Jim and I never tied the knot."

"You and Jim? Were…"

"Together? Oh yeah. For half a second, twenty-one years ago. He was a character, and I dug his sarongs." She winks. "I'm only human."

I feel more emotion at this news than I did about hearing Jim was my biological father.

"I keep waiting for some big emotion to hit me about the whole father thing," I hear myself admit. "Anger, grief, something. But I had two great moms. And Jim's choices aren't the ones I would have made, but he never signed up to be a dad. He didn't owe me anything, but he left me his treehouse. So maybe… maybe I shouldn't have any big feelings."

Ada shrugs. "I don't know that *should* has anything to do with it. Neither does biology, when it comes down to it. He gave you what he had to give, and what you do with the things he gave you, whether it's your hair or that tree-house, is all up to you."

That hits me hard because I've spent the past week and a half trying to figure out what Jim would want. Piecing together clues to figure out who Jim even was and why he did the things he did. But she's right. Whatever I do with my life or the treehouse is up to me.

"That's… helpful, Ada," I say softly. "Thanks."

"So many men think I'm just a pretty face." She grins. "That's how I lure 'em in. Then I spring my intelligence on 'em when it's too late."

Laughing, I climb up on the stepladder to clothespin the JG Flummery poster to the bunting, still processing everything Ada said. I stretch to reach the perfect spot… when the shop door suddenly bangs open.

I startle so hard the ladder tilts sideways, and for a horrifying moment, I'm falling backward with my arms windmilling uselessly—

Strong hands catch me around the waist, steadying both me and the ladder, and I find my face pressed against a broad, solid chest. I breathe in the scent of sawdust and pine.

A scent so *good* and already so familiar I'd recognize it anywhere.

For a heartbeat, neither of us moves. Beckett's hands are warm and sure around my waist, and his breath tickles my ear. My whole body flashes hot, and I'm suddenly very aware of how our bodies fit together, how his thumbs are resting in what's become their designated parking spot just above my hip bones and my face is pressed against warm flannel.

I tilt my head back just a little, and our gazes lock.

"We've got to stop meeting like this," I say in a voice gone whistly.

"You okay?" he asks roughly.

"Yeah, I…" I clear my throat and try to force my brain to make words. "Yes. Thank you."

It takes another beat before he seems to remember that he should set me back on my feet, and even then, his hands linger on my waist a moment longer than necessary.

"So it's like that, is it?" Ada murmurs under her breath, thoroughly entertained.

Beckett steps back quickly, cheeks going pink above his beard.

Sadly, from the heat in my own cheeks, I know he's not the only one blushing.

"My, ah… my mom asked me to bring you this." He picks up a small, well-wrapped package he dropped on the floor and hands it to Ada. "She said you needed it for your window display?"

"Perfect timing!" Ada crows. "Vivian offered to have Truett carve me some pickle ornaments. Winsome is lucky to have so much local talent, aren't we, Beckett?"

"Uh…" Beckett frowns. "Sure?"

She smiles mischievously. "I was just thinking Griffin needs to see more of our local charm. The shops and restaurants, galleries and artisans. You know, to improve the tourism marketing campaign he'll be sharing with the town at Hello, Winsome."

I narrow my eyes, not sure what part of our Big Dill strategy involves telling the competition what we're doing. "I've seen plenty of places already," I say. "And researched even more."

"But you've barely scratched the surface! How many local eateries have you visited, for example? You can't talk about the food scene in Winsome if you've only ever been to Watchfire. Not that there's anything wrong with Watchfire, of course," she adds to Beckett, who's still wearing a confused frown.

"I've been to the farmer's market," I protest. "And Fox Creamery. And I ate muffins from Ruby's Diner—"

"Pfft. Muffins." She shakes her head. "Beckett, you've been to Ruby's a time or two. What's your favorite thing on the menu?"

"I, uh… waffles?" Beckett shakes his head. "Anyway, I'd better get back to work—"

"Waffles!" Ada closes her eyes like she's about to faint

from ecstasy. "Oh, god. The ones with the apple cinnamon topping and the whipped cream!"

Beckett and I exchange a confused glance, and I shrug. I have no idea what's happening right now.

Ada's eyes pop open. "Well, there you go, then. Hello, Winsome's only a few days away, and Griffin can't possibly present his marketing campaign on Sunday until he's tried the waffles. Isn't that right, Beckett?"

Beckett looks like a deer caught in headlights. "I didn't say—"

"So you should take him over," she concludes. "Now."

"Ohhhh, no—" Beckett and I say at the same time.

Before either of us can finish our protests, though, the door chimes again, and one of the women from the Brine planning committee comes in.

"Ada, I was hoping to catch you—oh, sorry to interrupt!" She spots me and Beckett and smiles. "Hello, Beckett. And Griffin! I'm Eleanor Hartwell, town council."

"Nice to meet you," I manage, shaking her hand. I try to ignore that Beckett's standing just close enough for me to feel the warmth radiating off him, but I'm sure my awareness shows on my face.

"Eleanor, Griffin and Beckett here were just about to head over to the diner for waffles. Isn't that wonderful?" Ada says innocently.

Eleanor's eyes light up with interest. "It is! Research for this tourism marketing campaign of yours, Griffin? I've heard good things. I'm excited for Hello, Winsome on Sunday! And Beckett's the perfect guide. I bet he knows every inch of this town, don't you, Beckett?"

And just like that, we're trapped. Neither of us wants to say no and risk seeming rude to a council member.

Which is how, five minutes later, I'm back in my fleece, walking down Whether Street with Beckett.

Or, more accurately, Beckett's striding down the street silently while I double-time to keep up and try not to obsess about how his hands felt on my waist.

When a delivery truck rumbles past a little too close to the sidewalk, Beckett instinctively steps closer, creating a barrier between me and the street. It's such a small gesture, but it makes my whole chest warm.

"This is ridiculous," I say, stopping short. "We did the scavenger hunt together. We went on a woodland adventure. You yanked me out of a tree. Surely we can eat waffles without being weird."

Beckett crosses his arms over his chest and raises a skeptical eyebrow. If the edge of his lips hadn't twitched, I might have thought he blamed me for this surprise waffle attack.

"Seriously," I insist. "We just won't talk about... you know. Certain things."

He laughs. "Which things? Are we not talking about the easement? Or the Big Dill? Or..." He steps closer. "The sound you make when you're choking on my dick?"

I shoot him a glare because *way to make it very weird.* "All of that," I say firmly.

Amusement flickers across his face. "Fine, then what *should* we talk about? Wanna tell me all about this tourism marketing campaign of yours, city boy?"

I roll my eyes. "I'm sure you're dying to know, given how much you hate outsiders."

Beckett shakes his head. "You've got to stop listening to Derek Sullivan."

"How'd you know it was him?" I ask.

"Because Derek Sullivan has it out for Axford Lumber, which means he has it out for *me*. That's why he made you that neighborly offer to buy your land yesterday."

Guilt tries to sink its claws in me, even as I lift my chin. "I know you're business rivals, but that has nothing to do with me. All I did was listen to his offer. I haven't agreed to sell anything to anyone. Yet."

Though I can't lie, the offer was tempting.

I didn't want it to be. After hearing Beckett talk about the forest last weekend, about how logging "done right" preserves the land, after coming to know him (and I mean that biblically), it had felt weird and wrong to consider selling out to his competitor. Like a betrayal.

But that's my dick-straction talking. The numbers Derek mentioned would be life-changing. Enough to set me up for my next chapter *and* give my moms some money for renovations at the B&B that they've been daydreaming about. I can't just dismiss that because Beckett and I have hooked up…

Two and a half times.

"Besides, are you saying Derek's wrong?" I press. "Because you sure didn't seem eager to welcome an outsider when you were trying to tow my car."

Beckett runs a hand through his thick hair, looking uncomfortable. "That was the product of a difficult few weeks and a bad morning," he says almost apologetically. "And if it makes you feel better, my crew's been giving me endless shit about my behavior. The other day, Carlos started waving a fork at Rocky, telling him to *unhand* his chicken salad, and Rocky said to cool it before the boss threw his fork in a tree." He grimaces. "Freddy keeps giving me these sad looks like he's not mad, just disappointed."

I snort laugh so loud I clap a hand over my mouth. I can just picture the big man doing that exact thing.

"That does make me feel somewhat better," I admit. "Though… to be fair, I wasn't at my most diplomatic that morning. Vermont had already tried to kill me multiple times, just on the drive in."

His lips twitch. "Look, I know I'm not the friendliest person in Winsome, and people find me intimidating—"

I can't help it. I laugh out loud. "You wish." I shove his shoulder, though it doesn't move a centimeter. "You're a seven-foot-tall, inscrutable teddy bear. You're bossy as fuck, and you yank people out of trees against their will, but you're *not* intimidating. Do I seem intimidated by you?"

"No," he says slowly. "Except maybe when you were…" One side of his mouth quirks up, and he lowers his voice to a whisper. "Doing that thing we're not talking about."

I just *know* he means choking on his cock, and my face sets itself on fire.

"What you are is annoying," I say crisply, continuing our walk. "Which is worse than intimidating by *far*."

Beckett chuckles low as he falls into step beside me. "I'm only six three," he says.

I roll my eyes. "Great. That changes everything. You're practically petite," I shoot back. "A petite pain in the ass."

He chuckles again, and I feel a surge of something like pride. That's, what, four laughs in five minutes? Not that I'm counting because that would be absurd and black-banana-level *mushy*.

We're almost to the diner when an older man in coveralls calls out, "Beckett!" and rushes over. "Hey! I wanted to thank you again for helping me work out that payment plan. I signed all the paperwork and emailed it back."

Beckett looks nearly as uncomfortable as he did back at Ada's. "Oh. Good. And, uh… no problem. Thanks for agreeing to formalize things."

The man shakes Beckett's hand with both of his, then continues on his way.

"So intimidating," I say with a mock shiver. "I'm terrified right now."

Beckett knocks his arm into mine, but he still seems amused. "Shut it."

"What was that about?" I ask curiously. "A payment plan?"

He shrugs. "You remember I told you my dad and I have different opinions about running the business?"

When I nod, he continues. "My dad was pressing me to extend Ed credit, so I did… but I had him sign a formal agreement. Sort of a compromise between Dad's way and mine. No more handshake deals, though. Protecting the business is too important to me to just trust people willy-nilly. It's what I wanted to do with Jim, to get the easement in writing," he adds. "He agreed, but he didn't get to sign the papers before… you know."

"Oh," I say in a small voice.

Now I *do* feel guilty because for the last week and a half, I've been thinking of my own needs regarding the easement. How I want to protect my inheritance, protect Jim's legacy, from this powerful family who seems to run the town.

I haven't let myself think about what it's doing to Beckett's bottom line.

"Is not having an easement going to be a problem for —?" I begin.

Serious blue eyes meet mine. "We're not talking about that, remember? I shouldn't have even mentioned it."

"Right." I nod. "No. Good."

For a wild second there, I'd considered offering Beckett some kind of temporary agreement, but it's good that he stopped me. This is exactly what Milo warned me about.

The restaurant is what you'd expect from a place called Ruby's Diner—red vinyl booths with silver-edged tables, black-and-white checkered floors, everything permeated by the scent of a million cups of coffee. We slide into a booth by the window, and when Ruby comes over, Beckett orders us waffles, and she fills our coffee mugs without asking.

"You boys picked the right day," she says with a grin. "Got in some apples from an orchard up in Little Pippin Hollow." She points left to wherever she's talking about. "The apple cinnamon sauce is extra saucy."

While we're waiting, Beckett stirs his coffee and watches me over the table. "So, this tourism campaign."

I tilt my head, trying to decide if he's serious. "You really want to hear about it? Or you want to size up the competition?"

"Both? Mostly, I'm curious what you'd do differently. What turns Mr. Marketing Degree's crank..." He smiles and adds, "About this town, I mean."

I shake my head, fighting a smile. "Fine, then. But I warn you, the presentation's going to be *way* better at

Hello, Winsome. I'm putting together a whole audio-visual thing."

"Now *I'm* intimidated," he says, not sounding intimidated at all.

I decide to use this as a trial run and launch into the presentation I've been working on. The campaign started out as a way to win Big Dill, but I've been missing the marketing game so much, I've thrown myself into it and spent the last few nights brainstorming.

"I've come up with some ideas for cross-promotional partnerships with businesses both local and distant. Like, how fun would it be to see a Winsome Pickle Martini on the menu at a bar in the Village? At least for those who don't shudder at the thought of a pickle martini."

I go on to explain a few facts and figures supporting some of my ideas.

"I also researched the possibility of adding more cell towers to get rid of the cell-signal dead zones just outside town but realized pretty quickly that there'd be an environmental impact. So instead, I dreamed up the idea to— hear me out—call those zones 'Winsome Peace Pockets.' With proper signage that warns people in advance and encourages them to take those few miles to be fully present in nature, it could make the experience a feature, not a bug."

Beckett's eyebrows lift with interest. "Huh. That's cute."

"Right?" I continue telling him about including the stuff he told me about the rock walls in the forest and the change in the landscape over time. "That stuff will really appeal to naturalists."

Beckett listens to my spiel with his full attention,

nodding along and looking both thoughtful and impressed. I hate how nice that feels.

I finish just as Ruby delivers our waffles and refills our coffee, and Beckett sighs.

"Damn. That's… really fucking good, city boy," he says, and I hate how his approval hits me like rain on parched earth.

"It's funny," I say, following Beckett's lead and smearing whipped cream and apples all over my steaming waffle. "Usually, creating marketing campaigns is about creating an aspirational lifestyle story. Like, *drink this vodka, eat these wholesome granola bars, wear these leggings, and you too can be as social, healthy, and picture-perfect as these paid models!*"

Beckett laughs as he cuts into his waffle. "Yeah, how do you do that for Winsome? Eat these pickles, participate in these weird festival rituals, commune with the forest, and you too can be the subject of small-town gossip for the rest of your life?"

I frown a little. "Is that really how you see life here?"

He lifts one big shoulder, uncomfortable. "I dunno. Maybe a little. I've never really thought about it. Except for a few years in college, Winsome's all I've ever known. And the busybodies are a lot. There's always someone around, up in your business."

I nod. "That's true. Sometimes I'm like, *how do all these people know who I am?*"

Beckett flicks his wrist and spreads his fingers as if to say, *There you go.*

"But… I don't know," I say, fork suspended in midair. "The longer I'm here, the more I think it's kind of cool that people are so… open? I mean, don't get me wrong, it's definitely weird as fuck and nothing like New York. But the story here is that there's something in this town for everyone—natural beauty, kitschy charm, fine dining. You can come as you are and enjoy yourself. *Be* yourself. I mean, I haven't felt like anyone's wanted me to change who I am."

He frowns hard, but he doesn't look angry so much as... thoughtful.

"You'd know better than I do," I say with a shrug. "It's just that coming up with this campaign feels... organic, I guess? Like I'm not creating the story, I'm just telling it." I laugh lightly. "I'm almost sad I won't be around to see my ideas come to fruition."

"But only *almost*," he teases.

"Right," I agree, scooping up a bite of waffle. "Only almost."

I take my bite, and honest to god, I moan.

The waffle's perfectly crispy on the outside but fluffy inside, and the apple cinnamon topping is like autumn distilled into edible form—sweet but with just enough spice to warm my throat.

"Okay, maybe slightly more than almost," I say, forking up another bite.

Beckett laughs, but it sounds strangled, and when I glance up, he's watching me with intent. "The noise you make when you eat something delicious is another thing we won't be talking about," he says darkly.

My stomach gives a happy swoop that has not a damn thing to do with waffles.

"If it isn't our two *biggest* Big Dill competitors out for a nice brunch," Ramona Pratt says, materializing beside us, and I realize I'd forgotten for a minute that we were in a crowded diner. "Griffin, dear, how are you getting on?"

Something in her tone makes my hackles rise, though I can't put my finger on it. "I'm researching local businesses for my campaign, and Beckett's helping. Putting aside our competition for the good of Winsome is what it's all about, right?"

"Of course." She smiles fondly at me, then looks at Beckett with faint disapproval and says, "Nice to see you actually talking to someone for once, Beckett."

Beckett closes his eyes briefly. "Mrs. Pratt, I told you that was a misunderstanding—"

She purses her lips, and when she sees my confusion, she explains, "Beckett once spent an entire book club meeting in my living room without saying a single word."

I blink. "Beckett was in a book club?"

Beckett's cheeks are red. "As I told Mrs. Pratt at the time, I was just there dropping off a pie my mother had baked—"

"Didn't even pretend to eat the cookies I made!" she huffs. "Rude."

Something hot and protective flares in my chest that I definitely won't be telling Milo about. Is she seriously giving Beckett grief over this? No wonder he thinks people find him intimidating.

"Actually, Beckett's been incredibly charming," I interrupt with a bland smile before the man has a chance to respond. I feel like I'm channeling the old Griffin, the Manhattan Griffin who could handle the trickiest, crankiest clients. "My marketing campaign's made Beckett see Winsome in a new light, and I hope it encourages other Winsomefolk to look at things differently too. It's funny how we can become blind to what's right in front of us, isn't it?"

I can't tell which of the three of us is more surprised by me rushing to Beckett's defense, but Ramona recovers first.

Her expression shifts from disapproval to something more speculative as she glances between us. "Hmm. Well, I'll be interested to hear this presentation," she says. "Very interested. And I'll see you both at the Brine and Dandy tomorrow."

She walks away, leaving us sitting there in the aftermath. I focus on my waffles since I can't quite meet Beckett's gaze, but I don't really taste them anymore. *What was I thinking?*

"I'm seeing Winsome in a new light, huh?" Beckett teases.

I lift my chin and glare at him challengingly. "Well, aren't you?"

He smirks and takes another bite of waffle. "Maybe so."

"Do I want to know what this Brine and Dandy thing is?" I ask.

He shakes his head, giving me a look that makes my stomach loop-de-loop. "Definitely not, city boy."

*Fuck.* I want Beckett Axford. I shouldn't, but I do.

But Winsome was only ever supposed to be a stop on my comeback tour. A place where I could lay low and reinvent myself before heading back to the real world. I wasn't supposed to like it, and I sure as fuck wasn't supposed to get mushy for a lumberjack I barely know.

Fortunately, just as I'm getting back in my car to go home, I get an email notification. And for the first time in forever, it's not a bank statement or a Pottery Barn sales flyer, but an actual honest-to-god communication from Conor, an old business school classmate, saying he wants to talk to me about the possibility of a job back in the city.

The fact that I hesitate for a second and consider that the job's not *precisely* in my field is a sign of just how weird I'm being lately. It's in New York, for god's sake! What am I waiting for?

I'm starting to wonder if Milo's right... this town is making me bananas.

# CHAPTER TWELVE

WHEN FRIDAY AFTERNOON ROLLS AROUND, I'm bone-tired and pissed at myself.

I spent the second half of yesterday joining my crew out in the North Lot, marking the next rotation of crop trees and checking the access road conditions before we move the loader in. I spent yesterday evening going over the paperwork Ed had sent back and making sure all the details about delivery schedules and payment deadlines were locked down tight. And then I spent this morning hauling chainsaw fuel and bar oil up to the Hemlock Ridge site *on foot* because the rain we got last night means the access trail's still too soft for the ATV.

And all the hours in between yesterday evening and this morning? All those moments I should've been sleeping? I spent those tossing and turning in my bed, thinking about Griffin.

Griffin's body under my hands when he fell off the ladder at Ada's.

The excitement in Griffin's face when he talks about his marketing project.

The fucking thrill of Griffin defending me to Ramona Pratt.

The sexy moan Griffin makes when he eats waffles.

Since I was hard as a rock at that point, I'd had to slide my hand into my boxers to give myself some relief and came in literally two strokes… which means I will never be able to eat those waffles again without getting a semi.

And honestly, that's the least of my problems.

I keep telling myself to stay away from Griffin because the guy's a short-timer in this town, and I don't want to get attached—not to his pretty eyes, not to our ridiculous conversations, not even to his dick. But I can't seem to make myself listen.

So with these cheery thoughts in my head, it's no surprise that when True knocks on the open door of my office and says, "Got a second to talk?" I'm not feeling it.

The only thing that saves me from shutting him down is the fact that my middle sibling doesn't *do* spontaneous talks. Hell, True barely does necessary talks. He's the opposite of the stereotypical middle child, in fact. He's always been economical with words, and since his wife left him a couple of years ago, he's become even quieter. He spends his days in his shop, making incredible furniture pieces, like that's how he communicates.

"*You* want to talk?" I repeat. I sit back in my chair. "Okay, what's up?"

True shrugs as he takes a seat in front of my desk. He's wearing his usual uniform—faded jeans, a T-shirt from some band I've never heard of, and a Carhartt jacket that's absorbed so many years of sawdust it always smells like pine. "Just checking in. How are you?"

"Fine," I say warily. I do not add, *aside from a small issue with waffles.* "You?"

"Fine. Mom's doing family dinner on Saturday this week. You coming?"

Whatever I'd been expecting, it wasn't that. "Uh. I guess so, yeah."

He nods, clearly pleased. "I wasn't sure, what with… everything."

I don't know what *everything* he's talking about. "Well, Brine and Dandy's tonight and Hello, Winsome's Sunday, so I think I can squeeze you in tomorrow without compromising my hectic Big Dill social calendar," I joke.

"Good." He smiles. "But I meant you and Dad."

Oh. *That* everything.

I sigh and fiddle with a pencil on my desk. "I realize I haven't handled that well," I finally say. "Dad disapproves of how I'm running Axford Lumber, and that's not gonna change. But me distancing myself from the rest of you so that you won't be affected… it's like trying to hide an elephant in plain sight."

I don't know what I was thinking. That my siblings wouldn't notice I was missing? That my mom wouldn't? None of them are stupid, and they don't take things quietly. The more surprising thing is that it's taken them this long to get in my face about it. But in the past couple of weeks, Holden's brought it up, Ames lured me to family dinner, my mom reverse-psychologied me into socializing via the Big Dill thing, Eliza's doing her best to manage my campaign, and now my silent middle sibling's dropped by to "chat."

They're not subtle. But knowing they love me, even when I'm being a jackass, makes me realize how fucking lucky I am to be an Axford.

The truth is, I've been thinking about Griffin and his moms, and whatever secrets they were keeping that made him desperate enough to call me last Sunday rather than be alone. I feel like it was about more than them knowing Jim built a treehouse and wrote some books… though Griffin hasn't shared anything else about it.

I mean, not that he would, right? We've hooked up, but that doesn't mean he trusts me. It doesn't mean we're close.

"I'm not sure you're right about that," True says thoughtfully.

I blink, trying to remember what we were talking about. "You mean I *should* distance myself?"

"No, dumbass." True gives me an exasperated look. "I don't think Dad disapproves of you."

"Oh." I snort. "No, he definitely does. You remember how he and Mom sat me down when he was still in the hospital and said Dad was retiring as of that moment? He said he trusted me to run the company, to uphold the legacy, Mom got all teary, I felt like I was getting knighted or some shit?"

True nods. He knows this part. Everyone does. So I fill him in on the part I've been keeping to myself.

"Three weeks later, he's home from the rehab place, barely able to put on his own bathrobe, but saying, 'Beckett, let me show you the right way to categorize things in QuickBooks,' and 'I had a plan for x-y-z, so maybe I'll just handle it myself,' and 'Put relationships first! That's the Axford way.' And on and on like that." I break off with a shake of my head. "Not sure what you think I'm misinterpreting. I bet as far as Dad's concerned, I deserve that stupid 'Axe' nickname Derek Sullivan gave me because all I've done is wreck stuff lately."

The business. My family relationships. Every damn boundary I've tried to set with Griffin.

"You really are a dumbass," True says fondly. "Now, tell me why you and Griffin were at the diner yesterday."

*Shit.* How the heck does he know about that? "It was an accident. A… matchmaking accident. Ada Wickham got her claws in us."

"And forced you to share a meal?" He whistles low. "Diabolical."

"Shut up. It wasn't like… whatever you're thinking, okay? Griffin's a good guy. He explained the marketing presentation he's doing for Hello, Winsome—which reminds me, I don't have a single thing to talk about on Sunday, since Eliza says I'm not allowed to suggest widening the parking spaces on Whether Street so I can park my truck more easily." I wince and decide to save that problem for tomorrow. "But that's all it was."

True raises an eyebrow.

"I'm serious. That's all it *can* be. If it wasn't clear before yesterday, it's crystal fucking clear to me now that Griffin does not belong in Winsome. And it's not just about his fancy boots and fancy hair product and fancy fake-rugged outdoor wear."

Even though I'm starting to find his city-boy outfits kind of sexy.

"Griffin's passionate about marketing the same way I'm passionate about the forest," I explain, since True doesn't seem convinced. "And he's talented as fuck. Hell, his marketing thing nearly sold *me* on Winsome, and I already freaking live here. There's no way he'll stick around for long, and why would he want to? So… take that back to Mom or whoever else you're reporting to on the Winsome gossip chain."

He laughs softly to himself. "Damn, you're defensive."

"Griffin's my rival. My opponent for Big Dill." I fold my arms over my chest. "The guy preventing me from accessing our land."

"So you really like him, huh?"

I open my mouth and shut it again. "That is the exact opposite of what I—"

True grins. "Stop pretending you don't want things just because wanting them feels risky, Beck. If you want something badly enough, you'll figure out how to get it. Remember, 'axes' don't just wreck things; they help clear away the old shit so new things can be built."

"And now he's a fortune cookie," I complain to the ceiling. "Have you considered talking less, True?"

His laughter echoes out into the chilly October afternoon, and then he's gone, leaving me with the uncomfortable feeling that the most reticent Axford just saw right through me.

BY THE TIME I lock up the office, I've nearly convinced myself I shouldn't go to the Brine and Dandy tonight. After hearing about his tourism thing, it's clear Griffin's got Big Dill on lock, especially since I have no amazing ideas of my own.

Which is why, when I get to the end of the driveway, I

hesitate. Everything in me wants to turn right and go home. Let Griffin have this one and spend a little time getting my head on straight, remembering why I need to avoid the guy for my own peace of mind. But before I even have a chance to consider what I'm doing, I hang a left and head into town.

The Shed on a Friday night during the Brine is exactly what you'd expect from Winsome's most beloved—and only—watering hole. It's warm, it's loud, and it's packed to the rafters with a mix of locals and tourists who've all had just enough alcohol to think they're best friends.

The place itself is a dive bar, but Vermont-style. Weathered wood paneling covers every surface, dotted with vintage signs advertising long-gone breweries and faded photos of New England sports teams. Mismatched tables and chairs are clustered together, and string lights cast everything in a warm, golden glow that makes even Hussein's five-o'clock shadow look romantic. There's a small stage area that sometimes hosts folk musicians or '80s cover bands, but tonight, it's been cleared for what I can only assume will be our public humiliation.

I grab a spot at the bar and order a beer, watching the crowd. Half the town seems to be here, along with a decent number of tourists who probably think they've lucked into the quintessential Winsome experience. Which I guess they have.

A cute woman from Boston asks to buy me a drink, which isn't altogether unusual—plenty of folks come to town looking for a hookup, and that's been my favorite way to blow off steam for years—but I turn her down.

Several locals offer me friendly back-slaps, beer, and chats about our Pop Warner team's chances in the league, and that *is* unusual. Was my half-assed attempt at friendliness really all it took?

Then Griffin walks in, and I forget about all of it.

I notice him immediately and not just because he's gorgeous, though the green V-neck sweater and ass-molding jeans he's wearing don't exactly hurt the cause. It's because he's got a fucking fan club.

"Griffin!" someone calls from a corner table. "Over here! Join our team!"

"Griffin!" Mrs. Chen from the post office yells. "I want to chat about Celine's college application essays. Do you think you could—"

Griffin laughs—a genuine, surprised laugh I'm starting to recognize—and makes his way through the crowd, stopping to chat with people as he goes. Perky Halloran shakes his hand. Even Walt Lehmann, who's been suspicious of outsiders since Bush was president, claps Griffin on the shoulder like they're old friends.

Griffin doesn't seem to know how to take it. He's not unhappy, but… uncertain. His gaze roves over the crowd like he's looking for something.

And then locks on me.

The second our eyes meet, I feel a *snap* of connection. An invisible tether stretching between us across the bar. It's like the whole tightly packed crowd falls away, and it's just him and me. My pulse kicks so hard I can feel it in my throat. I can't look away. I can't even blink—

"You know," a voice above my shoulder says, "you keep staring at him like that, folks are going to start talking."

Startled, I break my gaze from Griffin's—a good thing

—and glare at Holden instead. "Don't you have some little old ladies to pull over for speeding?" I demand.

He grins. "So what's the strategy tonight, bro? Charm offensive? Strategic alliance?" He lowers his voice suggestively. "Aggressive flirtation?"

"No."

"You sure?" His brown eyes gleam with humor. "Because the way you were looking at each other at the farmer's market could heat entire cities. And Ames said that after the scavenger hunt—"

*I can just imagine what Ames said.* "Ames talks too much."

"—Griffin hung out with him and was really sweet. He said he thought if you two could just discuss the easement issue, Griffin would be reasonable about it."

I grunt. He doesn't know the easement is on the list of things Griffin and I definitely *aren't* talking about while we're busy eating waffles, solving riddles, finding hidden rope bridges to fairy-tale pickle-barrel turrets, and... you know... fucking.

It's not that I've forgotten about the easement. Not when my logging schedule and my pending deliveries mock me every time I sit down at my desk.

"Beckett! There you are!" Eliza pushes through the crowd and greets us both with a cheek kiss.

She's traded her scrubs for jeans and a sweater but is wearing her determined look that means I'm about to be voluntold to do something. And sure enough, she starts in with, "I've been making the rounds, analyzing the crowd before the competition, and I think we need to—oh! Hi, Griffin!"

Griffin appears beside me, and suddenly, the bar's fifty degrees warmer. *Too* warm. Some might say… hot.

"Hey," he says, and I can't tell if it's my imagination or if his smile when he looks up at me is different from the one he's been giving everyone else. He focuses on my sister. "I don't think we've met—"

"Not officially," Eliza agrees, shaking his hand. "I'm—"

"Dr. Eliza Axford, who never got the message she was the *second*-born Axford and has been bossing us all around since preschool," Holden teases.

Eliza shoots him a look that says she's planning to boss him harder from now on. "I was just telling Beck, the Brine and Dandy starts in ten minutes. Everyone's breaking into tables of four, and you'll compete against the other people at your table. Nearly every table wants one of you to join them, so I think—"

"I can see them wanting Griffin," I interrupt. "They think they can outdrink him. I highly doubt they want me."

Eliza raises one dark eyebrow. "Despite being built like a brick shit house and able to hold your liquor, you're known for being easily riled in Griffin's presence."

She doesn't know the half of it.

"Which means they want a show," Holden says.

"Correct," Eliza says happily. "And it can only mean good exposure for both of you."

Griffin's eyes widen. "Me, compete with this guy?" His face is pink, and he can't quite meet my eyes. "He can probably pound shots with impunity. That doesn't seem fair."

"Glad you agree! Now, go sit with Ames and Ry Marek." Eliza takes Griffin by the shoulder, turns him, and points to a high-top table in the corner, proving that her bossing extends to more than just her own brothers. She lowers her voice. "I think they're supposed to be on a date, and Ames needs a rescue."

She's not wrong. From this distance, it looks like Ry's pumping out energy like a nuclear reactor, which I'm learning is kind of his thing. Meanwhile, Ames looks like he's being held at gunpoint. His smile is anemic, his eyes are dull, and I've seen lunchmeat with more personality.

"Ooof," Griffin says softly, not arguing anymore. "What about Holden? Whose table will you be at?"

Holden's teasing grin softens into something more genuine. "Oh, I'm just here for the party. And to make sure folks like this guy…" He claps me on the shoulder. "… who probably didn't plan ahead, get home safely."

I grimace because… he's not wrong. I hadn't actually considered how I'd get home. Which just goes to show how rarely I do shit like this.

A cheerful voice comes over the sound system. "Time for the main event, everyone! The Brine and Dandy Competition!"

The crowd cheers, and people finalize their teams, as friends, couples, families. It's a kind of easy camaraderie I've been watching with a raised eyebrow from the side-lines for years. It feels fucking strange to be in the throes of it now.

"Do your thing," Griffin says, nudging me in the side.

It takes me a second to realize "my thing" is acting as a battering ram to get us through the crowd like I did during the scavenger hunt.

I chuckle. But instead of letting Griffin follow behind, I sling a friendly arm around his shoulders and drag him along beside me. I'm not sure why I do this, exactly, but let's pretend there's some premeditated, logical reason that doesn't involve his citrus scent, or the way he feels under my arm, or how much I like it when, after a moment of hesitation, he clasps me back in a similar way.

Like we're just two pals, a couple of amigos, hamming it up for the crowd.

"Griffin, sit with us," Ramona Pratt insists as we pass her table. "I want to hear more about your fresh ideas!"

"Beckett! Beck! Getcherass over here," Patrick Turner yells before telling the woman beside him, "Bet Beck's never tossed a pickle in his life!"

Griffin shakes his head and gives both of them a polite smile, thumbing over his shoulder at me. "Sorry, guys. I'm sitting with him. Beckett's mine for tonight."

It's a throwaway comment. I mean, *fuck*. Obviously, it is. Griffin and I aren't together.

But I hear True's voice in my head telling me to stop pretending I don't want things just because they feel risky, so I don't pull away from Griffin or correct whatever bull-shit calculus I see happening on Patrick's face as he watches the two of us pass. I just... enjoy the feeling of Griffin's hand on me. The sweetly painful sensation of being claimed by someone.

"Beck! Griffin!" Ames says when we get close. He looks almost relieved. "You guys our competition?"

Ry doesn't seem upset that Griffin and I have crashed his date. He's as eager-beaver as ever, jumping off his stool to give Griffin a hug—which Griffin endures with a stiff smile—and shake my hand.

"Cool!" Ry says. "Cool, cool. I thought... I mean... I figured we'd be competing with Robbie and Lissa, since

Robbie and Ames are, you know…" He twines two fingers together, then shrugs and darts a look around the bar. "But I guess the lovebirds ditched us?"

"They went out back about… fourteen minutes ago," Ames confirms with a forced smile. "Give or take. Pretty sure they're not coming back."

Griffin rolls his lips together and gives Ames a sympathetic look. I feel like I'm missing something.

"Well, we're here, for whatever that's worth." Griffin slides onto the stool beside Ry and gestures me to the one beside Ames. "I don't actually know how this event works, and I wasn't really paying attention when Ada explained it yesterday, but it's some kind of drinking game, yes?"

Ry explains the rules while servers distribute shot glasses and bottles. The concept is simple enough—a bell rings every fifteen minutes to start a new round, and there are five rounds in total. Each competitor takes a shot of a pickle-infused vodka they call "The Brine" to start the round, and then we each complete a challenge. If we can't complete it, we take another shot. At the end of the five rounds, the person at our table who's taken the fewest shots wins.

"The alcohol is… pickle flavored?" Griffin whispers as he inspects a bottle. His face is a little green.

Ames raises his hand, and Raisa, the bar owner, comes over. "What do we do if someone at our table's physically incapable of taking a brine shot?"

Raisa doesn't blink. She raises her mic and says, "Great question! If someone on your team can't han-*dill* the Brine-infused vodka shots, they'll need to take a shot and *a half* of the Dandy instead. These are maple rye." She holds up one of the smaller bottles on the table for the rest of the room to see. "And remember, we have plenty of nonalcoholic options available for those who'd rather refrain, like my own sweet bride." She winks across the room at a woman I recognize as Posy from the Wild Gherkin Chase, who blushes. "Though, I'll warn you, the apple-ginger Dandy still packs a punch, and it'll clear your sinuses."

Griffin exhales. "Thank fuck. Maple rye sounds fine."

Ames huffs into his beer. His laugh's thin, but it's better than the hollow smile he's been wearing. His eyes keep darting toward the back door like he's trying not to look.

"Everything okay, Ames?" I ask, low enough for only him to hear.

He takes a breath and nods. "Just… you know. Rob and I won the Brine and Dandy last year, so I thought… but it's fine! Really. I'm going to have fun," he says, like a man being led to a guillotine. But it's clear he doesn't want to talk about it, so I frown and nod.

I meet Holden's eyes across the bar and tilt my head toward Ames. Holden nods back, and I know I can trust him to make sure Ames gets home safely. I'm swamped with affection for these fuckers. I love knowing I can rely on them.

Then a bell clangs, and Raisa's voice is back. "Okay, round one! Do your Brine shots, and then… show your skills with the garnish toss! Land two pickles on your target, or get Brined again!"

Ames and Ry toss back their shots of Brine, while I pour three shots of rye. When I'm done pouring, I slide one of the glasses to Griffin.

"You don't like pickles either?" he demands.

I shrug. "I don't care one way or the other. But if I'm going to win—and I am—I'm gonna make sure it's fair and not because you're a lightweight."

Griffin's face morphs into a mixture of insult and… fondness. And I decide, as I knock back two of the three shots, then guzzle a glass of water, that's a win.

When Griffin realizes I took his half shot, the look on his face intensifies and warms my belly more than the liquor.

Volunteers come around again with a basket of pickle chips and cocktail toothpicks stuck to a foam board, and suddenly, the bar is a giant cafeteria food fight, with grown adults in various states of inebriation hurling pickle slices at the targets and also at each other.

Ames tosses two without looking and lands them both. So do I. Ry tosses so hard, both his pickle slices fly off the table. Griffin appears to be calculating the trajectory of his shots. He lands one but not the other.

He and Ry take their penalty shots. Griffin, who's now had two and a half shots in ten minutes, coughs and sputters.

"Y'okay?" I demand.

"*Dandy*," he says, sticking his chin high in the air.

Someone at the table next to ours overhears and repeats it to his teammates. They all *howl*, like it's the wittiest thing they've heard in years, and yell, "That's the spirit, Griffin."

I roll my eyes because *come on*, but I feel my face stretch into a grin against my will.

Griffin's pun doesn't get me, but his chin tilt does.

"You look ridiculous right now," I mutter, reaching out a finger to flick that raised chin.

Hazel eyes flick to mine. "And yet you keep looking."

*True.*

Round two is the Brine-Balance Sprint. Think tape line on the floor, mini gherkin on a spoon held high above our heads, and, *once again*, a bunch of people who have jobs and mortgages and the right to vote taking turns racing around the bar.

Ry goes first, tongue between his teeth, one arm holding the spoon high and the other out for balance. Ames takes the spoon from him and does his lap, steady as a metronome.

Griffin's three and a half shots in at this point, and when his turn comes, I see his hands aren't particularly steady. I move in behind him without thinking, my palm hovering over his lower back as he lifts the pickle spoon above his head.

"Short steps," I advise.

He shifts just enough to lean into my hand. "Bossy," he murmurs.

He makes it around without losing his pickle—*yes, I hear myself; no, I cannot believe it*—and when he hands me the spoon, our fingers brush in a way that hits me harder than alcohol.

Somehow, my hands think Griffin's back, his skin, are their jurisdiction.

When I finish the round with no calamities, Ames laughs.

"That summer you spent impersonating a tree's really paying off there, bruh." He lifts his own arms like distorted branches until I fling a leftover pickle chip at him, and he dissolves into tipsy laughter again.

"You did what?" Griffin demands.

"Grandpa Syrup, the sugar maple," Ames explains gleefully as I look around for more pickle chips to shut him up. "The kids loved him."

"It was in college," I say, still glaring at Ames. "My mom's friend runs the Koasek Highlands Tourism and Visitors' Center, and they gave me a small scholarship that came with certain… obligations."

Ames pipes up in an obnoxiously deep voice, "'*Grandpa Syrup says, I'mmmm rooting for you, kids!*' Go on, sing us the photosynthesis song."

I clamp my mouth shut, hot with embarrassment. Was I feeling fond of my siblings? I take it all back.

Griffin's already holding his stomach, doubled over with laughter. Ry's eyes are filled with wonder.

"*I get my energy from the sun! It helps me grow and have some fun!*" Ames sings.

"Oh my gosh! Could you write that down for me?" Ry demands. "My students would love it."

Griffin laughs so hard he can't catch his breath. "That is the best thing I've ever, ever heard," he gasps, leaning his head against my arm.

And I decide maybe it wasn't so embarrassing after all.

Round three somehow gets even sillier, which I truly didn't think was possible.

"Tilly-Dilly Tongue Twisters!" Raisa announces. "You need to read the words on your card three times, no mistakes."

"Easy," Griffin says as I sneak the extra shot away from him again. Three times, he repeats, "Six slick Big Dills downed a dainty Dandy."

Ry can't get through it without spraying vinegary consonants all over our table and ends up taking his punishment shot. Ames doesn't even try. He reaches for the rye and tosses back a couple of shots like he's decided to just get hammered.

When it's my turn, I get through two rounds before Griffin, who's tipsy as fuck and adorable with it, starts giggling at me.

"Sorry, sorry!" he gasps, face flushed. "It's just… your mouth… saying those words… I can't not laugh."

He's doubled over, so his arm's pressed against mine. The citrus-smoky fragrance of him is all around me, and once again, the noise starts to fade. It's just him and me in this bar, and he's so fucking beautiful. I want to tell him—

"Come on," Ry encourages me. "Say the words."

It takes me a minute to realize what the fuck he's talking about, and then my own face heats.

"Sex slick dills—" I begin.

Ames barks out a laugh and claps a hand over his mouth. "Sorry, bro—"

"Awww." Griffin leans over and pats my thigh in commiseration. His eyes are warm and teasing. "I thought you were better with your tongue than that, Axford."

I clench my teeth against the need to remind him just how good I can be with my tongue. But when I lean forward to take my punishment shots, Griffin's hand slides up my thigh, his fingers curling around, clenching into my muscle, and he doesn't move it.

Heat knifes through me so fast I forget to breathe. I look down at his long, capable fingers, then up at him. He doesn't pull back. He watches me watch him, chin tilted, cheeks rosy.

*Okay.* Fuck.

"Y'okay?" he asks, soft and smart-assed all at once.

"*Dandy*," I breathe, for his ears only. And I lay my palm over his knuckles, not to move him but to keep him.

Round four is "Pickle Pong"—basically beer pong, but with miniature mason jars and pickle juice instead of beer. The goal is to land ping-pong balls in your teammates' jars, and if you miss all three shots, you drink.

Griffin's gotten progressively more relaxed as the night's gone on, his usual sharp edges softened by alcohol and what I'm starting to see is genuine enjoyment. When he leans over the table to line up his first shot, I find myself studying the curve of his spine, the way his sweater rides up just enough to show a sliver of pale skin.

"Focus, city boy," I taunt.

"I *am* focused," he shoots back, not taking his eyes off the target. But his first shot bounces off the rim, and his second goes wide.

"You're trying to get in my head," he announces, straightening. Since I'm still sitting on my stool, he's a couple of inches taller than me, and I can tell he's enjoying that.

I feel like this is only fair since I can't get him out of mine, but I simply smirk. "Is it working?"

Griffin narrows his eyes, sets his shoulders, and goes back to lining up his third shot. "You know, my Aunt Jill was a drill instructor in the Marines. Before I went to college, she and Aunt Della decided they didn't want me getting hustled by frat boys, so they taught me beer pong."

"Yeah?" I say, intrigued despite myself.

"But Aunt Jill stood behind me the whole time yelling, 'YOU THROW LIKE MY GRANDMOTHER'S POODLE!' at the top of her lungs." He grins at the memory. "She said if I could sink shots while she was screaming at me, college boys would be easy." He bends over and lines up his shot again.

"YOU THROW LIKE MY GRANDMOTHER'S POODLE!" I bellow suddenly.

The whole bar turns to look at me, but Griffin doesn't flinch. His shot lands with a satisfying *plunk*.

"Yes! Told you! Suck it, Axford." He spins around, grinning, and stumbles slightly.

Without thinking, I catch him around the waist, and for a breath, we're pressed together—his hands on my shoulders, my hands at his waistband just under his sweater.

I move one finger—just one—in an arc across his bare skin, and he sucks in a breath like he's been electrocuted.

"Suck… what, exactly?" I murmur roughly.

Ry clears his throat loudly. "Uh, guys? It's Beckett's turn."

I reluctantly let go of Griffin, and he steps away, but only slightly. I can't tell if this is because he's feeling the same magnetic draw I am or because he's trying to distract me. Either way, I don't care. I'm just drunk enough to like him exactly where he is and to forget all the reasons I shouldn't.

"With those women in your life," I say as I get ready to take my shot. "I guess it's no wonder you don't find me intimidating."

Griffin's grin turns wicked, and he lowers his voice so only I can hear him. "Except when I'm doing… that thing we're not talking about."

The memory of Sunday night hits me like a freight train—Griffin on the couch, breathless and demanding—and my concentration completely shatters. My first shot goes so wide it nearly hits Ry at the next table.

"Fuck," I mutter, and Griffin's laugh is pure satisfaction.

Fortunately, I land the next shot easily.

"Beer pong champion of my freshman dorm," I brag unapologetically. "It was a big dorm."

He shakes his head sadly and teases, "I feel like you were one of those boys Aunt Jill warned me about."

"You're saying you would've avoided me?" I press a hand to my chest.

"No." His hazel eyes are brighter than the neon lights over the bar. "I'm saying I'd have challenged the fuck out of you every chance I got."

By round five, half the teams around the bar have forfeited. They're still doing the challenges, just for the fun of it, but they're too inebriated to actually follow the rules.

At our table, Ames is drunk but functional. Ry's gotten quieter as the night's worn on, which is interesting and probably for the best. Griffin's cheeks are flushed, his eyes are bright, and every time he laughs at something, the sound pinballs around my chest, lighting up several places.

I can't lie, at this point, I don't know the score, and I don't give a shit who wins or loses. I'm not drunk, but I'm pleasantly buzzed, and I want nothing more than to get Griffin alone somewhere. Fuck, *anywhere*. But he still seems to be having a good time, and I'm enough of a competitive bastard that as long as he's in, I'm in too.

"Final round!" Raisa announces. "The Pickle-Eating Contest! Each team member needs to eat a whole dill pickle as fast as possible. Last person to finish on each team takes a double Brine *or* a quadruple Dandy."

Griffin goes pale. "Oh, fuck."

I glance at him, then at the massive dill pickles being distributed—easily six inches long and thick as my thumb. I'm not thrilled about this challenge, myself, but Griffin looks like he's been asked to eat live scorpions.

"You really can't do pickles, huh?" I ask quietly.

"I will literally throw up on this table." He wrinkles his nose. "I hate to say it. I really hate to say it. But I think I'm gonna have to…"

"Hold up! Isn't there a pickle substitute?" I demand, just as Raisa's about to ring the bell. I'm not as polite as Ames, so I don't raise my hand and wait to be acknowledged.

"Not this time, I'm afraid," she says with a sympathetic wince for Griffin.

"We'll all forfeit!" Ames says firmly, though he can't quite seem to focus on Griffin's face. "In solidarity with our vinegar-hating brethren!"

Ry's already taken a bite of his pickle, but he puts it down immediately. "Yeah. Yes. Right. Solidarity!"

Griffin shakes his head. He looks solemn, and I wonder if he's drunker than I thought. "No, please. I don't want everyone to lose! I don't want *anyone* to lose—"

I take a deep breath and sigh it out, then grab Griffin's pickle—*don't* say it, seriously don't—and eat it along with my own, as fast as humanly possible.

"What are you doing?" Griffin demands.

"Told you I'd be your Vermont bodyguard," I mutter, reaching for a glass of water. "Apparently, that extends to pickles."

Is eating an enormous pickle the stupidest thing anyone's ever done for a guy he's attracted to? Considering I don't know shit about music but once learned how to play a Lynyrd Skynyrd song to impress a guy I had a crush on, I'm not sure I'm the best judge. It's not exactly slaying-dragons, highlight-reel-worthy shit.

But Griffin's staring at me like I've performed actual magic, so, you know. That kinda makes up for the fact that my bloodstream is now half sodium and I'll be entering a vinegar-induced delirium any minute.

"Why?" Griffin says softly.

I grin because I love that *why* has become an inside joke between us now. Griffin's genuine questions about Jim's treehouse have become a kind of shorthand for all the things that don't make logical sense... but feel right anyway.

"For the same reason my great-uncle built half a bridge," I say. "Because sometimes you just start building, even when you don't know where you're going."

The words hang between us, piercing the alcohol haze and making me wonder what the fuck I'm doing. I don't build bridges, period.

But then Raisa's voice says, "Alright! Choose your winners, teams!"

Ry says, "Shit, Griffin, you won!" and grabs Griffin's arm to hold it up.

One of Raisa's volunteers drops a blue ribbon with a pickle-shaped charm into his palm.

And Griffin launches himself at me in a hug that's pure joy. Well, joy and alcohol.

I stand and catch him around the waist again, lifting him slightly off his feet, and at that moment, I don't care who's watching or what it looks like. He's warm and solid in my arms, and the way he's looking at me makes me feel like my brain's been pumped full of helium.

He steps back quickly and looks at the charm. It says "Brine and Dandy Winner" along with the year, but Griffin's staring at it with quirked lips and shining eyes, like it's something more meaningful than a cheap trinket.

He lifts his gaze finally and looks at Ames, Ry, and me. "I don't deserve this," he protests, still clutching the charm. "I didn't actually win. Beckett ate my pickle!"

Several people at nearby tables dissolve into laughter at that, and Griffin turns red. I shake my head and groan.

"That's not—I didn't mean—"

"Quit while you're ahead, Mercer," I tease, and for once, he doesn't argue but subsides with a huff.

Raisa turns on some music, the volunteers clean up the remains of the Brine, and the room settles into this warm, communal feel. Like surviving this silly adventure together has brought us some kind of closeness.

It's strange because I've grown up in this town, you know? I've lived here my whole life, except for a few years at school. But somehow, in this moment, I feel like I *get* it for the first time.

Or, shit, maybe that's just the alcohol too.

But when Griffin's hand lands on my thigh a moment later, right where it was before, I don't fight the giddy feeling it stirs in me. I take his hand and press it harder against my leg, and he spreads his fingers against the denim. For a second, I let myself imagine I'm not just here with him, but *here with him*. That this is a feeling that could last for more than a minute. That, like True said, if I want something badly enough, I can figure out how to get it.

The noise of the bar continues around us—people congratulating each other, ordering a round, starting to think about heading home. But at our table, there's a bubble of quiet. Ry and Ames are having their own conversation about something in low voices, leaving Griffin and me in our own world.

Griffin's thumb traces a small circle on my leg, and I have to suppress a groan. When I look at him, his hazel eyes are dark and focused despite the alcohol.

"What are we doing here, Beckett?" he asks quietly, his voice barely audible.

There are a lot of answers to that question. Is he talking about tonight? About the Big Dill? About the fact that we haven't resolved anything regarding our easement dispute? About this thing that keeps drawing us together despite every reason we have to stay apart? About the way I keep touching him like I have a right to... and he keeps *letting me*?

I look down at his hand on my thigh, then back up at his face—flushed from the alcohol and the warmth of the bar, his eyes soft and questioning and a little vulnerable.

"No fucking clue," I admit. "But I don't want to stop."

# CHAPTER THIRTEEN

## GRIFFIN

After we get Ames to his apartment above Watchfire, the ride home is a blur of Holden's country music and the heart-thrumming sensation of Beckett pressed against me in the back seat. Since Holden's driving his official sheriff's vehicle, this means he's separated from us by a cage-type thing, which adds to the illicit feeling that I'm doing something I shouldn't.

Not that there's any law against one legal adult hoping to get railed so hard by another legal adult that he can feel it for a week. Not in Vermont, anyway.

But Beckett confessing, "I don't want to stop," keeps sloshing around in my head, along with the five thousand shots of rye I took and the message I got yesterday from Conor offering me a job—well, the possibility of one— back in New York.

And all of it's making me twitch with nervous energy.

Part of me knows I should, at this minute, be messaging Conor back to ask for a meet-up. Hell, I should have done it immediately yesterday. That I should be excited about the prospect that I might be employable again, in the *city* again, even if the job's not exactly what I'd hoped for.

Instead, I continued to leave his message on read and went to the Brine and Dandy.

*Foolish, foolish, foolish.*

I've never been a risk taker. I'm whatever the opposite of Jim's free spirit is. Beer pong with Aunt Jill aside, just knowing something could impede my climb up the corporate ladder was enough to get me to avoid it.

Beckett Axford is the first terrible idea I've been unable to resist. In fact, as Holden sings along to Kacey Musgraves about how love can make the ordinary shine, and Beckett grins at me sideways while his fingers toy with mine, I feel like I'm actively embracing it.

"Sure you can walk home from here, Griffin?" Holden asks with a knowing grin as he pulls a few feet into Beckett's driveway and the two of us climb out. "Chilly out there tonight."

I glance down the dark road, toward where my driveway should be on the opposite side. It looks very far away and very dark, but fortunately, I'm not actually planning on walking anywhere.

"Definitely." I wave a hand. "I'm highly adaptable. I can practically see in the dark. It's no problem."

"I believe you." Holden grins, and I decide he might be my second favorite Axford.

I don't realize I've said this out loud until Holden laughs and demands to know which sibling's beaten him out for the top slot. "It's Ames," he teases. "Isn't it?"

Beckett glares dangerously. "Aren't there some ducklings crossing the road somewhere who need your assistance, Sheriff?"

Holden's grin widens. "Have fun, boys. Play nice."

Beckett flips him off, which only makes Holden laugh again as he drives away and leaves Beckett and me in the cold, dark woods.

Once we're alone, Beckett turns to me and brushes the hair off my forehead. If he were anyone else, I'd probably dodge away, but thanks to some strange magic—or possibly multiple previous orgasms—Beckett's gotten beneath my personal space force field. It no longer recognizes him as *other*.

"Hi," Beckett says.

I shiver slightly inside my fleece, and not from the chilly autumn bite in the air. "H-hi."

He curls an arm around me and pulls me against his side. "I was hoping you'd come inside for a drink, but if you—"

"Yes!" I blurt. I feel myself go hot despite the cold, despite everything. The last thing I need is more to drink, but I'm hoping Beckett means *drink* in the sense of *fuck*.

Beckett wraps his arm around my shoulders as we walk up the rest of the long driveway, his steps sure and certain despite the alcohol and the near-total darkness.

"Quiet out here, huh?" I whisper, and for the first time, I mean it in a good way. I *like* that the only sounds I can hear are our mingled breaths, the sounds of our feet crunching the leaves in sync.

"Not so quiet," Beckett disagrees. "But you have to be still to hear the sounds. When I was a kid, I'd drag a sleeping bag into this clearing in the woods. I'd try to stay perfectly silent so the animals would forget I was there just so I could feel like part of the forest."

I laugh because I can picture it. "Meanwhile, I dragged a blanket out onto the fire escape so I could listen to the sirens and the people playing music down the block and feel like part of the city."

Beckett leads me up the three porch steps to his cabin. It's a squat little house that's almost exactly what I had in mind when I learned I'd inherited Jim's property, and it's every bit as homey, if not nearly as whimsical. The living room is all warm wood and comfortable furniture—a worn leather sofa, a coffee table, plaid fleece blankets, and a crocheted afghan—arranged in front of a fireplace laid with actual logs. On the wall over the couch hangs an acoustic guitar.

I grin. "You liar! You said you don't play anymore."

"I don't," Beckett insists, heading for the kitchen. "I like how it looks, but I haven't played in decades."

"Not since that boy sophomore year broke the music in you?" I lean against the kitchen door. "I think I saw a Disney Channel movie just like that. Or was it the photosynthesis song that made you give it all up?"

Beckett snorts, and the look he gives me is heated, but he asks, "You want water, whiskey, or both?"

"How about… neither." I step across the small kitchen and slide both hands up his chest.

He immediately sucks in a breath. He's so much bigger than me, but it turns out I really like that. I might have accused him of being bossy, but when he and I are together, there's not a doubt in my mind he'd rather cut off those big hands than use them in any way I don't want him to.

"I was hoping that the *come in for a drink* thing was code," I say. "For *come in and get naked.*"

"It was…" he admits, wrapping those big hands around my waist. His hands push my sweater up just far enough that his calloused thumbs rub the skin of my ribs. It's just a thing he does. A habit, and it's kind of a mind-fuck that I've been with Beckett enough that we have *habits.*

I'm so damn mushy.

"…and it wasn't," he finishes.

Already I'm struggling to hold on to the conversation. Like every time Beckett touches me, I get this electric hum in my blood, this feeling that part of me wants to savor the anticipation of what's about to happen and part of me wants him to hurry up, to tear my clothes off *right now*, to put those thick fingers around my cock or in my ass.

The other part of me, the Sensible Griffin who wants to remind me that being with Beckett is just a deflection from the myriad things I don't want to think about, has had enough alcohol that he's bound and gagged in the corner of my brain, which is convenient.

"It was *and* wasn't? What's that mean?" I demand, moving closer to feel the solid heat of him against me.

"It means I wanted to be with you. For sex, yeah, but also to talk about… shit, I don't know. Your pickle aversion, or the kind of music you like, or your weird aunts, or why you think Vermont's trying to kill you but you're apparently still determined to lure tourists to come visit, why you decided to come here in the first place?" He shrugs. "Any of those things, really."

My fingers slide up to clench in the hair that curls over his nape. "Okay. Well. That's… You're not what I expected," I hear myself say, and I wish I could blame alcohol, but I can't entirely. For saying it out loud, maybe, but not for feeling it.

"Same," he admits. "It was easier when I thought you were an entitled city boy out to destroy my company. The guy standing between me and what I needed to keep my business afloat. But then you turned out to be funny. And smart. And you get along with my siblings better than I do. And…"

Beckett's hands move up my sides—only an inch, but there's *possession* in that inch. I want that. To be possessed by him. I have no fucking idea what's happening to me right now.

I dart my tongue out to wet my lips. "And?"

"And you're so goddamn *hot*." His fingers clench into my skin, and my breath catches. "I can't see you and not want to touch you. To have you look at me. To see you smile. I feel like…"

"Like I'm losing my mind," I breathe.

"*Yes*," he groans.

And then I'm kissing him, and he's kissing me, and it tastes a little like maple rye and a whole lot like possibility.

This isn't like last time or the times before. There's heat —god, so much glorious heat—but no anger, no feeling that I'm using Beckett as a distraction. There is nowhere in the world I want to be except right here.

I sink into it, into the warmth and the wanting. I forget about land disputes and family fuckery, about all the reasons this isn't just complicated but impossible.

His hands frame my face, thumbs stroking over my cheekbones as he kisses me, and I make a sound more soft and helpless than I thought I was capable of. But there's no room for self-consciousness when Beckett's tongue is in my mouth, when his hands are clasping my back and reaching down to mold my ass, forcing me to stop thinking and just feel.

"Tell me what you want," he demands breathlessly.

Oh fuck. So many things.

I want to forget about Derek Sullivan and the town council and the ticking clock on my time in Winsome. I want to stop thinking about my uncertain future and complicated legacies and just… just *be*. I want him to touch me everywhere, and for me to touch him back. I want to hear the sounds he makes when he comes apart.

"You," I say, since that encompasses all of it. "I want you to fuck me. Please, Beckett."

Heat flares in his eyes, and then he's kissing me again, deeper this time, his hands moving up my sides again to pull my sweater over my head.

Cool air hits my skin, but before I have time to shiver, Beckett's mouth is at my throat, my collarbone, sucking bruises into the skin where my neck meets my shoulder. His beard scrapes against the sensitized skin, and I arch into him, wanting more.

He backs me into the kitchen table, which I belatedly realize is covered in paperwork and a laptop only when I reach back my hands to brace myself.

"Bedroom," I gasp. "Bed. Room. *Now*."

"And you say I'm bossy," he teases.

He wraps his arms around my waist and half carries, half pushes me down a short hallway to a bedroom lit by a single bedside lamp.

I am not a person given to being manhandled—I'm way too big and some might say too prickly—but when

Beckett grabs me by the waist and deposits me on his huge bed, I can barely get out a cry of protest before he's climbing over me, pressing me into flannel sheets that smell like him, and then he's kissing me again.

I suddenly wonder if maybe there's something to this being-manhandled business after all.

When Beckett climbs off to shed his henley and jeans, I make a noise of appreciation. God, the man is built like he was carved from a tree—thick thighs, muscular chest scattered with dark hair, arms that could bench-press a small car… or lift a whole-ass New Yorker onto a bed, as the case might be. And his cock is so thick and long it makes my mouth water and my ass clench.

"Get the rest of this shit off." He reaches for my belt with a predatory grin that I feel in my balls.

"I say you're bossy because you *are* bossy," I feel the need to point out.

"And you love it," he shoots back, which is…

Accurate. *Fuck.*

He pulls down my jeans and boxers, and I lift my hips to help him. Then he stands by the side of the bed and stares down at me.

It should feel weird or clinical, the way he's looking me over. I'm twelve shades of pale, thin but not muscular, while he is, through some unfair whim of DNA, a golden-tan, dark-haired Adonis from head to toe. But the way he's looking at me—it feels like *worship*.

My dick's so hard it's aching, and I can't help reaching down to stroke myself once.

Beckett's eyes darken as he watches me touch myself, his own cock twitching in response. "Fuck, you're gorgeous," he growls, his voice rough. "Look at you, already so hard for me. You want my mouth on you, Griff?"

My hand stutters on my shaft. "I want your mouth everywhere," I admit, my voice breathy. "But I want your cock in me more."

He groans, low and guttural, and drops to his knees beside the bed. His hands grip my thighs, spreading them wide, and then his mouth is on my cock—hot, wet, and relentless. I gasp, my back arching off the bed as he takes me deep, his tongue swirling around the head before he pulls back just enough to say, "You taste so fucking good."

"Fuck, Beckett—" My fingers tangle in his hair, not guiding, just holding on as he works me over, his lips tight, his tongue doing things that make my toes curl. But as good as it feels, it's not what I need. "I want you inside me. Now."

He pulls off with a wet pop, his lips glistening, and grins up at me. "Patience, city boy. I'm gonna make you beg for it."

I whimper, my hips jerking up. "I *am* begging. Please, Beckett, I need you to fuck me."

He chuckles, the sound dark and satisfied, and presses a kiss to the inside of my thigh. "Not yet." His breath is hot against my skin as he moves lower, his tongue dragging over my balls before he nips at the sensitive skin behind them. I shudder, my legs trembling.

*Oh. My. God.*

Then his mouth is on my hole, his tongue flat and insistent. His hands grasp the backs of my thighs, pressing them to my chest, and no word of a lie, no hint of exaggeration—I see stars. Entire constellations of them, pinwheeling against the backs of my eyelids. "Oh fuck. That's—fuck, Beckett—"

"You like that?" His voice is a rumble against my skin, his fingers spreading me open as he licks again, slow and deliberate. "You like my tongue in your ass?"

"Yes—god, yes—" My voice breaks, my hands fisting in the sheets. The sensation is overwhelming, the wet heat of his mouth, the brush and scrape of his beard, the way he's holding me open like I'm his to devour. The way I *want* to be his to devour. "More. Please, more."

He doesn't make me ask twice. His tongue pushes inside, fucking me in slow, deep strokes that have me babbling, my cock leaking onto my stomach. "You're so tight," he murmurs, pulling back just enough to speak. "Gonna have to stretch you out good before I can get my cock in here."

I groan, my head thrashing on the pillow. "Just do it. I don't care. Get in there."

Beckett chuckles again, the vibration making me whimper. "*I* care," he says gently. "I'm not hurting you." He reaches for the nightstand, pulling out lube and a condom. I watch, dazed, as he rolls the condom on, his cock thick and veined, the sight of it making my hole clench in anticipation.

He slicks his fingers, pressing one against my already-wet rim. "Relax, baby. Let me in."

I try, but I'm wound so tight, I'm literally trembling with need. His first finger slides in easily, though, and I moan, my hips rocking down to meet it. "M-more. Now. I can take it."

"Greedy little thing," he murmurs with something like

affection, adding a second finger, scissoring them to stretch me. "Gonna feel so good around my cock."

"Fuck, yes—" I'm panting now, my body burning, my skin too sensitive. "Beckett, please—"

He adds a third finger, crooking them just right, and I cry out, my cock jerking. "There it is," he growls. "Right there. You're gonna come so hard when I hit this spot with my dick."

"Fuck me," I demand. My voice is desperate, and I don't care one bit. "Why are you taking so long?"

He chuckles and pulls his fingers out, lining his cock up with my entrance. "You ready?"

"Fuck you."

He pushes in slowly, inch by inch, blue eyes locked on mine. The stretch burns, but it's so, so *good*, especially when he bottoms out and I feel him everywhere.

"Christ, Griffin," he groans. "You feel incredible."

I want to agree, but I can't even form words. So I just nod, my nails digging into his thick shoulders as he starts to move. He's big, so big, and it's been a while, but the way he's filling me, the way he's looking at me—it's worth every second of the burn.

"You okay?" he asks, his voice strained.

"Move," I gasp. "P-please. Please!"

"So polite, city boy," he teases. But he does move, finally, pulling out almost all the way before slamming back in, and when I cry out, it's like the sound is torn from my throat. "Like that?"

"Yes—fuck, yes—"

He sets a punishing rhythm, his hips snapping against mine, his cock hitting my prostate so perfectly that my vision whites out.

"This ass is mine now," he growls, his hands gripping my hips hard enough to bruise. "Say it."

I hesitate. Beckett doesn't know it, but I don't say shit like that. Not even in bed. I've built a whole life where all of me is *my own*, and that's exactly how I like it.

But in that moment, with Beckett moving inside of me, with the smell of cedar and sex all over me... I want to be his. I want it to be true. At least for right now.

"It's yours," I moan, the words spilling out. "Fuck, all yours."

"Damn right." His thrusts get harder, deeper, his breath coming in ragged gasps. "Gonna make you come so hard you forget your own name."

I can feel it building, the pressure coiling tight in my gut. My cock is trapped between us, leaking, aching. "I need... Beckett... I need to touch myself," I beg. "I need to come."

"Yeah?" He wraps his hand around my shaft instead, and it's a thousand... a *million*... times better. "Give it up to me, Griffin. Let me feel you."

I don't know if I have any say in the matter. My orgasm crashes over me, my cock pulses in his grip, my ass clenches around him, and I come harder than I ever have in my life.

Beckett groans and stills, his eyes burning into mine as he watches me like he's soaking in every ounce of my pleasure, and I swear my empty balls give one last spurt just from the look in his eyes.

He pulls out of me gently, and I whimper, my empty hole twitching at the loss. But then he rips off the condom, runs a hand over the mess I made of my stomach, and starts jacking himself.

*Dear. Fucking. God.*

He's working himself roughly, showing off for me as he kneels between my thighs, letting me see just how much he loves this. His thighs tremble, his breath hitches every time his thumb grazes the head of his dick, his fist makes an obscene *shlick shlick shlick* sound as it slides over his glistening cock, and I think, *That's me all over him. My* cum marking his skin, like he's every bit as much *mine* as I am *his.*

Once again, I get that sensation that I've only ever had with Beckett. That letting him have me doesn't make me weak; it makes me fucking powerful.

I want to taste him like I did the other day. I want to lick his fingers clean. Want to throw him down and kiss every fucking inch of his too-perfect skin until he's begging. But I'm too spent to move. So instead, I lie there watching him like he watched me earlier and try to show him just how fucking gorgeous I think he is.

"Come on," I whisper. "Come for me, baby."

Yeah, I don't know where the *baby* comes from, but the word feels right. And the second it leaves my lips, Beckett's eyes flare, his breathing stutters, his cock jerks, and his whole body tenses. His lips part, and his eyes roll back, and then his cum lands in thick stripes against my stomach, mixing us together.

It's glorious, and that… freaks me right the fuck out.

This was supposed to be a physical thing. Just sex. But I'm very afraid I've gone and caught feelings. I'm not just a little mushy. I'm… I'm gone for this guy.

*Dear god.* What have I done?

While I'm lying there, letting this avalanche of reality hit me full-on, Beckett has gotten up and gone… somewhere. He comes back a minute later with a warm, wet cloth and starts to clean me off.

"I'll do it!" I croak, grabbing for the washcloth. "I'm perfectly capable of—"

"Of course you can, but I want to," he says, not stopping. "So let me."

He says *let him* like it's no big thing. I don't think he understands that for me, it really is.

When he's done, he throws the towel aside, flops beside me in the bed, and pulls a soft blanket up to cover us, tucking us in for the night.

I should move. I should get up and walk myself home. No part of me is drunk anymore, and my thoughts are buzzing around my head like gnats. I've never had a panic attack come out of nowhere before, but if I had, I imagine this is what it would feel like. A creeping cold, starting at my extremities and moving toward my heart, while I can't remember how to move or even how to breathe.

"Griffin," Beckett says, rolling into me and laying one huge arm over my middle. "Stay." He presses a kiss to my hair and whispers, "Just... stay."

For a while? For the night? For... longer?

I should know the answers to these things. I shouldn't keep doing this until I know what I'm doing. But *god*, the warmth of him pressed up next to me seeps into my skin and deeper, into my bones. It pushes back the cold. It stops the buzzing.

"Okay," I whisper. "Yeah. Okay."

I wake up early the next morning, needing to pee. My mouth is dry as the Sahara, but my head's surprisingly clear, considering how many Dandies I downed. Someone —Beckett, clearly—left a light on in the living room and plugged my phone into a charger on the nightstand, which is really freaking sweet.

When I grab the phone, the display reads 4:47 AM. Even Beckett, who I assume operates on some rise-at-dawn lumberjacky internal clock, is dead to the world beside me, his arm thrown over his face, his breathing deep and even.

I read a book once where the author described someone's face as being "relaxed in sleep," and I thought I knew what it meant. But Beckett's face is somehow even more appealing when he's sleeping. He looks vulnerable. Gorgeously, entirely mortal. His mouth is pouty, without the usual tension that keeps it smirking or scowling, and I have the most terrifying urge to trace his bottom lip with my finger. Or my tongue.

And this, friends, is why I don't do sleepovers. Way too much opportunity for mushiness. I can feel the mush taking me over.

I slip out of bed quietly, trying not to wake Beckett, and find my discarded clothes on the dresser. I grab them and head for the bathroom.

The guy in the mirror looks nothing like me. Not only did my brain decide to stop functioning last night, but so did my hair product. My hair is a horrifying mess of dandelion fluff sticking straight off my head. Thank fuck Beckett didn't see *me* asleep.

One more reason I don't do sleepovers.

I retrieve my shoes from Beckett's room and creep toward the door. I'll text him later. I'll explain my early departure… somehow.

But as I pass through the living room, I notice that under the guitar is a little gallery of photos hung in a line.

All the frames are matching, and they're arranged in a cute pattern that makes me think Vivian had a hand in this.

I dart a glance at the bedroom, then pad closer to the pictures to take just a quick peek.

My reward is immediate because the first picture is of a man standing in front of an Axford Lumber sign, holding an adorable baby who's obviously his copy/paste miniature, right down to their jeans and flannel shirts. The baby's got four teeth, and they're all on display as he scowls ferociously at the camera from his father's arms, and I snicker because I'd know that scowl anywhere.

The next is of a teenage Beckett with an axe thrown over his shoulder and a mop of brown hair flopping over his forehead like he was trying for emo rocker and ended up serving Justin Bieber. He's standing in the woods with his arm slung around another Axford, while a littler boy with a sunshiny grin—Ames—hams it up in the foreground, and their father looks on with a smile.

The next is of Beckett in a cap and gown at college graduation, flanked by beaming parents.

Mixed in with these are other shots—Beckett and Eliza with a blue-ribbon pumpkin, all the Axford siblings in Red Sox T-shirts, dangling from tree branches. And inexplicably, there's a photo of what appears to be a very tall sugar maple wearing a ranger hat, which makes me bite my lip to keep from laughing out loud.

But it's the ones of Beckett and his dad that get me for some reason. Beckett says his dad doesn't like how he's running Axford Lumber, and it's hard to reconcile that with the pride and love in these pictures.

"I swear to god, if you make fun of my teenage hair,

I'm resigning as your bodyguard. Vermont can have at you."

I jump a foot and whirl to find Beckett, wearing only a pair of low-slung pajama pants, leaning against the doorway. His dark hair is messy, and his smile is so relaxed and happy it makes my breath go wonky.

"Hey," I say. "Did I wake you? I was just..." I glance down at the shoes in my hand.

"Spying?" Beckett quirks an eyebrow. "Trying to dig up dirt on your Big Dill competition?"

I laugh despite myself. How does he *do* that?

"You caught me," I say. "I was looking for evidence of your guitar-playing days and the boy who broke your heart—"

"Jesus. I don't think I've thought about Thad Gates as much in twenty years as I have since you came to town." Beckett yawns and scratches his chest before pushing off the doorframe. "You want some coffee?"

I follow him to the kitchen, still clutching my escape shoes, because I can't *not*. Because I like him so much it overwhelms my common sense.

He heads for the coffee maker, and I drop my shoes and sit at the table, nudging aside the laptop and papers scattered across the surface. "I have a fascination with Thad Gates. I imagine him moving to Boston is where your dislike of city folk began. Your poor broken heart."

Beckett laughs, the sound warm and genuine. "Remind me again what you do for a living? Because you could totally write for a soap opera."

"Drawn from the pages of my own life," I agree. "Marketing professional from the big city loses job, becomes

TikTok scandal, inherits weird treehouse in a tiny town, meets local lumberjack—"

"We prefer the term *forestry professional*," Beckett corrects. He winks, and then his expression grows more serious. "You, ah, mentioned something the other day about being… unemployable? But then yesterday, that presentation you came up with was amazing. So… what happened?"

I suck in a breath. Beckett Axford seems like one of the few people in the world who hasn't seen the billboard video trending on social media. But that also means he's one of the few people I can tell this story who doesn't already have any preconceptions.

So I pour out my tale of billboard woe, and the words come easier in the pre-dawn quiet of Beckett's kitchen, with coffee brewing and his patient attention focused entirely on me as he leans against the counter.

I tell him about my years of work and my dreams of making a big splash. About how I'd poured my heart into the Rise campaign, and I'd been so sure I was getting a promotion. How it felt when that big splash started with a forty-two-story fall from grace. How I'd felt betrayed by Erick and Alan… hell, by the whole city of New York.

"I loved that job," I say, because that's the part that still hurts the most. "I know it sounds stupid, loving marketing of all things, but I was really good at it. And now I'll forever be remembered as the guy who greenlit the most expensive dick joke in Times Square history."

Beckett's expression has darkened as he listened, and when I'm done, he growls, "Jesus, I want to find this Erick kid and beat the crap out of him until he tells the truth."

Hearing that feels better than it should.

"Yeah, well, even if Erick came clean tomorrow, I can't imagine an employer would believe it. Not enough to hand me a million-dollar ad campaign. I'd still have to prove myself again. Rebuild from the beginning. Or build something new." I meet his eyes and admit, "I got a job offer yesterday. Or at least an offer to talk about the possibility of a job."

"You did? Back in New York?" He studies my face and frowns. "Wait, that's... that's a good thing, right?"

"Yes. Probably?" My hands flail a little. "An old friend from college is starting an image consulting company. It's more PR than creative marketing and would mean starting at the very bottom again. Maybe lower than the bottom, if people remember my name. And we haven't talked salary yet. But... it might be fun. And would get me back to New York. So... I don't know."

Beckett pours two cups of coffee and brings me one, settling in the chair across from me.

"I don't know what the fuck I'm doing," I admit. "It's like I took a wrong turn somewhere, and I have no map for getting where I want to go."

"I understand," Beckett says quietly, his gaze drifting toward the living room, where the pictures of him with his father hang.

Something in his voice makes me look at him more closely. "Your dad?"

He nods abstractedly. "My dad and I were close. I mean, he loved all his kids equally, but he and I... we both love this land, the forest. I was his shadow. I wanted to be Grant Axford when I grew up. And he, uh... he made some not-great business decisions, before he had his heart attack. I didn't—don't—know how to reconcile that mess with the responsible guy I knew. *Know.* And it's not enough that I'm fixing the mess, he's gotta critique the way I'm doing it. *Let me show you how it's done, Beckett.* And I want to say, *You were the one who fucked it all up.* He gave me a legacy to protect, but protecting it means losing my relationship with him, and—fuck. Sorry. I didn't mean to dump all this on you."

I focus on my coffee because... good lord. I'd been trying to sneak out to *avoid* this kind of closeness, but here I am, reveling in it.

And suddenly, I *hate* that there's a list of things we're not supposed to talk about.

"Beckett, about the easement—"

"Stop." Serious blue eyes meet mine. "Look, I've been thinking about that, and I'm not going to pressure you about an easement anymore. That's not... any part of what this is."

"But Axford Lumber still needs access to that land." I frown. "It's hurting your business, not being able to access it."

Beckett shrugs, a nonanswer. "That's not on you, Griff. You want to keep the property intact and protect your inheritance, to take your time to think about the decision, and I get it. If I'd been thinking rationally, I'd have admitted that from the beginning."

"But—"

"Look, I'm not saying I'm giving up on the easement. Not at all. I'm just saying... we'll let the town council decide. Or the court. Or, I don't know, maybe I can work out a deal with whoever you sell the land to when you move back to New York." He forces a smile that sits wrong on his handsome face. "Assuming it's not Derek Sullivan.

I'm saying I want you to make the choice that's right for you on your own time, okay? You've had enough choices taken away from you recently."

My eyes sting, and the mushiness is spreading, suffusing my whole body. "You mean that?"

"Absolutely." His smile shifts and warms.

"Thank you," I whisper. "Because what I really want to do, what I'm *choosing* to do, is offer you a temporary agreement. You can bring your trucks through Monday and access your land to… cut whatever you need to cut for right now. And then, after I've talked to an attorney about it, we can reassess."

"No," he argues. "Griffin—"

"You said you're supporting my choices. Supporting me doing what I want. Well, that's what I want," I say fiercely. And the second it's out of my mouth, it feels so right, I wish I'd done this two weeks ago. I wish I hadn't been too *scared* to do it then. "I know you'd prefer something official, and you don't want to rely on handshake deals, but I—"

Beckett stands up and holds out a hand. "From you? I'll take the handshake."

The moment our palms connect, something electric passes between us. His hand is warm and calloused and steady, and for a second, I can't let go.

*Does he trust me that much?*

"Thank you," he says simply, and the sincerity squeezes my heart just as surely as his hand squeezes mine.

I pull my hand back. "Maybe, um… maybe you should talk to your dad. I mean, I know jack shit about father-son stuff, but… only a fool would care more about a legacy than his relationship with you. And the guy in those pictures—" I gesture toward the living room. "He looks like a person who loves his son."

The words hit me as soon as I say them. Beckett's father cares more about his son than about any legacy.

Unlike Jim, who built me a treehouse but never wanted me to know he was my father. Who left me this inheritance but opted not to have a relationship with me as an adult while he was still alive.

All of a sudden, the kitchen feels too small, too warm. Beckett's looking at me with concern, and I can see him starting to reach across the table, but I refuse to fall apart.

"I should go," I say abruptly, pushing back from the table. "I promised Milo I'd buy him a dozen jars of pickles, if you can believe it, so he can share the health benefits with his new wellness influencer friends. Which, like, should be against some kind of friendship code, right? Given how pickles are against my religion?" I'm babbling brightly, and I can't stop it.

"Griffin—" Beckett says.

But I'm already grabbing my shoes, fumbling with the laces. "Thanks for coffee. And for… you know. Last night. It was fun. Right?"

He nods slowly. "Sure."

"But we both know it's…" My hands flail. "It's complicated."

"Right." Beckett narrows his eyes. "Griff, baby, are you okay?"

*Ugh.* The *baby* hits me square in the chest, making me feel warm and terrified at the same time.

"Yeah, of course," I manage around a smile that feels like it might crack my face. "I'm always okay."

I practically run for the door. I hear Beckett say my name again, but I'm already outside in the cold morning air, sucking in deep breaths. Part of me wants to turn back, but leaving feels cleaner. *Safer.*

Only when I'm halfway down his driveway do I realize that I feel *less* safe the further from Beckett Axford I get. And the closer I get to Jim's treehouse—my treehouse— the more the burning behind my eyes intensifies.

I should be happy about the temporary truce, about the job offer, about having some kind of plan again.

But I have no fucking idea what I want anymore.

And I am definitely not okay.

# CHAPTER FOURTEEN

## BECKETT

I'M THINKING about Griffin as I walk down Whether Street later that morning, after Eliza gave me a ride to town to pick up my truck.

This is not new. It feels like I've been thinking about nothing *but* Griffin for the past couple of weeks. Now I just have a whole bunch of new stuff to obsess over.

Like the goofy grin on his face when he looked at the photos Mom and Eliza hung on my wall, and how vulnerable he'd looked when he talked about losing the job he loved… and the way he practically fled my cabin like it was on fire later.

The temporary truce he offered should make me feel better, but instead, I'm worried about him. The man who teased me and claimed me at the Brine and Dandy, who turned off the gravity in my brain last night, was shaken.

I don't know how to fix those problems if he doesn't want to talk to me, though. And fuck knows, I have problems of my own I've been avoiding…

Shit I'm not putting off any longer.

When I arrive at Watchfire, my dad's already sitting in his usual booth by the window, nursing a cup of coffee and staring out at the street with the distant look he gets when he's thinking too hard about something. His crossword puzzle sits untouched at his elbow.

But he's here. And that says something.

I slide into the booth across from him, and he looks up with a smile.

"Thanks for meeting me," I say.

"Course. I was glad to get your text." He gestures to Tania, one of Ames's servers, and she brings over another cup of coffee. "I was planning to help your mother with the fall decorations over at the Abigail. We were gonna play my favorite game, *That Garland's Too High, Grant! That Garland's Too Low, Grant!*" He shakes his head fondly. "When she heard you texted, she got Ames to pinch-hit for the first round."

I laugh, and it's so freaking normal and good—easier than we've talked in ages—that I *almost* take it as a conversational peace offering. And almost punt the hard stuff.

But Holden was right that this has gone on too long, and True's words are still playing in my head. Even Griffin saw something in those photos that made him sure I've been misinterpreting things. It's past time I stop running from this conversation.

That doesn't mean I know how to start it, though.

I take a deep breath. "So, ah… we have temporary access to the Far Tract, starting Monday. In case you were stressing about that."

His eyebrows shoot up. "Griffin agreed to let you through?"

"He did. This morning."

Dad nods. "And that's why you texted?" He gives me a lopsided grin and taps his chest. "Wanted to make sure I wasn't putting too much stress on the ticker?"

"That, yeah." I pause. "Actually, that's not the only thing I wanted to talk about. I've been… I think I've been handling things wrong. Between us, I mean."

Dad sets down his coffee cup and gives me his full attention.

"I was angry at you," I admit. "About the land sale. About the finances. About you not telling me. And I know… I know you were doing your best, so maybe that's not fair of me, but—"

"I fucked up," Dad interrupts. "I know it, Beck. I knew it, even while it was happening." He turns his mug carefully one way and then the other. For a long moment, he doesn't say anything, just stares out the window at the morning foot traffic. Finally, he sighs. "I just thought I'd have plenty of time to make it right before you ever had to know."

I wasn't expecting him to admit it so directly. A weight that's been sitting on my chest for a year starts to lift. "Dad—"

"Let me finish. Please. I've wanted to talk to you about this for a while, but I… I guess I didn't know how." His eyes, a match to my own, meet mine across the table. "From the moment you showed the first sign of loving Axford Lumber, of wanting it to be your future, I had a dream of leaving you a strong, thriving business. A solid foundation that you could launch even higher. Instead, I left you with a mess, scrambling to save something I should've saved myself. And I'm sorry about that. Really damn sorry."

Tania bustles over to deliver my coffee and a plate of cinnamon rolls she says Ames baked this morning. Dad gives her a polite smile, but as soon as she's gone, his smile fades.

"It's like this, Beck: I was ashamed. I didn't want to admit I'd messed up. That's why I didn't tell you. It was pride, pure and simple. I believed in the way I was running things. I believe in helping our neighbors, in serving our community. But folks had a few bad years, couldn't pay when they should. I took out loans I thought were temporary… And I let it go too far."

He looks tired, and my throat tightens because I can see how much this conversation is costing him. Before I can say that, though, he leans forward and speaks again.

"It sucks getting old, son. And that's not an excuse, I'm not trying to make it one. I just want you to understand where my head's been at, okay?"

When I nod, he continues. "I lived my life like I had unlimited time left. I always figured it was fine to delay the vacations your mom wanted to take, to keep doing what I'd been doing with the business, because I knew in my heart it was right. I believed things would settle down eventually, and *then* I could make changes I knew I needed to make."

"It didn't work like that."

"I don't think it works like that for *anyone*, but yeah, it damn sure didn't for me." He shakes his head ruefully and taps his chest again. "Five stents were not part of the game plan. And that meant it fell to you to fix my mistakes. And let me tell you, there's nothing more humbling than watching your kid, the man you taught to be take-charge and responsible, struggling with the weight of a burden you gave him."

"But if you know you messed up, why do you keep criticizing how I'm doing things?" The question comes out gentler than I expected. "I'm trying to take care of the business like you taught me—"

"Criticize?" He looks honestly confused. "Beckett, I've only been trying to help you. I'm *worried* about you. You're killing yourself, just like I did. Making the same mistakes I made, just shooting yourself in the opposite foot, so to speak."

I frown. "What's that supposed to mean?"

He holds up a hand like he can tell I'm getting defensive. "You've decided the problems with Axford are *yours alone* to solve. You don't want to burden anyone else or ask for help from your family. And the harder it gets, the lonelier you feel."

I close my mouth because… fuck. He's not wrong.

Dad's lips twitch. "I didn't do everything right, Beck. But I did learn *some* things over the years. And I know what stubborn pride looks like. Now that I'm not the guy running the office, working the schedules, writing out the insurance checks every month… I see other things a little more clearly too. For one, I see the toll it's taking on you."

"It's manageable—"

"Beckett," he chides.

"Okay, it's hard sometimes. But it was hard for you too. That's just… how it goes."

"But it isn't, son. It's not supposed to be. And if that's what you learned from me, then I fucked up even bigger than I thought. Of course there'll be long days and lean seasons, but that's when you need to rely on your family, on your crew, on your community. And if running the business is coming between you and your family, between you and having a support system? Then shut it down, Beck. Simple as that. Shut. It. Down."

I stare at him. I literally never dreamed he'd say such a thing.

"I won't be the guy who lets Axford Lumber fail four generations in," I argue. "Besides, I love the company. The crew. The *land*. Protecting the forest and sustaining it for the future is all I've ever wanted to do. You taught me that."

Dad nods. "And I felt the same. Which meant I needed to be the one to keep it going. It was *my* company, right? And all that single-minded focus cost me was my health and, to some extent, my relationship with you." His mouth twists, and he looks pained. "Some things aren't worth the sacrifice."

*Jesus.* My nose tingles, and I have to look down at my coffee. All this time, I've been so focused on fixing his mistakes that I never stopped to consider how he felt about making them.

"When's the last time you went to the Shed just to have a drink with friends?" he demands. "When's the last time you let the town support you instead of holding everyone at arm's length?"

"Actually," I say slowly. "Last night. I was at the Brine and Dandy." I fill him in on the events of the night... at least the part that happened at the bar.

Dad snorts. "Well, if that's what comes of you going out for Big Dill, then I guess it's worth it. So... you and Griffin are getting along, huh?"

The caginess in his voice makes me groan. "Please don't. There are enough matchmakers in this town."

He laughs out loud. "I'll stick to my crossword puzzles," he promises. "But I am curious what changed this kid's mind about the land access."

"Griffin's not a kid," I say firmly. "He's a good man, and he was trying to do the right thing. To look out for his property and not make rash decisions. He's been going through a stressful time too."

Dad's eyebrows rise slightly. "That so?"

"Yeah, and…" I hesitate, then figure *what the hell*. "He's leaving Winsome soon. He's already got one job offer back in New York. He'll be back in the city before long."

And I'll still be here.

There will be no early morning coffees with laughter. No stupid arguments about *Extreme Wilderness Adventure*. No seeing his chin tip up when he gets pissy… and then needing to kiss him until he forgets what he was pissed about.

Which is why I'm not letting myself even think about wanting those things.

Dad studies my face. "Well, New York's not so far. Wouldn't hurt to have a friend in the city, would it?"

The way he says "friend" makes it clear he doesn't think that's all Griffin would be. But I don't know what else he *could* be. The city's full of hot guys, and Griffin's not going to want to keep an occasional fuck buddy around as a souvenir of his time in Winsome. Ada sells knickknacks that would fit the bill a lot better. Things he could stuff in a drawer when he's done with them.

I force a smile. "We'll see. Anyway, since we're admitting shit, I… I should've approached the whole thing with him differently from the beginning. I was… focused on the bottom line and not building a relationship with him as a person. I get what you're saying about needing to balance the two."

Dad looks surprised.

I scratch my beard. "Funnily enough, though, it's only because Griffin and I were competing for Big Dill that I got to know him." My eyes snap to his. "Do *not* tell Mom that."

He laughs—the loud, booming laughter I remember from childhood and haven't heard much lately. The kind that makes me want to laugh too.

"Wouldn't dream of it," he says. "But I do wonder if maybe we should thank him as a family. Have him to dinner sometime."

The very idea is like a gut punch because I can fucking *see* it. Griffin at our dinner table, charming my mother, getting into heated debates with Eliza about god knows what, probably teaming up with Ames to tease Robbie. He'd fit perfectly, I know he would.

And he'd weave himself deeper into my life just as he's about to leave it.

"Oh, Jesus, don't do that," I tell my dad, hoping my voice sounds light. "Too many Axfords at once would be a punishment, not a reward. Just… let it be."

That's what I should do too. Take the out Griffin gave me this morning, remember how complicated things are, and stop thinking about him all the damn time.

Dad just gives me that knowing look that says he's filing this information away for later.

His phone chirps in his pocket, and when he looks at it, his face splits in a grin. "Would you look at that? Your mother says Ames just abandoned her mid-garland hanging. Can't think why!"

I huff out a laugh. "So she needs you?"

"Well, she doesn't say that, exactly." He grins. "But after nearly forty years of marriage, I know better than to wait for her to say she needs me. When you love someone, you want to make their life better. Easier, anyway." He stands. "Speaking of which, if you want, I can give you a hand at the office one of these days. Just to talk things through and be a listening ear. Nothing that'll stress my heart... or your mother. And nothing that'll stress you out either. You let me know."

"Yeah," I say, thinking of how good he is at fixing crew schedules. "That'd be... that'd be good. I'll do that. I'll text you next week."

"See you at dinner, kiddo." Dad pats my shoulder as he leaves, and I exhale slowly. It feels like I've been holding my breath for years.

But the peaceful feeling doesn't last long. When I get back to my truck, my thoughts drift right back to Griffin.

I force myself not to drive by his place on the way to the office, though I really want to check on him after the way he bolted this morning. Instead, I throw myself into paperwork for the rest of the afternoon, then head home to shower and change for dinner before enjoying family dinner.

But when I pull up at my parents' house later, I see a familiar car with New York plates in the driveway and realize that I made a critical error.

My *dad* might be capable of letting things be, but I don't think Vivian Axford understands the concept, especially not when she thinks her children's happiness is at stake.

Sure enough, when I walk into the kitchen, there's an extra plate setting squeezed in at the table. And when my mother turns from some flowers she's been arranging on the counter to greet me, she wraps her arm around the shoulders of the man I haven't been able to stop thinking about.

"Beckett, honey! Look who's here."

Oh, I'm looking alright. Griffin's wearing a gray V-necked sweater and dark jeans that fit him like a glove. His golden hair's been pomaded within an inch of its life with whatever he uses that makes it smell like citrus. His pale skin is pink with embarrassment. His hazel eyes can't quite meet mine, but he lifts his chin—of course he does—defiantly.

Just seeing that gorgeous face has happiness searing through me like a flash fire. And I realize this is exactly what I was afraid of.

I don't just want Griffin in my bed. I want him in my life. Full stop.

Which means I'm officially *fucked*.

# CHAPTER FIFTEEN

## GRIFFIN

It turns out I'm shit at saying no.

And I'm *especially* shit at saying no to nice women who low-key remind me of my mothers.

When Vivian Axford greeted me at the grocery store while I was grabbing Milo's pickles, embraced me like I was a lost child who'd been returned to her, and apologized for not bringing me over an apple cake, I'd gotten this weird, earthquakey sort of feeling in my gut.

Her perfume's the same Ombre Rose scent my Mama Laine wears, and something about it made me feel like a kid again. At least, that's my excuse for not immediately pulling back the way I usually do when confronted with a hugger. Instead, I'd taken a deep breath and hugged her back.

And after all that hugging and quaking, I wasn't thinking straight. So when she said she'd love to have me over for dinner—just *"a casual thing, honey"*—I'd instinctively agreed. You know, the way you do when a colleague or classmate says, "We absolutely *have* to schedule dinner soon! I'm *dying* to catch up!" but you both know "soon" won't happen for another month or year or *ever*?

I keep forgetting Winsome's not the city. Insincere platitudes aren't the norm here. People mean what they say.

So when Vivian beamed at me and said, "Wonderful! We'll see you tonight around six. Grant will be so pleased!" I hadn't known how to backtrack. I mean, she's the sweetest woman on the planet, so I didn't want to hurt her feelings, obviously.

And… okay, yeah, maybe I'd been a bit curious to see where Beckett came from.

I also hadn't been opposed to having something to distract me from thinking about all the things I'd been putting off thinking about while plastering on my most *okay* face all day. Like job offers, and treehouses, and my moms, and Hello, Winsome, and my non-feelings about my biological father, and my too-many-feelings about a certain lumberjack.

Pardon me, *forestry professional*.

But now that I'm standing on the Axfords' porch, clutching some flowers I hastily purchased at the Basket, I don't know what the fuck I agreed to. Because judging by the number of cars parked in the drive, this is not a *casual thing, honey*. Not like any casual thing I've ever been to, anyway.

"Griffin!" Vivian beams as she opens the door. She's wearing a pumpkin-colored sweater and cute plaid pants. "Come in, sweetheart!"

She leads me through the front hall and into the kitchen, introducing me to everyone. In the kitchen,

Holden waves from the stove, where he's stirring something, and Ames pauses in his critique of Holden's technique long enough to give me a quick hug. Truett, the brother I haven't met yet, waves briefly from the big wooden table, where he's playing with an adorable golden Lab Vivian calls Greta. In the living room, Eliza introduces me to her fiancé, Luis, and her cousin Wilder before they go back to discussing their wedding plans, while Wilder sneaks glances at the college football game on TV in the background.

When we get to Beckett's father, he sets down a book of crosswords and gets up from his recliner to greet me with a handshake.

"So you're Beck's Griffin? Good to meet you, son. Call me Grant."

Look, I know how to act around people, okay? I've handled high-profile client meetings. I've made cold calls a million times. I'm the opposite of a shrinking violet.

But shaking Grant's hand after he called me "Beck's Griffin"? Yeah, I have no frame of reference for this. I'm confident my face is a shade of red that coordinates nicely with the grocery store bouquet I'm still clutching in my hand.

"These... are for you," I manage in a strangled voice, thrusting the chrysanthemums at Vivian.

She clutches them to her chest like I've given her a priceless treasure. "Oh, honey! How beautiful! Come help me arrange them. Ames!" she shouts. "Get down my blue vase, please?"

Being with the Axfords is like being in the path of a whirlwind. A very friendly and accepting tornado. I'm not sure where to put my attention.

And then Beckett arrives.

He pauses in the kitchen doorway, scanning the room, and when his eyes find mine, I lose control of my breathing. He's wearing his usual uniform—a henley, dark blue today, boots, and jeans that are nicely broken in, in all the right places. His hair, as usual, looks like he's been running both hands through it.

And somehow, the whirlwind just... stops. Just... calms. The winds die down, and everything feels normal again. *I* feel normal again.

"Sorry I'm late," he says. He's talking to his mother, but his blue eyes are fixed on me. "I was finishing up the invoicing."

"You're right on time," Vivian assures him. "Dinner's almost ready. Everyone, wash up. Griffin, honey, you and Beckett wash up in the bathroom. Beckett will show you."

Beckett nods his head toward the hall, and the two of us crowd together, hip to hip, in front of the sink in the tiny half bath while he turns on the faucet and washes his hands quickly before grabbing the hand towel and giving me room to take a turn at the sink.

"Your mom asked me," I say quietly, running my hands under the water. "At the grocery store. She was so sweet. And I didn't think— I'm so sorry if I'm intruding. I know this is probably the last thing you wanted—*mmph.*"

Beckett stops my spill of words with a quick, hard kiss.

"No, it's not," he whispers, rubbing a thumb over my cheek. "I'm glad you're here, city boy."

He heads back to the kitchen, leaving me dripping over the sink, thinking about how fucking good he makes me feel... and why that scares me so hard.

When I get to the table, there's one spot left, right

between Beckett and True. Eliza hands me a glass of red wine, and Vivian passes me a platter of golden roast chicken and root vegetables, while Ames continues the story he's telling.

"So then this morning, Perky comes in, asking if I'll cater his book club," Ames says, grinning wildly. "Since he heard I was catering Eliza's wedding."

"Oh my god, no!" Eliza says. "Not the romance book club! They're *so* extra."

"Eliza!" Vivian chides. "I think the Winsome Ardor Society is lovely! I wish I could make it to more meetings. They're so much fun."

"They do themes," True tells me with a shrug when I look confused. "Romance themes."

Beckett leans close and whispers in my ear, "The members call themselves the Ar-dorables."

I can't hold back a laugh. "Please don't tell me this is the same club Mrs. Pratt's part of?"

"The very same. And since it's Halloween this month, the theme is *vampires*," Ames continues. "They're reading a novel about a vampire chef, and they'd like 'thematically appropriate' food. So there I am telling Perky I don't know how to make food that's both elegant and blood-themed. But he told me if I could figure it out and serve it in costume, he'd pay me double. So apparently, next Tuesday, I'll be serving a garlic-free menu while wearing a cape." While everyone laughs, he adds, "If anyone has any ideas about the food…?"

"Red velvet cake," Eliza says immediately.

"Chocolate-dipped strawberries," Wilder volunteers.

"Blood orange sangria," I suggest. "And something with roast beef."

Ames's eyes widen, and a slow grin spreads across his face. "*Yes*. I have the best family."

"Obviously," Holden says, reaching for more vegetables.

I reach for my wine so I'm not tempted to imagine what it would feel like to actually be part of this family. Thank god the wine's delicious and mild, with just a hint of spice.

"Griffin," Vivian says, looking at me with the kind of maternal attention I bet she gives everyone. "How are you settling in? I can only imagine how different Winsome is from New York."

I feel the heat of Beckett's gaze on my face as I answer. "Really well, thank you. Everyone's been friendly. Mostly." I kick my shoe against Beckett's under the table, and from the corner of my eye, I see him shake his head slowly. "It's *very* different from New York, but not in a bad way. It's like a space out of time. A unicorn of a town. And it did seem a little quiet to me, at first. But since I started doing all the Big Dill events, I can't believe how quickly time has passed."

I can't believe how quickly my time here will be up.

Grant sets down his wineglass. "That's an interesting perspective. Remind me again what kind of work you do back in the city."

"Marketing," I say, summoning a smile. "Corporate campaigns, mostly."

"Griffin's the Rise Athletics guy," Holden volunteers as he eats. "You know, the billboard that went viral?"

"Oh." Eliza looks at me in surprise. "That was you?"

I think I've been low-key dreading this moment since I

arrived in Winsome. I mean, it was only a matter of time, really.

"Holden," Beckett nearly growls. "Seriously?"

"What?" Holden glances from Beckett to me mid-chew, and when he sees my face, he swallows, and his eyes go wide. "Oh, shi—*shoot*," he corrects with a glance at Vivian. "I'm sorry. Was that a secret or something?"

"No," I say quickly. "Don't apologize. Hardly a secret. I think the whole world's seen the video by now."

"I haven't," Beckett says, still growling.

I turn to him in surprise. "You didn't look it up after I told you about it?"

"Why would I?" he demands. "*I* didn't think it was funny." He gives Holden another heated glare.

I probably shouldn't be ready to cry about the fact that Beckett's willing to go to war with his own brother on my behalf, should I? It's fucking ridiculous of me, I know, but having Beckett in my corner, ready to shut down a family conversation just to spare me discomfort… it's like the last emotional straw this very overloaded camel can handle.

"What? I said sorry!" Holden lifts both hands in surrender. "I saw the video before I knew you, Griffin, but then after you got to town, I put two and two together. I didn't bring it up to make fun of you or anything. In fact, I thought the ad was brilliant. Really subversive."

"Totally. I was just showing it to Luis the other night. Rise Athletics has all these questionable family values policies," Eliza explains to the rest of the table. "And Griffin's billboard was like a statement about how the company's happy to profit off sexy images but won't actually embrace sexuality, especially when it comes to the gay community. You're a hero on this Reddit board I follow."

I blink at her. "That, uh… wasn't intentional. I almost wish it was. My intern switched the files at the last minute, I'm almost positive, and then left me to take the fall. I don't blame you for finding the video funny, though," I add quickly. "I might, too, if it hadn't destroyed my career."

"Oh, damn," Ames says. "Destroyed your career?"

"Yeah. The video of the billboard went viral and got stitched a million times. And, ah… let's just say the corporate marketing community doesn't share the same ideals as your Reddit board. Wasting millions, shining the wrong kind of spotlight on my client? I'm the *opposite* of a hero. I got fired, and no one else wanted to hire me. That's why I came to Winsome after Jim left me his treehouse."

"Well, I think that's awful," Vivian says fiercely. "You know, I have a friend at the Koasek Highlands Tourism and Visitors' Center. You just say the word, sweetheart. I'm sure she'd love to have you on their team."

"Oh, wow, that's so kind—" I begin.

"You could be a talking tree, like Beckett!" Ames says cheerfully.

Vivian *tsks*. "That's not what I meant at all."

Beckett rests one big hand on my knee under the table. "Mom, that's really sweet, but I don't know that Griffin wants to live up here. His life's in New York." He grins. "He likes listening to the sirens. He likes the bustle. I think that would be like asking one of us Axfords to move out of Winsome."

Damn, I love that he was listening. That he remembers I said that.

Vivian frowns across the table at me. "But… are you sure, Griffin?"

I open my mouth, then close it again, and think, *I'm almost sure I'm sure. Does that count?*

"A friend from med school lives in New York," Eliza offers before I can reply. "His wife's in advertising, but I don't know exactly what she does. I could ask if she knows of any openings."

"That'd be great. I'll take any leads I can get," I say.

"And Griff has a job offer already." Beckett gives me an encouraging look. "Or an offer to talk about one. Right?"

I nod, not nearly as enthusiastic as I should be. "It's more of a public relations thing. Not my favorite. But it's a good sign, so we'll see."

"Well, as long as you're happy, sweetheart," Vivian tells me. "And in the meantime, I'm so excited for your presentation tomorrow night. Speaking of which… Beckett, what will you be doing for Hello, Winsome?"

"I, uh…" Beckett winces. "I don't know."

"You don't *know*?" I demand.

"I figured I'd wing it." Beckett shrugs. "Eliza shot down all my brilliant ideas, so—"

"Your brilliant ideas were about widening truck parking on Whether Street and banning—direct quote here —'that ugly-ass kind of fake shiplap that looks like plastic.'"

"Shoulda been done a long time ago," Beckett grumbles, and I can't help laughing out loud again. "Besides, we all know whatever I come up with wouldn't be as amazing as Griffin's presentation anyway."

"Unless," Ames says slyly, "you sang the photosynthesis song. That would get the crowd rocking."

I press my lips together to hold back laughter as Beckett gives him an eye roll.

"No, wait, Ames might be onto something," Vivian says, eyes wide. "I think it would be *lovely* if you played guitar, Beckett! I know it's been a long time, but it's probably like riding a bike, right? You could just... pick it back up!"

"Mom, no—" Beckett begins.

"Especially since you only ever knew a couple chords!" Wilder says with a teasing grin. "How hard could it be?"

Eliza, who stood to get more wine, ruffles Beckett's hair on her way back. "Can you wear it Bieber style? For me?"

"Absolutely not." Beckett shoves the strands back, clearly aggrieved. "And thank you all so much for your eagerness to see me humiliate myself in front of all our neighbors. Not gonna happen."

I laugh out loud. Beckett turns to me, his face softens, and for a second it's like it's just the two of us in this room full of people.

"Well, I know Ed Hawkins will think you're the bees' knees, even if you get up there and recite the alphabet, Beck," Grant says. "He came into the Abigail today and was thanking me up and down for the payment plan. Said he prefers having everything in writing." He looks at his son with obvious pride. "Nice work."

Beckett looks across the table, the ghost of a smile still lingering on his face, and nods.

Up and down the table, the other Axfords exchange grins, like this is momentous. And it is, if it means Beckett and his dad have cleared the air and come to some sort of peace. I'm happy for him.

But when I watch this simple exchange—father proud of son, son accepting that pride—and I feel this giant fissure that's been growing inside me crack open a little more.

Too much to hide, apparently, because Beckett turns to me in concern.

"You okay?" he asks quietly, just as he did earlier.

I nod. But when Vivian starts clearing plates and talking about coffee and dessert, it's as if all the feelings I've been holding back, all the realizations I haven't wanted to face, all the not-okay I've been trying to hide, are about to come crashing down on me.

Like how I had these amazing moms, a bunch of wonderful aunts, but it still fucking *hurts* that my biological father was able to walk away from me so easily and didn't want to know me as an adult.

Like how Jim took all the fun parts of me—the kid-Griffin parts—and built this treehouse as a kind of shrine to them but didn't want to see who I'd actually become.

Like how I worked and worked for *years* to achieve success, but I still didn't measure up.

Like how I've achieved more connection and acceptance in two freaking *weeks* in Winsome than I did after decades in New York, and I haven't done a damn thing to deserve any of that.

I feel like a little kid throwing a pity party. Surely at thirty years old, I should know the world isn't fair, right? But I guess deep down, I thought it was, and now it feels like all the foundations I've built my life on have shifted, and all the *shoulds* in the world can't hold back this avalanche of feelings.

I can't stay in this lovely house with these lovely people another minute.

I push to my feet and summon a huge smile. "Vivian,

thank you so much for dinner, but I just remembered I have a… a thing tonight. I'm sorry to duck out so suddenly—"

"Oh. Gosh. Well, will you take some pie with you?"

"I can't," I say. It comes out high-pitched and wrong. "I can't. Thank you, though. Thank you for… just, everything."

The goodbyes blur together. Ames telling me to stop by Watchfire. Eliza wishing me luck tomorrow. Vivian hugging me tight. Grant patting my shoulder and telling me, "Beckett says you're a good man. Glad you found your way to Winsome."

I head for the door, dimly aware that my cracks are showing, that I don't seem remotely normal, but I can't keep up the facade any longer.

Beckett follows me to the front door, because of course he does. He's bossy and wonderful, and my breakdown is not something he should have to witness.

"Griffin, can we talk about—"

"Sorry, Beckett! I'm sorry. I've got… you know. Email. For the work thing?"

It seemed like he could see right through me, and the tender concern on his face is more than I can handle. Thankfully, he lets me go. "Right. No, I get it. Thanks for coming."

I drive back to the treehouse in the dark. My head's spinning, my eyes are wet, and if a moose wandered into my path tonight, I'd be toast. But Vermont is kind to me, this once, and I get home safely.

Inside, I sit on Jim's ridiculous velvet couch and stare at my laptop. The email about the job interview is still there. All I have to do is type "yes" and hit Send.

All I have to do is choose the life I planned and not the one I never saw coming.

My fingers hover over the keyboard, and I suck in a deep breath.

The path ahead was so clear to me only a few days ago, so why the fuck does it seem so impossible now?

# CHAPTER SIXTEEN

## BECKETT

I STAND ON MY PARENTS' porch long after Griffin's taillights disappear, feeling like I'm watching a part of myself drive away. I can't decide if that means I should race after him… or let him go once and for all, and save myself from feeling even worse when he finally leaves Winsome for good.

But the truth is, I don't know if I'm capable of that anymore.

Dinner had been good. Really good. Watching Griffin laugh at my siblings' antics, talking to my dad, smiling at my mom, it had been even better than I would have imagined. He'd fit so naturally into the chaos of my family. And somehow, with him at my side, I'd appreciated the whole experience more.

And then he'd left.

More accurately, he'd fled.

For the second time today.

I'm no relationship genius, but he was clearly feeling strong emotions about something.

"Is Griffin okay?" Mom asks, pulling a shawl around her as she steps out beside me. "Poor man seemed upset."

"He did." I scratch my beard, still staring down the driveway. "I don't know what's going on with him, though."

"Well, he's probably feeling some kind of way about Jim," she says in a gently rebuking tone, like that's something I should've considered. "Must be hard being around a big family, especially now." She shakes her head and sighs. "I should've thought of that. Asked him to lunch instead of a family dinner."

"What do you mean, about Jim? Like… a delayed grief thing?" I frown. "Griff and Jim weren't that close. They haven't seen each other since Griffin was eight."

Mom stares at me like I've grown two additional heads. "No, honey, I meant Griffin learning Jim was his biological father. I bet seeing you with your dad dredged up all kinds of emotions."

My jaw literally drops. "Jim is—was—his biological father?"

Her eyes widen in the porch lights. "You didn't know? I heard from Ada. She was worried about him and asked me the best way to handle it. I don't think she knew it was a secret. I sure didn't!"

I drive both hands through my hair. Jim Grange, Griffin's biological father?

Ah, fuck. Griffin had been searching high and low to figure out why Jim left him that treehouse. Then he'd found out his *why*… and the why sucked.

No wonder he was upset tonight. And this morning, after that whole long conversation about my dad? *Jesus.*

I dig my keys out of my pocket, ready to follow him.

Griffin needs comfort, and I let him go because I was busy trying to protect myself—

And because Griffin hadn't told me about Jim.

The thought makes me freeze.

Griffin obviously wanted to be alone, right? So I should respect that.

He could've told me about Jim on Sunday or any time since, and he hadn't, which meant he didn't want me to know.

And even if I went over there… fuck, I don't know how to comfort anyone. Just because I have feelings for him, just because I want him around me all the fucking time, doesn't mean the reverse is true.

Dad's voice calls from inside, asking if Mom wants him to bring out her jacket, and I remember what he said earlier today, at Watchfire. *"I know better than to wait for her to say she needs me. When you love someone, you want to make their life better. Easier, anyway."*

I squeeze my eyes shut as things fall into place with an almost audible *click*.

Goddamn it, I'm falling for Griffin Mercer.

I wait for this realization to feel wrong or to scare the shit out of me. But instead, it steadies me. Shores me up like hardwood. And makes me realize that while I'm sitting here dillydallying, Griffin's out there alone.

Which is absolutely unacceptable.

I know he probably doesn't return my feelings. I know he's leaving soon, and his future plans don't involve me. But I also know that *if* I can be there for him, *whenever* I can be there for him, for as *long* as he might want me to be there for him, that's exactly where I want to be.

"I'll check in later, Mom," I call, already heading for my truck.

She doesn't sound remotely surprised. "Give Griffin a hug from me," she yells after me.

When I pull into Griffin's place ten minutes later, I don't have to look far to find him.

Though I can see the lights shining through the darkness from the treehouse windows, Griffin's standing in the driveway, at the scene of our first meeting... and our second. His blond hair's shining like a beacon in the moonlight... and he's glowering up at the tennis racket lodged in the branches of a giant oak.

He doesn't seem to hear the crunch of my tires on the gravel or my boots as I step cautiously closer to him. It's like he's lost in his own head, staring down that racket.

"Hey," I say softly.

His head whips around at the sound of my voice. His hair's a mess, his sweater's covered in pine needles, and there are silver tear tracks on his face. He looks miserable... and it breaks my heart a little bit.

I have no idea what to say or do. How to fix this for him. When people want comfort, they turn to my mother. To Ames or True. To Eliza, in a pinch.

I've spent so long pushing people away, I don't know how to be what Griffin needs.

So I do what feels right.

"Come here, baby," I call softly. Then I close the distance between us and gently pull the brave, brilliant man I'm falling for into my arms and cradle him against my chest.

Griffin just exhales and melts into me, like he's been holding himself together by sheer force of will and finally has permission to fall apart. His shoulders shake against my chest.

"If you want the racket down, I'll get it down," I murmur into his hair.

"You know, he said this racket was lucky." Griffin's voice is muffled against my shirt.

"Jim did? When?"

"It was hanging in a glass box in his living room—*my* living room—labeled 'Good Luck Charm, Break in Case of Emergency.'"

I nod slowly. "That sounds… Jim-like." By which I mean ridiculous and generally harmless.

His gaze lifts to mine, and fresh tears flow down his cheeks. "Yeah? I wouldn't know that because I barely knew the man. *You* knew him. Perky at the grocery store knew him. Freakin' Posy at the scavenger hunt knew him. Not me, though. All I have is a treehouse, and a rope bridge to an empty room, a bunch of books about a guy with my name, and a stupid letter that tells me fucking *nothing*."

He inhales a ragged stutter-breath. His hazel eyes are so bright it's like he's burning from the inside. "I didn't care. I don't care. It doesn't matter that he's…" He breaks off and shakes his head.

"Your biological father," I finish. "That's what your moms told you last week, right?"

Griffin's eyes squeeze shut, causing more tears to spill out, and he nods. "I'm sorry if you think I should have told you. I wasn't sure how I felt about it. If I felt *anything* about it. I felt like… like I *shouldn't* feel anything about it."

"Griffin, baby—"

"Jim didn't want me to know he was my biological

father. He didn't think he had it in him to be a father to me or something. And that's fine! Genuinely fine. It *should* be fine. Like, so what if I didn't have a father like you had, when I had a pack of ten lesbian aunts who taught me to play T-ball and beer pong, you know? I didn't need a father. I didn't *want* him to be my father. But why does it hurt so much that Jim didn't want me in his life, even as his nephew? That he didn't want me to know him, even if it wasn't as his son? That he didn't let me thank him for this inheritance he gifted me before he died? I'm being so s-stupid. A-and I'm crying, and I *hate* crying."

I hold him tighter.

"Griffin, stop thinking about what you owe other people." The words come out fiercer than I intended. "Stop thinking there's a right way to feel. I fell into that trap with my dad, and you helped me get out of it. What Jim wanted or needed, the way he handled this… that's on him. And… I guess a little on your moms. But it has not one damn thing to do with who you are or what you're worth. You're *everything*."

Griffin's expression twists into something raw and vulnerable. I have the overwhelming desire to keep him in my arms forever and make sure nothing hurts him again.

"It's not just Jim," he whispers. "I gave my whole life to my career, Beckett. I wanted to build something stable. Something no one could take from me. But it's like I told you before. I took a wrong turn somewhere. I had it all wrong. I failed. And now I just… "

"Bullshit." I cup his face in my hands, tilt his chin up for him, since for once he can't seem to manage a defiant chin lift on his own. "You are brilliant. People in New York knew it. Everyone in this damn town knows it. *I* know it.

You're smart, and you're brave. And you had some shit luck. You trusted someone who fucked you over. But if you want that career in New York, you'll get it. And I will do whatever I can to help you."

His eyes search mine in the moonlight like he's trying to read the truth in them. "But... why would you do that?"

My expression melts. "Why? Because I care about you, city boy. Because you're so fucking special, I can't *not*."

Griffin stares at me for a long moment, his expression shifting from raw pain to something like wonder, as if he can't believe what I'm saying.

If I stop to think about it, neither can I. This sweet man has turned my entire life upside down in just a few short weeks.

I brush away his tears with my thumbs. "Cold out here," I say. "Let's go inside."

He nods and leans against me as we walk up the stairs to the treehouse, wrapping his arm around my back.

Inside, the house is warm and quiet, with lamplight spilling golden across the purple sofa and all the mushroom knickknacks.

"I think," I begin.

But Griffin immediately reaches for the hem of my shirt, tugging it upward so he can work at my belt. "You remember I told you that I like you not-thinking?" he teases.

"Hey." I catch his hands gently, stilling him. "Griffin. Baby, there's no rush."

"There is, though." His voice is rough. "Please... I can't..."

"You want to push it all back?" I murmur, tugging a strand of his hair. "Focus on something else?"

He nods.

"I get it," I say softly. "But come sit with me a minute. Just let me hold you."

Griffin resists at first, because of course he does, but he lets me pull him down on the sofa beside me. He stretches out his legs along the cushion, plasters himself against my side, and buries his face in my neck.

I hate that he's in pain, but the way he's letting me hold him, letting me help him…

I didn't know I wanted this. In fact, I would have told you I actively didn't. But now, I can't imagine giving it up.

I lift one booted foot onto the coffee table to stretch out and accidentally bump something there.

"Shit, sorry." I lift my foot to see what I kicked and find a hardcover of the first *Whispers* book. The copy Griffin dragged out of the pickle barrel turret the other day.

"Were you reading that?" I ask.

Griffin glances up to see what I'm talking about, and then his gaze skitters away. "I thought about it, but I can't even make myself open it." He plucks at a spot on my shirt. "It feels like… like he chose the Sprout in the book instead of me. The fictional guy instead of the real one."

I snort. "If he did, he was an idiot."

Griffin's eyes fly to mine, and he manages a little smile. "Right."

"I say you open it." I lean forward to grab the book and prop it against my stomach. "Just rip the Band-Aid off. Prove it doesn't have power over you. And if you're still pissed off, I'll take it out in the yard and yeet it, as the kids say. Give the racket some company."

He lifts his head, and his laughing hazel eyes meet mine. "Beckett, no kids actually say that anymore." But he glances down at the book and sighs. "You're right. I mean, Jesus, the book's not actual magic. It's wood pulp and ink."

"Exactly."

He sits up, and I position him so his back is to my chest and my arms are around him. His hands shake slightly as he opens to the first page, so I lay my hands over his to hold the book steady.

I watch his face in profile as he reads the dedication. When he finishes, his eyes are shiny again and he shifts the book over for me to read.

> *For Sprout.*
>
> *Keep risking those scraped knees to chase down adventures.*
>
> *Keep asking the good questions and giving the good answers.*
>
> *Find your way home, no matter what obstacles you face.*
> *Love like the clouds do, wild and brave...*
>
> *And know that somewhere there's a mushroom who loves you back.*

"This doesn't change anything," Griffin says, but he sniffs loudly as he shuts the cover. "It's a book about a kid who gets lost in the woods, you said, and he talks to mushrooms—"

"While trying to find his way home, yeah."

Griffin nods down at the book for a minute, then touches the cover and sets it on the table. "If he loved me, I don't understand why he did things the way he did."

I shrug. "Me neither. But from what I knew of Jim, he wasn't... conventional. I think he prided himself on being a nomad. This was his home base, but he was gone a *lot*, especially years ago. Maybe he didn't know how to reconcile really caring about someone while living his life the way he wanted to. He gave you what he thought he had to give. Which has nothing to do with what you deserve."

He takes a deep, shuddering breath. "Ada said... she said I'm like him."

"No." I snort. "God. Not even a little."

"But maybe... maybe she was right, in a way. Maybe I don't know how to reconcile those things, either. I want a stable life the way Jim wanted the opposite. But we're making the same mistakes."

I huff out a breath.

Griffin turns to face me. "Why's that funny?"

"My dad said something similar to *me* earlier today." I run my fingers absently along his stubbled jaw, his sculpted cheekbones, his plush lips. "We sat down and actually talked, and he said he's been worried I'm making the same mistakes he made. Pushing too far in the opposite direction but for the same stubborn reasons. Thinking I need to do it all on my own. This whole time, I thought he was trying to jump in and fix things because I wasn't doing it right, but he was actually trying to help in his own way."

"And things are good with you two now? At dinner, it seemed like you were getting along."

"They're better," I say cautiously. "My default is to assume, when he offers me something, that it's because *I'm* not doing it right. It'll take time to change that." I tap his chin. "Maybe you and I both need to work on that."

Griffin huffs and drops his forehead to my chest. "I don't know how you do it," he murmurs. "But you somehow make things quieter in my head. Make things feel easier. Or at least… doable."

I laugh. "And here I was, thinking you make things *louder* in my head. In a good way. Like I've been half-asleep for a long time and you woke me up."

He tilts his head up, and his hazel eyes are soft but intent enough to make my heart race. I lean in and kiss him, slow and hot, but pull back before either of us is satisfied.

"You need rest," I remind him, running a hand over his hair.

I've never considered myself sweet by nature, but there's nothing I want more than to be sweet to this man.

Griffin grumbles but lets me pull him to his feet and kiss the top of his head. "Have I reminded you today how bossy you are?"

"Have I reminded you that you love it?" I counter.

While Griffin showers, I send a text to my crew, asking if any of them are available to do me a favor in the morning. When Griffin reappears, shower-damp and half-naked, in the doorway of his bedroom and finds me sitting on the edge of his bed, I immediately slide my phone away.

"So… I mean… I'm fine. Clearly." He runs one bare foot down the leg of his pajama pants. "And I appreciate you coming over, but you don't need to babysit me, if you—"

I back him against the doorframe with my body and force him to look up at me. "*You* don't need to pretend to be okay if you're not," I say softly. "And whether you're okay or not, I still want to be here, if you want me to be. I kinda like you, city boy."

"You care about me, you said." Fuck, it kills me when he looks this vulnerable.

"I do," I say simply. "Do you want me to stay?"

He nods.

"Then I will."

I take off my jeans and shirt and climb under the blankets in just my boxers.

And for all the second- and third-guessing we've done with each other, once we're pressed together in his small bed, it's the easiest and most natural thing in the world to wrap my arms around him, to pull him against me, to kiss the top of his head when he murmurs "so warm," and to let him fall asleep in my arms.

Sometime later, Griffin's fingers brush my collarbone, and I open my eyes in the thick, velvety dark. His touch is so light I might've thought I'd imagined it, but then his voice, rough with sleep, whispers, "Hi."

I turn my head and find his head on the pillow beside mine. Our faces are inches apart, and his breath's warm against my lips.

"Hi," I say, smiling sleepily.

He lifts his head a little and runs his thumb along my beard. "Beckett…"

I reach for the lamp in the darkness, and with a *click*, dim golden light spills over us. It's just enough for me to see the flush on Griffin's cheeks, the dark hunger in his eyes, the way his cock is already tenting the front of his pajamas.

I don't answer in words. Instead, I grab his wrist, press my lips to his palm, and look at him in return, letting him see the hunger in my gaze. His breath hitches, and his fingers tremble.

I shuck my boxers.

I roll toward him, and our bodies align perfectly despite our size difference, chest to chest and hip to hip. My hands map the dip of Griffin's waist, the ridge of his hip bone, that I've already claimed as my own, and he arches into me, his lashes fluttering.

I kiss the hollow of his throat, where his heartbeat thumps, and part my lips to taste him. He moans, body melting into the sheets, so pliant and silent in this, at least.

After shucking off his pajamas, I run my hand down his creamy skin, finding his length, hard and aching. I palm his cock once, twice, slow and measured.

Griffin groans, eyes closing as his thighs fall open in blatant invitation.

"Look at me," I murmur, and he obeys, dragging his eyes open.

"Lube and condoms?" I demand.

"D-drawer." He motions toward the nightstand.

After I've retrieved them and straddled him again, his breath catches. My first touch is gentle—just the pad of my finger circling and teasing his hole. His body tenses, then relaxes, his thighs spreading wider. I press in just a little, letting him adjust, but just that small motion has his fingers digging into my shoulders, his nails biting into my skin. I crook my finger, finding his prostate, and he lets out a soft, needy whine.

"Fuck, you're beautiful like this," I whisper as I add a second finger, stretching him open. My free hand grips his hip to hold him still.

Griffin's only answer is the clench of his body around my finger, the gasps that say he's forgotten how to breathe, and the way his cock leaves a sticky trail along my stomach.

By the time I line myself up, he's trembling, but I pause there, my tip just breaching his ring, my forehead resting against his, our breaths mingling.

"Mine," I breathe.

The last time we did this, I claimed him in a physical way. Claimed his skin, his cock, his ass, those hip bones.

But that physical claiming's not enough now. I want him in every way. In my bed, at my table, by my side. And I don't know how to make that happen, but for maybe the first time, I don't need details.

With this contrary, compelling man, I'm willing to make a handshake deal.

With Griffin, I'm willing to trust.

He nods back at me, eyes shining, and I think he feels it too.

I push forward, watching his face as I enter him inch by inch. His lips part, gold-tipped lashes brush the tops of his cheeks, and those pretty eyes that caught me from the first minute glaze over with pure *want*.

"B-Beckett," Griffin whispers, like my name says everything.

His hands find mine, and he threads our fingers together, gripping tight as I bottom out inside him.

*Fuck. How is it possible that this man already feels like home?*

I kiss Griffin, our lips clinging just as our bodies are locked together, and set a lazy rhythm because I want this to last as long as possible. Want to draw it out all night, if I can.

But the way his dick jumps and his breath punches out

of him every time I tag his prostate, his mindless, needy whimpers every time I drag myself out of him, make it impossible to keep up the slow pace.

Griffin's legs wrap around my waist, and his heels dig into the small of my back, pulling me closer, deeper, begging me to go faster.

I bury my face in the crook of his neck, breathing in the scent of him—sweat and skin and that damn citrus hair product that makes me lose my mind. Every single thing about him is fucking perfect, every sound he makes tightening low in my belly.

Griffin's body clenches around me, breath ragged. "Beckett," he whines again.

I answer by reaching between us, wrapping my hand around his cock in the way he likes, tugging him firmly while my thumb rubs over his tip.

He comes on a choked cry, like his orgasm snuck up on him. And the way his ass tightens around me, milks me, makes it impossible for me to hold back.

I come in slow waves and sigh his name into the skin of his shoulder.

Afterward, we stay like that, sweaty bodies tangled together with me still inside him, most of my weight braced on my forearms. His fingers trace random patterns up my spine and over my shoulders, and I try to memorize his features in the golden light.

I press a kiss to his temple, letting my lips linger there. "Mine," I whisper again.

Griffin turns his face just enough to catch my mouth in a slow, deep kiss. Then he sighs, soft and content.

When his sigh turns into a yawn, I chuckle, pull out of him, and dispose of the condom. I find my boxers somewhere at the end of the bed and clean us both off, and then I turn off the light. Within seconds, Griffin has rolled himself practically on top of me.

I hold him tight, one arm around his back and the other threading into his messy golden hair.

And as I follow him into sleep, I think this is the most peaceful I've ever felt.

I WAKE TO ABSOLUTE CHAOS.

There's beeping somewhere, like an alarm blaring, and voices outside are shouting. For a second, I don't understand where I am or what's happening, but then Griffin pulls out of my arms and grumbles, "The fuck? Again?"

He stumbles out of bed a heartbeat before I do and rushes, naked, to the living room. I catch him around the waist just as he's about to throw open the front door.

"No way," I growl, my eyes still at half-mast. "Whatever's happening out there, you're getting dressed this time."

"Bossy," Griffin breathes, sinking back against me for just a second.

A second is precisely long enough for me to realize my eyelids are not the only thing at half-mast and that Griffin's ass rubbing against me is a surefire way to get me to full mast in no time.

He turns in my arms and lifts up to kiss me, and I groan the second our tongues touch. Griffin is light, and I am a moth, and I'm incapable of not wanting him.

I've just decided whatever's happening outside can

happen without us, when a feminine voice outside gives a shrill yell.

"No, sir, you will *not* bring that truck onto my son's property! He said *no* logging trucks! You will not encroach on his land!"

"Don't make us call our friends and turn this into a topless protest!" another woman yells.

"Please, ma'am," a voice that sounds like Freddy's begs. "We're just helping out—"

While someone else says, "I wouldn't mind a topless —" The rest is garbled.

Griffin's body stiffens in my arms, and he pulls back just far enough for me to see that his eyes are fucking *huge*.

"Oh, shit," he breathes. "Beckett! My mothers are here!"

"And my crew," I confirm. "Fuck."

"Get dressed!" he wails.

We run back to the bedroom, trying to find the clothes we discarded. I quickly pull on my jeans and henley. Griffin jumps into his pajama pants but then starts running in panicked circles. "I can't... I don't... Beckett, where's my sweater?"

I grab him by the shoulders and force him to stop. "You weren't wearing it when we went to bed. Find a new shirt!"

"Right. Good call." He opens a drawer, pulls out a shirt at random, and tucks it under his arm. "Wait, shoes!"

We're back in the living room, sliding our feet into boots, when another voice joins the fray. "Oh my gosh, you must be Griffin's mothers! So wonderful to meet you! I'm Vivian Axford. Would you like some apple cake?"

I freeze. Griffin's eyes widen.

He stomps into his boots and pulls his shirt over his head as I'm throwing the door open… and then I stop.

The shirt Griffin picked is *my* shirt—the flannel I lent him weeks ago. And it still hangs on his frame, like he's covered in *me* from shoulders to thigh.

"Holy fuck," I growl. I grab him by the buttons and haul him against me, because even in crisis mode, the sight of him in my clothes does things to me. "You are so goddamn sexy."

He resists for only half a second, then groans and kisses me back…

Until another voice outside, cultured and urbane, drawls, "I assure you, madam, I have no interest in paving anyone's paradise! My business is with *Griffin Mercer*, so please let go of my son before I have to call the authorities!"

Griffin gasps and pulls away. "Holy… Beckett, that's my *boss*!"

"I'm also here to see Griffin," another male voice insists. "I've made him a business offer, and he's going to want to see me first."

"Is that… Derek Sullivan? What the fuck?" I demand.

Griffin shakes his head helplessly.

As we head down the treehouse stairs hand in hand, I'm unsure what is waiting for us. But I also know it has the potential to change absolutely everything.

# CHAPTER SEVENTEEN

## GRIFFIN

WHEN WE REACH the bottom of the treehouse stairs, absolute chaos greets us.

There's an Axford Lumber logging truck with a crane parked at the edge of my driveway, and my mothers are standing in front of it with their arms spread wide like human shields. Vivian Axford's trying to mediate the situation as best she can while holding a cake carrier in both hands. Erick Nelson, of all people, looks like he's trying to melt himself into the forest floor, and two men in expensive suits—Alan Nelson and Derek Sullivan—appear to be arguing with everyone at once.

"Join hands with me, Tish," Mama Laine calls, staring daggers at Carlos, who's standing beside the crane looking bewildered. "They can't move both of us!"

"Ma'am," says Freddy. "I mean… Ma'ams. Please, if you'd just listen for a second—" He's built like the Jolly Green Giant's whiter, friendlier brother, and he's literally wringing his hands.

As if that weren't enough, the sheriff's SUV pulls up

behind the crane, and Holden emerges, wearing his uniform and shiny sunglasses. "I got a call from an Alan Nelson about some kind of disturbance," he says, taking in the scene. Then he takes off his sunglasses and shakes his head at his brother. "Beck, what the hell is going on here?"

Everyone starts talking at once, voices layering over each other in a cacophony that makes my head spin. I turn to Beckett, feeling overwhelmed. "See? *This* is why a man needs a lucky tennis racket to brandish," I mutter.

Beckett's standing at my shoulder, both arms folded over his chest. "You don't need a tennis racket, baby," he says. Then he puts two fingers to his lips and lets out an ear-piercing whistle.

Everyone stops talking immediately.

"Griffin will talk to each of you when he's good and ready, so chill out and shut the fuck up," Beckett says in his most authoritative voice. Then he adds as an afterthought, "I know, Mom. Language."

Vivian presses her lips together like she's fighting a smile. "It seems appropriate," she says. "Under the circumstances."

I stare at Beckett, a little awed. It's kind of wonderful having that grumpiness working *for* me. I can almost see how other people find him intimidating.

Then he shoots me a wink, and I want to laugh out loud.

Still not intimidating to *me*. Never to *me*.

"Griffin, sweetie!" Mama Laine completely ignores Beckett's warning and rushes over, Mama Tish right behind her. They both wrap me in fierce hugs that smell like home—vanilla and incense and the faint scent of the art supplies Mama Tish always has on her hands.

"We were so worried about you," Mama Tish says, squeezing me tight. "I know we said we'd give you space, and we will. But we needed to see you. To make sure you were okay."

"We remembered what you said about your house being small." Mama Laine peers through the trees like she's still looking for the treehouse. "We were able to get a room for the night at the most adorable little inn, right in the center of town. But we wanted to come here first, and then we found these men trying to sneak their trucks onto your land!"

"We brought the boom truck to get the racket down, boss," Carlos says. "Just like you asked us last night. But then these ladies said Griffin didn't want trucks on the property, and we didn't wanna cause trouble."

I turn my head to look at Beckett, something hot and… yes, fine, *banana-y*… blooming in my chest. Even while the man was holding me last night, even while he was putting me together piece by piece after I emoted all over him, he was thinking about the tennis racket. Thinking about the tiniest thing I might want or need. And doing something to help me get it.

*God*, I really like this guy.

More than like. I've fallen.

I am one hundred percent mush, and I don't give a single shit. In fact, I embrace it.

"Things have changed," I tell my mothers, and I'm aware of Beckett nodding emphatically beside me.

That simple gesture steadies me completely. Somehow —and I still don't know how—this man has become the quiet in the storm that is the rest of my life. He's solid as an oak tree, unshakable as bedrock. Standing here wearing

Beckett's flannel shirt, with his support behind me, I feel like I've come back to myself.

Or, I don't know, like I was the land, the forest, that had been clear-cut and planted with crops it wasn't meant to grow, but now I'm letting myself become forest again. Wild and free, and exactly as I was meant to be.

I feel clearheaded for the first time in a while.

"Griffin," Alan Nelson calls impatiently. "I didn't drive out here for the fun of it. We need to talk."

"I'm starting to see the appeal of the rope bridge," I murmur just low enough that only Beckett can hear it. "Think we could make it if we run?"

Beckett snorts and unfolds his arms, but only so he can lay a hand at the small of my back. His palm is warm and grounding through the flannel. "You know, I think I'd follow you anywhere, city boy."

That touch, that quiet confidence, reminds me I am not a person who has to handle shit alone anymore. I'm not the same man who stood in this driveway weeks ago, half-naked and furious and completely out of his depth.

I turn to Vivian first. "Would you mind putting the cake in the house? Thank you so much."

"Of course, sweetheart." She beams at me and then at Beckett with a trace of maternal pride. "I wanted to check on you after last night. You seemed upset. But we'll chat later." She pats my arm as she heads past me toward the treehouse.

"Is that your apple cake?" Holden asks hopefully, but Vivian ignores him, and Beckett snorts.

Hearing Vivian, my moms' expressions grow even more concerned.

"We knew something was off," Mama Laine says softly.

"Honey, remember talking is sometimes the best way to process your emotions." Mama Tish adds.

"I know," I tell her. I sway closer to Beckett so my arm's brushing his. "I promise, I know." *And I'd really like to get back to talking to the man beside me, if everyone would leave us alone.*

Then I turn to Beckett's guys. "Please go ahead and get the racket down. Thank you guys for coming out on a Sunday."

"Sure thing," Carlos says, clearly relieved to have a task. He jumps into the basket of the crane-thing.

"Anything for a Brine and Dandy winner," Freddy says with a wink before he turns and brings the engine on the crane to life.

"Mama Laine, Mama Tish," I begin, but they're both staring past me with narrowed eyes at where Derek Sullivan's pushing toward me. Beckett's body stiffens next to me, but he keeps his mouth closed.

"Griffin," Derek begins. "Before you make the mistake of letting Axford Lumber onto your precious land, I wanted to reiterate the offer I made you the other day. I promise, the numbers I offered are more than fair, but if you'd like to discuss, I'd be willing to—"

I'm already shaking my head when Mama Laine says, "Griff, honey, tell me you're not selling to *him*." She gives Derek a scathing glance like he's something she'd scrape off her shoe.

"No." I take a deep breath and give Derek an apologetic smile. "Thank you for the offer. I agree, it was very fair. But I'm not interested in selling at this time—"

"Really?" Beckett asks. He's dropped his intimidating-ish facade, and his voice is surprised and hopeful.

I meet his eyes, seeing the question there. "Really. In fact, I—"

"Thank goodness," Mama Tish interrupts. "Do you know who this man is, Griffin? That's right, I recognize you, Derwin Sherman!" she adds, glaring at Derek.

"Simpkins," Mama Laine corrects under her breath. "I keep telling you, sweetie, it's Derwin Simpkins."

"Wait." I frown at them, trying to remember where I've heard that name. "Who's—?"

"The man who tried to build the eco resort near us!" Mama Tish continues.

Derek's face pales. "I don't know what you're talking about," he says, but I'm pretty sure everyone can see that he's bluffing. Even Erick Nelson looks skeptical.

"Is that so?" Mama Laine steps forward, and Derek actually takes a step back. "He bought up pristine land in Williamstown, claiming he wanted to build a luxury, eco-friendly resort there. But there wasn't a single thing eco-friendly about it, was there, *Derwin*? Substandard building materials, reprocessed to add fake eco-friendly labels," she scoffs. "We protested for months and finally got enough attention on the matter for the state environmental agency to start investigating, but then Derwin here suddenly abandoned the whole project and disappeared."

Beckett stares at Derek, understanding dawning on his face. "Oh, fuck. *That's* how you're doing it! I *knew* you didn't have enough harvestable acres for all the eco-friendly lumber you were claiming to supply—"

"Interesting," Holden says, looking at Derek with new attention. He turns to my mothers. "Do you ladies have any proof of these allegations? Know who was handling this investigation?"

"Absolutely, we do," Mama Tish says.

"And what we don't know, our friends do," Mama Laine confirms.

"That's utterly ridiculous," Derek protests, backing toward his BMW. "Griffin, we can discuss my offer later, when you've had a chance to come to your senses and—"

There's a loud crack from above, followed by Carlos yelling, "Oops! My bad!" And then the tennis racket comes plummeting down, whacking Derek squarely on the arm and knocking his key fob out of his hand and into the bushes.

"Holy shit. The racket really *was* lucky," I whisper.

"Derek," Holden says, patting him on the shoulder. "Why don't you come with me for a chat? We can discuss your… business ventures at the station."

As Holden leads an increasingly pale Derek toward his SUV, my mothers immediately try to corner me again, but I hold up a hand.

"I love you so much for coming to check on me, and I will talk to you both, I promise," I say. "But could you go inside with Vivian for a minute, please? I need to handle something first."

"But," Mama Tish begins to protest.

"This is my boundary. I will talk when I'm ready," I tell her gently.

She sucks in a breath and looks disappointed but nods firmly and takes Mama Laine's arm. "Okay, sweetie."

I'm already low-key exhausted when I turn to Alan Nelson, who's been watching this entire circus with barely concealed irritation. Erick stands behind him, darting his eyes toward the trees like he's considering making a run for it.

"Griffin, my son has something to say, and we thought it best to say it in person." Alan nudges Erick forward, none too gently. "Don't you, Erick?"

Erick's model-beautiful face turns red, and he lifts his eyes to mine. "I'm sorry," he says quietly. "It was me who changed the text on the Rise campaign billboard. I figure you already knew that, but I wanted you to know that I... I admitted everything to my father and to Bill Tiden."

I press a hand to my sternum and lean into Beckett. "Oh, god." I never imagined he'd admit it. "But... why? Did you hate me that much, Erick?"

Erick shakes his head forcefully. "No. No way. You were amazing to work with, Griffin. You gave me a chance to prove myself, and you taught me so much. I just..." He squeezes his eyes shut. "I hated working for Bill. I hate Rise. I hate his stupid 'family values' bullshit. I never wanted us to take them on as a client, but Dad wouldn't listen—"

"Jesus, Erick," Alan scoffs. "Business is business."

Erick sets his jaw. "I didn't think it through," he continues. "I wanted Rise to fire *us*. The Nelson Group. So we wouldn't be associated with them anymore. I didn't want *you* to get blamed. But then when everything happened... I panicked. And I fucked up—"

"Yes, you did," Alan snaps.

*Fuck.* I'm looking at Erick when it all clicks into place. He went about it the absolute wrong way, but Erick Nelson had more integrity than I did. Why had I been spending my life working on campaigns for brands I didn't believe in, for people I didn't like? Was that really the brilliant life I'd envisioned for myself?

Standing in this forest, with this man at my side, my life in New York feels like the palest imitation of happiness. The most hollow definition of success.

Carlos, who's been coiling up crane cables, suddenly speaks up. "Alright, enough. He said he was sorry." He steps closer to Erick and gives Alan a glare that rivals Beckett's glower.

Erick glances at Carlos curiously, and a faint blush creeps up his neck.

"I, ah…" Erick clears his throat. "I want you to know, I resigned from the Nelson Group. I'm going to find a job in education. I've always wanted to be a preschool teacher, believe it or not—"

"It's a phase," Alan says dismissively. "Which you'll regret. Thriving family businesses don't come around twice."

Carlos grins fiercely. "Yeah, well, I say that's kick-ass! My sister-in-law's a preschool teacher. Those guys are heroes!"

Erick's smile is small but genuine. Beckett and I exchange a look, and Beckett shrugs with what might be amusement.

Alan clears his throat impatiently. "The Nelson Group would like to offer you your old job back, Griffin. With a five percent raise. Obviously, we'll also make a public statement declaring you blameless regarding the billboard incident. You can start back Monday."

*Monday.*

The air goes still. Even the breeze seems to pause. I

don't think Beckett's breathing anymore, and for a second, I'm not either.

Then everything falls into place again.

Into its right place.

And suddenly, I can see exactly where I'm going.

I know exactly what I want.

"I can't," I say slowly. "I have—" I gesture toward the treehouse, toward the life I'm building in Winsome. "I have things here."

Alan looks around the woods skeptically, probably the same way I looked at this place when I first arrived. But now, his dismissive expression pisses me off.

"Your choice," Alan says, narrowing his eyes. "If this is a negotiation tactic, just know this is my only and final offer. I'll see you Monday. Come on, Erick."

"No," Erick says. When Alan turns to him with a frown, Erick says, "The car ride here was miserable. I'll find my own way home."

Alan huffs and stalks off to his car, slamming the door harder than necessary. Then he speeds off in a cloud of gravel.

I'm vaguely aware of Carlos offering Erick a ride to town, but honestly, I don't care. All I need and want at that moment is to talk to Beckett.

Just Beckett.

But when I turn toward him, I find him looking down at his phone with a frown.

"Hey," I say. "Fuck, I'm so sorry about all this. Is everything okay?"

He starts to answer when *another fucking car*, this one with New Jersey plates, comes rolling up my driveway and parks behind Derek's abandoned BMW.

"What the actual hell?" I mutter, running a hand through my hair and not even caring that I probably look like a mad scientist. I didn't think I knew this many people, and suddenly, they're all fucking *here*, right where I don't want them.

A pleasant-looking woman in her fifties steps out of the modest sedan and greets me with a smile. "Hi, there. I'm looking for Griffin Mercer."

"You found him," I say shortly. "But—"

"I'm Jim Grange's attorney," she continues. "I heard you had questions about your trust."

Shit. I turn to Beckett, mostly to see his reaction, but he's staring down at his phone again.

"Ames," he tells me. "He needs my help and says it's urgent." He looks at the attorney, and then at me. "I don't want to leave you to deal with all this, but…"

I don't want him to leave either, but I can't ask him to stay when his family needs him. "Go," I say. "Talk later?"

Beckett huffs out a laugh and rubs the back of his neck. "Definitely, baby. We, ah… we have a lot to talk about, don't we?"

He kisses my forehead quickly and rushes off to his truck, leaving me standing in the driveway.

As I watch him drive away, I wish we'd just fled to the damn rope bridge earlier after all. I don't like the forced quality of his smile, and all I want is to have a moment alone with him to make sure we're on the same page.

Does he think Alan showing up here and offering me my job changes things?

Fuck, maybe he does. Maybe things weren't as settled as I'd thought they were.

"Mr. Mercer?" the attorney prompts gently. "I think you're really going to want to hear what I have to say."

"I do. I want to hear all about my inheritance. About what happened to Jim. But…" I sigh. "I have kind of a lot going on right now."

And I'm drawing another boundary because enough is enough.

We make a plan to meet early the following morning at the Abigail, where she's staying. Then I head inside the treehouse to find my mothers and Vivian drinking coffee and eating apple cake.

All of them look at me with varying degrees of concern and curiosity. I know they want to hear every single thing that's going on with me, to make sure I'm okay, and I love that. I do.

But all *I* want is to chase after Beckett. To show him that I'm all in on Winsome. On *him*. On this… this thing that we're building together.

When Vivian says, "Griffin, sweetheart, I was just telling your mothers they picked the best time to come! We're all going to see you give your presentation on tourism at Hello, Winsome tonight!" I want to groan.

I'd forgotten all about the damn presentation. And does it even matter anymore? Beckett can have the easement. Hell, I want Beckett to have *everything*.

But then an idea hits me—a way I can make my intentions absolutely clear, not just to Beckett but to everyone in town. Something that will show them exactly who Griffin Mercer is… and what he wants his life to look like.

# CHAPTER EIGHTEEN

## BECKETT

I BURST through the community center doors, my boots squeaking against the polished floor as I skid to a stop, ten minutes late and breathing hard from my sprint across the parking lot.

This whole day has felt like one upheaval after another, starting with the fuckery in Griffin's driveway and followed by Ames's sous-chef, Jenna, texting to say there was something wrong with Ames. If it hadn't been important, I never would've left Griffin's side.

Griffin was strong and brave, no doubt about it. But after the emotional turmoil last night, I wanted to be there in case he needed me.

Hell, who was I kidding? After the emotional turmoil of last night, *I* needed *him*.

I'd planned to talk to him this morning, to lay it all out there—that I was falling for him and I wanted to be with him, whatever that looked like. My dad had pointed out New York wasn't all that far away, and that was true. Long distance would suck, but I'd do it if it meant keeping Griffin in my life. And if things worked out… hell, maybe they needed a forestry professional in New York. They had parks and stuff there, right? I could run Axford Lumber from a distance, or… fuck, I didn't know, but I was willing to consider all the possibilities.

The most important thing was that Griffin could have what he needed—his job in the city, which had been restored to him with a raise on top—and I could have what I needed too. Namely, Griffin.

Assuming Griffin wanted me too.

"Where've you been, bro?" Holden's voice cuts through my racing thoughts. He's leaning against the wall near the closed auditorium doors. "Griffin was looking for you."

"Did he seem upset?" I demand.

Holden shrugs. "Kinda? More like nervous. Kept muttering about last-minute changes. But his moms seem sweet. They wanted to know all about Derek Sullivan. Speaking of which, you'll be happy to know—"

*Nervous? Really?* Griffin's been working hard on this presentation, and I know he's already demoed it with a bunch of people. Besides which, Griffin's good at public speaking. He had to have given a million presentations back at his job.

I interrupt Holden to demand, "Where's Griffin now?"

While I might care later, right now, I could give two shits about what happened to Derek Sullivan.

Holden gives me an amused look. "Down in the front row, along with all the other people who'll be speaking and performing tonight. You know, where *you're* supposed to be?"

I wave this off, already moving toward the aisle. At this point, I don't care about winning Big Dill. Griffin can have it if it'll make him happy.

And I already got everything I wanted to get and then some—a deal for the easement and a city boy I'm absolutely crazy about.

I try to slip down the aisle unnoticed, but that's basically impossible in this town. The moment I step past the back rows, heads turn in my direction like I'm a neon sign, and I'm showered with friendly, approving glances that are… well, kind of unusual for me but make my chest warm anyway.

On stage, Sandy Navarro is finishing her baton act with a flourish, the sequins on her outfit catching the stage lights, and the crowd erupts in applause and whistles. But I'm still making my way toward the front row when I hear Griffin's name called.

He stands up, and even from here, I can see his deep breath and the way he squares his shoulders like he's readying for battle. He's wearing jeans and a sweater with a collared shirt underneath, and his hair's perfectly styled. I recognize these signs as his armor.

He's so brave and so fucking gorgeous, I can't look away, even though I know every damn person in town is watching me watch him.

*Fuck it*. Let them see.

I manage to make it to the front just as Griffin reaches the stage, and I slide my ass into his now-empty chair next to Ry Marek. Griffin clears his throat at the microphone, and the sound echoes through the packed auditorium.

His face is pale under the stage lights, and I think Holden's right—Griffin definitely looks nervous. I lean forward in my seat, trying to send him calming vibes through sheer force of will.

"Hello, Winsome!" Griffin's voice rings out, and the crowd responds with enthusiastic claps and whistles. He pauses, gripping the microphone stand. "I'm Griffin Mercer. And I know most of you came here today to hear the tourism marketing presentation I've been working on, but, ah… change of plans."

He swallows hard, his Adam's apple bobbing, and I frown.

*What change of plans?*

"Tonight, I have a different kind of presentation. More like a, um, story, really?" He huffs out a nervous laugh, and I dig my fingers into my thighs like I'm forcing myself to stay in place. "Now, I wouldn't call myself a storyteller —though, I guess they say marketing is kind of like storytelling. But most of you probably know I've been living in this whimsical treehouse, and… it feels like I'm kind of in a fairy tale, so I thought it was appropriate. I hope you'll indulge me."

The crowd murmurs a bit, clearly as surprised as I am. He'd worked his ass off on his project. What made him change his mind?

Then Griffin begins, and from his first words, I'm completely locked in.

"Once upon a time, there was a bridge builder who lived in a kingdom where everyone judged you by how grand and shiny your bridges were. Our builder spent years building a spectacular golden bridge. A bridge he thought was so shiny, so magnificent, it would stand for all eternity."

His voice grows stronger, more confident as he settles in, and he stands a little straighter.

"But bad luck hit our bridge builder. An evil spell was cast that made everyone see only rust and decay where his beautiful bridge had once stood. The bridge builder watched helplessly as his life's work crumbled. He didn't know how to fix it. He didn't know why."

Griffin's mouth twists into a wry smile—the one he gets when he's being self-deprecating. My hands clench in my lap.

"Heartbroken, the bridge builder fled to an enchanted forest, where a mysterious wizard who loved mushrooms had left him a magical treehouse. The builder figured he'd live there quietly for a time, speaking only to pine trees, and wait for the evil spell to fade."

A few people in the audience chuckle at the mushroom reference—clearly thinking of Jim. I barely hear them.

"But it wasn't that easy. The builder quickly started to believe that the enchanted forest was trying to hex him because it sent him a variety of challenges, large and small."

More laughter ripples through the crowd. Someone behind me whispers, "Is he talking about Vermont?"

"But perhaps the biggest challenge was the giant grumpy troll who guarded the forest… and who immediately started a property dispute with our bridge builder."

Griffin lifts his head, and his gaze locks directly onto mine like he knew I was there all along. My heart's beating so fast I'm sure everyone can hear it.

"It turned out, the troll had been trying to build his own bridge for years—nothing fancy, no shiny gold for this troll, but one made with sturdy logs and honest craftsmanship. The troll had been building alone, though, and he couldn't understand why his bridges kept collapsing. Why he only ever managed to build half a bridge. Why it wasn't working out the way he hoped."

I swallow hard, my mouth suddenly dry.

"At first, the bridge builder and the troll fought constantly. The troll thought the builder was going to dismantle his whole forest and take all his bridge-building supplies away. The builder thought the troll was being difficult—and let's be honest, he kind of *was*."

Griffin's eyes are still on me, sparkling with mischief now, like he's speaking only to me. "'I will get that troll if it's the last thing I do,' the bridge builder insisted." Griffin shakes his fist at the sky.

I'm grinning like a fool.

He's got me, alright. For as long as he wants me.

"But as they kept clashing, the builder started to notice things about the troll. Like, that he was really smart. And funny. And skilled. And dedicated. And not at all intimidating—"

I huff out a laugh.

"—and that actually, the troll was kind of gorgeous, when you looked past his troll-y facade."

Laughter erupts around me, warm and delighted. Someone near the back whoops. I can feel my face heating, but I can't look away from Griffin.

"And the bridge builder started to notice things about *himself* too. Like, that when he was with the troll, he felt happier, safer, and more free to be himself than he'd ever felt in his glorious kingdom. And that he'd started seeing life as an adventure again. He'd remembered bridges were most beautiful when they were sturdy and had purpose and weren't just a means to an end."

Griffin's hazel eyes *glow* with emotion, and I sit there utterly transfixed.

"It turned out the enchanted forest wasn't actually out to get him, because the whole forest began teaching the builder too. Things he'd never learned while he was toiling in the kingdom."

I watch him gesture toward different sections of the audience as he continues.

"The friendly shopkeeper taught him that even something weird and awful like pickles could connect people. The innkeeper taught him that true hospitality meant making everyone feel like a part of the community, even if you had to use reverse psychology to do it—"

Somewhere in the crowd, I hear my mom make a soft "Awww" sound.

"The village chef taught him that kindness and friendship sometimes come in the form of a sandwich. And the rest of the villagers taught him that sometimes enchanted forests are better than glorious kingdoms."

My chest tightened, and my eyes filled. Was he saying what I thought he was saying?

Griffin continues, his voice growing more serious. "But here's what really amazed the bridge builder: he realized the troll hadn't been protecting the forest for himself. He'd been carrying on work his family had started generations ago—work that kept the streams clean, the wildlife safe, the ancient trees standing tall. The troll's father had shouldered this enormous responsibility alone, and when his heart grew weak, he'd passed the burden to his son. The troll had been struggling under the weight of legacy and duty, thinking he had to be strong enough to bear it all by himself."

I have to blink hard against the tears threatening to fall. *He sees me.*

"'Why, the troll's not a troll at all,' the bridge builder realized. 'He's actually freaking amazing.' And that's when the bridge builder realized he'd been looking at things wrong for a long, long time. He'd spent years building bridges to impress people who didn't matter, fighting battles with ogres who weren't worth his time. But he realized maybe there was a different kind of bridge worth building, as long as he had someone to build with at his side."

Griffin's hazel eyes blaze across the feet that separate us, and a slow smile spreads across my face despite the emotion clogging my throat.

I place my hand over my heart and hope he knows I'd hand it to him if I could.

"So the bridge builder decided to start building again, right there in the enchanted forest, where he'd found himself a home, but this time, he didn't want to build fancy bridges that led nowhere. He wanted to build bridges that connect people. Bridges that were whole. Bridges that couldn't crumble. Bridges that matter. With… with people who matter. Specifically with the beautiful, wild, grumpy, and not-at-all-troll-like man, who…" Griffin takes a deep breath, his voice dropping. "…who the bridge builder had fallen madly in love with."

*Oh, fuck.*

The last words come out as a whisper, but in the

sudden silence of the auditorium, they ring like a bell. Griffin comes to a stop and swallows hard, his cheeks bright red under the lights.

He's so beautiful that just looking at him makes my chest hurt.

"Thank you, everyone," he says simply, setting the mic back into the stand.

I'm on my feet before I can think twice, crossing the floor and up the three stairs to the stage. Behind me, the audience erupts into cheers and applause, but all I can see is Griffin.

"Wait, how does it end?" Perky's voice cuts through the noise. "You can't end a fairy tale like that!"

Griffin's eyes are wide as I approach, but he doesn't move a muscle. "I don't exactly know how it ends yet, Perky—" he begins.

I reach him then and slot my hands into their place at his sides. "I do," I tell him, my words carrying through the mic. "We live happily ever after."

And then I kiss the shit out of Griffin, right there on-stage in front of the whole town.

The crowd goes wild—cheers and whistles and applause that folks in the next county can probably hear. But all I care about is Griffin's mouth under mine, the way he melts into me, the soft sound of relief and surrender he makes that the microphone definitely picks up.

I pull back just enough to whisper against his lips, "I love you, Griffin Mercer. I will build bridges with you any day of the week, whether it's here or in New York. Whatever you want, we'll figure it out."

Griffin's eyes go wide. "Wait, really? You'd be okay if I went to New York?"

"If that's where your dream job is, baby." I cup his face in my hands, thumbs brushing over his pink cheeks. "And all this troll wants is for you to be happy."

Griffin's smile lights up the whole stage. "I love you too, Beckett Axford. But I told Alan no... and I already turned down the other offer last night. I want to stay in Winsome. I want to build a life here. With you." He kisses me again, quick and sweet.

I honestly don't know what to do with myself. I'm so relieved, so fucking thrilled, I'm lightheaded.

So when Griffin pulls back with a teasing look and says, "But there might be one *tiny* thing that would make me even happier..." I don't hesitate.

"Anything," I say, and I mean it.

"Would you..." He bites his lip. "Would you sing the photosynthesis song for me?"

I open my mouth, then shut it again. "You could have anything, city boy, and that's what you pick?"

Griffin's smile is wide and full of affection. "When I'm with you, I'm already happier than I've been in a long time."

And that is how I, Beckett Axford, full-grown adult, forestry professional, and (very) recently reformed intimidating troll, found myself standing on-stage in front of the entire town of Winsome, with Griffin's arm around my waist, doing an impression of a tree while singing about converting sunlight into energy... and not giving a good goddamn that Holden was recording the whole thing on his phone.

Because like a tree, I'd been stunted and struggling, all my energy spent just staying upright. Then the gorgeous man at my side had brought sunshine to my life. He'd woken me up. He'd reminded me of my roots. He'd expanded my mind, nourished my soul, and encouraged me to flourish.

And I knew in my bones that the love Griffin and I shared would continue to grow just like the forest around us, climbing straight and true and toward the light.

# EPILOGUE
## GRIFFIN - FOUR MONTHS LATER

THE FEBRUARY AIR'S so cold it makes my cheeks sting and my breath puff out in white clouds as Beckett and I hurry down Whether Street toward Watchfire. I'm bundled in my heavy coat, and Beckett's wearing his thick brown Carhartt jacket over a flannel, looking exactly like every rugged mountain man fantasy I never knew I had. When the arm around my shoulders squeezes me tight, I swear I can feel the warmth of his palm even through the layers.

Or maybe it's just that every part of me feels warmer since I fell in love with this man.

I'm so busy looking at Beckett, soaking him in, I barely notice that every shop on Whether Street is decked out with shiny paper hearts and light-up cupids that twinkle against the snow. I also don't notice the pedestrians we're passing, trusting Beckett to steer us a path, as usual.

Judging by how many times he has to pull me out of the way to do just that, it's clear the town is hopping tonight, and I understand why. After a couple of weeks of relentless snowfall, we Winsomefolk are happy for an excuse to break hibernation.

"Jesus Christ, Fred, watch where you're going," Beckett mutters as one of his crew passes us in the opposite direction.

Okay, all but *one* of us Winsomefolk.

I hide a smile in the neck of my coat. "You know, we really didn't have to come out tonight," I remind Beckett.

I've been extra busy this week, and so has Beckett. My work for the Koasek Highlands Tourism and Visitors' Center is nothing like my high-stress job in New York, but it turns out I love that. Right now, we're launching a new campaign to draw in visitors this summer—one that uses a lot of the ideas I came up with for my Big Dill campaign— so I've been busier than usual. Beckett's been working nonstop, assessing some new forest areas and doing snow removal. It's not like Beckett and I haven't woken up together every morning, either in my bed or his, but we haven't had as much time to just *be* together as I'd like.

"Of course we did, baby," Beckett insists, just as he did when we had this same conversation an hour ago. "It's Valentine's Day, and you're the love of my life. We're celebrating."

But he glares at Charlie and Dolores Newman as they nearly walk into us, and I have to stifle a laugh.

The moment we step through Watchfire's door, Vivian appears like she's been waiting for us, which she probably has. Her face lights up, and she comes over with that warm smile that made me understand how Beckett turned out to be such a good man, despite his attempts to hide it behind his Resting Intimidation Face.

"Happy Valentine's Day, boys," she says, pulling us

both into hugs. "I have the perfect table for you." She gives Beckett a wink and says, "Secluded, just like you asked for."

Before leading us anywhere, though, she pauses and looks at me with gentle concern. "Griffin, sweetheart, how are you doing with the… the Jim thing?"

"Mom…" Beckett says, reaching for my hand in a gesture that's become as natural as breathing. The way he immediately presents us as a united front still makes me mushy. Probably always will.

I smile at her, squeezing Beckett's fingers. "I'm doing okay, Vivian. Really."

I don't blame her for asking because "the Jim thing," as she calls it, was kind of a mindfuck, and I wasn't always okay with it.

When Jim's attorney came to Winsome for a visit back in early October, she'd mentioned that I'd really want to hear what she had to say, and she'd been right.

Beckett and I had gone to meet her the morning after Hello, Winsome, and the conversation had gone something like this:

*Me: Hello, I'd like to know more about my inheritance and how Jim died, please.*

*Her: Yes, you mentioned 'inheritance' yesterday. I'm afraid there's been a terrible mistake. Jim Grange isn't dead.*

No, seriously. What the actual fuck, right?

I think the attorney thought I'd be delighted. Instead, my predominant emotion had been a kind of horrified embarrassment.

Turns out, when a man like Jim tells you he's gone to the Big Drum Circle in the Sky, he literally means he's gone to a fucking *drum circle* in *Big Sky, Montana*, in his

Magic Mushroom Mobile. What I'd thought was an inheritance trust was actually a trust tied to my thirtieth birthday, which I'd barely even celebrated with all the fallout from the Rise campaign.

The lawyer had apologized profusely for this miscommunication—her word—and explained she'd been on leave for a few weeks, helping her daughter through a difficult pregnancy. She said she'd included Jim's phone number on the paperwork, assuming I'd call him for info, but obviously, calling a dead man had never occurred to me.

This revelation, which Milo claims puts my life squarely in *Days of Our Griffin* territory, threw me for a loop. Talking to my therapist the past few months helped me regain perspective. Having Beckett by my side helped even more.

And meeting with Jim for the first time last week had also been surprisingly good, not because Jim and I had some fantastic, immediate connection… but because we really hadn't.

Jim isn't my parent and had never intended to be. He's a man who did a nice thing for two women he once knew, and an even nicer thing for the grown man he'd known as a child. I'm learning his lack of involvement in my life isn't a judgment on my worth; it's about him being true to himself. Now that I'm being true to *my*self, I really get it.

If there's one thing I've learned from my own mothers and from being around the Axfords, it's that biology doesn't make someone a parent, and being a parent— biological or not—doesn't entitle someone to a place in your life.

The only people I want in my life are the ones who

stick around through difficult times. Who do the best they can and also acknowledge when their "best" still hurts you. Then they take steps to do better and let you do better too.

"You can tell my moms to stop worrying," I add, taking Beckett's hand more firmly and smiling up at him. "I'm in good hands."

Vivian and my moms now have a group chat that I privately refer to as the Is Griffin Okay chat. The answer's been Yes for just about four months now, and I don't see it changing anytime soon. I feel more grounded than I have in… well, ever.

Beckett grumbles under his breath, "I think he'd be doing better if he could get some privacy with his boyfriend."

I snicker at his mock-grouchy tone. "Patience, mountain man."

Vivian laughs and shakes her head. "Come on, Griffin. Let me show you to your table before my son spontaneously combusts."

We pass another couple having a romantic date, and I realize it's Ry Marek, Winsome's current Big Dill. Beckett and I officially withdrew our names from contention the morning after Hello, Winsome. Beckett because he hadn't actually wanted the position, and me because it became clear pretty quickly that I had other stuff to focus on. But Ry's been amazing at it. He got the new crosswalk installed near the school right away, and he's brought his Captain Fun energy to all his ceremonial appearances, which is exactly what the town deserved.

Once we're seated next to each other at a cozy, candlelit corner table near the front window, Beckett finally relaxes.

He reaches over to trace his fingers over my knuckles, and the simple touch sends heat racing up my arm.

"I want tonight to be special," he says, his voice low and private in the way that makes my heartbeat quicken.

I lean forward, close enough to smell that pine and cedar scent that clings to his skin. "Baby, every single day is special when I'm with you." I drop my voice to match his, and I don't even care that the shit coming out of my mouth is so gooey it would have mortified past-Griffin. I revel in this shit now. The gooier the better. "And it'll get even more special when we get home. I have plans for you in the pickle turret. Remember last time?"

The pickle-barrel room has now become a kind of office. Beckett dragged up a comfortable desk chair, and I've decorated the space with framed artwork and a gorgeous carved oak tree sculpture True made me for Christmas. We also moved the old living room couch up there so I could get some more functional furniture since I've been having lots of friends and family over.

The other night, Beckett climbed up to the turret via the rope bridge to surprise me while I was working on a secret project… and let's just say the brothel couch lived up to its name.

Beckett's eyes dilate and darken with want in the candlelight, and I know we're *both* remembering. I'm worried that the whole restaurant will know, too, since my cheeks are so hot. Unfortunately, my tendency to blush like a tomato remains unchanged.

Beckett leans closer—close enough for me to breathe in the woodsy, outdoor scent that's become home to me— and says, "Griffin Mercer, those blushes are going to be the death of me," and I decide maybe I don't mind my blushing so much.

Before I can respond, the door opens, and Carlos, one of Beckett's crew guys, walks in. He's wearing a suit, carrying a single red rose, and looking nervous as hell.

As soon as he spots us, he heads in our direction.

Beckett groans under his breath as he separates from me, and I smirk at his expression.

"Hey, boss," Carlos says. "Griff."

"Carlos." I jump up to give the man a quick hug. "How's your mom?"

"Better. Thanks for visiting her, man. Broken hip's a bummer. She's gotta micromanage me cooking from the couch in the living room. *Carlos, don't forget the azafran!* Like I haven't been watching her since I was a kid." He gives me a sheepish smile and clears his throat. "Anyway, just wanted to say thanks. I'll, ah… let you two get back to your night."

Vivian shows him to a two-person table on the far side of the room.

The second he walks off, Ames appears from the kitchen and heads over.

"Are they tag-teaming?" Beckett grumbles under his breath. "Don't they know it's fucking Valentine's Day?"

"Hey, guys!" Ames says with the kind of desperate brightness he's been exhibiting more and more often recently. "How's it going?"

Beckett's face softens slightly, but he still mutters, "Peachy. So far, we've had to talk to Mom, then that hot mess—" He nods at Carlos, who's chugging water and compulsively smoothing his hair. "—and now you. Could you, I don't know, hang some privacy curtains or something?"

"I think it's sweet," I argue. "Your mom wanted to make sure I was okay. And Carlos is adorable. I hope his date tonight's worth all the effort."

"The last woman he dated never let him get a word in edgewise, so tonight's lucky lady has to be better," Beckett says.

"Or gentleman," Ames says.

Beckett looks at him questioningly, and Ames flushes.

"I mean, don't assume his date's a woman." There's a hint of defensiveness in his voice. "Carlos could be bi or gay. It takes some guys longer to figure it out. That's allowed, Beck."

Beckett looks at his brother carefully. "Of course it is," he says slowly. "There's no timeframe. But I don't think it happens nearly as often as some people wish it would. It's not like in those novels the book club likes to read."

Ames's face goes as red as mine had been, and pain flickers across his features. He's been in a bad place since Robbie told him Lissa wanted to get married.

Though Ames has never admitted he's in love with Robbie, it's been pretty obvious, at least to me, that Ames has been dreading an engagement announcement. Seeing Beckett being so careful with his brother makes me think he's finally guessed the truth too.

"Ames!" Jenna calls from the kitchen, and he excuses himself to go talk to her.

Beckett watches him leave with a frown. "I don't like seeing him like this."

"Me neither." I reach for his hand again. "But Ames

will figure it out. And he won't be alone. He's got us. He's got a circle of people who support him."

Beckett's expression softens as he brings my hand to his lips. "I love that you're part of that circle now." He winks and adds in a sexy growl for my ears alone, "And not *just* because of what you did the other night in the barrel room."

I nearly choke on my water, remembering how I'd proved, once and for all, that I am definitely not intimidated by Beckett.

Not by any part of him.

*Ahem*.

Beckett grins wickedly. "Sorry, baby, was that on the revised list of things we're not supposed to talk about?"

I shake my head with mock annoyance. Beckett knows very well that there's nothing we can't talk about anymore. "Ideally, I'd prefer not to discuss that in *public*," I tell him, raising my chin. "And not when I'm wearing these jeans."

Beckett laughs and tweaks my chin with one finger. "You love it," he says, and he's right.

I love his smirky innuendos and his gruff sweetness. Mostly, I love the way he makes me feel safe and cherished and wanted every minute of the day.

Before I can tell him exactly how much I love it, we're interrupted again.

"Griffin!" Ada's clearly a little wine-drunk and isn't making any attempt to be quiet as she toddles over. "Did you hear the news?"

"Happy Valentine's Day, Ada," Beckett says a little sourly. "I hope you're enjoying the holiday."

Ada chuckles. "As a matter of fact, I am. I'm here with the Ardor Society. It's our Ar-dorable Valentine's Day Dinner." She points to a large table on the other side of the restaurant. "Ames outdid himself!"

Beckett and I exchange another wordless, amused look. After outdoing himself with the Halloween vampire menu last October, the Ar-dorables have decided Ames is one of them. He grumbles about it every month when he's coming up with new themed menus, but I secretly think he likes it.

"Anyway, enough of your interrupting, Axford," she says crisply, and I have to bite my lip at the look on Beckett's face. "I wanted to tell Griffin the latest news on Derek Sullivan."

She leans in conspiratorially, but she's still talking loud enough for the restaurant and probably some passersby on the street to hear. "The investigation down in Massachusetts is still ongoing, but I hear he's declared bankruptcy."

Beckett doesn't comment, but he does exhale a satisfied grunt. It's not a surprise, exactly. Derek has sold off pretty much his whole operation in Winsome already, just to pay his legal bills. Which means the guy who bought the land got himself a really good deal.

I grin at Beckett across the table, and his lips tip up in response.

When the lawyer came by last fall, she hadn't just dropped the news that Jim was alive; she'd also informed me that the trust Jim gave me also includes the royalties from the *Whispers* books. And since the money's been growing untouched for years, it had really added up.

Enough that I'd gotten a financial planner who'd advised me to invest in real estate.

Which means now, believe it or not—and sometimes I still cannot—I'm the owner of over a thousand acres of Vermont forest. A thousand acres of hardwoods and softwoods and all the creatures who call them home.

It's a huge responsibility… but fortunately, I know a guy who can make sure that forest is protected for generations to come, and I happily leased the land to him.

And I did it officially, even though he assured me he'd have taken a handshake deal.

After Ada returns to her book club, Beckett and I finally, *finally*, get a moment alone. He's stroking his thumb over my knuckles, and I feel the familiar flutter of contentment in my belly that still surprises me sometimes.

"I heard from Milo today," I tell him. "He's coming for another visit next month."

Beckett rolls his eyes. "Is he still claiming he's only coming to get more hydration pickles and hang with his new BFF?"

I chuckle. Milo claims he won't forgive me for my "betrayal" in moving to Vermont until my lumberjack and I have produced the required four children named in his honor, which I warned him won't be happening anytime soon… or ever. But he still comes to Winsome pretty much monthly, supposedly to hang with Vivian, who he says is his soulmate.

"He's actually going to spend the summer here," I add, watching Beckett's reaction. "Your mother's going to teach him to plant an herb garden, apparently."

"And where's he going to stay?" Beckett frowns. "The

treehouse is pretty cramped for two people, babe. Especially when one of them enjoys pickle-turret shenanigans on a regular basis."

"Actually…" I lean closer. "I thought I might give up pickle-turret shenanigans while he's here."

He narrows his eyes skeptically. "Is that so."

"Mmm." I run my fingers over his strong calloused hand and under the cuff of his shirt. "In fact, I was thinking I might see if this guy I know would let me stay with him in exchange for some… *forest-y* shenanigans."

"Some guy, huh?" Beckett's voice is a low rumble that makes my stomach somersault and all my blood head south.

"*My* guy," I correct softly. "My favorite guy. Who makes the best maple syrup pancakes, and gives really good back rubs, and looks fucking *hot* when he's handling an axe."

"Wow." Beckett's blue eyes darken again, and it's glorious. "Sounds like a catch, this guy."

"You have no idea," I murmur. Then I lean in and kiss him.

Beckett's lips are soft and warm, and as usual, once I taste him, I can't get enough. The kiss is sweet and dirty and full of love, as all of Beckett's kisses are.

I never take for granted the way we fit together. The freedom and safety I've found with him.

I'm just about to declare that we need to go home *immediately* and celebrate our first Valentine's Day at home, when there's a commotion at the door, and Robbie and Lissa come in. They're flushed from the cold, and Lissa is smiling from ear to ear.

Ames is just re-emerging from the kitchen when they come in, and he stops dead when he sees them.

Vivian hurries to the front and greets them with an apologetic smile. "Hey, you two. I'm sorry, but we're completely full tonight. Quite the crowd for Valentine's Day—"

"Oh, I figured!" Lissa's practically bouncing in her high heels. "But we're not here for dinner." She thrusts out her left hand, and my stomach plummets. "We wanted Ames to be the first to know... we're engaged."

The restaurant erupts in congratulations and excited chatter. Everyone here is in love with love and eager to celebrate.

Almost everyone.

Ames's face drains of color right before my eyes.

Robbie notices and takes a hesitant step in his direction. "Amesie, I—"

The door opens again, and someone new walks into this mess. Ames's gaze darts to the newcomer like a drowning man in search of a lifeline.

Ames's eyes widen, and so do mine because the man who walks in is none other than Erick Nelson, wearing a long wool trench coat I'd bet my brothel couch is this year's Bruno Cucinelli.

"Oh my god! Erick?" I wave and half rise out of my chair. "I had no idea you were coming to Winsome."

Erick clocks the dozens of eyes staring at him and swallows nervously. "Oh. Well, actually, I'm here to meet—"

"Me!" Ames strides forward and wraps an arm around Erick's waist. "He's here to meet me! Because Erick and I have an announcement too. Surprise! We're... together."

He squeezes Erick enthusiastically. "Tell them, honey bunch."

"The fuck you say," a male voice that sounds suspiciously like Beckett's Carlos growls from somewhere in the restaurant.

Robbie's whole face contracts in shock and suspicion.

Vivian's eyes widen, but she smiles gamely and says, "How wonderful! It's lovely to see you again, Erick."

Erick looks utterly poleaxed. Like he opened the door to Watchfire and ended up in an alternate dimension. But all he says is, "Th-thanks?"

"Congratulations, Robbie and Lissa," Ames says brightly. He pulls Erick a bit more tightly against his side. "Now, come on back to the kitchen, pookie, and let's get our Valentine's Day on."

Erick takes a deep breath and casts a worried look toward the dining room in general but allows Ames to draw him away. Robbie looks like he wants to go after them, but Lissa grabs his arm and tows him toward the front door, babbling something about telling her parents, and he gives in.

Carlos gets up and marches toward the kitchen.

Beckett's hands clench into fists, and he half rises like he wants to follow, but I lay a comforting hand on his wrist, and he blows out a breath.

"That's… fucking weird," he breathes.

"Beyond weird. Starting tomorrow morning, we're gonna be all up in Ames's business," I say firmly. "And Erick's too, come to think of it. We'll get to the bottom of this."

Beckett's eyes soften as he looks at me, and he turns his hand over to thread our fingers together. "The day you came to Winsome was the best day of my life, city boy," he says gruffly, and I know he means every word. "Even if I didn't know it at the time."

Not for the first time, I am swamped with love for this man. For the life we're living. For the future we're building together.

I came to Vermont all those months ago thinking I was a guy who'd lost.

Now I know I was a guy who *was* lost. A man who'd forgotten that life could be an adventure with all sorts of unexpected twists and turns and that it didn't have to be a solo endeavor with winners and losers.

Now I know there's no extra points awarded for doing life alone, and no weakness in wanting to share it with people who make you feel good and happy, safe and strong.

Looking around Watchfire—at Vivian fussing over customers, at Ada and her book club drinking wine and discussing romance tropes, and most importantly at the man in front of me, who looks at me like I'm the most important and cherished person in his world—I realize Vermont gave me something I hadn't even known I was missing.

A home.

*Not ready to say goodbye to Griffin and Beckett just yet? Sign up for my newsletter to read* Up a Tree, *a* Kiss My Axe *bonus story, here → https://readerlinks.com/l/5015414*

*Discover what's going on between Ames and Robbie in the second book in the Axford Brothers series,* **Hot Axe.** *Visit https://readerlinks.com/l/5015377 to get your copy!*

*Want more small town shenanigans? Ruby mentions Little Pippin Hollow, the setting for my Sunday Brothers series, and it's full of small town charm! Start the series with* **Pick Me,** *available here → https://readerlinks.com/l/4420112*

## ABOUT MAY ARCHER

May is an M/M author who lives in Boston. She spends her days planning vacations, mainlining diet soda, avoiding the gym, reading M/M romance, and when all other forms of procrastination fail, writing it.

Visit her website at mayarcher.com to sign up for her newsletter to hear about sales and upcoming releases, freebies and behind the scenes info and more! Or join her Facebook group, Club May!

facebook.com/may.archer.author

instagram.com/mayarcherauthor

patreon.com/MayArcherRomance

bookbub.com/authors/may-archer

# ALSO BY MAY ARCHER

Find me online → https://mayarcher.com/links/

Love in O'Leary Series

Whispering Key Series

The Sunday Brothers Series

Copper County Series

The Way Home Series

Licking Thicket Series

*(cowritten with Lucy Lennox)*

Champion Security Series

*(cowritten with Lucy Lennox)*

Honeybridge Series

*(cowritten with Lucy Lennox)*

For a comprehensive list of titles, audio samples, freebies, suggested reading order, and more, visit my website at www.MayArcher.com!